RETRIBUTION;

Elizabet M...

THE MURDER AT THE OLD DYKE.

A Romance.

Murder most foul, as at the best it is,
But this, most foul, strange, and unnatural.
SHAKSPEARE.

LONDON:

PUBLISHED BY E. LLOYD, AT THE OFFICE OF THE ILLUSTRATED EDITIONS
OF STANDARD WORKS, 12, SALISBURY SQUARE, FLEET STREET.

1847.

PREFACE.

In concluding the Romance of "RETRIBUTION, OR THE MURDER AT THE OLD DYKE," the Author feels that he is imperatively called upon to return his best thanks to the public for the large share of patronage it has been pleased to bestow upon the work so named.

It becomes a matter of absolute and stern necessity, in the delineation of human life and character, to paint vice as well as virtue, and it was only with the conviction that such a necessity must be yielded to, that could have brought the Author to the task of recording the frightful crimes of Margaret Wyvill.

Let us hope, for the honour of human nature, that there are few, very few, such as she is, or rather was; and that such a character served but as a marked and strange exception from the general kindliness and social excellence of woman's nature.

Some of the incidents recorded in this Tale actually took place, and indeed all that we have set down as the general characteristics of the family of the Fosters is strictly true.

The Dyke House, or rather the blackened ruins of what was once the Dyke House, still remains in the romantic mountain pass which connects two of the most lovely valleys of South Wales; but, as may be well supposed, notwithstanding all the actors in this eventful drama of real life have changed to dust, we have altered their names, from the dread that the slightest pang could be inflicted upon any of their descendants.

The moral of the Romance—and why should not a romance have a great moral?—consists most unquestionably in the fact, that persons should never jump at conclusions, to the detriment of others, too hastily; but that the slowest possible credence should be given to suspicious circumstances; and separations of the loved and the loveable should never be permitted to take place through the intervention solely of third parties fetching and carrying their venomous information.

One half-hour's interview between Emily Wyvill and her husband would have sufficed to scatter to the winds all the flimsy devices of Margaret, and have enabled both to see her in her true colours.

With these few remarks, we dismiss the work in its completed form to the literary public, who have already given it so favourable a reception in its fragmental state.

LONDON,
February, 1847.

RETRIBUTION:

OR, THE

MURDER AT THE OLD DYKE.

A Romance.

BY THE AUTHOR OF "NEWGATE." ETC.

CHAPTER I.

THE BENIGHTED TRAVELLER.—THE CHILD'S RESCUE.—THE MURDER.—THE SPECTRE THE VAULT OF DEATH.

In one of the most mountainous districts of Wales, there is a long narrow pass or gorge, of a serpentine shape in some places, in order to avoid huge masses of rock which rise nearly perpendicularly, and in some places seem as if they were ready to topple over on any chance passenger who might be beneath. It is a wild

No. 1.

and rugged spot, a spot which superstition had peopled with terror, and which tradition had made up with tales of the wild and of the wonderful. And yet, as is commonly the case in that country of abounding natural beauties, the sterile mountains, and uncongenial tract of country, is bounded by two of the most beautiful valleys in all the principality. The inhabitants of that region are not a migratory race; they are home-liking, home-keeping people, like the Swiss, and mountaineers in general; and, although this sterile part of country through which passes the narrow gorge-like pathway, is not above four miles in extent, there were many persons residing at each extremity, who had never tempted the passage, and who knew nothing of the aspect of nature beyond that sterile boundary. Perchance there might have been some of them who found too much enjoyment in the relation of the natural wonders of this mountain pass, to disturb their dream of fancy by an actual inspection of it. It was said, that from time to time, dreadful deeds had been committed by predatory ruffians who found security and rest among the fastnesses of the mountains.

There was but one human habitation in the pass, and that was a kind of change house, or rural inn, inhabited by persons who had a great reputation for sanctity, and whose very residence on that spot, seemed sufficient almost to rob them of it, and to spread the odour of immorality about and around it. The house was a ruin, propped up, patched and supported by more materials than, if properly bestowed, would have rebuilt one of double its dimensions; but its inhabitants seemed to cling to it with a kind of veneration, and repudiated all advice which tended to produce great alteration in their dwelling.

A swinging sign announced good entertainment for man and beast, for the pass was just wide enough to allow a couple of country carts to pass each other, and those who commonly traversed it of the better class, on pleasure or on business, usually did so, mounted upon one of the rough sure footed ponies of the district. It was a picturesque dwelling, where the sun shone upon it, and even in the depth of winter when the snow lay heaped up against its door, and the winds howled round its dilapidated chimneys, it was still a print in the landscape, upon which the traveller might rest his eye with the feeling that he was not quite isolated from the whole human race.

It is October, a soft and mellow autumn has succeeded a summer of beauty, the hardy mountain vegetation appears, as yet, to have suffered but little from the near approach of winter; the early night is closing in, and a peculiar chillness in the air proclaims that the vernal season is passing away to give place to that of a colder and less congenial aspect. There were peculiar appearances too, on this particular evening, in the atmosphere; now and then the breath, as if of a hot-wind, would sweep across the plain, then to be succeeded by a chilly dampness, and once, a startling peal of thunder seemed to shake the heavens and to toss some of the huge clouds which obscured the sky, into strange and shapeless masses. A distant clock struck the hour of seven, as, contrary to advice and almost supplication, a man of gentlemanly and prepossessing aspect, leading by the hand a child, apparently not above five years of age, entered the mountain pass; he turned for a moment and smiled, as he waived his hand to the occupiers of a cottage in the valley, where he had stayed some time for repose and refreshment; they returned the salute, and in another minute he was hidden from their view, round an abrupt angle of rock which stood near the entrance of the gorge. For a moment then he recoiled a step, for the reflected light, which was in the valley, had deceived him as to the progress of the night, and to walk into that narrow mountain pass seemed like going into a cavern, so dark, so profound and mysterious did it look. A shudder passed across his frame as he then, by some impulse that he could not control, for there was no particular cause for him at that moment to do so, lifted the child in his arms and folded it to his breast, he kissed its cheek, its lips, its brow, and in a voice of saddened but deep emotion, he said—" Dear, dear one, I cannot love you less, that you so resemble your mother, but I fear that it will make me ever love you with a kind of sadness, because, with the abounding joy of ever seeing you near me, will be mngled sad remembrances of the past." The child twined its arms round his neck, and, with all the trusting confidence of happy innocence, nestled in his breas and laughed gleefully in his face, understanding not the melancholy of his words, but in a blissful ignorance of all but one feeling, that it was caressed. And now he carried his little charge and walked a few paces through the mountain pass : a cold feeling crept across him and he turned twice completely round as if he feared that something evil was behind him. "What is this? What is this?" he said ; " am I to become the slave of such fancies; I, who have stood the brunt of battle, and looked, unmoved, on death in every shape? my feet seem made of lead, and something at my heart, each step I take, seems tugging at it to pull me back again." A sudden gust of wind swept through some crannies in the rocks, producing a wailing shrieking sound that might well be mistaken for a human voice, expressive of the agony of some departing spirit. " My Eliza! my Eliza!" he said, " my heart, to-night, is full of thee ; and I can almost fancy thy gentle, uncomplaining spirit, standing by my side. I have wronged thee not in thyself but in the spirit of thy child, and it knows not the injustice I have done it ; but, a deeper vengeance is in its clinging to me thus, in trusting fondness, than as if it loved me not : but, why do I tarry, home is before me, that, however, which shall be a haven of rest to thee, dearest and best."

" But father," said the child, " they call me Mary."

" My dear one, I was not speaking to you or of you; you are Mary, it is your mother whose name was Eliza."

The child shrunk closer to him, and said, in whispered accents, " Are you afraid of the dark ?"

" No, dearest."

" Yes ; you tremble—they say I tremble in the dark."

" Nay ; there is no fear. I said that I would carry you, if you walked from the cottage door some distance, and now you see I am performing my promise."

The child clung closer to him, and he walked on ; but he did not walk on with the confidence that a man should walk—there was a shifting, uneasy movement of his eye, now and then a tremulous step or two, and once, in every hundred yards or so, he by some irresistible impulse—an impulse which he could neither resist nor desire, turned and looked behind him as though he heard pursuit. Once, too, he entirely paused, and said to himself, half aloud,—

" Shall I go back ?" and then, as if ashamed of the impulse which had prompted the remark, he walked on again more hurriedly, like one who dreads his own power of perseverance, and wishes, by a show of haste, to banish some uncomfortable thoughts. He had got about a mile along the pass, when the moaning wind, which had hitherto whistled through the narrow defile, suddenly ceased, and there succeeded to it a calmness which had about it that marked and particular character which, in mountainous districts more than any other, is the sure precursor of some great strife of the elements.

The stranger who carried the child, and who seemed for some particular objec to be intent that night on getting completely through the pass, felt assured, now that the prognostications of the people in the valley he had left, concerning the, probability of a furious storm arising, were about to be verified ; and it became to him a matter of consideration whether he should return the distance he had already traversed, or now that he had got so far, push on and endeavour to achieve the whole of the distance. Probably, but for one mental suggestion, he would have chosen the former alternative. In fact he had turned round to retrace his steps, when he suddenly exclaimed,—

" I had forgotten ; there is the Dyke House, as it is called, only about another mile a-head, where I can have both food and shelter if a storm should really ensue. The Fosters are very worthy people."

As he spoke, he turned again with his face up the pass, and then he added, " What can be the meaning of this ? Just now, while my face was turned in the other direction, a feeling of surprising satisfaction came over me, which now is reversed for one of dread and alarm. Is this a presentiment of some evil which I ought to give way to, or is it but a piece of nervousness which, once to encourage, would be for ever afterwards to give it a sort of control over me."

A loud peal of thunder rattled above.

"I'm the better for that sound," he said; "it reminds me of ordnance in the field of battle, of the rush of arms and the clangour of the trumpet, at which my heart has often leaped in enthusiasm—besides, I have a piece of stern justice to do to-night. I have not only, when I reach home, to pluck from my bosom a serpent that has stung me, but I have to show it that it is so plucked, and that retribution has come at last."

A fresh courage appeared to come to his aid, and he strode forward now with rapidity, which would soon enable him to traverse the mile which yet lay between him and that dismal habitation called the Dyke House. This conviction urged him on, and rapidly he made his way, thinking lightly of the burden of the child, and likewise lightly of the storm that now began to howl wildly and beat about him. It seemed as if the elements, in all their majesty of wrathfulness and might, had agreed to assemble in that mountain pass for a terrific contest, during the continuance of which an utter heedlessness of the mischief they might occasion was their chief characteristic. The blustering wind howled, shrieked, and flew up the narrow pass, scattering before it every loose particle of material that was not sufficiently ponderous to resist its power. The blue, jagged lightning streamed across the sky, seeming to strike like flaring arrows against the surfaces of the rocks, and then to spread out in lurid sheets of flame with a hissing sound; and ever and anon the loud thunder pealed from heaven to earth, awaking endless echoes in the mountainous region, so that the reverberation of one tremendous peal had not ceased, ere heaven's artillery again thundered forth its terrific sounds to keep the war of tumult alive.

The child wept and sobbed, and clung to the breast of its father, and more than once that stout-hearted man quailed and cowered beneath the fury of the storm. But there was no shelter; if he stood beneath a beetling mass of rock for a moment, the dread that it might fall upon him and involve him in a terrible death forced him again from its apparently friendly covert, and he struggled on, panting almost for breath as the wind came in his face almost with a bodily power that was sufficient to force him back.

But these furious elemental strifes, like human passions, are briefest when most intense. He knew that such a warfare could not last long; and so, covering the child more closely in his cloak, he uttered a prayer, which took more the form of an ejaculation, and pressed on.

The wind, as it careered up the mountain pass with such terrific violence, soon swept all obstacles from before it; so that dust and the [debris of stony matter no longer impeded the traveller's vision—and he fancied that, some distance a-head, he saw the faint glimmer of a light.

"It is the Dyke House—it is the Dyke House," he said. "I shall soon be in shelter now."

Even as he spoke a terrific sound, some distance behind him, announced the fall of a large mass of rock, which, had it but a few moments sooner loosened itself from its hold, would have buried him beneath its incumbent pressure, together with that young and beautiful being whom he folded to his heart, and who as yet stood but upon the very threshold of that world into which heaven had sent it—surely with a better and a higher purpose than to meet with such a death.

He shuddered as he heard the sound, and well he might—it was different from the loud-mouthed brawling thunder, and well he knew what it portended.

"On, on," he cried. "This is an awful night! Is not my purpose holy and full of righteousness? Yes, yes; as heaven is my judge, it is for good that I am thus striving, and for the happiness of this dear creature who now reposes on my breast. What sound was that?"

He paused instinctively, as a low wailing sound came to his ears, which was followed by one of a sharper and more sudden intonation, that partook of the character of a half-stifled shriek.

For a moment he thought that it came from some distance a-head of him: but then again he got bewildered with the numerous echoes with which the place abounded; and, for a moment or two, whilst there was a partial lull in the tempest, it seemed to him as if he were surrounded by a legion of evil spirits, shrieking and wailing into his ears some note of warning, which his heart panted to understand more fully, but which possessed only abundant dread, but nothing explanatory. Then again came the roar and the shout of the mighty wind; and he had to bend all his energies to the task of proceeding in the face of so violent a foe. He could not well wander from his path, that mountain gorge was so narrow, and so shut in by perpendicular rock; but still he kept his eyes fixed upon the twinkling light afar, viewing it as an indication that there, at least, was a haven of rest, which soon would welcome him. The child was sobbing upon his breast, but he silenced it by caresses.

"Hush, darling, hush," he said, "it is but the wind: you're safe, you know, in your father's arms; be still and tranquil. There, look, dear Mary, you can look now. See you not a light? Nay, weep not: it is almost kind of the wind to dash aside those clustering curls that you may see the clearer. You will smile yet to-night, my little one; and in your dreams you will only remember that you were held closely to your father's heart, and not that there was anything to dread in the mountain pass that led you to your happy home."

The child was too young fully to understand the words that were uttered to it by that man who was unused to the prattle of the young; but the tone was gentle and kindly, and full of the most profound affection: that it was which spoke to the heart of the little innocent, and calmed its fears. The girl ceased to weep, but it clung closer still to its protector, and hid its face completely in his neck.

If there be anything in human nature more than another calculated to teach the sternest heart the gentlest and sweetest dictates of humanity, surely it is the trusting confidence of a young child; a confidence which knows no doubt, acknowledges no fear—but is a feeling of the whole soul, and different, essentially, from any other which in after life can take possession of the mind.

That father felt the full force of the silent appeal to his protection which was made to him in the child's caresses. There needed no words from that young thing to tell him how he was trusted and beloved.

"Heaven help you," he said: "and I have held to my heart one who would have injured thee, my child; but not again beneath my roof shall that betrayer of affection sleep; it would be treason to thy caresses, my Mary, to allow her to breathe the same atmosphere with thee."

The light in the distance became clearer and more distinct: each moment added to its strength and size; and soon, while yet there scarcely seemed an abatement of the fury of the storm, he could see that it proceeded from a latticed window, and he felt assured that he was in the immediate neighbourhood of the Dyke House.

The almost immediate certainty now of safety and succour for the child gave him fresh strength, he folded the travelling cloak he wore more tightly around him, so as to present the smallest surface he could for the wind to act upon, and in a short time he found himself close to the mysterious and lonely dwelling, which occupied the place half way through the mountain pass. He raised his voice and shouted loudly, although he doubted but that the wind would carry it away, and if, amid the roar of sounds that must have been saluting the ears of the inhabitants of the Dyke House, he could be heard. The only indication that he had, and that was an immediate one, of his having not shouted in vain, consisted in the sudden and immediate removal of the light, which had been placed in the window apparently as a beacon for travellers. All was then black darkness, and on such a night as that it was impossible to distingush the outlines of the house from the large masses of rock which backed it. He thought it strange, that in order to admit him, that light should be removed, but before he had time to give this a moment's sound consideration it was replaced, and then he heard some one unbarring the door, and he could not but feel surprised at the unusual precaution of keeping it so fast. The moment the outer door was

Opened, a confused banging and clattering within testified to the force of the current of air which had immediately rushed into the dwelling. A man appeared with a lantern in his hand, the dark side of which he held towards himself, so that it was only by a very dim and reflected kind of light that the traveller could see him. He knew him however, and called him by his name, crossing the threshold with his child as he spoke.

"Foster," he said, "don't you know me?"

The man retreated backwards as the traveller entered, and then he said in a voice which any one could have sworn to be artificial—

"Praises be to the Lord, to him be the praise; walk in, Sir Anthony; what a night, it is. We have been lifting up our hearts in thanksgivings, miserable sinners that we all are, worms and reptiles, worms and reptiles."

"I perceive," said the traveller as Foster now commenced barring the door, "that you still affect the language and twang of the conventicle now, the same as you did when last I saw you."

"Yes," said Foster, "the Lord willing, always. Do you fancy, Sir Anthony, that I was going to slide back in so short a space—no, I hope that I still walk in the grace of faith, the beauty of righteousness, and the glory of—"

"Foster, you know that this kind of thing is very distasteful to me. I give you credit for sincerity, but don't inflict upon me the particular language which you consider it necessary to clothe your religious sentiments in."

"Ah, well," said Foster, with a snuffle, as he finished barring the door, "man is a weak vessel."

"Well, well, I've heard that before."

"Even like a piece of potter's clay, not well annealed in the furnace, liable to cracks and flaws,—damme if there don't go one of the windows up stairs—Amen! the Lord be with us."

"Why, Foster," said Sir Anthony, "what was that? I'm afraid now and then you can be a little rational; but, however, all I want of you is a shelter till the storm is over; perchance I may trespass upon your hospitality for the night, for to tell the truth, I want some news from you as well."

"Ah, yes," said Foster, "there's nobody within but Judith, and Elsbeth, and Ben, so that there's a spare bed that belongs to Goliah."

"Belongs to whom?"

"To Goliah, my eldest son."

"Oh, I had forgotten."

"Oh, I wish I could forget."

"Well, don't make such a hideous groan of it."

"It's nothing to the groans I have groaned, he wouldn't walk in the ways of grace, but he chose a thorny path, and now he has walked his walk into——"

"Where?"

"The county gaol, amen!"

"A promising subject truly; probably the county will say amen upon the occasion as well as you, Foster. I admire your philosophy, if I don't your religion: but why do you bar your door so cuatiously?"

"It has been blown open twice by the wind, and once when I was passing it, I think Satan assisted a little, for it hit me a grievous blow on the side of the head; but will it please you, Sir Anthony, to walk in? there's a blazing fire of forest logs upon the hearth, and we will find you something to comfort the mortal vessel. Would you object to a psalm?"

"Most decidedly; it's the mortal vessel, and the mortal vessel only, which wants comforting just now,—but you can sing a psalm if you like in some other room, while I eat my supper."

"Ah, truly."

Foster led the way down a narrow passage, and then flung open a door; it disclosed a low-roofed spacious apartment, so rude and rough in its appointments, that it scarcely seemed to belong to the age in which it had been built. The roof was composed of so many massive beams, and there were so many cross supports in all directions to the walls, that it seemed as if it must have been built by some cunning architect, whose only notion of the subject consisted in placing an enormous mass of wood-work together, so as to leave some sort of hollow space in the middle of it, which he called a room.

There was yet an air of rude comfort about the place which perhaps it would not have had in daylight, for there blazed an ample fire of logs upon the hearth, which threw a ruddy and a plesant tint upon every object in the apartment, giving them a beauty of expression which their natural colour could not have aspired to. A coarse wooden table, more like a butcher's block than anything else, stood in the centre of the room, and around it were several wooden stools of the rudest manufacture. There seemed to be no end of hiding places and cupboards in this apartment, and one end of it was partitioned off into a sort of imitation of a public-house bar, behind which, hung a number of tankards, and upon several shelves an array of glasses exhibited themselves. Crouched down by the fire and swaying to and fro, as she muttered something which was quite unintelligible, was a woman, while there lay at full length in a corner, the huge form of a hulking looking young man who seemed either drunk or asleep.

If Mr. Foster had purposely delayed Sir Anthony outside until his family had assumed a decent appearance to receive the visitor with, it seemed as if he certainly might have spared himself that trouble. As he came into the room he said, in a louder voice then he usually spoke in, " The Lord of Hosts has sent us Sir Anthony Wyvill as a guest."

Nobody took any notice of the announcement, and Foster knit his brows as he advanced towards the woman who was crouching at the fire, and touched her shoulder.

"Do you hear?" he said? "we have a honoured guest ; I pray you attend to him."

The woman sprung to her feet and looked wildly about her for a moment, like one awakened from a dream.

" Yes, yes," she said ; "I recollect—a hundred pounds, was it not, if done effectually ? "

"Amen," said Foster, in a voice that made the place ring again.

The woman shrunk back, and then in an extremely altered tone, she said—

" Be seated, sir, be seated ; it's a long time indeed since we had your honour in our humble home. What can we do to make you comfortable, while you honour us with your presence ?"

" My comfort," said Sir Anthony Wyvill, "is of little consequence compared to the comfort of this darling of my heart."

He threw aside his cloak as he spoke, and shewed for the first time, the child to the inhabitants of the Dyke House.

Foster and his wife started back in amazement; "A child !" he said

"Whose child ?" said the woman.

"My own," said Sir Anthony Wyvill; " the child of my deceased wife, Eliza, whom I loved, and to whom I have behaved unjustly, although not unkindly. Look in this infant's face both of you, for you've seen its mother, and tell me if you do not think it marvellously like her ?"

" Wonderful !" said Foster, " amen."

" It has her eyes," said the woman, as if more conversing with herself than replying to Sir Anthony. "It has her eyes and they look through me."

Foster stepped forward and made a gesture of impatience towards his wife.

"Truly, Sir Anthony," he said, "you have surprised me ; first by your own visit, and then by showing me your companion ; bless its heart, it's to be hoped it will continually go on walking in the ways of grace, keeping its eyes continually fixed upon its latter end."

" I think," said Sir Anthony, " we both require rest and refreshment."

" Let me take the little innocent," said Mrs. Foster.

" No!" said the child, firmly.

" But, my darling——" said the father.

" No, no, no."

"Nay, come tc me," said Mrs. Foster; "what a little beauty."

"No!"

"Well, well," said Sir Anthony, "there is no accounting for the wills of childre let her be with me, I have been petting and humouring her for a few days now, a no wonder she clings to me."

"Ah, it's dreadful," said Mr. Foster, "to think that one so young, and wi such dimples on its cheek, should, with the original curse, be likely to go dov below."

"Mr. Foster," said Sir Anthony, "you may say what you like about yourse and I'm not very particular what you say about me, but when you talk of n child you tread upon ticklish ground—be warned!"

"Amen!" said Foster.

"Well, I say, amen, too," said Sir Anthony; "now you understand me."

"Ah! the Lord's above us, and the other place beneath us. It's a stout ro of faith that would drag a swimmer upwards, and when he gets there, he mu knock with a heavy hand, and say—God bless my soul, who's that?"

There was such a thundering knock at the outer door, that the pious M Foster very nearly slipped off his stool. Mrs. Foster looked alarmed, and tl sleeping young man in the corner got half up, and growled out his dissati faction.

"Some one like myself," said Sir Anthony, "who is benighted, wishes for shelter."

Bang, bang, bang, came at the door.

"Be it who it may," said Foster, "he might have more patience."

He ground his teeth together, apparently with vexation, as he went to adm the new comer.

There was a pause of some minutes' duration, and then, he returned, ar flinging open the door of the apartment in which sat Sir Anthony Wyvill, l said,—

"It's Soft Bill, the idiot; who'd have thought of him being out in such night as this!"

"Yes, it's me," said a singular looking being, walking into the room, "It me; how the wind blows! It's a nice night for flying kites; somebody's bee playing at bowls; I heard it, as I came along, 'Rumble tumble, rumb tumble, Soft Bill.' 'My mates,' says I, 'did you ever see a man with a brow wig, standing on his head, and balancing a donkey on his great toe—'cos if yo never did, nor more did I, and I think you never will—clever people's scarce i these parts.'"

Such an unconscious, idiotic, quiet sort of smile played upon the features (the idiot, as he spoke, that Sir Anthony, as he looked at him, and he knew hii well, could hardly connect his words, in which there was a strange ramblin sort of method, with his appearance.

"What brings you abroad to-night?" said Foster.

"Ah! fool-like," said the idiot, "I must needs be gadding—but about this ma and the donkey; they tell me that if he could get the donkey on to his toe, h could do it, but the great difficulty is to coax him there."

"I should say it was," said Sir Anthony.

"Yes; you may stand on your head till all the blood's gone out of your fee and still he won't come. 'Ass, ass, ass,' says you, but he won't come."

Soft Billy took quiet possession of one of the stools, and commenced roastin his hands at the blaze of the log fire, occasionally muttering to himself a objuration to the supposed donkey, consisting of—

"Now, ass, if you please, stand on my toe: twenty guineas is the prize—d it at once—here I am on my head."

He was boyish in appearance, and small of stature; he wore a suit of clothe: which some one had given him, that was a world too large, and he had singular looking white hat, or a hat that had once been white, round whicl was a bit of rusty-looking crape : a very mockery of mourning, when worn by such a person.

"He's worse than ever," said Foster, "ten times worse than ever."

"Why, he's not likely to improve, poor fellow," remarked Sir Anthony. "I've not seen him for some time, but he looks to me just the same. Soft Bill, do you know me?"

"Aye, to be sure," said the idiot, slowly taking off his hat, and smoothing out the bit of crape that was about it ; "know you—yes. I'll wear this for you to-morrow."

"For me?"

"Yes, I can see it on your face."

"What madness is this?" said Foster suddenly, "really, when folly takes this dangerous shape—"

"What dangerous shape?" said Sir Anthony.

"Why, he—he—he—intimated your death, and thought—"

"He's a clever fellow," said Soft Bill, pointing in the face of Foster ; "ah, well, its all the same in a hundred years hence. Did you ever see a pig put his tail up at a Dutch auction, and when he found nobody to bid for it, hang himself in despair."

"Ah! bah, bah," said Foster, "this is his old folly. The Lord is willing he should be an idiot."

"Why, so it seems," said Sir Anthony.

Mrs. Foster, during this time, had busied herself in providing some refreshment for her guests ; she placed some cold meat and bread before Sir Anthony Wyvill, as well as some mountain ale, which was really of an exquisite quality ; but when the idiot attempted to draw some of the viands towards him, she interposed ; but Sir Anthony Wyvill checked her, saying, "nay, is this your christian charity, with so much profession of religion ; at least have one of the cardinal virtues, hospitality."

"Oh, I was only going to bring him some more, and to prevent him touching this, Sir Anthony."

"Amen!" said the idiot ; and it was so close an imitation of Foster, that he turned round and started again.

"Very good," said Sir Anthony, "be it so."

It was strange to see with what instinctive kind of abhorrence the child looked upon Foster and his wife, it would not leave its father's arms, but it laughed glee-fully, at some of the idiot's grimaces. Meanwhile, the storm gave ample evidence, as it dashed against the windows of the Dyke House, that it was very far, indeed, from being appeased ; and, Sir Anthony Wyvill began to think that, after all, he should be compelled to remain there for the night, however contrary to his arrange-ments it was to do so. He looked all the vexation that he felt at such a necessity ; and the more he heard the wind rattling the windows, and the dashing hail falling as it did, like chaff against them, the more he instinctively clasped his child to his heart, and felt a wish to proceed home instead of remaining at the Dyke House. And, yet, if he had been asked, candidly to state, what objections he really had to passing the night beneath the roof of the Foster's, he would have found it very difficult, indeed, to give any tangible reason for his conduct. The real fact was, that beyond a general aversion to the society of persons, whom he considered must be either fanatics, or hypocrites, he could not say that he knew anything of the Foster's which could reasonably induce him to entertain a worse opinion of them than of their neighbours. To be sure, candidly speaking, he did, in the recesses of his own mind, think that there was a great deal more of hypocrisy than fanaticism about them, and he could not help imagining that the affected religious fever they professed, acted like a large cloak which covered a multitude of sins.

Sir Anthony Wyvill, however, was what is commonly called, a religious man ; and, therefore, he had charity and goodness enough not to judge hastily, or harshly of any one ; and, even the Foster's he gave a sort of negative credit for virtue to, so long as he knew not of any precise act of villany, which they might have committed. Which is very far from being the case with religious people, who fancy

No. 2.

that if a man's opinions differ a little from theirs, he is, of course, capable of the commission of any enormity whatever.

When the idiot fancied that the child was pleased with him, and paid attention to what he did, and said, he bestowed a great deal of his talk upon the little creature ; and, while Sir Anthony, affecting a state of considerable mental abstraction, slowly partook of the refreshments that had been placed before him, quite a sort of acquaintanceship sprung up between those two persons, the idiot and the child.

The most uneasy thing in the world, to Foster and his wife, appeared to be silence ; so the former, after a time, broke that which ensued, by saying, " Sir Anthony, this is one of the most continuous storms I have noticed for a long time indeed, my own opinion of it is, that it will last the whole of the night."

" Think you so?"

" Yes, Sir Anthony, and should that be the case you know you would never with the dear little one, be able to get past the ford in safety."

" True," remarked Sir Anthony, in a low tone of voice, as if he were now communing with himself ; then, answering to him, " True, I did not think of the ford ; these showers of rain, hail, and sleet, will render it difficult to pass under any circumstances ; and a matter, almost of utter impossibility, with my little darling here in my arms."

" And in the dark, too,'" put in Foster.

" Yes, in the dark, too. I begin to fear that I must trespass upon you for the spare room you talked of ; and, for which I will, of course, pay you."

" Oh, do not mention that, Sir Anthony, do not mention that ; the honour of having you for a guest, at the Dyke House, is quite sufficient ; and, the Lord always willing, we will endeavour to make you as comfortable as we possibly can."

" Amen !" said the idiot again, in Foster's exact tone ; and the malignant expression of anger that came across the face of the latter, for about the space of a moment, and no longer, certainly went far to belie the effect of religion—or mock religion—of one of his temperament.

" Say that again ! say that again ! said the child."

" I must not," replied the idiot ; " Master Foster will cut me up if I say it again. But, I will tell you a story, if you like ?"

" Oh, do. Papa, the good one is going to tell me a story."

" The who, my darling ?"

" The good one ; that's the good one, papa," and she pointed to the idiot ; " and that's the bad one," and she indicated Foster.

" My dear, my dear, you must not draw such hasty conclusions."

" Ah !" said Foster with a sigh, " when the evil one—"

" Amen !" interrupted the idiot. " Now, for my story : I was running one night through the dyke here, and thought I heard a cry of despair ; and I lay down and fell asleep, and dreamt that he who uttered the cry, never uttered another—that's all—it has the merit of being short, has it not? It was only a sort of murder, I think, after all.

" A murder !" cried Foster, " what do you mean by saying a murder—how the hail rattles against the windows, to be sure."

" It aint hail at all," said the idiot, " you ought to know better ; its dead men knocking against the window panes, with their large finger nails, that's what it is ; it sounds like hail, but I know better.'"

Foster seemed to lose all patience, and springing forward, in a threatening attitude, he exclaimed :—

" I will not have you here at all ; troop, troop, I say, get out, I will not have you. In my opinion you are more knave than fool. Do you fancy that I will have the peace of my family disturbed for your fancies. No, by heaven, I will not ; get out, I say, get out, get out."

" What !" cried Sir Anthony Wyvill, rising, while the child clung to him in terror,—" would you, religious Mr. Foster, turn such a poor creature as that out at this time of night, and amid the howling of such a hurricane as now rattles round this building. Do you not hear how terrific is the storm, and how it dashes past your door-way, as if intent upon the destruction of every thing that comes within its way? For shame, man, for shame, I will take upon myself all the charges of this poor fellow's entertainment. For shame, I say; he shall not, while I have a voice potential in the matter, be turned from this door."

" The Lord," said Foster, " has made me a man of short amount of patience, although he has given me abundance of grace—let the idiot remain."

The poor demented creature stepped up to Sir Anthony Wyvill, and laid both his hands upon his arm. He looked up in his face with a composed expression, and then he passed his hand across his brow, as if striving to recollect something which, despite all his efforts, would escape his memory.

" What is it you would say," asked Sir Anthony, mildly.

" There's at least a dozen things I wanted to say to you, but I cannot recollect one of them. Heaven help you, and as Anthony Foster says—amen ! —one good turn deserves another. You shall sleep Sir Anthony, but I will watch."

" My friend," said Sir Anthony, " I think there is no occasion to watch."

" Not the least, not the least," said Foster ; " it is part of this poor creature's fatuity that he is suspicious. The Lord help us ! we are poor, but abundantly honest. And see the young infant's eyes drooping weariness. 'Early to bed, and early to rise,' they say, ' maketh men healthy, wealthy, and wise.'"

" I am sufficiently wearied," said Sir Anthony Wyvill, " to need no great inducement to retire to rest ; and now, that I have partaken of some refreshment, if you will show me to the chamber which is destined for me, I will gladly lie down in it, and taste of nature's sweet restorer—sleep. I have a weary and frightful task to go through to-morrow, and I tremble even to think of it. Come, my little Mary, come, we will to rest ; and may the shadow of your poor mother watch over you."

The child nestled into its father's bosom, and Sir Anthony—with his eyes fixed upon the darling's face, and his mind so absorbed in that blessed contemplation, that all other ideas, for the moment, flitted from his memory—walked towards the door of that large straggling apartment, followed closely by Foster, who had hastily snatched up a light in order to conduct his guest to a chamber. A glance of frightful intelligence between Foster and his wife, as the latter watched him out at the door, and then not a word was spoken ; as, passing before Sir Anthony Wyvill, he ushered the way up the creaking staircase which led to the rooms above. This upper floor of the Dyke House appeared to have been laid out and subdivided in a most curious manner ; for there were chambers and passages, leading the one to the other, in so intricate a manner, that no one unacquainted with the locality would possibly have found his way amid such a maze. Weariness was, however, upon the eyelids of Sir Anthony Wyvill ; and he followed Foster—without at all marking the route he took—until they reached a cold and cheerless looking chamber, in which was a faded melancholy looking bed, that to all appearance had not been slept on for a long time.

" Perhaps," said Foster, as he held up the light, " your worship would like a fire kindled on the hearth."

" No, no," said Sir Anthony, " never mind it ; little Mary and I will lie down as we are ; we must be early on foot in the morning, for I have an object in reaching home before the family are at all astir."

" Certainly, Sir Anthony Wyvill, certainly, sir," said Foster, as he put down the light and rubbed his hands together in an uncomfortable manner. " You will find all comfortable here, very comfortable, and extremely quiet ; the wind may howl a little, but that you know we cannot help ; and as for safety, you might sleep here for a hundred years and no one approach you, for yonder window looks out upon the dry face of the rock, down or up the precipitous side of which, nothing human could ever hope to get."

" I am satisfied—I am satisfied !" said Sir Anthony ; " good night, and should I not awaken early in the morning you arouse me, for, as I said before, I want to be early on foot."

"The Lord be with you," said Foster, "and angels guard your sleep ; and may the blessing—" By this time he had closed the door and stood upon the landing ; so that, he abruptly paused in his evangelical oration, and a humble sinister expression came across his countenance. "A hundred pounds," he said, "a large sum for such a simple deed. Does he suspect us ? I never knew a man to be so utterly confiding ! Hush ! hush ! hush !"

CHAPTER II.

THE EVIL SPIRIT AND THE GUARDIAN ANGEL.

FOSTER groped his way down in the dark, until he had descended about half the staircase ; and then felt carefully over the wall with both hands, until he felt a small handle, which he turned, and then a door opened ; which, amid the rough wood of which the wall was composed, might easily escape detection. To glide into a small apartment and to close the door behind him, was the work of a moment. And now, let us introduce another character of our eventful narrative, who occupied, and had occupied for hours, a place in the small room to which Foster had now made his way. Sitting in the easy chair which the place afforded and in nearly the very centre of the apartment, was a woman—perhaps from her attire we should say a lady ; for she was richly dressed, although incongruously, as regards colour and fashion. It seemed as though, hurriedly, she had laid hold of some articles of her wardrobe and heaped them upon her without form or order. But it was the attitude in which she sat that would have excited the marked attention of any one ; her hands were clasped and resting in her lap—her eyes were fixed with a frightful kind of gaze upon vacancy, and the only indication of life that she presented was a restless movement of the lips, as if she was whispering to herself some dreadful truths too horrible to speak aloud. She seemed not to exceed thirty years of age, and as far as we might judge from the sitting posture in which she was, her stature was above the ordinary stature of woman, and of a commanding and noble order of beauty. The features, upon which the light of a solitary candle which was in the apartment glared with a dubious and flickering ray, were of a ghastly paleness ; but still cast in one of nature's fairest moulds.

She was just of the order of beings who are beautiful, without being loveable ; whom we cannot but feel are entitled to our admiration, at the same time that we cannot bestow upon them any warmer tribute of regard. She was evidently unconscious of the appearance of Foster—wrapped up was she completely in some soul-absorbing contemplation of her own, which engrossed all her senses. Had a thunderbolt fallen at her feet, she would have scarcely been conscious of its presence.

"Oh, indeed !" said Foster, in a very different tone from the sanctimonious one which he sometimes used, "oh, indeed, she thinks much of it—that ought to enhance the reward—how absorbed in thought she is."

He stepped up to her and laid his hand upon her arm as he said :—

"Madam !"

With a shriek she sprung to her feet.

"No, no," she cried, "mercy—heaven—help, help, save him yet—look at the blood—it follows me wherever I go—outstrips me if I fly as fleetly as the wind— comes creeping after me if I become a laggard on the way. Oh horror, horror, horror ! Is it—is it all over yet ? Speak, murderer, speak !"

"Are you mad ?" said Foster ; and he clutched her wrist with so tight a grasp, that she shrunk back with pain, "are you mad, that you speak in such a strain ? go home as I advised you from the first."

"Hush ! no, I am not mad, perchance I may be; and do not speak so loud—where is he now ; and the child, you will save the child ?"

"No, it may not be, both, or neither must fall."

"No, no, you do not mean that ?"

"Do you retract, madam, if so, say at once you do not wish the deed to be done."
She covered her face with her hands and shook violently.

"Disgrace," she muttered, "contumely, reproach, triumph, degradation, despair—ah, no, no, were it a very sea of blood, I would wade through it, to escape such evils on the shore."

"It is enough," said Foster; "you do not waver in your determination, you may come down with safety now, or at least in a few minutes. We have no stranger now in the house, but the idiot who wanders about the dyke, and I'll soon turn him out, or silence him for ever, which perhaps would be the best plan."

"No no, not that, no unnecessary deed; and I will not come down, let me remain here, with my own thoughts thronging round me for frightful company. Come to me again when all is over, but not before, not before."

"As you please," said Foster; and turning abruptly, he left the apartment and closed the door after him. He then descended to the common room below, where the idiot was lounging against one of the wooden benches, with his eyes fixed upon the door way. Foster marched up to him at once, and in a voice of suppressed passion, he said:—

"Tramp, tramp, we'll have no trampers in the Dyke House, get out I say, get out."

"Not yet, Master Foster, would you turn a dog into such a storm as this. If I had a pocket mirror, I could show you how a man looked that was just going to do a murder."

"Now by all that's damnable," cried Foster, "I'll have his life."

He sprang to the fire as he spoke, and seized one of the burning logs of wood, with which no doubt he would have struck the idiot; but his wife clung to him crying, "Foster, Foster, are you mad, do you not see he's going, hush! man, hush! Well, well, a fool may go his own gate, do as you please, rouse your guest above stairs, do, it will be like your wisdom."

"Get out," cried Foster, hoarse with passion, "get out, or by the living God, I'll—"

"I'm going," said the idiot, "I never meant to sleep beneath your roof, but don't touch me, Foster, for the Lord willing, as you say, I'll knock you down. God took away my brains, but he shaped them into bones and muscle, and gave them to me instead."

Placing his hat jauntily on one side of his head, and trolling as he went, the burden of some merry song, he leisurely walked down the passage leading to the door of the Dyke House, followed at a few paces distance by Foster, who still flourished the smoking brand he had snatched from the fire in a threatening attitude. The idiot himself took down the bar from the door, and then the roaring wind lashed it open in a moment.

Foster with an implication, flung the brand after him, and then advanced to close the portal of his dwelling, but before he could successfully do so against the raving current of the wind that set in that direction, it was flung back again like a dart, and hitting him in the face, covered him with hot charcoal and millions of bright sparks. Foster dashed forward, and was out into the night air; but a second thought convinced him, of how, worse than useless, it would be to attempt to pursue his foe through such a storm as was still raging, although certainly with decreased violence. Muttering curses, both loud and deep, the highly religious man turned, and promising to himself vengeance on a future day, he again closed and barred his door with a determination not again on that night, to open it to any one.

There was a remarkable and strange sort of stillness now in the Dyke House, a stillness which had a sympathetic effect upon Foster; for whereas, before, he had seemed to be quite regardless of the tumult he had created in turning out the idiot, he now trod so softly, that one would have supposed him actuated with the extremest caution in his movements. In this state he reached the room in which he had left his wife, they both looked at each other for a few moments, like guilty beings as they were, and then ensued a whispered conference, with the details of which we need not trouble the reader.

*　　*　　*　　*　　*　　*　　*

The wind still howled without, moaning round the Dyke House in the most melancholy manner; and ever and anon, the dashing hail would come again and again against the windows, threatening to force them into the interior of the dwelling; while, occasionally, the rumble of thunder might be heard awaking the echoes of that mountainous region.

Sir Anthony Wyvill, when he found himself alone with his beautiful child, felt the sensation of weariness so strongly upon him, that he at once cast himself upon the bed, and nestling the child in his bosom, in a few moments fell fast asleep. How long this rest lasted he could not well tell; but, from strange and sudden impulse he awoke, and all the feeling of weariness that had before beset him completely vanished. It was evident that he could not have slept long; because, although the wick of the candle wore a long and particular appearance, yet, the cotton was by no means exhausted, but lent flicking and uncertain radiance to the apartment. There was just sufficient light for him to distinguish objects around him; and, for the first time since his entrance into that room, he did look narrowly around it and saw how desolate and how fearful looking a place it really was. As he looked, a strange uncomfortable feeling crept over him; a feeling, almost approaching to positive dread; and yet he knew not why, except it might be, that the wind which howled without sounded like a human voice full of despairing cadences, bidding him beware of some insidious and impending evil.

"I'm not usually nervous," he said, "or alarmed at trifles; and but seldom does a superstition which is current in my family recur to my imagination. It is said, that those of my race who are near their end, are warned of approaching dissolution by a wailing sound coming upon the night air, as if some living thing were in mortal agony and uttering its plaints to heaven. It is a terrific superstition, and one that I have ever cast aside from my imagination as most unworthy to be indulged in, and yet by some strange means it clings to me to-night, with a more than ordinary power. I must shake it off, I must shake it off. And yet back again—what sound is that—I cannot be mistaken." He listened with an intentiveness that seemed as if his whole soul was thrown into the act, and then he could have almost sworn that the howling sound that met his ears could be not only the one that was really at the same time joined to some voice, human or preternatural, which was warning him of something dreadful about to occur. Once, twice, thrice, he heard the strange wailing sound; and, no wonder, that at such a time, even such a man as he shuddered, and felt himself not wholly free from superstitious forebodings, after all that had occurred on that really fearful night of storm and uproar.

"'Tis very strange, passing strange, that, but a short time since, so complete a weariness should have been upon my eyelids, that I could have sworn it would have taken hours of repose to have recovered me; to feel as alert and full of life as I unquestionably am at present; and, with what a preternatural soundness my child sleeps, my beautiful Mary. No presages of evil disturb your young repose; may you always rest thus, as soundly and as calmly as upon your father's breast, dreaming not of aught ill, and awaking but to feel the charm of an existence which it is his best and earnest prayer may ever be gilded with delight. There again, there again, God of Heaven! there it is again, that frightful sound. Yes, it came again more terrific if possible, than it had done before, and Sir Anthony Wyvill felt there was no longer any sleep for him in the Dyke House—without being a superstitious man; how could he listen to such a tone of terror, and not feel shaken. The inhabitants of mountainous districts are, it is well known, more prone to cherish those strange fancies, than persons residing in different regions, so that we may not expect even, that an educated man like Sir Anthony, would be wholly free from them. The child slept soundly, and then a sensation of gratitude to heaven came across him, that it did so; "for surely," he said, "if that really be the omen of death which haunts my family, it comes not to threaten this fair scion of the ancient stock, but we, who can better be spared, than one so young, with, I will hope, a long happy and prosperous life before her."

There was a lull in the wind, at this moment, and by some species of infatuation he fixed his eyes upon the window, and then suddenly, without there being any susceptible current of air to produce such an effect, it was evidently shaken; and before he could recover from the surprise occasioned by this circumstance, one of the latticed panes was dashed in, and some heavy substance fell at his feet. He thanked heaven that he had a light still burning; and, upon casting his eyes to the floor, he saw that it was a heavy stone which had been cast into the window, round which, was roughly wrapped a soiled looking piece of paper, which at first he was disposed to disregard, but which, a second thought induced him to examine carefully by the aid of the light; when, to his consternation, he read upon it the following words, evidently hastily written, and in pencil:—"Sir Anthony beware! you are in a house of murder, or else evil spirits scream at midnight instead of the souls of dead men; save yourself, you and your child are doomed to the knife—keep yourself alive for two hours and help will come to you, God have mercy upon us all."

Twice, thrice, did Sir Anthony Wyvill read these hurried lines, and then the paper dropped from his hands. "It is true, it is true," he said; "a horrible suspicion haunted me below—my child! my little one heaven look down upon thee!"

CHAPTER IV.

THE NIGHT OF HORROR.—THE MURDER.

AFTER the paper had dropped from his hands in the manner we have related, Sir Anthony Wyvill stood, with all the appearance of a man in a state of stupefaction. His thoughts seemed to be in a complete whirl, and he was evidently incapable for many minutes of coming to any just conclusion, with regard to the circumstances in which he was placed. He had uttered the few frantic exclamations concerning the child, and as he did so he had moved towards the bed, but there it lay soundly sleeping, so calm, and so gentle in its repose, that he stopped, abruptly, as if some powerful hand arrested his progress—and dreaded to awake the sleeping innocent.

"Two hours," he said—"two mortal hours before help can come; and am I till then a prisoner, unarmed, with no means of even selling my life dearly. Oh, that I were alone! Oh, that I were alone! It is the thought of this little one that will unman me; and yet, that thought should give me nerve and strength. Oh, is there no hope, is there no hope!"

He clasped his head, and felt as if his brain was on fire—then, staggering rather than walking to one end of the room, where there was water, he dashed some upon his face and temples, saying as he did so—

"Now, God grant me the greatest of gifts, at such a time as this—self-possession."

His prayer seemed to be answered, for he turned comparatively calm, and was able to reason upon his position.

"Firstly," he said, "is this a false alarm, or can it be really the truth, that some of the evil reports spread about regarding the Dyke House, are about to be verified in my own person. I will read the paper again."

He did so, and there was an air of deep earnestness about it, which brought a sad and dreadful conviction to his heart.

"I will test the truth of it," he said, "for if I be permitted to leave the chamber, I shall not think it likely that any such dreadful deed is meditated; but, if I am a prisoner here, I am certain that it is for my destruction."

He went towards the door of the apartment, and essayed to open it. It was perfectly fast, and he felt convinced that the fastening without was of such a nature that it would be impossible to force it; indeed, from the sort of resistance the door offered to his exertions, he felt certain that there was a bar across it, which held it in its place.

He turned, hopelessly, from the door, and approached the window, which, it will be remembered, Foster himself remarked opened upon a precipitous rock.

In addition to its so opening, Sir Anthony Wyvill, by the aid of his light could perceive that there was some iron work outside ; which, while it doubtless had the appearance of being placed there to resist any invasion of the premises, presented a great bar to any one escaping from the window, even had they been inclined to risk being dashed to pieces down the face of the precipice, while in the attempt.

"And, am I to die thus caged, in such a room as this ?" he said. " I who have fought the battles of my country, and come out unscathed from a hundred fights— no weapons, and no hope. Courage, courage, I will not abandon hope. Surely, surely, I may succeed in protracting my existence for these two hours, at the termination of which aid is offered me. Oh! speed, speed, with your promised assistance; you who have written this short admonition, speed, I charge you, not for my own sake, but for the sake of this dear little one, whose life I would willingly purchase at the sacrifice of my own."

He stood in the centre of the apartment, and held the light high above his head, in order to take an accurate survey of all within it ; and then, for the first time since he had set foot across its threshold, he became thoroughly alive to its gloomy and desolate aspect. He was fearful to awake the child, and, therefore, he trod softly and noiselessly across the floor ; in pursuance of a resolution to make a thorough examination of everything within the room, cherishing a hope that some weapon of defence might present itself to him during the course of the search. The walls were composed of wood-work, patched in a variety of places, similar to the room below ; and, more than once, Sir Anthony thought there must be a cupboard or door-way of some sort in the wall, without being able to find the means of thoroughly satisfying himself upon the point. In one corner of the apartment lay some lumber, consisting of short pieces of wood and broken furniture, but there was nothing among it with which he could have made the slightest efficient resistance to any attack. Then, not satisfied with his first examination of the place, he again went over every portion of it with increased care ; and, at length he felt convinced that there was a cupboard in one corner, which however defied his efforts to open it. A quarter of an hour might have elapsed in this anxious manner, but not more ; and then, it suddenly struck him, that in all his researches, he had omitted to look beneath the bed, which was one of those old-fashioned cumbrous-looking pieces of furniture, that were very low to the ground. He stooped with the candle in his hand, and lifting up the faded, bleached drapery, he looked long and earnestly beneath this antique piece of furniture. At first he could see nothing but a mass of blackness, which might be a shadow for all he knew, but yet, it seemed too dark ; and he crouched down on the floor, and reached his hand under to feel if any tangible substance was there. He laid hold of some clothing which he dragged out, it was apparel of a superior description, but by the appearance of it, had been laid by for a long time ; it had a horrible smell about it now that it was disturbed, and some of the different articles seemed actually caked together with what, upon a close examination, Sir Anthony Wyvill told himself, with a shudder, was blood. With the cold perspiration standing in heavy drops upon his brow, he pursued his inquiries, and dragged out, piece by piece, numerous articles of apparel, all in the same frightful condition ; the very floor, too, he saw was stained of a deep dull crimson hue. Horrible discovery! could there be any longer now a doubt with regard to all the terrors of his situation? he was doomed—doomed to a death, probably of the most terrific character—at the hands of a person from whom there was no means of escape.

" And have I lived so long for this ?" he exclaimed, " is this, after all, to be the fulfilment of my frightful destiny, but I will not fall untamely ; unarmed as I am, except with the strength which heaven has given me, I will battle for my life, they shall not find a tame and heartless foe ; oh! for a trusty sword, such as I have wielded in the battle's strife."

He turned his eyes again upon those ghastly articles of apparel which he had dragged from beneath the bed, sickening at the fœtid odour which exhaled from them, he restored them to their hiding-place. All was still in the house, and that very silence had about it an ominous and fearful character, it looked as if all preparations were made, instead of to be made, for his destruction; the candle was near expiring, and for ought he knew, its extinction might be the signal for the onslaughter to be made, which was to insure his death. But, while there was still a dim radiance emitted from it, he staggered, rather than walked, towards the bed, to look, while yet he might, upon the face of the slumbering infant, whom he had brought so far to meet so fearful a destiny.

"My child—my beautiful—my joy," he cried, "what can thy life avail to murderers; will they not be moved by thy beauty, and thy aspect of angelic innocence? They surely will, they must, and even at the last moment they will save you; oh, if by the immediate sacrifice of my own life, I could insure your own safety, how gladly would that sacrifice be made."

Suddenly he heard a sound in the room below, it came only lightly upon his ears, but he remembered that he had there seen a clock, and now he felt convinced, that it was striking the hour, and that, consequently, he had been sure when about half the time specified by his unknown friend, as that which would be required to bring him assistance. Alas! during the next hour, what frightful tragedy might not be enacted; was there not time for a thousand murders, and was it not likely that those who intended to take his life, would hesitate so long before the accomplishment of their end? No; he was doomed, he felt assured he was, and that help, if it came, would come too late to save him. "But, am I not too calm," he cried, "shall I wait here, supinely, the coming of events—to hasten which can scarcely be a calamity—if, by the process of so doing, I can gather the slightest hope of rescue, what strength I have shall be now exerted, and at once?" He stooped to kiss the child as it still lay sleeping; the sleep of innocence and guilelessness upon the bed, and, as he did so, he shrunk with horror, to observe, that even the very bed-clothing, in many places, was of that unsanguined hue, which, like the apparel beneath the bedstead, proclaimed the dreadful deeds that had been committed within it. "Not another moment," he said, "not another moment can I let my darling repose in such a place as this; no—no—that blood is pollution." He placed the candle upon the bed, securely, and then he gently moved the child on one side; surely that was an interposition of a Divine Providence, which induced him, at that moment to remove it from where it was resting, for, scarcely had he done so, when a strange crackling noise came upon his ear, as if marching of some sort was suddenly set into action, and, to his astonishment, there shot up, right through the bed from beneath, a sanguinary looking blade, of, apparently, a double-edged sword, but much thicker, which, had he, or the child, been lying upon the spot, must have pierced them through and through. A cry of astonishment, not unmingled with fear, at such a moment, came from his lips, and, there he stood, with the half-awakened child, clasped to his breast, gazing upon the singular spectacle of that sword-blade, glittering before him, as it stood up, a sufficient height from the bed, to have prevented the possibility of any victim escaping from it whom it had once pierced. A fearful silence of about five minutes duration, succeeded; he could not speak, and, although the child had opened its eyes, the terror that it saw depicted in its father's face, froze up its faculties and prevented it from giving utterance to the slightest sound. All was still too below, and now that it was presumed, no doubt, by his would-be murderers, that the deed was surely done, it would seem as if they had abandoned the apparatus, which had caused the ascent of the blade, and were resolved to wait patiently until there was an assurance of their victim having breathed his last. Each moment now the candle was burning dimmer, and a glance towards it from the terrific object which had enchained his attention, convinced him, that in a few moments more, he must be left in darkness. Darkness—ah! with what additional terrors would that invest his situation—darkness, of which he never before had any dread, but which presented itself to him as the most terrific of added evils to those which already possessed him—yes; a darkness, as of the very grave, was creeping slowly about the place, which seemed, in all probability, destined to become a sepulchre for him,

"Father! father!" half shrieked the child, as she recovered, sufficiently from her fright, to speak to him and to cling closer to his heart.

No. 3.

" Hush, darling, hush," he said, " not a word—not a word—God of heaven, let me think ; can nothing be done—nothing—while yet there is a glimmering light to do it ; oh, inspire me, heaven, with some happy thought that may preserve this fair object of thy creation, this young and innocent being to whom, surely, life has not been given in order that it should be taken away again, by such horrible means ; save it, save it, oh heaven ! save it ! " He sunk upon his knees, and while the young child, with frantic eagerness, and bitter sobs, clung to him, and tried to flinch away from his face, his hands, with which he covered it, he prayed to heaven for mercy on the head of that little one.

This prayer was over, and led us to believe that it was heard ; for a thought came across him which presented, at all events, a chance of safety for the child, if not for himself. With rapidity almost of thought itself, he dragged some of the polluted bed clothes, saturated with blood as they were, from the bed, and with an eagerness and a desperation that lent him strength to do it, he tore them into strips. These strips, in an incredible short space of time, he tied firmly together, and then he wound one end round the child, and adding to the length by his cloak, he approached the window with the hope, that by such means he might be enabled to lower the little innocent down the face of the rock on to some firm footing below. This window, it will be remembered, was at the back of the house, and so it was possible that even he himself might escape by such a means ; and, at all events, he told himself that death in the attempt were better than to await it with all its accumulated horrors in that frightful chamber. The child sobbed, and called upon him by the most endearing epithets not to leave it. His heart was wrung almost to the breaking, but he went to the window resolved that if he had to tear it down piecemeal from its frame-work, he would, at all events, secure an opening through it. And this he soon found was an idle declamation, for he had actually to do, so as the window did not seem adapted to open, but to have been let in solidly in the wood-work comprising this side of the texture. Time with him was everything—consequences nothing ; and he at once dashed his hands through some of the panes and began tearing away the leaden lattice-work that held them. He worked like a madman, stopping for nothing—heeding not the laceration which he endured during the course of this progress until at length, although his hands were covered with blood, and at any other time or under any other circumstances he would have doubtless felt great pain from his wounds ; he then felt nothing, thought of nothing, but the possibility of saving his beloved little one. We have before said, that exterior to the window there was some iron-work which would have been a serious obstacle to any one attempting to leave the room by such means ; but although that cheveux—a pin, for such it was—might have prevented him, without much personal injury by leaving the apartment from the window, it by no means interposed so great an obstacle to his standing out the child, because he saw that he could reach beyond it with his previous burthen, and so probably succeed in lowering it down. Although this was done in a much shorter space of time than it has taken us to relate it, and now having accomplished thus much, it were a sight enough to make any heart bleed to see the farewell which he took of that dearest, best treasure of his existence. Oh, how he strained her to his breast ! how he blest it ! prayed for it, and repeated its name in all the accents of tenderest affection.

" My own, my best, my dearest, he said !" " Live for joy such as should be thine, and may thy poor father's fate never dim the lustre of thy happiness which he would fain bestow upon thee, my beautiful Mary ; if this indeed be a farewell, for aye and for ever, may a halo of your father's purest and best affection cling around you ; may you be all that he would wish you in loveliness and intelligence ; in purity of heart and soul ; may the smile of heaven ever linger on your path, lighting to you the noblest and best deeds of which poor humanity is capable. Farewell, dearest ; dearest, it may be a farewell for ever."

He walked to the window with the child in his arms, trailing behind him the long pieces of the bed-clothing which he had tied together, and at that instant the light went out. He stood for a moment as if bewildered, for his eyes were unaccustomed to the darkness ; but then as he looked at the window it assumed a brighter aspect, and he remembered, that for some time he had not heard the blusterous wind, for the storm had become hushed, and a calm serenity had come over the face of nature. He knew that the moon too, ought soon to rise, and he fancied that he saw the faint blush of its earliest beams amid the darkness of the night air.

"Father, father," said the child as she clung to him round the neck, "you will not throw me from the window; oh, you will not throw me from the window!"

"Hush, darling, hush!"

"No, no, father, you will not, you will not; I have done nothing; no, no, no."

It was like tugging at his own heart-strings to force from their hold those tiny fingers which clasped his neck, but there was a stern and terrible necessity for doing so, and although he could not speak, he did it. The child uttered a shriek as he lifted it over the iron-work, and it hung suspended in the air.

"Now, God's mercy," he cried, "look down upon me: this is worse than death."

He shook frightfully, and, for the first time since the years of earliest childhood, the hot tears gushed from his eyes as slowly he lowered the child into the abyss below.

"Hark, hark! what sound is that? It comes from afar, borne gently upon the wings of the night wind; there again—there again—yes, 'tis louder now." Oh! well he knows that sound—on the battle-field he has heard it—it is the measured tramp of military; and ever and anon there came upon the air the rattle of drums and the shrill-piercing cry of the fife.

"They come—they come!" he said, as he clasped his hands, "and I may yet be saved."

Alas! in the excitement of the moment he had let go his hold of the long strips of clothing, and like lightning they rushed out of the window. There was a faint, smothered shriek. It was answered by the bereaved father in a yell of agony, as in an instant he awakened to a consciousness of what he had done. Then he fell backwards from the window with a heavy blow upon the floor, as one might have fallen suddenly deprived of life by the irresistible fiat of the Almighty.

CHAPTER IV.

THE COMPLETION OF THE CRIME.—THE MILITARY POSSESSION OF THE DYKE HOUSE.

Not only to Sir Anthony Wyvill's ears did the sound of those drums and fifes from afar come, but consternation was spread through the guilty family of the Fosters, as they sat gloomily below ruminating upon the consequences of the crime which they believed themselves to have committed.

"Do you hear that?" said the heavy looking son, who had been sleeping in one of the rooms on the arrival of the baronet and his child; "do you hear that? Damnation! What brings troops into the mountain region at such a time? Where can they come from?

"From Newport, the Lord willing," said Foster.

It was at this moment Sir Anthony Wyvill fell so heavily upon the floor, after allowing the child to slip in such a manner from his fingers as he had done, and the whole family started to their feet at the most unexpected sound.

"What's the meaning of that?" said Foster.

"By all that's damnable," said the son, "he's got off the bed, where never man got off before that once yon machine sought to confine; you had better go up and see—there will be the devil's own mess."

Foster shrunk back, as he said, in a low tone, "Will you go? You are younger than I, and I must confess myself somewhat nervous."

"Somewhat cowardly you mean, I fancy."

Foster pretended not to hear the remark, and the heavy, hulking-looking son proceeded to the side of the fire-place, where there hung a massive cleaver, such as is used for chopping meat. This he took down, and, swaying it in his hand for a moment, he, with a grim smile, left the apartment.

"A likely lad," said Foster, looking askant at his wife.

"Yes, for a gallows here, and hell hereafter."

"Ah! the Lord willing," said Foster. "Hark! is not that a noise above? Yes, most certainly he has got off the bed. There again—there again. Can it be that he is only slightly hurt? Aye! I must go and help."

There was a shuffling noise above stairs, and Foster slowly walked to the staircase.

"Hoi! hoi!" cried the son. "Come up here; I'll be damned if I know what's happened, but he's thrown the child out of window, and I'm going after it, for if its found, our necks are not worth the price of the ropes that will hang us.

"Stop, stop," shouted Foster, "you'll kill yourself if you attempt to get out of that window."

"Not I; I've learnt how to do it before to-day."

"He will die the death," said Foster, as he ran up the stairs. "Why, Sir Anthony must have got mad from some wound to throw the child from the window."

The scuffling noise continued as Foster proceeded up stairs, but before he reached the door there was a sudden crash as of broken glass, and then all was still.

"The heedless fellow," said Foster, "he has gone from the window. Well, thank the Lord, its his own neck, not mine, and he can do with it what he likes. What's he done with the light, I wonder?"

When Foster reached the room door all was darkness, save the faint rays which came in from the scarcely risen moon, which had but just presented its silver ridge over the horizon. He groped his way into the room with his hands cautiously held out before him. All was still, but he felt the keen air as it blew in from the broken window, and saw that it was a complete wreck, and then he stumbled over something, which, upon picking up, he found was the cleaver which had been taken up stairs by his hopeful son.

"Then he has gone from the window," he said, "the mad-brain fool. Hilloa, what is this lying before me?—the body of Sir Anthony Wyvill, I'll be bound. I wish the moon had risen a little higher that I might see if he were quite dead or not. He is motionless enough too; and yet it may have happened that the ascending steel had only wounded him. He knelt down by the side of the prostrate body, and placed his hand over the region of the heart. To his alarm he felt it distinctly throbbing, and then a deep groan came from the lips, which assured him that his purposed victim lived.

"It is your murder," he muttered in low tones, "or my hanging now. I prefer the former'"

There was a pause of a moment or two, during which he perceptibly trembled, and during that pause he again heard the drums and fifes of some advancing party of the military. With a bitter oath he raised the cleaver in both hands; he knew that it was over the face of his victim—he shut his eyes, and then he brought it down with a sickening crash.

Bone and muscle alike gave way beneath that frightful blow; the feet of the murdered man were brought up for a moment, and then shot out with terrific violence. Foster tried to raise the cleaver again, but it had stuck fast among the bones of the head—he felt the steam of the hot blood rising in his face; indeed some splashes had come upon him, and now, shaking like a man in an ague, he retreated backwards from that apartment, and, forgetting in his terror where he was going, he fell headlong down into the passage below.

At the sound of this sudden and frightful fall of Foster, his wife raised a shriek of dismay, and believing that something had occurred above stairs, which, in all likelihood, would be productive of personal danger to herself, she at once made a rush to the front door to escape if need, wherefrom the vengeance of Sir

Anthony Wyvill, who, for all she knew, might yet be living, and by some desperate means have conquered completely her husband and her son. She indeed ran out some few paces from the dwelling in the suddenness of her fright, nor paused until another step or two would have had the effect of bringing her over the edge of a precipice which was close at hand, and apparently yearning to receive her. All was still in the house now, for Foster had struck his head and stunned himself by his fall, so that after the first shock of terror and surprise that had come from his lips upon going so unexpectedly and so precipitately from one story of his house to the other, he remained motionless. How beautifully now the moonlight beamed up the mountain pass, and what a marked and wonderful change had taken place in the aspect of all things. That mountainous region, which a short time before seemed to have been given up to the very spirit of the storm, now presented such an aspect of perfect and beautiful repose, that it was delightful to look upon it—that is to say, delightful to any one whose mind was sufficiently calmed by circumstance to enable the imagination to dwell with rapture upon the beauties of that world, which, with a language that cannot be mistaken, proclaims the greatness of its beneficent Creator.

But Mrs. Foster was not one of those blessed spirits who can look into their hearts, saying, " Here there are errors, but there are no crimes ;" and so she shrunk, as the guilty always do shrink, before all the most beautiful phenomena of nature.

"All is still," she said; " what can have happened in the house ? I—I must return and see. Whenever the moon shines in such a manner as it does to-night—from out the clear blue sky—I wish that I were dead. Yes, yes!—dead and forgotten— forgotten by heaven ! "

She was about, with slow steps, to make her way back to the Dyke House, when —proceeding along a narrow ridge of rock which led to a fort of the mountain pass, a considerable distance higher up than the Dyke House was situated—she saw the form of a man. In an instant she was still : her straining eyeballs seemed as if they would burst from their sockets, and she shook like one wrestling with the last dread pangs of death.

"'Tis he, 'tis he!" she shrieked; and then she fell in a swoon, some few paces from the door of the Dyke House. The figure whom she had seen, and that had called forth so frantic an exclamation, continued picking its way carefully along the mountain ridge; and although the cry of Mrs. Foster must certainly have reached its ears, it paid not the least apparent attention to the sound. But what was that figure like ? What hideous or what dull form did it resemble, that pierced the soul of that guilty woman with terror at the sight. He bore the general outward appearance of the murdered man—of Sir Anthony Wyvill—who, she had all the reason in the world to feel assured, lay dead in the upper room of the Dyke House. There was the cloak—there was the hat—and, to all appearance—although the back of the figure was turned towards her, so that she could not say for certain— he carried in his arms the child. At least so she, from the stooping attitude and the position of the arms, judged. What, then, could it be but the spirit of the murdered ? What else could account for such an appearance at such an hour ? Yes, it must be so—and henceforward that face was to be a region of unmitigated terror to the guilty. Alas, alas ! what a dreadful amount of punishment had she brought upon herself by her continued iniquities !

For a few moments only, the figure with the cloak appeared in sight; and then, as the mountain ridge on which it had been seen sharply descended to meet the narrow pathway of the defile, it disappeared. Scarcely had it gone, when Foster rose to his feet much bewildered by the blow he had struck his head, but still sufficiently recovered from its effects to understand how it had happened.

"Curses on my own folly ! " he exclaimed, "I might have killed myself.. Never before have I been so weak and foolish in the execution of my plans; and this affair, which has really been the most profitable of all, has been conducted with terrible and foolish confusion. Hilloa, there ! who is without? Wife, wife! I say, where are you ?"

He stepped across the threshold, and there he saw the form of his wife lying close to his feet. He started back in amazement, as he exclaimed—

" Why, what is this ?   Is she dead ?   Will the events of this night never cease ? There is danger, perhaps, yet."

He stooped, and, raising the form of his wife in his arms, rushed into the house with her, and laid her down on the floor of the room which the reader is well acquainted with.   Then he proceeded to the outer door and listened ; and, as he did so, he heard again, with great distinctness, the roll of the drums and the shrill cry of the fifes, which had for some time announced the arrival of a military party.

" What can be the meaning," he muttered, " of a march in such a night—for they must have started in the storm—and at such a time of night ?   Oh, perhaps some new change of quarters ; and the whim of the commander has made the march take place in the night, instead of in the day."

Notwithstanding Foster strove thus to explain to himself what gave him so much disquietude, that disquietude was none the less ; and the more he thought of the circumstance the more strongly it came across his imagination, that the military might come along the mountain pass, and make a halt at the Dyke House, in which case he stood in a dreadful risk of some of the evidences of murder showing themselves.

With this idea foremost in his mind he made the outer door fast, and returned to the room in which he had left his wife, who was sitting by the fire in her usual crawling position—swaying to and fro ; and now and then uttering a low groan, as she thought of some more than usually harassing subject for contemplation, or as memory —that curse of the bad and blessing of the virtuous—brought to her mind the dim remembrance of many a deed of blood.

CHAPTER V.

A RETROSPECT.

Precisely on that day five years before on which such dreadful scenes had taken place at the Dyke House, there sat in one of the chambers of Sir Anthony Wyvill's splendid mansion a young and beautiful girl. Perhaps we ought not to apply to her that term " girl," for she was a wife ; yet was there something so exquisitely girl-like and beautiful in the youthful aspect which she bore that one could hardly look upon her as aught else than one of the most finished and beautiful specimens of the English girl that it would be possible to find. And can there be a more loveable being than such a one as shall fully realize all that we would express when we use the words " a beautiful English girl."   He who writes these pages has had the fortune to see the young and the beautiful of most of the Continental nations ; but with a freshness, and with whole or renewed charm has there ever come before him one of those mildly intelligent and sweet countenances belonging to the girls of his own native land.

Some one has said that the nearest approach we can find to what the artist would paint as perfectly angelic, is a young girl, not of an age to care for, or to enter into, the cabals of life, and whom nature has favoured with the externals of beauty, as well as a mind full of the very grandeur, as well as the simplicity, of virtue. And let who will have uttered that sentiment, it is a true one.   There does seem about such beautiful and interesting beings a something more than mortal ; and such a one was she who sat, with a half smile upon her face, in an apartment of Wyvill House, as it was called, while a newspaper that she had been reading lay negligently on her lap, and her thoughts seemed for the moment to be far away.

And now before we proceed further with a description of what she did and said upon this occasion, we will briefly tell the reader who and what she is, and her present circumstances.

Sir Anthony Wyvill had early in life met with one of these disappointments of the heart which some men pass over as things of little moment, but which upon others produce the most lasting and sensible effects.   One whom he had loved with all his heart had been false to him, and had wedded with a wealthier rival for the glitter of a coronet, and such worldly advantages as are unwise, fortune may be supposed to bring to one who builds up all her hopes of happiness upon so frail a basis. No wonder then that he should, being a man of a nervous and enthusiastic temperament, consider that there was placed for ever a barrier between himself and that sex, one of whom had played him so sorry a trick.

Disgusted, as he told himself he was with society, he went into the army, leaving his estates, which were considerable, wholly in the care of Margaret Wyvill, his elder sister, although not by the same mother.

By one of those strange anomalies which sometimes occur among members of the same family, there was the greatest possible dissimilarity of disposition between Sir Anthony Wyvill and this sister Margaret of his ; for, whereas, he possessed all the characteristics of a great and noble, and a devoted spirit ; she appeared, on the contrary, to have devoted her intellect to everything that was despicable and mean. And yet, she possessed the most wonderful art in glazing over these errors of her disposition ; and, with refined hypocrisy, she was able to convince superficial observers of human nature, that she possessed a world of virtue which she knew nothing of but by name. She was one of those who seemed to consider throughout their entire life, that the better and nobler feelings of humanity are only useful, inasmuch as they may be assumed to get the better of the unwary : a mask behind which vice may hide herself, and more securely commit her depredations upon the innocent and just.

She had education and talent : but, alas ! both were perverted from their legitimate purposes, and made to serve the worst instead of the best of objects. In preference to taking the broad and even path, a path so simple that a child might tread it, which leads to happiness, with honour and honesty for guides, she chose the tangled and intricate ways of iniquity; fancying she was to achieve a something, heaven only knows what, by plotting and by planning, and undermining the happiness of all around her.

A restless desire to command, and to rise superior to every one around her, was the besetting sin of her disposition. Early enough in life she discovered the slavish adulation which all pay to wealth, and from that time avarice grew up in her head, and she grasped at wealth as one of the most ready means for the acquisition of power. In person she was commanding, not unhandsome in features, although there was a haughty, stern rigidity about her countenance ; and, occasionally, a flashing of her dark eye, which betrayed something of the quality of the restless spirit that dwelt within.

That this woman should succeed in inducing a belief in the mind of Sir Anthony Wyvill that she was just and honourable, and that those flashes of a darker disposition that occasionally appeared, were only to be attributed to the temper, and not to any inherent badness of disposition, is scarcely to be wondered at ; for he was a man ever disposed to look with the utmost lenience upon human nature—a man who fancied that more good was to be found in poor humanity than many persons gave it credit for. Moreover, he was of ready and credulous belief in what was said to him, and could scarcely think it possible but what there must be much exaggeration in the records of villany with which the history of mankind teems.

Such a man as this was not likely to think evil of one so nearly allied to him as Margaret Wyvill—he certainly thought her rather infeminine in character, and that he fell into the common and foolish error of attributing to a more matured intellect than her sex usually possessed, as if it were necessary because a woman was sensible that she should be likewise disagreeable, and divest herself of those feminine graces which are ever so attractive and so beautiful.

What share this Margaret Wyvill had in inducing the early disappointment which Sir Anthony had suffered in the one grand passion of his existence, it is not for us now to inquire.

That is an episode in his existence which has passed away, and it is of another that we have to speak. Delighted was she to be left in such unlimited authority over her brother's possessions. It gave her a consequence and a power, such as in no other way could she have aspired to; and she hailed his absence with pleasure, because it left the power uncurbed, by the conscientiousness that in him there was a court of appeal, against any too arbitrary exercise of it.

She considered, and she had ample grounds for so considering, that he was not a man likely again to entangle himself in the meshes of affection. She looked upon herself as the absolute mistress of the Wyvill estates, and she lorded it over every one who came within her influence in a manner which sufficiently proved she fully intended to show, that she did indeed consider herself in unlimited authority.

And so, half heart-broken, Sir Anthony Wyvill had gone abroad, little dreaming that ever again he should feel the soft rapturous feeling of affection for aught that was human. But the crisis in his destiny had not arrived, although he thought it had passed. He had yet to learn that it was possible to feel a second time the heart warmed to an affection which poets tell us can only be felt but once. Perhaps, after all though, they are right, and the first passion of Sir Anthony Wyvill might have been a spurious one ; this second feeling being the real out-pouring of an affection which, sooner or later, was sure to portray itself to some beloved object. Abroad he became intimate with a family of English origin, which boasted, as its chiefest ornament, a young and beautiful creature of that age when first the daring intellect begins to release itself from the trammels of childhood, and to look about upon the great world with something of an observant eye.

Her beauty was her least recommendation ; although she was all that the most fervid imagination could fancy as lovely in that sex, which certainly has monopolised the principal charms that heaven has bestowed upon earth ; but it was in her pure and lustrous intellect, child-like and trusting as it was, that the magic of her fascination lay. She knew no guile, suspected none, the world to her was an untrodden garden ; alas ! she knew nothing of the storms that would soon convert the love of her imagination into a very wilderness of gloom.

Sir Anthony Wyvill saw her and he admired her ; the admiration deepened into love, although for a while he combatted against the passion. It seemed a sort of treason to the grief which he felt from his previous bitter disappointment to fancy it possible that he could love again. And yet, thrown as he was by the hospitality of her friends in her society, he could not refuse from entertaining for her in a short time a genuine and deep affection ; which, although he told himself it had not all the wild fervour and passionate excitement of his first love, was likely to be more lasting, by being based upon more reflection and better principles. And she was not insensible to the handsome appearance and the many sterling qualities of Sir Anthony Wyvill ; she nourished in her breast, what she considered a gentle and a friendly preference for his society—she was not learned enough in the world's ways to know that it was love alone had unfurled his radient ensign in her heart. But soon a test of their mutual affections arrived. Sir Anthony Wyvill was recalled home with his regiment, contrary to his expectations, and to all his wishes ; for he had joined the corps of the army that he considered would have remained in active service for many years, and so saved him the pain of re-visiting the scene— of re-visiting the place of his former disappointment and love.

But what were these circumstances compared to the agony of parting with this new object of his heart's adoration ? Then, and not till then, he found out how deep had been the impression made upon him by that young and beautiful creature, who had chased melancholy from his soul, and healed the wounds which disappointment had given him—those wounds which he could not have vamped up by any other method.

And she, too, heard the news with trembling apprehension—she felt that her heart had received the impression of his virtues and his nobleness ; as though it had been of wax upon which an image could have been indelibly impressed. She told herself that so entwined were the threads of mutual affection, that an attempt to disentangle them would be to deprive her of all that rendered life dear to her, and to leave the shaft of disappointment bristling in her heart.

He came to bid her adieu ; it needed but one look at her tearful aspect to show him the true state of her affections ; his bosom's lord sat lightly on its throne, when he was able to whisper to himself " She loves me ! yes, she loves me ! " Oh what a world of unspeakable bliss is concentrated in those few words, when they can be repeated with a deep and trusting conviction of their truthfulness. In vain he attempted to utter the word, 'farewell!' Like the amen of Macbeth, it stuck in his throat; but not like the murderous Thane had he much need of blessing, for was he not blessed indeed, with the consciousness of having awakened a feeling of affection in the breast of one so true, so beautiful, so, in every way, calculated to smoothen the rugged path of life, and to be, as it were, a ministering angel through existence.

It was a moment of excitement far from premeditated or even dreamt of, but he told her that he loved her, with all the fond eloquence that characterises a truthful

attachment, that knows no bounds, but is as enduring as the universe itself; he told her that from the first moment he had looked upon her, the love of excellence, which from his earliest years had found being within his breast, had become personified in her; that she was the living image of his dreams; that he would love her while life remained to him, and that his dearest hope in a consummation of that life which was to come, would consist in the glorious expectation of meeting with her again, and treading with her the paths of immortality and eternal joy. And she had listened as one entranced, to that soft confession from one, who, when in the fond

No. 4.

enthusiasm of a girlish heart, she had taught herself to look upon as something more than human, for she was of that enthusiastic order of beings who are prone almost to deify the thing they adore.

He ceased, and he looked into her face as some one who felt that life or death hung upon the breath of another; she did not speak but she placed her hand in his, the gesture was sufficient, he felt—he knew that he was beloved; he knew now that the heart in which he had garnered up his best affections returned fully and completely all the passion, or rather all the sentiment with which he himself was inspired, and then he could speak even more freely than before.

"Dearest," he cried, "dearest and best; were I to range the great world through, I could not find one who could light the fire of affection in my heart, to the extent that you in the very simplicity of your goodness have achieved. Like fragrant incense from an altar, the vapour of which ascends to heaven, will my best prayers ever be uttered for thee, and I will love thee well and truly; the blush of wrong shall never dye thy cheek, and never shall you find me a bar to that happiness which should be yours. In my inmost heart I have registered your virtues, and had I left you now without this declaration, those who knew me best might have pointed to me in after years, with a bitter exclamation, 'He flew from affections;' and then, how distasteful would the world, with all its hopes and fears, have been to me; I should have felt like one done with humanity; who had accepted the cowl, and sought in a life of monasticism, that serenity which he could not otherwise enjoy."

"Speak on," said she, "your words are music."

"Ah, but what can I say more? not that I have yet exhausted love's eloquence, but that my heart is almost too full for utterance; I might have traversed many lands, and might have swept the ocean, and lingered upon many a hearth, ere I found one who could have responded to my purest dream of affection as you have done."

"No, no, there are many who could have loved you."

"But none whom I could have loved as I love thee; the fire of life would have grown dim; no more would those bright shades—scintillations of those glorious spirits within us have ascended to heaven, and my crushed affections would not, as they have, phœnix-like, sprung from their own ashes into a new and glorious existence."

"And can you love me so?"

"Aye, until I mingle with the dust."

It was in such a romantic strain that Sir Anthony Wyvill woo'd and won this paragon of excellence; he made her his own, and instead of returning to England, a desolate and solitary man, he left behind him the thunder of war, and lightened his leisure by the presence of all that was beautiful. Oh! it was a reign of pure enjoyment, the clouds of fate might lower in vain, but secure in the haven of his heart's best affections, he could hold at arm's length the accidents of fortune, and cry, all hail! to any fate.

How strangely possible it is for one human creature to wind itself tempestuously round the heart of another, and in the very hurricane of passion to find a calmness unknown to ordinary mortals. The sea of human troubles may wave to and fro its unhappy victims, and like bubbles upon the crested head of the mighty billows, man may become the slave of circumstances; and if he love truly, and that love be returned as truly, then he may be happy until the last sands of life have run through the glass of time. He reached his native shores, and sped towards that home of his infancy which he had scarcely thought to see again; he had given no notice of his approach, for he thought it would be an agreeable surprise to his sister Margaret, not only to see him so happy, but to see him so unexpectedly. Alas, little did he know, the disposition of the individual for whom he was planning, what he vainly considered this agreeable surprise; little did he know the feeling of jealousy, of envy, aye, of absolute rage with which she would be sure to look upon that home and beautiful being whose fate he had linked with his, and to whom he had made a promise of such happiness to come. With all the fond partiality which he felt towards Margaret Wyvill, he had informed the chosen of his affections, his own gentle and beloved Emily, that she was not to expect softness or tenderness from his sister, but that she was to look for, and surely would find, all the sterling virtues that could belong to human nature. He told her that she was truth itself, even to bluntness, for to that frightful extent had he mistaken the character of the being whom he madly chose as a companion of that young, innocent, ardent, and beautiful creature that heaven had permitted him to call his own. And in this way was Emily prepared, for she trusted implicitly to all that was related to her to respect and to venerate, if she could not absolutely love that stern sister of her husband.

By short and easy stages they reached Wyvill Hall, and the first intimation that was given of the approach of its owner consisted in a travelling carriage, the panels of which were unemblazoned, driving up to the lodge gates, and Sir Anthony himself alighting from it. The first object his eyes alighted upon was the aged lodge-keeper, who was familiar to his earliest boyish recollections; the old man knew him, and blessed the haply chance that brought the master of Wyvill House once again within the shadow of his ancient home. Tears flowed down his furrowed cheeks as he welcomed his master; and this is scarcely a matter of singularity, when we consider that in many of the districts of Wales the old feudal spirit still remains, and the system of vassalage, although unsanctioned by the law, has got so strong a hold of the country people, that they look upon their superiors as if they were beings fashioned altogether of a different clay from that of which they were composed. But when Sir Anthony Wyvill handed the beautiful creature he had torn from the cave, the old man's admiration was as boundless as his respect. He looked upon her as some angel descended to the earth to bless with her glorious presence that scion of an ancient race. And she spoke to him so gently, and with such a tone of kindly inquiry that she won his heart as well as his eyes; and as she walked up that long and graceful avenue which led to the entrance of the ancient Hall, he bent upon his staff and looked after her with something of a melancholy aspect upon his face.

"Heaven preserve her," he said, "heaven preserve her—she is too happy and too beautiful for it to last very long. God help her—a presentiment of evil creeps over my old heart."

He turned, and with faltering steps re-entered his lodge, and so impressed was the old man with some feeling of coming evil towards that young and beautiful lady, that to the surprise of his old dame, who had not issued forth, in consequence of what she called a romantic pain in the back, he wept abundantly. But let us follow Sir Anthony, and his fair young bride. Margaret Wyvill sat in an ancient apartment, looking upon the magnificent gardens of the Hall; she was deeply congratulating herself upon the advantages of her position, and into her calculations of the future no thought of her brother's return even obtruded itself. In point of fact, she considered that she was entirely and totally mistress of the Wyvill estates; and she had almost got the length of grudging the amount of money which she was required to pay into the hands of her brother's agents in London every quarter, as the rentals came due, to meet his drafts; she thought of controlling this amount of expenditure, and was turning over in her mind the best method of leading him into a belief that the estates were not so productive as they had been, when she heard a heavy tread upon the gravel path which led close up to the house. A feeling of dread came over her, and yet she was far from guessing that that tread bespoke the arrival of her brother. Had an angel from heaven appeared before her and told her he was present and within a few paces of her, she would have considered the news as too apocryphal and doubtful to be relied upon.

"Who can this be?" she said to herself, "how my heart beats—I feel an unusual tremor stealing over me—what can it mean?—something is about to happen—the footsteps come this way—is it human? It seems to come upon my ears with a familiar credence, as if I had heard it many a time before."

She paused for a moment and listened attentively—then with a sneer upon her countenance, she added:

"Have I turned superstitious at last—this is some chimera of fancy which shall not govern me—nearer, nearer it comes. I have no feeling but curiosity, and that

I care not to own to—it is one which belongs to me, but not in its meanest features."

She rose and walked close to the window, so that she should be sure, in the course of a few moments, to see who it was that was advancing up the garden avenue. And too soon indeed for her peace did she make that discovery; for a moment, her senses almost left her, and she shook from head to foot as she observed that it was her brother, whose formerly well-known footsteps had struck upon her ear, as something familiar to memory, while upon his arm there hung a female, who, from her general contour and appearance, Margaret felt certain, was young and beautiful. There was no time now for reflection—in another instant, Sir Anthony, and his fair young bride, reached the door of his own Hall.

"Be this who it may," exclaimed Margaret, "and let what will be about to happen, I must act my old part of seeming affection."

No sooner had she uttered these words, than schooling her features into an expression of delighted surprise, she flew to the threshold of the door and fell upon her brother's neck. It was an accomplished piece of acting—those who knew her not would have given her credit for the most genuine affection; and the young wife was charmed to think, that he, upon whom she had fixed her heart's best affections, should be possessed of so near and dear a relative.

"Margaret," said Sir Anthony Wyvill, "I have no doubt surprised you by my sudden appearance; believe me, I did not think so soon to have revisited the home of my father, but there is one whom I must introduce to you—this is my wife.'

"Thank heaven!" exclaimed Margaret, "then you are happy."

She took both the hands of Emily in her own, and as she looked in her face, and marked, with a jealous pang the wondrous beauty that then shone forth, she said—

" This is all like a dream to me; but, I need not say that I will try to love you for my own brother's sake, I will love all that he loves."

"Can I ask or hope for more?" said Emily, in that sweet, rich voice, which was peculiar to her; "you make me but too happy by such kind words."

It was thus conversing, that they made their way out of one of the principal rooms of the Hall. The whole establishment was set into commotion, and refreshments were immediately placed before them, while nothing could exceed the kind attention of Margaret Wyvill to their wants.

Emily was enchanted with her husband's home; she had pictured it to herself as something pleasant and great, but not in the wildest dreams of her imagination had it assumed such an aspect as now it really wore. There was nothing wanting to make it quite happy—especially, received, as she was, by that husband's sister, with such a profusion of real kindness.

CHAPTER VI.

THE INTERVIEW.—HYPOCRISY OF MARGARET.—A HAPPY MONTH.—THE DEPARTURE OF SIR ANTHONY WYVILL.—WAR'S ALARMS.—THE WIFE AND THE SISTER.—A MOTHER'S CARES.—THE LETTER.

" SISTER," said Sir Anthony, when the servants had withdrawn, and they sat alone, "sister, I the more appreciate your kind reception of us, because you are as yet in utter ignorance of the circumstances which have brought me back to England so unexpectedly."

" I am satisfied," said Margaret, " to see that you are happy."

" Nay, but I owe you an apology for not communicating to you the causes of my happiness. I have made no secret to Emily of my former history; she knows well that I had an attachment to another once, but, with that knowledge, she knows that I love her well and truly."

Emily looked upon her husband trustingly and fondly, while the colour, for a moment, fled from Margaret's cheeks, for she felt, that what Sir Anthony Wyvill had uttered, at once deprived her of one strong weapon of attack.

During the time that they had been partaking of the refreshments, that she had, so immediately ordered to be placed before them, she had concluded, almost as a matter of course, that the young wife knew nothing of the previous disappointment in his affections, which Sir Anthony Wyvill had undergone ; and she had calculated, with the rapidity of thought upon the power, which a knowledge of such a secret would give her over her brother. But to find that he had been so candid as to inform his young wife of everything, was a severe blow to Margaret's calculations, and she was compelled, consequently, to fall back upon minor sources of consolation.

" Yes," continued Sir Anthony Wyvill, " I have told Emily all ; and she loves me not the less, that my heart has been before sensible of an attachment, to one, who acted unworthily."

" I have nothing," said Emily, " to do with the past, the present suffices for me ; I am happy in your love, and why should I repine because you may once have spoken words of tenderness to another ?"

" Excellent and best of beings !" said Sir Anthony, " how can I sufficiently appreciate such an affection as yours ?"

" Most easily," she replied ; " you do so, fully, by reciprocating it. I ask no other recompense for my own heart's devotion."

" But you were about to tell me" said Margaret, " how you became acquainted with her, who, I feel convinced, will gild the remainder of your existence."

" True, I was."

" Then gratify me by the recital."

Sir Anthony Wyvill then related to his sister, how he had become acquainted with Emily, and how her beauty and goodness, had gradually achieved a conquest of his heart's best affections. And, as he spoke, he looked with such eyes of fondness upon his bride, that Margaret trembled for an empire over him, and began to suspect that the task of maintaining anything like her usual position, at Wyvill Hall, would be hard, indeed ; but she dissembled these sensations, and with a face of seeming interest, she listened to the recital, and, when it was concluded, with a mock smile, she turned to Emily, saying,—

" You will, and you ought to be, happy. I do not envy you, although I feel that in the society of my dear brother, whose many excellencies and virtues I know well you will arrive at as great contentment as, probably, this world is capable of affording you."

' I'm sure of that," said Emily.

" And do not think that I flatter you, when I tell you, that I believe you deserve such happiness as that I paint."

" I will strive to do so ; and if I fall short in my dessert, it shall not be for want of a desire to be all that I ought to be to one, who had lifted me to a summit of happiness I never before dared to hope, or expect, I should enjoy."

" Nay, there you are wrong," said Sir Anthony Wyvill, " it is I who ought to have made a speech, not you, my Emily. It is you, who have lifted me from a state of unhappiness, that, otherwise, I must have remained in while life remained to me. It is to you that I owe all, that I can now call, delight ; you have been my better angel, and have rescued me from a state of despondency, into which I had almost hopelessly fallen."

It was in such a conversation as this that an hour or two passed happily ; and so far did Margaret exert herself, to seem that which she was not, that Emily was charmed with her, and felt inclined to trust her with her whole soul ; so that, if chicanery and malice could accomplish anything, in consequence of the innocence of those, who trusted such feelings—disguised in the mask of virtue—Margaret was in a fair way of obtaining her object. And that object was one, which, from the first moment of Emily's appearance at Wyvill Hall, had found a home in her breast. It was to dispossess the young wife of her husband's confidence, and her husband's affections. It was not only to make her heart desolate, but the heart of Sir Anthony Wyvill, likewise; in order that she, Margaret, might still retain the power which accident had given her over those broad domains and smiling lands. And little she reeked what mischief she produced, little cared she what heart she broke, during her progress to her summit of ambition.

No, she said to herself, I am not one who will allow all my well-laid schemes of aggrandizement, to be set aside by a pretty face and a musical voice. I am not one to allow myself to be beaten by such shallow accomplishments; but I must dissemble, yes, deeply dissemble.

And, indeed, she did dissemble, and with a most fiendish skill that human nature could possibly lay claim to, she assumed the appearance of virtues that were completely foreign to her real character. She smiled when she could have frowned; she spoke in the soft accents of seeming affection, when she could have stormed with passion; and, Judas like, she kissed but to betray.

Alas, that such a creature as Emily Wyvill, which we must now call her, should fall into such cruel hands!

Some weeks flew by in uninterrupted bliss. Day succeeded day, but to produce some new enjoyments, invented by the very genius of affection, lest the time should pass heavily upon her hands. And none seemed more anxious than Margaret, to forward any little scheme of enjoyment projected by Sir Anthony Wyvill; so that, it seemed, as if the time were but one long summer's day of uninterrupted beauty and sunshine.

But this is not a period in the history of Sir Anthony and his lady, upon which we can afford to dwell, although we would fain linger upon it, did not sterner scenes call us to their delineation, and were we not compelled to be the chroniclers of a wildly different character.

*   *   *   *   *   *   *

A month has elapsed—a month, which seemed but a week, in such a career of uninterrupted happiness did it pass; and then, as Sir Anthony Wyvill and his smiling bride sat at breakfast, a letter was brought to him. He changed colour as he read it, and it fell from his hands upon the table. Emily marked the alteration in his countenance, and her fears took the alarm on the instant, although she by no means guessed the purport of that epistle. She hesitated a moment, and then he motioned her to read it. It was an official notice for him to join his regiment instanter, and proceed with it to the Continent, where war had broken out again, with apparently a greater violence, after a temporary and hollow peace which had been effected with the enemy.

"No, no," she cried, as she clasped her hands, "you shall not, must not, leave me."

His only reply was a deep sigh; and then, after a time, in answer to her earnest supplications that he would remain, he said,—

"My dearest Emily, I must feel that I am entitled, and that I act in a manner which shall still entitle me to your respect, as well as your affection. If I had but thought to leave the army during this period of peace, all would have been well, and I should have been honourably acquitted of my obligation to encounter again the alarms of war, but now, upon the first blush of a new contest, I dare not. You, dear Emily, would be the last to countenance me to any act that would sully the honour of him, to whom, I know, you look for all the happiness that this world can afford you."

She wept, for that is a woman's argument when her reason is convinced; she clung to him, and entreated him to stay, but yet his honour was very dear to her; and when he had, again and again, represented to her how he would suffer in the eyes of all who knew him, and how he would become obnoxious by the reproach of having forsaken the duties of a profession he had himself chosen whenever they became of an uncomfortable or dangerous character, she yielded, although she still wept.

"You must—you shall go," she said, "but let it be only for so long as shall suffice to vindicate your honour; just so long, and no longer, than shall be sufficient to free you from this fancied reproach, which, you think it possible, the world may cast upon you, and then, to return to love and to me."

This, we will imagine, was promised with all the eagerness of the utmost devotion, on the part of Sir Anthony Wyvill. The mandate, to join his regiment, was one which had to be obeyed within the short space of four-and-twenty hours; and, perhaps, for all parties concerned, it was better that that should be the case, for, since the parting was certain to come, it was but protracting the misery of all parties to put it off until a late moment.

She clung to him, for the short time he had yet to remain with her, as if, with some sort of strange feeling, that it would be long, indeed, before they met again. She looked in his face with that mournful earnestness with which we may be supposed to glance upon the countenances of those, whom the stern hand of death is taking from us.

She could not recover from the deep sense of depression which crept over her, and yet, now she used no arguments to induce him to stay, for, having once yielded the point, that it was for his honour to go, she would not imbitter the painfulness of so sacred a duty, by more regrets than were absolutely necessary.

It was in vain that he attempted, by a little affectionate dissimulation, to conceal from her the exact time of his departure. She dreaded those last few moments' interview with him, when she should feel assured that, under the most favourable circumstances, she was taking her last look upon him for a very considerable period. And so he would fain have cheated her of that burst of agony, but he could not, for she clung too closely to him; she would not lose a moment of the society of him whom she had made her heart's idol when she was so soon to leave him wholly.

"Emily," he said, "you will not let me deceive you; I would fain have left the Hall without saying to you that sad word, farewell! but you will not have it so, and now, dearest and best, we must part!"

She could not speak, but she clung to him with a convulsive energy; she could not say that word which he had hoped to avoid himself the utterance of, and, at length, he was forced to tear himself away, leaving her in the arms of Margaret in a state of half insensibility. But, although he had amused the mind of Emily with a hope that he would soon be able to leave the army and return once again to clasp her in his arms, he did not delude himself by any such feeling. The corps of the army to which he was attached was at the commencement of a most serious campaign—a campaign not likely to be quickly terminated, or terminated at all without numerous casualties. He, therefore, did not expect for some years to be able again to look upon his native land. As for making any attempt to leave the army while it was engaged in active warfare, that was a thing not to be thought of, and he could only hope that a speedier conclusion to hostilities might arrive than, in his own mind, he really expected.

And she—how did she, whom he loved with such devotion, and whose whole soul was concentrated in her affection for him alone, how did she pass her time during the long and weary days of his absence?

Alas! for a time most gloomily. That lordly home, with all its attendant charms, had no charms for her; the vastness of the apartments only struck her with a chilly awe, making her feel more acutely the want of him who would have lent a cheerfulness to them. The rich verdure that surrounded Wyvill Hall, and the tall trees which had taken centuries of growth to acquire their full maturity of beauty, no longer filled her mind with ideas of the great and of the sublime; the sunshine did not delight her nor did the perfume of the sweet flowers bring grateful feelings to her senses—the songs of the forest birds no longer were themes of listening delight, she saw every thing, she felt every thing, she heard every thing through the medium of her own disappointed hopes and feelings.

Amid the trees the pleasant murmur of the wind, as it played among the verdure of their branches, to her imagination was changed into sighs; the fragrance of the flowers brought back but recollections of what he who was far away had loved and praised, the songs of the birds were translated by her overwrought fancy into sweet pastoral lamentations—and so as love, in the fulness of its enjoyment, will alter every taste and feeling, making the rugged and the strange beautiful and great, so in its melancholy bereavement, will it convert those objects upon which nature has stamped the seat of its most exquisite enchantments into things of little moment or full of suggestive melancholy.

And such precisely was the condition of Emily Wyvill; through the false medium of her own melancholy feelings she viewed every thing, which otherwise would have been full of delight, but this was a feeling which, like the whole family of griefs to which humanity is subject, was sure to yield in some degree to time. In this case, likewise, time had a great auxiliary; for, before the first year had expired of the absence of Sir Anthony Wyvill from his home, Emily became a mother. In all the absorbing cares which occupied the maternal breast previous melancholies were forgotten. The first glance into the sweet face of the babe seemed as if it had opened to her a glimpse of heaven, which was so dear a recompense for all the past that, in the fulness of a young mother's delight, every thing but the joy of looking upon that young emanation of divinity was forgotten. It was something to her so new, so strange, and so beautiful, that this small thing of life should cling to her, and that that human face divine, in which she traced such a world of beauties, should have sprung so marvellously into existence.

It is not for us of the rougher sex to analyse or to understand the feelings of a mother as she looks upon her first-born, and feels it upon her breast throbbing and instinct with life; but we can faintly conceive the world of joy, the very emporium of happiness that must be her's as she looks upon that tiny being, which she almost feels she has created, and which looks to her with an instinctive fondness and a grateful clinging affection which neither time nor circumstance can ever change. Oh! if there be any thing in human nature which bespeaks the divinity of its origin, it is that holy, that rapturous love which is concentrated all upon those dear objects that are, in time which is to come, to represent ourselves and play our old accustomed parts in the great drama of existence. The man who loves not those little ones of whom are the kingdom of heaven, and who the world's great teacher desired might be brought unto Him, is something less than mortal; he who loves them best is something near to God.

We do not mean to say that Emily Wyvill forgot her husband, far from it; one of her chiefest pleasures was to consider what a joy it would be to present to him this living image of herself, this little creature whom she considered, and whom she knew he would likewise consider one of the greatest gifts of God. And it rescued her from all her melancholy thoughts and saddened fancies; she had now occupation, and it was an occupation which was all engrossing; she had no time, in the full joy of a young heart's happiness, to think of sorrow; and therefore little is it to be made a matter of wonder that soon the roses bloomed upon her cheek and at the opportunities that were presented to her to do so, she wrote to her husband letters full of hope, joy, and the most ardent affection.

We will not pause to analyze the feelings with which Sir Anthony Wyvill received the news that he was a father, engaged as he was in the stirring scenes of actual warfare, he had little time for the softer emotions of the human heart. But yet he snatched many a hour from the arduous duties, the fatigues, and the dangers of his profession, to write some words of love's greeting to her whom he had left at home to sigh for his return. And in those brief notes, for brief they necessarily were, he lamented that he had not yet looked upon that young and beautiful child of which she often breathed a fervent hope that the time would not be far distant when he would be enabled to press it to his heart, and hear it utter the endearing name of father!

* * * * * * *

And now we have, we hope, sufficiently explained to the reader, the state of affairs at Wyvill House, to enable us to continue our narrative in a fuller and more distinct form and it is necessary that we should call attention to two distinct episodes in this eventful history, and as we deem the lady has precedence upon all occasions we shall first take up that which more particularly belongs to Emily Wyvill, and then relate a something connected with Sir Anthony which enabled a third person, namely, Margaret Wyvill, to achieve results she might otherwise have sighed for in vain.

Sir Anthony had been absent about a year from his ancestral home, when one evening, as Emily was sitting looking upon the sweet colours which heralded the decline of day, while her child was sleeping in her bosom, a stranger was announced

as desiring to speak to her. Although no name was announced, nothing was so remarkable in the fact of any one calling upon her, that it should create much surprize; for her charities were so extensive, and she had so ardent a desire to do good to all around her, that she was frequently visited by persons who either came themselves to represent to her their deep distresses, or to paint in such language, as they thought best befitting, the miseries of some others in whom they felt deeply interested. She was told that it was a man who desired to see her, and that his appearance was that of one weary and travel worn.   He had said that he had come many a mile to speak to her; and the servant who brought the news of his approach, expatiated so largely upon the melancholy of his aspect, and the deep pathos of his tones, that Emily was insensibly led to a sympathetic feeling, and consented at once to see the stranger.

Resigning the child into the care of an attendant, she repaired to a room into which she had named he was to be shown; and, when she reached it, the colour forsook her cheeks, she clasped her hands and trembled, for in that travel-worn and weary looking stranger she recognised a brother, who long since had shaken off all ties of kindred, and who had been supposed to have gone to the tomb full of dishonour, and in some foreign land.

" Emily," he said, and he spoke in a tone which seemed to proclaim the contrition of a heart bowed down by suffering; " Emily, I have travelled hundreds of miles on foot to see you.   I heard that you were married, and that you were happy. Heaven forbid that I should be at all the means of disturbing your felicity, but I am destitute and friendless; can you, without prejudice to yourself, aid me ?"

" Oh, Robert, Robert ! " said Emily, " little did I think to look upon you; the question is, not whether I can aid you without prejudice to myself, but whether I can aid you at all."

" Say that you cannot," said the wanderer, " and I am gone."

" No, no, stay.   I owe everything to my husband, who has chosen me from amongst many where he could have fixed his choice; 'tis he who has made me what I am, and you may well think that I should shrink from bringing upon him obligations connected with my kindred, with which no law of morals, human or divine, can ask him to have sympathy ; but he is one among a million—generous, brave, and gifted ; do but show me, Robert, that you have resolved upon leading a new life, and I will show as much to him."

The weary man sat down, or rather, he staggered to a seat, and leaning his head upon his hands he wept.

" Sister Emily," he said, " I have quaffed even to the dregs the bitter draught of misery, and I have learnt experience from the cup ; I have sinned against man, and against God ; trampled upon the best feelings of human nature, and upon the holiest ordinances of my Creator ; but, I come to you, contrite and full of repentance."

" No more, no more, brother," she said ; " to own an error, is half to have compensated for it."

She spoke many words of comfort and consolation to this sorrow stricken man, but she could not induce him to have sufficient confidence in his position with Sir Anthony Wyvill, for him to remain at Wyvill Hall.

" No, no," he said, " I will not jeopardise for an instant the affections which your husband has for you, that must not be ; write to him dear Emily, and tell him that the brother, who, for his many vices and bad conduct you were compelled to repudiate, has repented him of the evil he has done, and turned aside from the paths of wickedness ; remind him that that is all that God requires of us, ask him to view leniently, a life of past errors ; and, if he can do me a service, request it of him in the name of that pure affection that he feels for you."

" I will, I will," said Emily, " and you shall be happy again Robert, the reminiscences of our happy childhood, when we have sported together in all the innocency and gaiety of youth, come full upon me,—fear nothing, and hope all things."

She supplied him with money for his immediate wants ; then, he left her, after loading with thanksgivings the very air she breathed, and calling down from heaven the choicest blessings on her head.   And Emily was very happy, for well she knew the noble nature of her husband, and that he, far from being the man to disapprove of that which she had done, would be the first to applaud her gentle virtue to the very echoe.   But when did gentle feeling, beauty, and humanity, escape detraction ; never, never, in this world; whatever those bright and glorious feelings may do in that which is to come. Margaret Wyvill heard from one of the servants of the Hall, that a stranger of mysterious aspect, who had given no name, desired an interview with Lady Wyvill, as Emily was called. She stooped to the meanness of listening, and so heard all that passed; and, when the interview was over she retired to a chamber, which since her residence in the Hall, she had exclusively appropriated to herself, and which bore the curious name of the Dead Turret, in consequence of i being shut up for many years from a conviction of its unsafeness, although recentt repairs of the Hall had rendered it perfectly secure. Let us take a glance at her as she there sits in the small apartment, which has witnessed many a combat between her guilty soul and her conscience. She is sitting in one of those antique chairs, the back of which lowers above her had, her hands are clasped and resting on her lap, her eyes are fixed on vacancy with that steady look, which proclaims that the mind is too busy with its own thoughts, to take in impressions of external objects; and, occasionally, her lips moved as if, to fix some idea in her mind with greater intensity it were necessary to repeat it in tangible language to herself. Hours passed, and yet there she sat in deep and mournful thoughts. It was an awful question that agitated her mind—the to be, or not to be, of guilt; the question was one which might have provoked high discussion in Pandemonium—was the innocent to be sacrificed at the shrine of avarice and ambition, or not? Yes, that was the dreadful question she propounded to her intellect; and, sufficiently worldly-wise and cunning in the exercise of that description of intellect, which works abundant mischief, was she to feel the advantage which time and circumstance had given her, over the pure, the beautiful, and the unsuspecting Emily. She knew her brother, Sir Anthony, well; she felt assured that his first disappointment in love, had sown in his heart the seeds of suspicion against the whole female sex, and that it needed but a little judicious cultivation to make those seeds produce most rank and luxurious shoots.

She felt, that since his marriage she had become as it were a mere nonentity; not the mistress of Wyvill House, and the large domains that belonged thereto, but a dependant upon the more legitimate mistress of that splendid property. She felt that she was tolerated and endured, rather than courted; all those dreams of ambition which allured her to think, that while she lived she would be able to hold sovereign sway in her brother's house, had vanished. Was she, then, a likely person to sit down contentedly, and tell herself that she had thus failed in the grandest scheme of her existence; was she a person to permit what she considered a mere elegant form, and an engaging countenance, to come between her and her heart's deep desires.

No, the very thought of such a disappointment was enough to awaken every slumbering passion in her bosom—to rouse into energy, every latent feeling of hatred and enmity, that lay, like reptiles of the mind, coiled up at the bottom of her heart. She could be scarcely said to have sat down in that apartment devoted to herself, to consider whether or not she should do something indicative of her enmity to her brother's wife, although she strove to ask that question many times. No, her mind was made up upon that point; although, perhaps, she would hardly have confessed that it was so, even to herself; and her principal thoughts were, not whether to do evil, or to leave it alone, but, how to do it with the greatest proximation to success, and with the greatest amount of personal safety. Margaret Wyvill, was cautious—very cautious; she was not one to plunge madly into any enterprise, the means of carrying out which she had not well considered—but, she was wonderfully bold, daring, and suggestive, as regarded those means; and what, to many persons, would have appeared insurmountable objections, appeared to her none whatever; but, with a wild and stubborn philosophy, the more daring and apparently desperate the plan of operation that arose to her mind, upon a slight examination would appear, the more was she inclined to carry it out fully, and to anticipate the greatest success. And now, as she sat alone, she did not do as many persons will do, when they contemplate crime, attempt to blink it to her own imagination, and make it appear less than it really was, but she told herself fairly and distinctly what she meant to do.

"My object," she said, "is the separation of my brother from his wife, or it is nothing—it is to make myself absolute and uncontrolled mistress of Wyvill Hall or it is nothing—the one event is a consequence of the other ; upon her degradation must I build my ambition ; and then, the man upon whom I have chosen to set the seal of my approbation, shall find that I can offer him such a home as he scarcely expects, or aspires to. But the means of accomplishing all this must be no common order. My brother is a man easily worked upon, if the proper feelings and emotions be brought before him in a proper manner, but a shallow plot he would detect at once. It must be something at once desperate and stunning, no matter how unexpected, it must crush opposition by its very strength. And how is that to be accomplished, what am I to do, and what am I to say ? This brother of Emily's—aye, this brother."

She leant her head upon her hands, and seemed to be lost in thought for a considerable time, and then she smiled. Surely some busy friend was whispering to her some dark and desperate plan of operation, whereby the peace of the innocent and virtuous was to be destroyed.

"Yes, this brother !" she exclaimed ; "from the first moment that I saw him here, and heard of his existence, I had a feeling come over me, that it was through him I should work my way to the position I would fain occupy. Yes, he shall be my instrument by which I will carve my road to fortune. Could I bear to live the mere minion, the guest, the dependant, no matter how honoured or treated with respect, of such a being as Emily Wyvill—no. And what follows if I cast off such a bondage ? Can I stoop to throw any personal exertions on my mind's capabilities, into what we call the ordinary channels of industry ? No, I will die first—I will make an effort to be greater than those around me— to attain that sovereignty over them, which wealth alone can give to a woman. But I will not condescend to acquire it by any of the beaten tracts to fortune. Some royal road alone can content me. If I fail in the attempt, it shall be a great failure—if I succeed, it shall be a great success. From this moment I dedicate myself to the work ; I will have no remorse, no tenderness—none of those human weaknesses, which are called affections, shall stand in my way—I will achieve my purpose or perish. And the world shall not say that I acted from deficient motives, for I have two of the greatest that human nature knows of—love and ambition. Yes, even I who have laughed to scorn the ordinary passions and feelings of my sex—I, who have treated with contempt all those tender alarms which make up the study of their existences, at last own to myself that I love ; and, he upon whom I will extend an affection only he could excite, shall find me no dowerless bride. I think he loves me, he has nearly said as much ; but, all I know, that fortune has not smiled upon him. He is too poor to wed, and yet the scion of an ancient stock —one of those old barons of the land whose names are famous in the history of the nation. He shall be mine, and master of Wyvill Hall. Then it shall be called Dacre Hall after him ; and, if he comport himself as I wish a husband of mine to do, he may be a happy man, and me well looked to ; but, he must not try to rule such a spirit as mine or he will find a contest arise, short but terrific, and in which he will be beaten. And now for the minor arrangements of my plan, something bold, resolute, and sudden, must be done ; let me think—let me think. How am I to place a gulph between my brother and his wife, that shall keep him away from his native land for ever, and at the same time prevent her from taking, even the faintest step, towards an explanation with him. That is the proposition, and it must be well considered—it shall be well considered."

*   *   *

And now, while Margaret Wyvill is in deep cogitation with her own guilty spirit, as to the means by which she shall accomplish the frightful act of treachery, she had secretly contemplated, events were occurring to Sir Anthony Wyvill abroad, which require a special notice from us ; because it seemed as if all the malignant fates at once had conspired to destroy the happiness of Sir Anthony and his wife, through the medium of their best feelings and holiest of affections.

It is nearly sun-set, on a summer's evening, after one of those fierce battles, which had ravaged the Spanish dominion for so many years, during that unhappy period, when that nation was made the battle-field, by other nations of Europe to fight out their quarrels upon. A sanguinary conflict had taken place, between the armies of the French republic, headed by the then General Buonaparte, and a combined force of Austrians and British, which had ended in the discomfiture of the future emperor of the French, and which, consequently is not chronicled in the annals of that glorious nation. The field was strewn with the dead and the dying, towards whom the Austrian officers betrayed an indifference, which provoked the British General Abercrombie to make use of some angry expressions ; and, among other things, he said, he would go himself and assist in picking up the wounded Frenchmen from the field. This, however, the officers of his staff, dissuaded him from ; but they could only accomplish that by promising to go themselves and undertake the duty ; which, of course, they did. Among those, who so went, was Sir Anthony Wyvill, then in command of a regiment of light cavalry. We will not pause in our narration, to enter into the particulars of the scene of horror that met them one very hand ; they almost waded in blood, and difficult was it to choose to whom to pay the first attention, amongst so many pitiful objects calling loudly upon their merciful considerations. Not the slightest distinction was made of rank, or-nation ; it was sufficient that a man lay wounded for him to receive the instant care of those, who in most cases were his victors ; and, it so happened, that Sir Anthony Wyvill came upon what he, at first considered was a dead body, around which was wrapped, in many folds, a flag of what, at the time, was called the Consular Legion, which afterwards verged into Napoleon's old guard. From the fact of this tri-coloured flag being so disposed about the person of the dead man, Sir Anthony Wyvill took him to be some different officer, who had been killed, and in his last moments thus endeavoured to secure the trust that had been confided to him. The possession of a few yards of silk, of different colours, fastened to a stick with a spike, and two tassels at the end of it, is considered a most brilliant achievement in the annals of war ; and, Sir Anthony Wyvill, had just entered into what is called, the spirit of the thing, sufficiently to induce him to unroll the colours from round the possessor of them in order to convey them to the British quarters. Before, however, he had proceded far in this process, he made two important discoveries ; the first was, that he, who had so wrapped himself up in the honourable rag, was not dead—and the second was, that he was an English officer of grenadiers who had taken it from some Frenchman, and after that, had been disabled himself from carrying it off the field. Sir Anthony Wyvill, of course, immediately interested himself in procuring the removal of his gallant countryman from the field, and he accompanied him to one of the regimental hospitals that had been hastily constructed for the purpose of receiving the wounded. Sir Anthony thought, by the cheerful manner in which this officer spoke, that he could not be badly hurt ; but he soon found occasion to alter his opinion after the report of the surgeon ; who made a skilful examination of his wounds, and then merely told him, to keep himself as comfortable and quiet as he could. This, Sir Anthony knew, was tantamount to a sentence of death, and he followed the surgeon from the side of the pallet, on which the wounded man lay ; " is he really dangerously hurt ? " said Sir Anthony.

" Yes ; his wound, of itself is not much, but it has mortified ; he will be a dead man in eight and forty hours, or less, we can do nothing for him."

" Good God ! but—"

" I beg your pardon, Colonel Wyvill, but we have quite enough to do, without listening to troublesome inquirers. There's a major of dragoons there, that's been wanting his leg off for this quarter of an hour—you'll excuse me if you please." And so the surgeon rushed off to attend to his duties.

Sir Anthony Wyvill, with a heavy heart, for he had taken a kindly feeling for the man whom he had rescued from the field of battle, approached the pallet on which he lay.

" Aare you in pain ? " said Sir Anthony.

The wounded officer fixed his eyes on his face for a few moments, and then he shook his head as he said in a low faint voice —

" No. I shall never be in pain again."

' Indeed.   What mean you ? "

" Nay, I know its kind of you—you wish to spare me a pang which I have already experienced. I am dying. The surgeon spoke too loud for caution, I heard him. Place your hand upon my wrist, you'll find no flutter there. I'm not afraid to die, but oh, there is a sore place in my heart for one whom, I—I must leave behind me to buffet with the rude world; and she's young and beautiful, and artless as she is beautiful, full of innocence, devotion, and kindly feelings. Oh, it was cruel, very cruel of me to link her fate with mine, when I knew not a moment that the fortune of war would lay me low—low as I am now."

He sighed deeply, and then Sir Anthony Wyvill spoke to him in a kind cheering voice, saying—

" Will you confide in me? We are not acquaintances, as the world goes, and translates the expression; but, if I can do anything to soothe the last moments of your existence, I will."

The dying man looked at him fixedly, and then he said—

" I will trust you, because you make no asseverations; you have not even said upon your honour you would do this, or you would do that; you speak like—like a man, who felt that his mere word ought to suffice."

" It has never been belied," said Sir Anthony.

" I am sure of that, or you could not utter those words in such a tone; and yet, there is nothing to confide, although much to hope. There is one who will miss me, and will fancy herself to be friendless, as she will be desolate when I am gone."

" A daughter, or a sister ? "

" Neither. A wife, young, beautiful, and innocent; she was the only child of one, who fell, even as I fell, upon the field of slaughter. I loved her the more, that she was alone and desolate in the wide world, and had no one to look upon her with the eyes of dear affection but myself, although hundreds would soon have told her that she was beautiful."

" And you married her ? "

" I did. I asked her if she would unite her fortune with one, who while he lived would be to her all he could be, a faithful friend, a counsellor in sorrow—a devoted husband; but I am dying now, already do I feel the chill hand of the destroyer upon my heart, and I must leave her to despair and to thee ! "

" Say on—say on."

" I conjure you, by all that you hold sacred, to seek her out; tell her that I died gently and painlessly, that my last thought was of her—my only prayer for her."

" All shall be done that you require, ere that head be at peace; I am, myself, a man who has felt the fond ties of affection. I have a wife in England, from whom I have torn myself to engage in this rough pastime of war. I will tell her the melancholy history, and she will befriend the chosen of your bosom."

The dying man stretched out his hand, and he turned his glazing eyes upon the face of Sir Anthony Wyvill.

" She is fond of flowers," he said; " and she says, of birds; take her into your pleasant orchard, through which a meandering stream bubbles such delightful music."

" He wanders in his mind," said Sir Anthony Wyvill, in a low tone, " he knows not where he is. And then," he added " you have forgotten to tell me your name and quality, and where she, of whom you speak, can be found."

There was no answer—death had done its worst. With a longing and a regretful looking expression, the eyes of the dead man were fixed upon Sir Anthony Wyvill, who soon saw that his protege was alike past all care, as he was past all consolation. Sir Anthony Wyvill now knew not what to do, for the officer had died so suddenly, that he neither knew his rank in the army, nor his name; and, consequently, was totally at a loss to think how he could possibly fulfil the promise he had made to look after his wife and be to her a friend. In this dilemma, all he could do was to go about and get soldiers of different regiments to come in and look at the body, with the hope that they might identify him. This, for a long time proved unsuccessful, until at last one man, the moment he looked upon him, exclaimed —

"It's Captain Angerstein, of the 60th Infantry, I know him well; a better man, or a braver officer never stepped in shoe leather!"

"Thank God, somebody knows him," said Colonel Wyvill, as he was more commonly called, than Sir Anthony. "Do you know where his wife is to be found?"

"Yes, sir, almost in the immediate vicinity."

"And who was she before she married him?"

"An only daughter, sir, of Major Jerningham, who was killed in action."

"Very well; can you take me to her, for I have the last words of her husband to communicate to her."

"I will, sir; although, poor thing, I think that those words are the last she'll hear in this world. She has been asking everybody if they have heard anything of him, and no one had; she suspects, but is not quite sure, that he has fallen—the certainty will kill her. But come this way, sir, and I will show you where she lodges."

Sir Anthony Wyvill now began to feel that he had accepted a most uncomfortable task; and it puzzled him exceedingly how he was to announce himself to the bereaved wife, as the bearer of such disastrous tidings as those which he brought to her. Every step that he followed the soldier, and which he felt convinced brought him nearer and nearer to where she was, made him more and more dread encountering her, until he got into such a state of nervousness that the look of his countenance was quite sufficient to proclaim the dread tidings he brought, without the necessity of his using any words in doing so. He shrunk almost from the door, when the soldier paused and pointed to a house in which he said that Captain Angerstein's wife was staying; but still, it was a duty which he had undertaken, and therefore, however it painted itself to him in uncomfortable colours, he would not shrink in performing it. The promise he had made to the dead was sacred, and he at once entered the house; which, as is the case with most Spanish, has its door upon the latch, so that any one might walk in who pleased, taking the risk, of course, of the reception he met with. It was something of a relief to Sir Anthony Wyvill to be told, that the captain's lady was not within; and the woman of the house added, "Poor thing, she's gone to search for her husband on the field of battle; I tried to dissuade her from it, but she said she would, and I have no doubt she has."

"She will search there in vain," said Sir Anthony; "for he is dead, and that is the intelligence which I come to bring her."

"Dead, sir!" exclaimed the woman.

"Yes, he was killed in the last battle, and—"

"Hush! she's on the threshold."

Sir Anthony Wyvill turned his eyes in the direction of the door, and then he beheld a young and beautiful female apparently so exhausted by fatigue that she could scarcely drag one step after the other. She entered the room, and sunk into the nearest chair; then resting her face upon her hands she wept bitterly, saying, between the intervals of her sobs, "No, no, I cannot find him—oh where is he?—I have searched long and painfully, but cannot see that well-remembered face. He is lost, lost to me!"

Sir Anthony Wyvill might well shrink from communicating the dreadful tidings that he brought, to one who evidently felt so keenly upon the subject which must form the staple matter of his communication; he did actually think of endeavouring to conceal the truth from her for a time, but he gave up the idea as after all a bad one; since eventually the shock must come, and let it come when it might it would be sure to be one of a most serious and distressful character.

"Tell her," he whispered to the woman of the house, "that a gentleman is here—an officer who knew something of her husband."

"Ah," said the woman, as she looked into Colonel Wyvill's face, enquiringly, "you know too much for her, poor thing; I can guess what you have to say."

"Hush, never mind, the evil is quite sufficient when it comes upon her.. Do as I bid you."

The woman shook her head in sorrow, and then turning to the young wife, she said to her, "An English officer is here who knows something of your husband."

That communication at once aroused the young wife to consciousness, she flew to Wyvill's side, exclaiming, " You knew him ?—you've seen him !—oh, tell me, tell me all."

" The gentleman," said the woman, " wishes to spare your feelings, he don't like telling you at once that your husband is dead."

" Woman, woman," said Sir Anthony, "how dare you afflict her thus suddenly ?"

" How dare I ?" said the woman, as she approached close to Sir Anthony Wyvill, " do you think you know better than I, a wife's feelings?—let the shock of such a piece of intelligence come at once, and then alleviate it afterwards ; you cannot tell a woman that she has lost all she holds dear by degrees ; the truth must be told eventually, better, therefore, tell it once. Look at her now, she suffers nothing."

" True," said Sir Anthony Wyvill, " because she has fainted—the shock of the intelligence has been too much for her."

And so indeed it was, for the captain's widow, although, until that moment she knew not herself as such, had fallen to the ground in a state of complete insensibility the moment she had heard those words which had fallen from the lips of the women of the house. She was carried up stairs, and Sir Anthony Wyvill waited below, until he should be told that she had sufficiently recovered to be able to speak with him. This, he doubted not, would be as soon as she recovered sufficient consciousness to know where she was, or what she was about ; and, when he was introduced to her, she overwhelmed him with a torrent of agonizing questions upon that trightful subject, which now she felt assured, he was well informed of. After the abrupt manner in which she had been told of the catastrophe, he felt that he need have no scruples in speaking of the subject; so, all he suppressed, was anything which might lead her to suppose that Captain Angerstein had suffered much—and alarmed was he at the fixedness of despair with which she listened to him. And when he told her of the promise he had made to her husband to look to her and added some kind and conciliating words, she shook her head saying :—

" No, no, that is a needless trouble—I'm no one's care now ; and need be no one's care—all is over; my life is passed away—leave me to die, that is all I ask of ye."

Of course, Sir Anthony Wyvill knew sufficient of human nature, to feel convinced that this was a state of mind not likely to last ; and, that when the first flush of her grief had had its way, she would be able to take a more rational view of her position. All he did then, accordingly, was to tell her to keep herself as quiet as she could, and to beg of her to consider, that as death was the ordinary lot of humanity, whether it came in the battle-field, or in the sick chamber, it was sure to come at last. She made him no answer to such topics of consolation, nor did he expect that she would ; but he left her with a promise of seeing her again on the morrow, and he told the woman of the house to see that she wanted for nothing, and that he would defray all costs and expences she might incur. What gentleman, or man of honour and feeling, could act otherwise than did Sir Anthony Wyvill on this occasion. He had promised to protect that young and desolate creature, and as he was not a man to promise anything heedlessly, he was one who ever kept up to the spirit, as well as the letter of his undertakings. I will take her to England with me, he said, and ascertain if she has any friends there ; and if she has none—Emily shall arrange to place her in some line of life which shall enable her to pass her life pleasantly. On the following day, punctual to his promise, he called upon Mrs. Angerstein. He had hoped to find her more composed under her misfortunes ; but he was doomed to be disappointed in that particular, for he found that she was confined to her bed by a fever, which had supervened in consequence of the great mental shock she had received. He got medical officers of the army to pay her every attention, so that she really had advice of the first quality, and in about a week she shewed signs of convalescence. During that time, a remarkable change had taken place in the aspect of continental affairs. The armies of the French had been defeated upon several points ; and, one of those hollow truces which were so repeatedly made by the French, during the long continental war, was executed for no other purpose than to allow them to gather force to be more aggressive. Some of the English regiments that had suffered most in several severe battles that had taken place were ordered home and among them, that of Sir Anthony Wyvill ; who, with a feeling of most exquisite satisfaction at his heart, found, that with honor and covered with renown—while he had escaped all the fearful dangers of war, he could again clasp to his heart his beloved Emily in his native land. But before his regiment marched to the coast, he had an interview with Mrs. Angerstein, who was sufficiently recovered to sit up and converse with those about her. It was a painful one, because she would insist upon

his describing to her the last words of her husband, and how he had come by his death. She wept abundantly, and seemed for a time inconsolable ; but she made Sir Anthony Wyvill repeat, over and over again, those bitterly painful incidents which had bereft her of all she had held dear ; but, when he concluded, and said to her in a kindly voice :—

"And now you must trust to time, the great healer of all griefs, to assuage yours," she shook her head and replied to him mournfully :—

"No, no, the blow has struck too deeply to my heart, ever to be healed ; I have

No. 6.

no hope—I look for—I expect—I desire no consolation. All is now dark and drear within my breast."

"Do not speak in so desponding a voice," he said, " you shall come with me to England; as I before told you, I have the means of throwing around you the shield of protection, and I am quite sure that she, whom I may call by the endearing appellation of wife, is one who will not suffer you to want anything that the most sisterly care and attontion can bestow upon you."

But for a long time he could not get her to listen to reason; and although she uttered many thanks to him, and seemed fully impressed with the most grateful feelings towards him for the generous offer he made her, her great calamity seemed too much to have broken down her spirit to enable her to wish or to hope for any thing in this world. This was a mood which he well knew would pass away, but he almost doubted if it would do so in time to enable her to accompany him to England. He therefore thought of a last resource for inducing her to do so, and feeling assured that she was a being full of the highest and noblest sentiments, he affected an air of displeasure, as if he had taken offence at her refusal of the kindness he offered her.

" Well, well," he said, " as you please ; I only sincerely hope that you will meet a friend who will be as sincerely disposed as I am, and as disinterestedly so to aid you. I have been thus urgent in endeavouring to persuade you to avail yourself of the protection of myself for the present; and, ultimately, of that of my will, in order that I might fulfil the dying request of your husband. His last moments were free from mental anxiety, because he fully believed that he had provided for you an efficient protection. If he could have but guessed that you would have been the party yourself to deprive him of that gratification in his dying moments, how little in comparison to what they were would those dying moments have been. But you will do as you please ; I cannot force you."

Sir Anthony Wyvill judged, that if those words had no effect upon her, nothing in the world that he could possibly say would, so he turned and walked leisurely to the door of the apartment, as though he were about to leave her for ever. He would not have done so ; but he was spared the pain of returning, and so showing that what he had said was a mere ruse for the purpose of inducing her to come to a hasty decision for her own benefit, for she called to him ere he had passed away from her sight.

" You have conquered," she said, " you have conquered ; but, oh ! in so long refusing your proffered kindness, do not suppose for a moment that I was ungrateful for it or undervalued it."

" I am very far, indeed," he said, " from supposing that, and am quite satisfied you had no such feelings. I rejoice that your better feeling has prompted you to adopt a course that must be conducive to your happiness."

From that moment he made every preparation to secure to his young and amiable protegé a pleasant transit from where they were to England. To be sure he had to endure a little raillery on the part of his brother officers ; bus that he little cared for, although some of them roundly accused him of killing the officer in order to take possession of his wife. But as this was said in so bantering a tone as to give it no importance, Sir Anthony Wyvill did not think it wise to take any notice of the matter, because, by so doing he could only have dragged the captain's widow into what, doubtless to her, would have been a most disagreeable publicity. His whole thought was to keep her as secure as possible ; and, conscious in the rectitude of his own intentions, he could afford, he thought, to allow such worthies to say what they pleased. The corps of the army to which he belonged was nearly in the centre of Spain, ard they had to traverse a vast extent of country before they could reach a port, from whence they could take shipping for England by way of the Bay of Biscay, and up the western shores of France. A considerable distance northward of the city of Leon was a maritime town, where such of the regiments as were to proceed homewards were ordered to assemble ; and accordingly he pushed on in that direction, accompanied by his fair companion, who, each hour he became acquainted wth her, presented to his observation some new theme for admiration. And besides, it must be considered that she was under the cloud of grief, and if then she seemed so amiable and fascinating a being, what would she be under different circumstances, when time had assuaged the bitterness of her anguish, and the more brilliant points of her character, which were now subdued, should show themselves in bolder relief.

These regiments which were ordered home were considered to be invalided, in consequence of the great losses they had sustained in the various actions, and indeed many wounded officers accompanied them, so that they went by slow stages, for the special accommodation of the latter; not travelling above fifteen miles in the day—a mode of proceeding, although it made a serious call upon the patience of some, yet enabled them to see and enjoy some of the most delightful scenery in the world; so that, even those who had first most deeply regretted the length of time that they were in reaching the coast, were compelled, ultimately, to admit how much they gained by the delay.

A kind of depôt of a great number of regiments was formed at the coast town, waiting for transports to convey them to England; so that at times, for weeks together, a number of officers, of all grades and ranks, met and messed together until their turn arrived for proceeding to their native land.

When Sir Anthony Wyvill, with his detachment, reached the place, he found his mortification that several transports had recently sailed; and that at least a fortnight would elapse before he could expect a passage home. This was provoking, especially, situated as he was, with one under his care whom he desired to place in security as quickly as possible.

His impatience, however, was a little assuaged by the fact, that a half courier, half spy—going over France with secret despatches to the English government—a service of great danger—volunteered, for a certain sum, to post letters for any English officer who chose to entrust them to him the moment he reached London. Of course, it was increasing his risk a thousand fold, but he had gone so often with impunity, that he laughed at the danger, although he charged a sum for his services, more commensurate with what other people thought of them than what he did himself.

Sir Anthony Wyvill gladly seized the opportunity to write a letter to Emily; and as that letter is fully expressive of his own feelings and sentiments, and shows how perfect was the understanding between him and the young and amiable girl whom he had induced to share his destinies, we give it entire:—

"Emily—I have two agreeable surprises for you, and I have vanity enough to hope that one will be more agreeable than the other; although the one, which I calculate as being the most agreeable, is more compounded of reality than romance, and, therefore, you will guess that that means myself, for I am not romantic, as you know, at all. Firstly, then, Emily, I am coming home, which I take upon myself to fancy will be as pleasant a piece of intelligence to you as it is a dear and delightful thought to me. Ah! Emily, there was a time when home to me brought no blissful recollections; but now it is replete with all the joys of a thousand dear associations—associations that lend it a charm beyond any that I could have supposed it capable of possessing—for are you not there, dear Emily? and, therefore, is not that home to me a very paradise of delight? And so much, dear Emily, as regards myself. And now I am going to awaken every feeling of jealousy that can find a place in your bosom. As if one wife at home was not sufficient for me, I have picked up somebody's else abroad. There, Emily, what think you of that—is not candid confession good for the soul? An officer was killed in action, his widow wanted another husband, and as I was a husband, and as volunteering in different services has been all the fashion lately in the army, how could I do otherwise than proffer mine to her? And now, shall I fancy, dear Emily—having written so much—a look of indignation upon that fair face, shall I fancy that the flush of injured pride has visited your brow? Ah no, Emily, you are well aware that you can trust me. Even although I am far—far away from you, you know that I am no truant to your affections, although I may be to your presence; dear Emily, you know that I am thine and thine only; so now for a plain unvarnished tale, that shall excite your sympathy but not your fears. A Captain Angerstein, a brave gallant officer, was mortally wounded in action. I picked him up from the field of contest, and attended his dying moments. In these dying moments he implored me, as I was a gentleman, a soldier, and loved honour and all its fair concomitants, that I would succour and be the friend, the champion, the protector of his young, friendless, and defenceless bride. Emily, need I tell you the answer that I made? from your own heart you can make it for me. I promised all that he required, and not heedlessly; for I meant, and have performed those promises. I can see that you applaud me. In my mind's eye, Emily, I can look upon your face and see the beaming pleasurable expression that, like sunshine, fresh from heaven, rests upon it. I can almost hear your approval uttered in some few short and gentle sentences. You can fancy how, if you had accompanied me to the field of battle, and I had fallen, how, in my last moments, I should have looked around me for some brave, generous spirit, to whom I would have said,—' I have a wife—young, innocent, and gentle. Will you befriend her until she reaches England; and, on your sacred honour, be to her a guardian and a protector?' I should have anticipated no refusal, but have died happy with the thought, that my greatest treasure was left in worthy hands. So now you know all, dearest Emily, and I hope shortly after you receive this missive to have the pleasure of introducing you to her, whom I would have been less than man not to have protected, and whom I am sure you will love when you become acquainted with her; for, candidly speaking, next to yourself, I know of no one better calculated to bewitch the affections.

"These are from, dear Emily, your own, "ANTHONY WYVILL.

"P. S.—Mrs. Angerstein is one of the loveliest brunettes ever I set my eyes upon. She has eyes like darkened diamonds, flashing through such long silken lashes, that really any man might be excused for loving her even to a pitch of adoration. "A. W."

This was the letter which Sir Anthony Wyvill entrusted to the care of the courier. He sealed it carefully, and addressed it to Lady Wyvill, at Wyvill Park, Wales, where the mansion was situated; and he finally hoped that it would reach its destination, and prepare the mind of his amiable wife for the arrival of the young and interesting stranger he had to introduce to her notice.

———

CHAPTER VII.

THE MESS DINNER.—THE DUEL.—THE GENTLEMAN WHO DID FOR THE NEWSPAPERS.

THAT fortnight which elapsed before Sir Anthony Wyvill and Mrs. Angerstein could proceed in effecting their departure from the Spanish port, was a period not doomed to pass away without its remarkable events, and those events we shall now proceed to detail.

Sir Anthony Wyvill succeeded in procuring a suitable home for her in a house kept by some very respectable people in the town, while he himself messed with the officers, who mostly lived together; and, by subscribing a comparatively small sum each, managed to realise a much greater amount of comfort than they could possibly have done individually. There were nearly thirty officers belonging to different brigades and regiments, and among so many, there were men of the very highest rank and reputation; while, at the same time, it must be confessed there were some who possessed neither of those qualifications. There are black sheep in every profession, and unless they happen to commit some overt act which at once places them beyond the pale of ordinary consideration, it is extremely difficult for those who are better disposed, to avoid mixing with them to some extent. As for Sir Anthony Wyvill, the majority of officers being strangers to him, made it extremely difficult, on his part, to discriminate between those who were eligible acquaintances and those who were not, so that he was compelled to adopt a uniform scale of civility, which confounded the one with the other.

A week had elapsed of the fortnight which he was told he had to wait; when, one day the wine was circulating rather freely at the mess-table, and various toasts and sentiments had been drunk off in the most recherché character—such as, to 'old friends,' and so on. A considerable amount of gaiety prevailed, and all was mirth and jollity, when a major of dragoons, of herculean frame, who had several times made himself conspicuous for the brutality of his remarks, and whose name was Grogan, suddenly rose, and said in a stentorian tone of voice, which commanded the whole attention of the company, "Gentlemen, I have a toast to propose to you."

There was a great knocking upon the table, for some sentiment was expected not at all of an evangelical character; and a smile sat upon every countenance.

"Gentlemen," continued Major Grogan, "I propose health and long life to Colonel Wyvill's legacy."

Now, it so happened that Colonel Wyvill did not know that Captain Angerstein went by that name among some of the officers of the various regiments, who knew of the circumstances under which he had placed her in his care; and his look of astonishment and puzzled inquiry produced a roar of laughter round the table.

"Health and long life" repeated Major Grogan, "to Colonel Wyvill's legacy!" and a something as near a shout as the officers chose to indulge in came from the throats of the guests, who were delighted at what now appeared a bit of practical fun; and right welcome it appeared to be, if one might judge by their faces.

In an instant, there was a refilling of glasses, and clinking of decanters, until the room resounded with them; and then, simultaneously, the whole of them rose, en masse, and lifting their glasses to their lips, repeated the words with much glee.

"Health and long life to Colonel Wyvill's legacy!"

Then came many a suppressed laugh; and every eye was turned upon Colonel Wyvill, who sat, in what might appear to be an equivocal position; but he was ignorant of the meaning of the toast, and sat calm enough—without a smile upon his countenance—wondering what all the hubbub was about; waiting until it calmed, before he should demand an explanation of its meaning.

Every one present drank the toast; and then rang through the room a hearty hurrah! as if the spirit of fun and mischief had seized them; the hurrah was repeated with a hearty gusto.

Then, after much laughter, they sat down; and something like order was restored among them.

"Now," said Colonel Wyvill, "now, that your duties to the toast are at an end, perhaps you will permit me to make a request to the proposer?"

"Oh! yes, certainly—certainly."

"Oh! certainly; any request you can make Major Grogan will grant. The major's —"

And then another provoking titter ran round the table.

"An explanation!" said one.

"Aye! that will be even better than the toast," said another, with great glee; "but, hush, Wyvill speaks."

"Since you permit me so much liberty, allow me to improve it; and while I have it, I will make my request; and, as Major Grogan has proposed a toast, he will be the best person to whom I can apply for an explanation of its import."

"Certainly; Grogan's the best man for that!" escaped from several lips at once; and those who were a moment before enjoying a laugh at Wyvill's expense, now prepared to do so at Grogan's.

"Yes, yes; Grogan's the man for an explanation. Give an explanation, Grogan."

"I cannot refuse Colonel Wyvill anything he may demand in reason ; but, I ask you all, gentlemen, whether I ought to comply with such a demand?"

"And why not?" inquired Wyvill.

"It is hardly a fair subject."

"And none could be fairer," said a young officer ; "for I have seen the legacy, and I declare, upon my honour, I never saw one more beautiful."

"Bravo! capital! hurrah!" shouted the officers

"I must beg, Major Grogan," said Colonel Wyvill, "as you have coupled my name and a legacy together, that you will afford me an explanation of what is meant by the legacy ; for, on my honour, I do not know what you mean by it, I beg you will favour me so far."

"Not know the legacy, Colonel Wyvill?" said an officer, near him ; "I am amazed."

"Such a thing couldn't happen to me, and I not know what it was by this time," said an officer opposite.

"Perhaps, sir, you will afford me the explanation I ask, since Major Grogan seems to object?"

"I have not objected to do so," retorted Grogan ; "I am ready to give it you, since you insist upon it"

"I have not insisted upon it," said Wyvill ; "I have asked you, as a gentleman, to inform me the meaning of the toast, and why my name is coupled with it?"

"Why," said Grogan, "the reason why your name is coupled with it, is, because it is so in fact."

"The fact itself I should be glad to become acquainted with," said Wyvill. "Surely, Major Grogan, I am entitled to some consideration and courtesy ; and from you, as the proposer of the toast, I demand an explanation of it."

"And you are unacquainted with the fact of your having a legacy, then?" said Grogan, with a provoking smile ; and there was a general laugh.

"I am," said Wyvill.

"Hum!" said the major ; and then, he added, "you have no pearl of price—no beauty, whose charms are so rare and precious, that you watch over with the jealousy of a Turk over a new sultána."

"Upon my word," said Wyvill, "you are pleased to speak in riddles. I cannot understand you."

"Well, it is unfortunate—there is no other resource, I see ; the truth must come out at last."

"Yes, yes, out with the truth," said several of the officers, who were emptying and re-filling their glasses, muttering as they drank, a health to Colonel Wyvill's legacy.

"Certainly, I desire the truth ; a man of honour never need shrink from the truth."

"It does not impugn your honour, colonel," said Grogan ; "but rather redounds to it, seeing it is no common man who could have obtained such favours."

"A truce to this, Grogan ; give the explanation, or refuse it broadly at once."

"The explanation, the explanation," cried those present ; "Grogan, give the explanation."

"Well, then," said Grogan ; "but first, Colonel Wyvill, permit me to ask you if there be not a certain beautiful widow that nestles beneath your wings? May your shadow never be less, as the Turks say."

"Well, sir."

"Mrs. Angerstein, the beautiful widow, is the legacy of Colonel Wyvill," said Grogan, gravely ; "and a legacy we can all of us envy you the possession of, and well may we say, 'We wish her health and long life.'"

Colonel Wyvill was silent for a moment or two, and his colour heightened when he looked round and saw a provoking smile ; or, as he would have termed it, a broad grin upon the countenances of his brother officers—there was such an air of intelligence about them, as much as to say, "We are well aware of what you are about to say, but you may as well save yourself the trouble ; because we can put our own construction upon what we hear and see."

"Gentlemen," said Colonel Wyvill, "the occurrence that seems to have given rise to your mirth is a painful one to me."

"I cannot see how that should be," said Grogan ; "we all know Colonel Wyvill's chivalrous spirit—he would never permit a beautiful woman to go a begging?"

"Sir——"

"I mean, that escapades like the present," continued Grogan, despite the coldness of Colonel Wyvill's demeanour, "are matters that may well be excused, for they will happen, and the best regulated minds never yet escaped."

"I am not aware of any escapade that I have made," said Wyvill ; if, fulfilling the request of a dying brother officer be an escapade, I have committed one."

"Undoubtedly," said Grogan, coolly ; "undoubtedly, and there lies the legacy."

This retort produced a general laugh, and the colonel grew somewhat warm, and the guests all appeared to think this was good fun ; that they might aid a quarrel seemed very probable—but that was not the less welcome to them ; and several said :—

"That is a very fair answer ; what more could you have of an explanation ? There is the legacy, and Colonel Wyvill has got it."

Colonel Wyvill thought it more incumbent upon himself to defend his conduct, not on his own account, but for the sake of the reputation of the lady.

"I would not care," he said "for myself, what construction you chose to put upon my conduct, but I cannot sit here and listen to that which is an implied calumny upon one whose virtue is as spotless as the snow on the mountains."

"The colonel is getting poetical."

"The snow is a very good thing to put wine in," said Grogan ; "but it is no likeness to a soldier's heart."

"What do you mean by that observation, Major Grogan?" demanded Wyvill.

"That the snow is cold, while the heart is warm ; the coldest and sternest of natures will melt before the beams of beauty ; and beauty—in distress, especially—demands our warmest admiration."

"Hear, hear, to Grogan," said several.

"Now, Wyvill, bring up the reserve, and pour a volley into him ; contradict that."

"The admiration and the aid of a sensualist will never be welcome to a virtuous woman," returned the colonel ; "and such aid is often destruction,"

"But I am no Platonist ; and I cannot understand how it is possible that such feelings—which are, in fact, but the rudiments of others—can exist in a heart warmer than ice ; but then, they change, and become something else in a very short time."

"Such they could not be charged in me."

"You have more command over yourself than most men," said Grogan ; "and I repeat, I am no Platonist, and never yet knew any one, who was really flesh and blood, that was ; and I think, Colonel Wyvill, you cannot point out an example to the contrary."

"I could point out many honorable men, sir, who could act as I have done in this matter, but you are not of that number."

"That, I can readily grant," said Grogan ; "very easily can I conceive that many men would have taken care of a beautiful travelling widow, which every one may look at with admiration, and yet the owner fears to touch ; she must be really more amiable than you think."

"You have a wife of your own, major ; just imagine you have made those observations upon her ; the lady, whom I have protected under such circumstances, is spotless, and as she is will be introduced to my own family."

"Colonel Wyvill," said Grogan, growing very angry, "you were pleased to make some remark respecting myself and my family, but you must remember they are not so placed, the lady you have by you is a widow."

" And as such demands my sympathies for her misfortune, which is the worst she can suffer."

" Doubtless, but we may hope the sympathy of Colonel Wyvill will make that loss as light as possible."

" Hear, hear, to Grogan ! " said several of those who had hoped there would have been a quarrel, but now they began to fear there would be none, and the threatened storm would blow over.

" I shall do my endeavours to such an end ; but, gentlemen, as a man of honour myself, I cannot conceive it possible that such a misinterpretation could have been put upon my words and acts; were I alone concerned, it would not so much matter, but the lady must not suffer from the folly and malignity of others."

" What do you mean by that?" inquired Grogan, sharply.

" Precisely what my words imply, Major Grogan," said Wyvill, coldly; " precisely what you can make of them ; and, I dare say, you stand in no need of an interpreter, unless, indeed, the wine has unduly bewildered you."

" This cannot be borne," said Grogan ; " you have got an intrigue, and want to make a virtuous affair of it. Ha ! ha ! ha ! upon my heart it is good.'"

" This arises, as I said before, from folly or malignancy—perhaps both," said Wyvill.

Before any reply was made, Grogan's eye sought the decanter, and his hand likewise, and then seizing it he hurled it full at the colonel, saying :

" Take that, Colonel Wyvill, as my answer."

There was a dead pause for some moments, and every eye watched the progress of the decanter, which went whirling through the air, spilling its contents over every one present, and struck, not Wyvill, but another officer who sat beside him, a blow across the head, which had the effect of oversetting him, chair and all.

In an instant there was a stir in the room ; every one had risen—all was noise and confusion ; some advanced to pick up the fallen officer, who had got entangled among the chairs, and being partially stunned, he got more amongst the legs than he need have done.

" Are you hurt, Major Stangroom ? "

" No, I believe not, Wyvill," said the major, who was helped to his feet by Wyvill ; " I am, I believe, only touched by a spent ball. Rascally bad artillery ! "

" Major Grogan ——," said Wyvill.

" Colonel Wyvill ——," returned the major, with wrath.

" Pistols and swords for two," said a young officer present, " and coffee for one ! Gunpowder mixed to every man's liking."

There was now a general hubbub ; and scarce could any one be heard so many were speaking at once—all apparently well pleased that there was likely to be a fray—it was so exciting ! However, when there was something approaching to a lull in the storm of voices that were heard, Wyvill's voice was heard, saying—

" Major Grogan, since your insult has been open, intended, and gross, I claim satisfaction at your hands."

" And, by heaven, you shall have it," exclaimed the major starting to his feet ——.

" Either an apology for your conduct, or a meeting."

" A meeting it shall be, and the sooner the better : the challenge is too open to admit of any delay."

" Bravo, Grogan ! You are a noble fellow to the back bone. You are indeed ! "

" Yes, yes," said Wyvill, " it had better be at once; this matter had better be settled now—before we move away from this house."

" Agreed, agreed," said Grogan; " anything and everything you please ; a fair field and no favour."

"! The only favour I seek is, an instant adjustment of time and place."

"Bravo! bravo!" shouted the officers, who were well warmed with wine; or all this wordy warfare had caused a great drought, and the noise helped to he same end; and they drank freely, and were ripe for anything, whatever might have been its character.

"Come, gentlemen," said Major Stangroom, "this must not be allowed; the rincipals must not be allowed to settle the preliminaries in this manner—there must be some third parties."

"Have as many as you please—a dozen."

"Colonel Wyvill, I will second you, if you will permit me. I had the crack on the head with the infernal decanter, intended for you. I have earned the distinction, I am sure, and very nearly paid expensively for it."

"I am obliged to you, Major Stangroom, and accept your offer with pleasure; I am obliged to you."

"My dear colonel, don't name it," said Stangroom, affectionately; "you are

No. 7.

most welcome to my services. You have been grossly insulted — most grossly."

" I have—I feel I have."

"You have, indeed ;" and then, turning to Major Grogan, he said to him in a deliberate tone—

"Major Grogan, I am the friend of Colonel Wyvill, and demand instant apology and retraction of the offensive meaning of what you have said, and for your conduct generally."

" Pooh, pooh ! Major Stangroom ; you know me too well to imagine anything of the kind of me ; I am not the man for an apology."

" Then I demand an instant meeting. You, in the name of your friend, Captain Irwin, will answer all inquiries respecting me," said Grogan, " and have my consent to do what he deems necessary."

There was now a little cessation in the house ; and every one awaited the result of the conference between the two seconds, on whom now rested the conducting of the affair ; and, as they were fighting men, there was little doubt how it would terminate ; and they set about it in earnest.

" One point is settled already," observed Major Stangroom, turning to Captain Irwin.

" May I inquire what it may be ?" said Captain Irwin ; " I am not aware anything had been settled."

" Oh, yes, there will be a fight ; both parties are determined upon that, I believe."

" Yes—quite."

" You have the choice of weapons," said Stangroom.

" Why, yes," said Irwin, " we have ; and, to equalise matters, I propose they should fire two shots, and, if no effect, they should take to their swords."

" I agree to that," observed Stangroom ; " I am sure there will be every disposition to afford them every facility to bring the affair to a conclusion."

" There is a large room above, which will give them ample space to settle this matter in ; there they can be accommodated, and every one can be allowed to see all is quite fair."

" Certainly ; that is all that one could wish it : this being settled, we may now assemble our men up-stairs, to their respective positions there."

" Yes, we may."

" Gentlemen," said Major Stangroom, " up-stairs we go ; there is a large room, suitable for our purposes."

There were immediately marks of approbation uttered by those present ; and a rush took place up-stairs, where there was a large room, one fit to hold a ball in : here the officers arranged themselves on either side of the room, leaving the two ends free for the passage of the balls.

" Now, Captain Smith," said Major Stangroom, to an officer close beside him, " I am afraid I shall be obliged to trouble you and some more gentlemen to hold candles up—there is little or no light."

" Lights, lights !" cried the officers ; and there was an immediate rush after candles and lights ; and, in less than five minutes, there were as many as twenty lights held up in the hands of those who were thus ranged on either side of the room, as spectators.

There were but few preliminaries now ; so the principals quitted the room, accompanied by their seconds.

" Are you satisfied with the arrangement ?" inquired Major Stangroom of Colonel Wyvill.

" I am quite satisfied ; everything is arranged as I could wish it. Do we fight here ?"

" Yes."

There was now a pause, and the two seconds took the weapons in their hands, and having loaded them and presented their swords, they returned and gave the arms into the hands of their principals ; and then Major Stangroom inquired in a strong voice—

"Are you ready?"

"Quite," said Captain Irwin; "give the word."

"Now, gentlemen, after I have given the word, you fire pistols; and proceed with your swords, until one falls. Are you both ready?"

"Quite," said Wyvill.

"Quite," responded Major Grogan.

"One, two, three—fire!"

The last word had scarcely passed the major's lips, when both pistols were discharged; and then, almost in an instant after, another brace of shots were heard from the combatants.

The spectators gazed upon them; but neither moved, or showed any signs of having been wounded, though they both paused, without any signs of life; then, as if seized by the self-same impulse, they threw away their empty pistols, and, drawing their swords, rushed to a close encounter, hand to hand.

This was not expected to last many minutes; they were too eager at it—though their swords rung with a tremendous sound as they met in hostile clash. It was like the sound of hammering iron on an anvil; rapid and fierce were their blows and thrusts, and each, you would have thought, would have ended a life.

Wyvill of the two was the coolest, and by far the better swordsman; and he intended to wait his time, for the impetuosity of Major Grogan gave him enough to do, and fully assured him of the skill of his rival.

In a few moments more, however, the fight was ended; for the major's sword snapped and was whizzing through the air, and the major received a stroke across the head from his adversary which laid him senseless on the floor.

Colonel Wyvill paused, and the seconds of the wounded officer now stepped forward, lifted him up, and carried him away bleeding from the room.

"You have done well," said Major Stangroom; "I thought you would be the best man at the sword, if you escaped the shot. You have acted bravely, and—"

"And I trust I shall no more be called upon to defend my conduct from aspersion, or the fair fame of one, whose situation alone ought, amongst us, to be a passport to our respect and sympathy."

CHAPTER VIII.

THE DEPARTURE FOR ENGLAND.—THE PROCEEDINGS OF MARGARET WYVILL.—HOME AGAIN,—AND THE WHITE CLIFFS OF ALBION.

DISTRESSED and afflicted as Colonel Wyvill was at the termination of his adventure, he still could not blame himself for any precipitancy in the business; and his principal care was expended in a desire to keep the matter from the knowledge of Mrs. Angerstein, who, he knew, would be much afflicted at the danger he had gone through, solely and entirely on her account.

The gallant and fearless manner in which he had conducted himself suffied to stop many persons from commenting upon the affair, who otherwise would have had their say, which might probably have reached her ears; but when it is found, among such individuals, that a man is not only ready to fight, but that he is capable of fighting well, they become a little cautious as to how far they venture in the career of provocation.

Hence was it that the affair of Major Grogan's purchased for Sir Anthony Wyvill a perfect impunity from the jests which had been so rife at his expense.

He heard no more of them, and, up to the day of his departure, was perfectly free and unmolested.

A favourable breeze from the south-west sped the vessel in which he and Mrs. Angerstein embarked rapidly up the beautiful western shores of France, and, in a much shorter time than might have been expected, they entered the English Channel, and with the same favourable wind sped on rapidly for Portsmouth, which was the port to which the vessel was chartered that conveyed them.

Sir Anthony Wyvill entertained of course no doubt whatever of the reception whch he and his fair companion would meet when he should reach Wyvill Hall, and this confidence was totally irrespective of the fact of his having written the letter, which we have laid before our readers, because it really was so doubtful an affair whether the letter ever really reached its destination, that he did not count upon it as an introduction for Mrs. Angerstein.

When she, as she several times did during their progress, shrunk from the possibility of arriving at Wyvill Hall without anything in the shape of a proper introduction, Sir Anthony laughed at her fears, telling her that if he had known she entertained any doubts regarding her reception, he certainly should not have written at all but have left the matter open, merely for the purpose of convincing her that the understanding between himself and Lady Wyvill was so perfect, that he could venture upon bringing home a visitor without any previous intimation that he was about to do so.

And so he succeeded in calming any apprehension of an adverse reception which he might, certainly, reasonably entertain.

Without libelling the ladies as a body, it is not every wife who could be expected to receive her husband with smiles upon his making his appearance at home, after a prolonged absence, with a young and beautiful female hanging upon his arm.

Confidence is a good thing and a great thing, but we may bend the most exquisitely-tempered bow till we break it, and so it is possible to test woman's best and noblest feelings a little overmuch.

By short and easy stages Colonel Wyvill proceeded towards his own estates, and, whilst he was doing so, let us draw attention to something which was going on at Wyvill Hall.

His letter did come to hand. The man who had undertaken the delivery of it had not deceived him, nor did he deceive himself in his anticipation of a completely successful journey through France, with the despatches of which he was the bearer.

And that letter reached Wyvill Hall in due course ; but, before Sir Anthony Wyvill had brought home his young and beautiful bride, Margaret had taken care that the domestics of the Hall should, from the very highest to the very lowest, be creatures of her bounty and of her will. One of her arrangements, immediately after the departure of her brother, was to the effect that all letters whatsoever, be they addressed to who they might, that came to the Hall, should be brought to her, and she would charge herself with the delivery of them to their respective owners.

That this was done for the express purpose of getting possession of any letter that her brother might write to his young and unsuspecting wife, there cannot be the shadow of a doubt; and in due time, accordingly, that epistle, so full of affection and the tenderest confidence, which we have had an opportunity of presenting to the reader entire, found its way to the hands of Margaret Wyvill.

Infamous and most unjustifiable as was the delay of it for a single moment, she scrupled not to take it with her to her own apartment, and there, by a sleight-of-hand that she had well practised, she opened it, knowing, from the handwriting upon the outside as well as by the seal, that it came from her brother.

But little did she expect that the contents would be so deeply interesting to her ; with what intense eagerness did she devour them when she found that they detailed circumstances so highly calculated to advance the objects she had in view !

Her looks of exultation would have been great had they been graced by a better cause ; her dark and subtle spirit saw in an instant how she might turn what she read to the greatest advantage, and impiously she declared that she believed that inscrutable power which people call Providence was really working in her favour, and assisting her in her nefarious designs.

"Can anything, by any possibility," she said, "be better than this? is it not the very thing to work all the mischief I can desire? Oh! I can make glorious use of this intelligence, having it wholly to myself, and, indeed, there are some parts of the letter which will well stand the exhibition. How strangely they are both working apparently to accomplish precisely what I wish; if I can but succeed now in keeping them apart for awhile, all will be well. She sat down with the open letter before her, and assumed that attitude which was customary to her when she was thinking over something which she considered was of more than ordinary moment and importance : it was an attitude which covered up her face completely, and shut out external objects, so that there was nothing to disturb her fixed attention to the one great subject that occupied her mind ; and there she remained an unusual time planning, plotting, and arranging the best and most likely method of producing more evil than, were she to try her utmost for the remainder of her existence, she could ever hope to undo. And, at last, a smile of demoniac triumph, seemed to announce that she had settled in her own mind how she was to achieve her diabolical purposes. She rose, and, with hurried footsteps and clasped hands, traversed the apartment ; and while her brow was bent, and her lips still curved by that unmirthful smile, she thus gave utterance to the dark and guilty feelings that found a home within her breast:—

"Yes, success is certain; it shall be so ; I must be mistress of Wyvill Hall; I will be its mistress, and I can be : I have but to be true to myself, and not to waver for a moment, and if not true to myself, to whom should I be true? I must have no qualms of that coward conscience, which is the foe to so many great and glorious attempts. I must proceed on, like some resistless conqueror in his path of glory, heeding little the suffering he inflicts on the mangled victims of his haughty policy, which he tramples upon as he pursues his career. Emily Wyvill, it has been your fate to cross me, and I am not one who will be crossed without making an effort to rid myself of the infliction. You will suffer ; not that I care that you should suffer, but you happen to be in the way, and therefore the advancing chariot of my ambition must crush you. And you too, Anthony Wyvill, my half-brother, child of the same father, but alien to my heart, inasmuch as we have no one feeling or sentiment in common—you too must suffer, and I pity you less than I should pity any, for you deceived me—you taught me to think that your heart was so crushed with the bitterness of disappointment which you could never forget, that I should be mistress of Wyvill Hall, and then you took to yourself another, forgot your past sufferings and disappointments, and, because you met with a pretty face that smiled upon you, made a fond girl your plaything, and destroyed my hopes.

"You had no right to do so ; and being, as I am, upon my own defence, I will prevent you doing so. I am not one to be thus trifled with—no, you ought to know me better than to suppose that I am weak enough to yield to such silly accidents of fortune, and yet I have taken pains to mask from you my real character ; you know me not as I know myself, but you will know me ere I have done with you ; and there may come a day—distant perchance, but come it will—when you will find that to trifle with Margaret Wyvill in her ambitious aspirations is no child's game. I would wade through blood to achieve my heart's desire. I want power—I will have power—I thirst to command ; and since, being a woman, it is denied to me to hold the rank and station that my heart yearns for, I must have gold—the rank and the station of wealth—power over those who are dependant on those who provide for them the means whereby they live. I must—I will arrogate to myself all that remnant of feudal authority which still lingers in this country between the tenant and the lord of the land which he holds. The estates of Wyvill Hall are broad, and prosperous, and beautiful ; they shall be mine—all mine ; and now for the means. Oh, I have them here clearly, all set down."

She placed her hand upon her brow as she spoke—

"Yes, I have them all arranged clearly, and with a power of definition which few can meet me in. The wife shall be taught to believe that the husband's protegée of compassion is the mistress of his grossest desires ; the husband shall be directed to think, without for one moment suspecting the relationship, that the brother of his beloved Emily is the blessed individual who has assuaged the wife's pangs during the husband's absence, and made up most amply for the want of those little domestic enjoyments which else with too much virtue have too much pride ; for,

> " Oh, it will work well—wondrously well ; Jealousy, it is indeed
> A monster, which doth make the meat it feeds on."

It is a passion, stupendous in result, and yet one which may be tickled into existence by a show. Most truly does it arouse all the dormant feelings of suspicion; and I will so arrange that they shall both be most suspicious, and then—

> " Trifles light as air shall seem to the suspicious mind
> Confirmation strong as proofs of holy writ ! "

That is the holy writ that does for fools, but not for me. I hope nothing but from my own exertions : I fear nothing—believe nothing, and so cannot be accused of superstition.   Oh, they shall find that they have aroused a spirit difficult to quell! And how delightful it is to feel that one is coalescing, at the same time that one's own objects are accomplished with what are called the best feelings of the most pious individuals !   Nothing can be done without the will of Heaven ; I separate the wife from the husband ;—it is the will of Heaven !   How delightful to think that such power is given me to use, and that I use it so piously.   I feel myself a kind of incarnation of divinity—a chosen thing of grace.   I never prayed ; but then, as it is the will of Heaven, I should not pray ; not to pray is to pray the best—a most logical conclusion ; truly, I am holy.   And so now for intrigue, for lying, chicanery, treachery, deceit, and, if need must be, blood ! "

At this word she stopped short, and a remarkable change took place in her countenance ; it seemed as if the utterance of it had shocked even her, and she shuddered from head to foot.

" No, no," she said, " not that, not that yet ; there will be no occasion.   Finesse will even achieve more than violence ; not that, certainly, not that !"

She walked to the door of her apartment and opened it, and suddenly—guilt is ever suspicious—and she feared, apparently, that some one might be there listening to her counsels, but all was still and lonely.   That room of hers was well chosen for such a person to hold these guilty revels of the imagination in.   It was situated at the extremity of a long corridor, so that there was no excuse for any one approaching it, unless they actually meant to come to it, and a lingering listener, therefore, could be detected in a moment.

And yet, what danger was there of any such ?   Who, in the wildest dreams of their imagination, would have suspected that she, Margaret Wyvill, was otherwise than happy—gratefully happy—in the protection and society of her brother's home?

Had she not all that to ordinary mortals would have rendered life desirable—the love of kindred, the respect of dependants—those luxuries of life that can only be aspired to by the opulent ? and was she not free from all those corroding cares which beset the ordinary run of human beings in the great struggle to live ? What, then, in the simplicity of goodness, had she to sigh for ?   What had she to make her unhappy that she should shut herself up in solitary apartments, and with brows knit with care, and agitated gestures, plot and plan as if she had the weight of a kingdom upon her head?

And yet, strange to say, she thought she was watched by everyone.   Suspicious of each person around her, she thought herself suspected by all ; and no small amount of the vitiated ingenuity which characterised her was expended in assuming the gloss of good feeling, and in a great pretence of satisfaction and pleasantness, most foreign, indeed to her real nature and feelings.

It would seem that after this—we were going to call it interview with herself—she appeared, without the slightest struggle of remorse, intent upon the prosecution her abominable plans.

The letter which she had succeeded in intercepting, and which we have given at length, she never delivered at all, but she religiously and carefully kept it, for she had an expectation that it might become of use—full of tenderness and beauty as it was—in the prosecution of her designs.

We are told that the author of all evil can quote gospel to serve his purposes, and why, therefore, might not Margaret Wyvill succeed even in turning some of the contents of that letter to the purpose of serving her own evil resolutions?

And she kept it, although without a defined motive for so doing; for as yet she was as one groping in the dark towards an object which she had determined to reach, but knew not what aids and appliances she might meet with on the way.

And now she cast about for the villain's right hand—a confederate—and, strange to say, she pitched upon the very man whom she had destined to become her husband. One would have thought that the individual whom Margaret Wyvill would have chosen from the mass of mankind—to have a legal as well as a moral mastery over her—would have been something different from the common herd. One would have thought he would have been an individual sufficiently marked and distinguished by some qualities, physical or intellectual, which would have highly recommended him—but such was not the case.

He was a man despised among men; but then he was the sort of man whom Margaret Wyvill could rule, if she chose it, to her heart's content; he was one who looked upon her as something most astonishing and beyond the run of common womanhood. He admired her for those qualities which an intellectual and high-minded man would have called unfeminine.

We can present this individual to our readers in a very few words: he was big and clumsy—of a fat and lazy intellect, such as too frequently belongs to those individuals of the human race, whom Nature has chosen to present with abundance of the material of human existence.

He moved along like a young elephant at play—there was not the steadiness of the mature animal about him; he was just the sort of creature that could be driven easier than he could be led—for to be led requires that the mind should see something delightful for the mind to follow it—it is a mental action, in which sometimes we surrender our better judgments to the fascinations of grace and beauty; but inferior animals, who have nothing but their physical endowments, are never courted along the road of life by

"Nods and becks, and wreathed smil s."

But society contents itself by goading them on from behind with such kicks and buffets as may be considered necessary.

And thus was it that Margaret Wyvill pitched upon this man, whom she disdained to lead to any purpose, but whom she knew that she could drive wheresoever she pleased. And Mr. Adolphus Dacre thought her quite a wonderful woman.

Mr. Adolphus Dacre could not be called a small farmer, for he was almost the largest one in the district, personally; and yet he was entitled to the former designation in consequence of being heir-at-law to certain lands and tenements which had belonged to his progenitors from time out of mind, and who had all in some degree partaken of the fat and comfortable aspect of their decidedly slow descendant. The property of which he became possessed upon the death of his father—who fell asleep one afternoon, after being wedged into his arm-chair as usual, and never awoke again in this world—was one which, in skilful hands, would have improved amazingly with the improvement of the times, but his brains had by far too somnorific a tendency to enable him to make any effort to place himself in a different position from that which the mere force of circumstances had plumped him down in. He was one of those men who smile blandly when improvements are mentioned, and the march of science is expatiated upon—a man who would put you down by telling you that his father and his grandfather did so before him, and then insinuate, rather than say, that that, of course, must be the best possible thing for him to do. And this was the man whom Margaret Wyvill had pitched upon to be the partner of her ambitious operations. She knew that she could not, without a husband, assume that rank in society and that social condition which she panted for, for she was one of those to whom wealth has little charms unless its shows and elaborations can be brought before the eyes of others most dazzlingly. And now she knew that not a moment was to be lost. She wrote to

Mr. Adolphus Dacre to come to her at twelve the next day, and sent a trusty messenger with the epistle to Dacre House, which was some twenty miles from Wyvill Hall. Their interview was somewhat curious, and therefore we will sketch it, for the amusement of the reader.

Adolphus Dacre was quite delighted at the summons to attend her whom he really considered the first of womankind, and he arrived at the appointed time, elate with the hope that at last she might have consented to make him what in ordinary parlance (and he always used ordinary parlance) is called a happy man. It was known to Lady Wyvill that the great Mr. Dacre, as she facetiously called him, was an acquaintance of Margaret's, so that his calling was not a matter of any suspicion at the Hall, and they were generally left to have a *tête-à-tête* together as long as they pleased. Margaret knew her subject well, and when she came into the room it was with a vehemence that was quite sufficient to deprive Adolphus Dacre of the little self-possession he possessed.

"Mr. Dacre," she exclaimed with vehemence, "I have something of a most horrible nature to communicate to you. Be seated."

A push sent him into an easy chair, which groaned audibly at the superincumbent pressure, and then, before he could gather breath to speak, she continued :—

"Mr. Dacre, something has occurred which will astonish you—something which your quiet and sensitive disposition has no idea of. Mr. Dacre, I fancy I see the incredulous look upon your countenance, when I explain to you that which it is my duty to relate, and in which you can give some assistance. You know that Sir Anthony Wyvill is abroad?"

"Yes, oh, dear, yes," gasped Mr. Dacre, who was quite terrified at this preface, which must, he conceived, come to some horrible communication.

"Well, you would hardly believe it, but during his absence there has been here a man of the name of Willoughby, who has been decidedly carrying on an intrigue with Lady Wyvill."

"No!" said Mr. Dacre.

"But I say yes. You must not, however, appear to know it. Your duty is plain and easy before you, and if anybody questions you upon the subject—should that person even be Sir Anthony Wyvill himself—you must not admit that I told you, but you must say that which you cannot deny; your knowledge of the fact— you had it from common report."

"What a remarkably good idea!" said Mr. Dacre.

"Yes, it is. Do you know Portsmouth?"

"No, I don't know many people thereabouts. You don't mean Bill Hare, the gamekeeper, do you?"

"No. Your wit will choke you some of these days. I mean the town of Portsmouth."

"Oh, ah—it's a good way off."

"But you can ride there—report names you an excellent horseman. Surely you can ride there for me—for me, you know, Mr. Adolphus Dacre? Do you think I could have a brother coming here to find out, after his arrival, the faithlessness of one upon whom he counted as his heart's best treasure? Do you think that I could endure so much? No—you must proceed to Portsmouth, where he soon will be, and meet him for the purpose of delivering to him a letter, with which I shall charge you—perhaps two. Are you prepared to start almost immediately, and then to wait there until transport ships shall arrive from the coast of Spain with some portion of the army that has been there fighting against the French?"

"I am ready," said Mr. Dacre, heaving a great sigh at the prospect of a journey, "I am ready to do anything in a reasonable way, I am sure; and as to going to Portsmouth to oblige you, Miss Wyvill, of course I'll do it; for I always do say, let me be where I may, that you're the first woman in the county. I should say now, if you're a bit, you're five-feet-five without your shoes, aint you?"

"Mr. Dacre, how can you make such remarks? But am I to understand that you will hold yourself at my disposal to-morrow morning to undertake this journey?"

"Oh, of course I do, Miss Wyvill. I'll saddle old Bellerophont, as steady a horse as ever went, and the only one I have that's equal to my weight. We'll soon do the distance; only you tell me what you want of me when I get there, and tell me so as I thoroughly understand, and I'll do it."

"What I want you to do," said Margaret, "shall be made evident to the meanest capacity."

"Thank ye, thank ye; there's nothing like being plain."

Margaret Wyvill now dismissed her cumbrous wooer; for she had got him into the line of just doing all that was required, and after that she wished to give him as little information as possible.

The public prints at that time were so full of the movements of the army that she had very little difficulty indeed in ascertaining when the expected arrival of Sir Anthony Wyvill's regiment was to take place, and hence she was enabled to take her measures accordingly for the destruction of those who merited a far different fate than to be made the tools of her terrific and overbearing ambition. But being determined not to throw a chance away, and caring little for the time or convenience

No. 8.

of Adolphus Dacre, she resolved at once upon sending him to Portsmouth, in order to obviate the possibility of a mistake.

On the following morning she despatched him with a letter, addressed to her brother, of which the following is a copy :—

" BROTHER,—I hesitate to address you for the first time in my existence. When I could talk to you of hope, of joy, and expatiate upon a wish that you should soon return to your ancient and much-loved home, I could be discursive, and write much ; but now that I never wish to see your face again beneath your own roof, I scarcely know how to shape the dictates of my mind into words.

" And yet I must be cruel to be kind. I must tell you that which will harrow your very soul, in order that you may not have yourself the agony of making a discovery that would come upon you most terrifically, blighting your every energy, and depriving you of all power of reflection.

" Oh, brother, well I know that you have garnered up your heart's best affections in your wife, and that you believed she was a piece of virtue upon which absence could have no more effect than the march of time upon those mighty pyramids of Egypt which have withstood its onward progress.

" And who can blame you for such noble, pleasant, and delightful confidence; who can take upon themselves to say that you were wrong when all the semblance of virtue was presented to you?

" Oh, brother, I can fancy that, in my mind's eye, I can see your fevered cheek, your saddened eye—and how your frame shakes and shivers with a consciousness of having been deceived where most you trusted—made thoroughly wretched and desolate, where most you looked for happiness and all the most delightful sympathies of human nature.

" Brother, I can write to you what I dare not say to you. I could not look you in the face, and tell you that your Emily was false, because your anger might light upon me before I had time to prove my accusation, although prove it I can, as fully and completely as ever anything in this world was proved.

" I have it from her own lips. She owns, she admits that there is a man named Willoughby, for whom she entertains a sufficiently tender regard to receive him in her own private apartment—that apartment, which you made a perfect gem of beauty by the crowd of beautiful images which you assembled within it— that apartment, which your thoughts deified by the presence of eternal love, has been polluted by the interviews between the adultress and her paramour.

" Oh, I can see the blush of shame upon your cheek, I can hear the indignant denial from your lips, but all is vain, you cannot gainsay proofs ; but if you want another yet more stringent than any I can offer, write to her, and ask her if there be. such a person in existence as Ernest Willoughby.

" Note her reply well, and if that be not sufficient to convince you of the guilt of her whom you have trusted, see her ; ask her if it be true that she has torn you from her heart, and listen to the words that she shall utter in your agony of self-condemnation.

" I ought to tell you clearly and distinctly how the affair occurred, of which I have now written the boldest particulars.

" When or where the acquaintanceship commenced I know not ; I must confine myself to what happened at Wyvill Hall. The day when I see you I can give you the very date and hour there came a stranger who desired to see the Lady Wyvill.

"He seemed certain of welcome, for when some demur was made to his admission, he smiled, and with a look of contempt desired that she should be immediately informed of his presence.

" She received him, and with looks of agitation, remarked even by the servants. One who passed the apartment heard some words of endearment fall from her lips, and being surprised, paused and listened, when more was uttered, which convinced that domestic that some old acquaintanceship must have existed between Lady Wyvill and that mysterious stranger.

" And now I fancy I can hear you ask me who and what he is ; and there I am at fault, for I cannot tell you. He has been repeatedly, yet no one knows him ;

Coarse in manner and appearance, he yet seems to rule the Lady Wyvill as he pleases.

"It is evident she dare not contradict him, for I am informed of a dialogue which took place between them, of which the following is the substance.

"The man spoke, saying :—

"' I will not thus willingly destroy your happiness ; make one effort to give me what you can, and I will leave you. We are both of us well aware of the nature of the claim we have one upon the other; of course it is one which you may easily cast off, if you please, but I do not expect such treatment from you, after so long a separation.'

"' No,' said Lady Wyvill, 'you have no reason to expect any treatment from me inconsistent with affection. I will take some means to serve you, and that effectually. In the meantime, let me see you often, for the pleasant revival of old recollections brings me much satisfaction, and as no one here suspects who you are, you can come and go with impunity.'

"These words were actually overheard, and I leave you to draw your own conclusion from them. You know that I am not one who would suddenly alarm thus your most sensitive feelings, but the fact is that I am likewise one who cannot sit idly by and see dishonour brought upon my family; but let me pray you, whatever you do, to act calmly and discreetly—let me beg of you to take especial care that you have abundance of evidence, before you move in this matter. Do not take my word, or anyone else's, but judge for yourself, and only think that I could not bear the idea of your coming home full of confidence and affection, when those feelings were misplaced. Let me know most especially, and, if possible, what hour, you expect to reach the Hall, so that I may make fitting preparations to receive you, and take care that nothing actually occurs to wound your feelings at the moment. But come—come, that you may be able for yourself to judge ; and so, afterwards, you will feel that what you do was not done hastily, or without sufficient grounds for proceeding. In a case like this, trust no one. We are all liable to err, and after all there may be some mistake, even on my part, although I have watched with an intensity that enables me, conscience free, to take my oath before Heaven, were it necessary, of the truth of the statement. "Believe me to be, your affectionate sister,

"MARGARET WYVILL."

This was the letter which Margaret Wyvill charged her emissary with, making it an especial point with him that he should deliver it quickly—aye, immediately upon the ascertained arrival of Sir Anthony at Portsmouth.

"If you do really," she said, "as you affect to do, value my regard, this is a matter in which you will be most urgent; so go at once."

And he did go—the poor fool, who was made thus to pander to the worst vices of a woman who despised him, and only attached herself to him because she felt that slender indeed would be the control she would have over any right-thinking honourable man, with capacities sufficient to question her conduct. Oh! it was daring, bold and desperate, this plan of Margaret Wyvill's ; perhaps, eminently calculated for success on that account. It took those whom it attacked positively by storm, leaving them little time for reflection, and stunning them with the impetuosity of her manner, and the complete nature of the charge she brought against them. She intimated nothing, urged no suspicions, but at once spoke of facts, as if they were thoroughly ascertained to be such, and so admitted of no denial whatever. With feverish anxiety she now waited some communication from Sir Anthony Wyvill, for that he would be enabled immediately to start from Portsmouth home she ascertained was not probable, inasmuch as the military rank he held would compel him to remain a short time, in order to assist in arrangements regarding the troops, which must be done in an official manner.

Upon what a slender thread now hung all the machinations of Margaret Wyvill! The least accident would have disturbed everything, and plunged all her schemes into confusion. It said something for the wonderful daring spirit of the woman that she should venture so far.

But then she was skilful enough still to secure herself something of a retreat, for should the truth really become apparent to Sir Anthony Wyvill—that is to say the truth that the supposed lover was a brother—it would be impossible for any one to contradict her when she chose to say that she thought the case was otherwise.

And then, if that failed, there was Adolphus Dacre, who, although comparatively poor, and not at all living in the style that Margaret was kept in, she still felt conscious she could inflict herself upon when she pleased ; and so with a bold and steady perseverance did this wrong-minded woman proceed onward in her course of evil.

But she had her own share of suffering, for the interval she passed, after sending Dacre with her letter to Portsmouth, and before it was at all likely she could receive an answer to it, was one of great anxiety.

And this brings us back to that portion of our story which has awakened all these retrospections. And again we call attention to that beautiful girl, in whom the reader will recognise the young wife, Emily Wyvill, sitting with her child in that antique apartment, crowded with all that was costly and beautiful, but herself the most beautiful and noblest piece of work of all.

So guileless, so pure, and so innocent ! Alas ! that such a being as thou art should be subjected to the frightful machinations of one who, like Margaret, knows no touch of human sympathy ; but like some being, the very personification of selfishness, stalks gloomily onward in the career of terror and destruction to all but herself, as she supposes, but ultimately to her own undoing.

CHAPTER IX.

THE INSIDIOUS INTERVIEW.—THE BROTHER'S CRIME.—THE MESSENGER FROM PORTSMOUTH.

Yes, there sat the young and beautiful Emily Wyvill. Oh! would that we could always see her thus—full of pleasant recollections of the past, and confidence in the future ! She had nothing to regret ; in the storehouse of her memory she had laid up no unpleasant episodes, and so pure and spotless had been her career, so guided by the best and holiest of natures, that had she had the choice to live over again—a choice which how many villains would have been glad to avail themselves of, with altered views and altered thoughts—she would have done but as she had done before.

She had been happy, too, as she thought, in trusting the serenity of her future life to one so deserving of such a trust as was Sir Anthony Wyvill.

Taking, then, her career from the first to the last, so far as it had gone, she had endured little, save those pangs which the disseverment of old connections by the stern hand of Death must occasionally inflict even upon the most fortunate.

She had always had some one to love her, to anticipate every wish, and indulge with a pleased affection, her very caprices.

A favoured child of fortune had she been, for she had gone from the arms of a fond and doating father to those of a husband who idolized her, and to whom with a conscious pride, she felt she was the charm of an existence that without her would have been spiritless and vapid.

But her day of gloom was coming ; the clouds of fate were gathering about her, and already, although she little guessed it, the first blow was struck at the very foundation of her happiness.

Yes, there she sat, looking more like one of those sweet mothers of Titian nursing the world's regenerators.

There was something so holy, so self-subdued, and so beautiful in her aspect as she looked upon her child, that, for the credit of human nature, we will believe that there are not many hearts which like Margaret Wyvill's could have held their purpose, after gazing upon that very picture of affection which that young mother presented.

Occasionally a touch of sadness would pass across her brow, and that was when she thought that Sir Anthony Wyvill might have written to her, for the affectionate letter he had written yet reposed in Margaret's writing-desk.

And now that spirit of evil—Margaret Wyvill—glided into the apartment, and the young mother looked up gently at her, and with a tenderness of speech, and that rich, glossy, musical voice in which she spoke to all—she bade her note some growing beauty in the child.

And how well did the arch-fiend dissemble! how she fawned upon the v ctim she intended to sacrifice—dressing her, as it were, in the garlands of pretended affection, ere she plunged the knife into her heart; but that would have been mercy in compassion to the withering sense of hopeless misery she there implanted.

"Is it not strange, Margaret," said Emily, "we have not heard from Wyvill?"

"I hope it is only strange," said Margaret; and then she started, as if she had said something abstractedly which she would fain recal, and in a hurried manner added :—"Yes, yes, it is strange; but you may depend that some accident has certainly happened to his letters or letter. There are people capable of even intercepting others' communications, and you know he must write under the disadvantage of having his letter brought through a hostile country."

"Yes; but how harmless is the epistle of a husband to his wife—surely, they make not war with the affections?"

"And yet, Emily, I am not surprised that Sir Anthony has not written—he may have many special reasons."

"I do not murmur, but will even content myself with the old adage, 'that no news of the absent is good news of them,' although it ever seemed to me that the proverb might be read the other way."

"True," said Margaret, "most true. I had a dream last night."

"Not a vision of evil, let me hope."

"I scarce know what to call it. Strange shapes in mingled confusion flitted before my disturbed fancy, and among them all I thought I saw you placing faded flowers upon a tomb."

"You alarm me; no, no, not alarm me—but still these visions have ever some effect upon the mind."

"Yes; but I seem to have a perception that the tomb was not a grave of aught human, which had given up its spirit to its Creator, but merely typical of the loss of some earthly feeling; and as this thought crossed my mind, a strange thought whispered to me :—

"Emily Wyvill still clings to the tomb of her lost affections."

Emily shuddered, as Margaret thus spoke.

"The tomb of my lost affections," she said, "what can that mean?" and as she uttered the question her eye glanced upon the child, and she seemed there to find an answer, for her eyes filled with tears, as sobbingly she held it to her heart, saying :—

"No, no; let me descend into the tomb, my own, my beautiful!"

This was not exactly the effect which Margaret had intended to produce, but still she had produced it; and how to counteract it became a matter of considerable difficulty. She was considering what she should say next when a servant brought in a note, which was respectfully handed to Emily.

This note coming by hand and not by post, thus found its way to its real destination, instead of into Margaret's hands, but the moment Emily had read it she clasped her hands in grief, and to the alarm of Margaret, whose busy fancy tortured everything that occurred into something inimical to her own plans and interests, seemed too much agitated for several minutes to speak.

"What has happened?" exclaimed Margaret, holding out her hand for the note; "tell me, Emily Wyvill, tell me what has happened! Speak, speak, I charge you!"

"Read, read," said Emily; "my brother—he whom I hoped had seen enough

of evil and its consequences—has committed a crime, and is even now in the
hands of justice."

Margaret snatched at the letter, and rapidly glancing her eye over it, she saw
that it briefly recounted some criminal adventure upon the high road, that the
authorities would not believe was other than a highway robbery, and in so
supposing they showed their skill in the detection of criminality, for that was
just what it was, and nothing else.

"Margaret, Margaret," said Emily Wyvill, "I do not understand these things.
What is to be done? If Sir Anthony were at home, I am sure that for my sake
he would do something to endeavour to rescue one so nearly allied to me from
such an evil course."

"He could not," said Margaret, "and he would not attempt to thwart justice;
besides, Emily, have you no knowledge of the innate pride of rectitude that
properly belongs to my brother? Can you not expect how he would revolt from
it being known that Lady Wyvill was connected with a criminal? And is it fair,
likewise, to expose him to such degradation?"

Emily shrunk aghast at this new aspect in which Margaret placed the affair.

"I expose him whom I love to degradation!" she exclaimed; "oh, no,
impossible! But I will be guided by you, Margaret, in whatever steps I take in
this distressing affair. I must do something—I cannot abandon him."

"Certainly not," said Margaret, "nor need you, always provided you make not
yourself the medium of any assistance you render him. Supply me with the
means and I will be the person to see that your bounty is applied as you wish
it. Write me a note, which shall be my credentials upon the occasion; and,
without personally involving yourself, or the name of Wyvill, you may succeed in
doing all that can be done, or that your wishes would prompt."

"True, true," said Emily; "believe me, Margaret, that I am most grateful for
this interference; without you I should not know what to do, and, as you say, I
might have compromised him whom it is my first and foremost duty to hold free
from all blemish. I have money amply at my disposal. Take it, Margaret, and
use it judiciously, as I know you can and will, for my brother."

"But you must write to him or he will be suspicious, and, knowing not from
what source the good comes to him, he may probably reject it."

"Think you so? then I will write; but what to say I know not. When your
heart is full, and you wish not to commit yourself or others, it is so difficult to
speak."

"It is. Would you write from my dictation?"

"Gladly—most gladly—if you will give it me."

Another moment saw writing materials placed before Emily, and Margaret
Wyvill stood by to dictate such a letter as she hoped and wished would serve her
turn well to produce at some future opportunity, when it might be wanted to fix
the wavering resolution of Sir Anthony Wyvill.

"Say on, Margaret, say on, I am ready," said the agitated Emily; "tell me what
to write?"

"You know, Emily, that letters of this kind, addressed to persons accused of
criminality, are always used by those engaged in the administration of justice."

"Indeed! is it so?"

"Yes; therefore it will be necessary to write with great caution."

"Oh, yes, yes, I understand!"

"Proceed, then, and commence thus abruptly—

"'You know my affection for you, and that under no circumstance could it be
more, nor can anything, however seeming unpromising to its continuances, make
it less.'

"I have written that," said Emily, "say on."

"'The affection of my husband places means at my disposal—means which I
shall not scruple to use in your behalf.'

"Yes, yes, that is true."

"'I have commissioned one whom I can trust to see you to bring] you money, and to tell you not to despair, but to rely always upon my affection, which is most enduring, and which nothing can obliterate. The remembrance of past happy times will always cling to me. Farewell, and doubt nothing—fear nothing while you know there is one that loves you as sincerely as EMILY WYVILL.'

"Shall I put my name? indeed," said Emily, "does that square with the caution you have instilled into me?"

"No, I had for the moment forgotten; erase it, so that it will be readable only to those who know it, while it is not at all so to any one who has no key to who is likely to be the writer: you understand me, Emily?"

"Yes, yes, well and completely—you see I have crossed it over and over, so that it may be read by those who would guess that it had come from me, but by none others."

"I think that that will do."

"Margaret, how strangely you uttered those words; I could almost have sworn that it was some other voice than yours that I heard."

"We are alone, therefore it must be either you or me who speak, but I will go at once upon your errand, and all will be well. You will have aided him you wish to aid, and yet incurred no danger by the act, nor compromised any one whom you love and are bound to honour and respect."

"True, true; and I have done all this through your kind instrumentality. What I should do without you, Margaret, I know not. We shall both thank you— Sir Anthony and myself—when I tell him how kindly you have got over this difficulty.'

"Yes," said Margaret, as she left the apartment, "when you tell him, I shall look for thanks—but not of the complexion you at present presume to be owing to me."

Margaret was not likely to leave the house upon such an errand, although she felt it was quite desirable that the brother should have the assistance, to a certain extent, which his sister wished him—not from any real wish for his welfare, or care for what fate he came to—but to prevent the possibility of his making a second application; and so, practically letting Emily know that she, Margaret, had broken her word. We have before hinted that the servants of the establishment were principally creatures of Margaret's, and she easily found one of them to whom she could entrust the missive. And well for her was it—or rather well for her schemes—that she did remain at Wyvill Hall; for scarce another half hour had elapsed, when, breathless and heated, Adolphus Dacre stood before her. His appearance betokened a long and hasty journey; and there was about as much agitation manifest in his countenance as so warped a collection of features could, under any circumstances, be well supposed to exhibit.

The appearance and manner of Margaret Wyvill was in striking contrast with that of her bulky admirer, for when she saw that he was in a state of agitation she immediately assumed a calmness and composure, which in reality was foreign from her feelings; for although by no means in the state of excitement in which he was, she could not but feel fully the critical position in which she had placed herself.

"Speak, speak!" she cried; "let me have your news quickly, and cease this idle grimacing."

"Idle grimacing, Mistress Margaret! I have ridden hard," he replied, "and all to do your bidding. Methinks I merited a better reception."

"Pshaw! this is no time to prate of receptions. Your news—your news—let me have it at once—I shall estimate you at its value."

"Why then, Mistress Margaret, I went to Portsmouth, according to your orders, and, after remaining there some time, sure enough, as you said he would Sir Anthony Wyvill arrived."

"Well, proceed—proceed—"

"I am proceeding as quickly as may be. Knowing then, or rather suspecting that the letter you had given me charge of was one of no trifling importance, I made up my mind to trust it to nobody, but deliver it myself. Thinks I to myself, it's something that will please him very much, no doubt, and I shall get all manner of compliments and an invitation to dinner."

" Well—well—"

" Nay; don't be so impatient, I'm telling you as quickly as I can—I went with the letter to an hotel at which he was staying, and sending up my name, I desired to see him; I don't suppose he knew me by the kind of message that was brought back, although, if you do recollect, mistress, we did meet once at the county ball, when he was in these parts."

Margaret made a gesture of impatience, and Adolphus Dacre continued—

" Well, I'm not going to detain you another moment. I was shown into a very handsome dining-room, and was requested to be seated until he should come to me; and, while I was sitting there—would you believe it, Mistress Margaret?—I was quite ravished ——."

" Quite what?" said Margaret, as she bent her haughty brows upon him.

" There you go again: you won't let me finish a sentence I was quite ravished by the sight of one of the most beautiful creatures I had ever set eyes upon. She came tripping into the apartment as playfully as a pet calf; and I do think, at the moment, she mistook me for Sir Anthony Wyvill: but, certainly, that's not to be wondered at—for both are fine men!"

" Who was she?" said Margaret. " Did you ascertain her name?"

" Oh, yes, I did: they called her Mrs. Captain Angerstein. Odd enough name for a female. A soldier, who had come over from Spain with her in the same ship, told me."

" And is she very beautiful?"

" Oh, an angel. I never saw anybody like her, nor ever shall."

" Indeed ! 'tis well—go on—go on."

" Yes: it's all very well for you to say ' 'tis well;' but there I sat, waiting for Sir Anthony Wyvill, with all the patience in the world; and not at all expecting that anything was amiss, and fully calculating upon the invitation to dinner. And at last in he came, as civil as you would ever wish to see anybody—begged that I would continue seated—begged that I would communicate my business; and so forth, *et cetera*."

" ' Why, Sir Anthony Wyvill,' said I, ' I have come a long way to deliver a letter to you.'

" ' Sir,' he said, ' I am much beholden to you. A letter of introduction, I presume.'

" Well, you know, Mistress Margaret, I thought there would be no harm in saying ' yes it was,'—so I did. So he smiled, and I smiled, and we both bowed, and I never felt so pleased in all my life; and then I got up and I went to the window in quite a genteel sort of way, so that he might have no interruption in reading his letter, which I am sure you will admit, on my part, was only decent and polite behaviour."

" Gracious Heavens !" said Margaret, " when will you cease this prolixity? Come to the point—come to the point—"

" That's just what I am coming to, I am sorry to say. The lady stood at the window, and in a very polite manner she said: it's charming weather, sir; so I not to be behindhand in wit, and to show her that I was a man of the world, said at once, with a bow and a smile—

" ' And ladies are charming likewise, madam;' which I think you'll own was rather smart on the spur of the moment."

" Idiot !" said Margaret, between her clenched teeth.

" What ! you don't think that was clever? Well, there are many people of many minds of course; but, however, before I could recover myself from the bow, which accompanied this remark, I protest, upon my honour, that I received a kick behind that I very nearly went through the window.

" The lady screamed, and as soon as I could I turned round, and there was Sir Anthony, with his face as red as fire, and that confounded letter in his hand."

" ' Scoundrel !'" he cried, ' how dared you tamper with me in this way?'

"'Scoundrel!' says I; 'Yes,' says he; 'where did you get this letter from?' 'Margaret Wyvill,' says I. 'Liar!' says he—'do you see,' says he, 'that door, and do you see that window?' says he—'now, if you don't get quickly out of the former, I shall be under the necessity of throwing you out of the latter,' says he.

So then up I got, and away I went.

"And do you mean to tell me you put up with all this indignity?"

'How could I help it? he took me unawares; but, between you and I, I consider that he thought I was cutting him out with the lady; and when he heard that remark of mine about the charming woman, no doubt he said to himself ' Here's a remarkable man, and I must get rid of him.' So thereupon he gave me that violent kick behind, as a beginning, to let me know I wasn't welcome."

Margaret paced the apartment with clasped hands, and such an expression upon her countenance, that, whenever it was turned towards him, Adolphus Dacre was positively frightened at it.

No. 9.

The fact was that this reception of the letter on the part of Sir Anthony Wyvill, went beyond all her calculations. It showed her that he looked upon it as a forgery, and that she would have all her work to do when he arrived.

And that that arrival would be soon, there could not be the remotest shadow of a doubt. Nay, even now he was doubtless upon the road, and, although he had given so furious a reception to Adolphus Dacre, it might be, that after-reflection had altered his views upon the subject, making him see it in a different light.

And when she came to consider, as she did quickly, for Margaret was a rapid thinker, that he knew her hand-writing well; and that, upon a re-examination of the letter, he would probably feel convinced of its genuineness, some of her fear abated, and, turning to Dacre, she said in a firm, clear, and decisive voice—

"Remain here till I come to you—I may want you. Do not stir; and mark me, speak to no one, as you value my friendship. You must be silent upon this affair. Of course, you can have no difficulty in perceiving, with your great skill and tact, that this lady whom you saw, and whose beauty you praise so much, is Sir Anthony's mistress."

"His mistress!" exclaimed Dacre, and then suddenly recollecting the compliment that Margaret had paid to his shrewdness, he added, "Oh—ah—yes, to be sure. Oh, yes, I saw it—I could not be very well off seeing, that you know—"

"You are so certain of it," said Margaret, stepping up close to him—so close, indeed, as almost to frighten him—"you're so certain of it that you could swear to it ?"

"Why, yes, in a manner of speaking."

"'Tis well. Now remember, Adolphus Dacre, you were at Portsmouth by accident, and happened to put up at the same hotel where Sir Anthony Wyvill and his lady were staying. You heard enough—you saw enough, to convince you of the tender nature of the connexion between them. You know I am not in the habit of mincing my words—you know she was living with him as his wife."

"Why, I may say, yes, I do."

"Now, mark me, falter in the least in that which you may have to say, and not only shall you never look upon my face again, but I will take care to have a revenge of you you little dream of."

So saying, she abruptly left the apartment; and from the manner in which Adolphus Dacre opened his eyes, it really seemed a doubtful case if he would ever get them closed again.

And now Margaret had her grand move to make—now she had that to do which was to mar her fortunes or to raise them. Well might she pause for a moment, and her guilty soul recoil at the thought of that which she had to do.

But it was only for a moment. The sterner nature that was within her impelled her onwards, and schooling her countenance to an appearance of composure, although it was ghastly pale, she with a firm step walked towards that apartment, which was the favourite one of the young mother's, because within it she passed so many happy hours with him, whom she now supposed far more distant from her than he was, and exposed to the perils of warfare, which in reality he had left far behind him.

————

CHAPTER X.

THE FEARFUL INTERVIEW.—THE PROOFS.—THE HEART'S AGONY.—THE FATAL
DETERMINATION.—GUILTY TRIUMPH.

MARGARET paused for a moment, with the handle of the lock in her hand; even she felt, for the second time, in her passage from the room in which she had left Adolphus Dacre to that where she knew she should find Emily Wyvill, some dread of the interview which was about to take place.

"Courage, courage," she said; "where now is my much-vaunted fortitude, where now is that boldness, which has hitherto carried me on towards every object upon which I had set my heart, heedless of consequences?

But nature will have its way; a faintness crept over her, and she was compelled to pause several minutes before she could enter the apartment. During that time, she heard the young mother singing to her child; it was an exquisite and simple ditty, full of affection, which she had heard when a child herself, and of which she entertained many a fond remembrance. Margaret felt as if choked, and clutched at her throat convulsively.

"Do I know myself?" she said; "is this the daring spirit that has conceived so much, but to falter at its execution? What to me are human hopes, fears, or affections, when they stand between me and the objects of my whole ambition? Nothing, nothing! I'm heedless of all—the blow must and shall be struck."

With these words she opened the door and at once entered the apartment.

At first Emily Wyvill did not notice that any one had come in, for so engrossed was she in attending to her child, that her mind had, as it were, shut out all external objects, and she thought of nothing, saw nothing but that little innocent who sat beside her, smiling in her face.

But this sight moved not Margaret: alike insensible was she to the actual sight of such dear affection, as to the sound of its existence, which she had heard before entering the apartment.

She had nerved herself to the execution of her task—it was a fearful one; but she had a fearful mind, adapted to it.

She was fated, however, once to feel that in most enterprises of pith and moment the first step is the greatest of the difficulties. She tried to speak, but her tongue apparently clave to the roof of her mouth, and so she stood for nearly five minutes, looking upon the mother and the child, while both were unconscious of that evil genius which was glaring upon them.

It was the child that saw her first, and it shrunk back instinctively closer to its mother's breast, making an exclamation of fear as it did so.

Margaret Wyvill's was far from being the sort of mind which could readily assimilate itself to the wants and wishes of childhood. If she could not stoop to the courtesies of existence usually, but with a haughty spirit defied them, it was not likely that she could unbend to those little ones, in whose artless prattle the greatest sages and philosophers the world ever saw have found the purest delight.

The action and the exclamation of the child caused the mother to look around her, and then for the first time she became conscious of the presence of Margaret Wyvill in the apartment.

A something of what was passing within her mind must surely have manifested itself upon Margaret's countenance—an expression of the dark and desperate design upon which she came must surely have been there; for Emily shuddered to the full as much as the child had done, and shrunk back, even like it, from that demoniac-looking visage, and those strange, lustrous-looking eyes, that were bent upon her.

"Do you not know me?" said Margaret, advancing, "that you shrink from me thus?"

"Not know you!" said Emily. "Margaret, of course I know you; but you look strange and altered. What has happened to you?"

"Indeed! you think I look strange and altered. It may be so. I will not—I cannot deny it—I think that it is so. Emily Wyvill, I have news for you."

"News—news of my husband?"

"Yes, a shrewd guess; news from your husband it is that I have for you."

"Oh, tell me, Margaret, tell me quickly—you know that all intelligence of and from that quarter is most welcome to me."

"Doubtless."

"Is he well—is he coming home, untouched by the battle's strife? Have my prayers availed—shall we see him soon again? Speak to me, Margaret, speak to me, and do not leave me in suspense another moment.

"Be calm," said Margaret, "and you shall know to the full all that I can tell you. It is my duty to communicate all to you: it is one from which I have shrunk, but one from which I will shrink no more."

The colour fled from Emily's cheeks, and clasping her hands in despair, she exclaimed—

"Oh, Heaven! my heart tells me but too truly he is lost to me for ever."

"Ah! say you so? what whispers such a thought to your mind?"

"Death—death has robbed me of him, and I am now desolate."

"No; he is well, extremely well: the alarm of war has passed him like a mere vapour; the foeman's sword has not touched him, and the leaden messengers of death have passed him by; full of health, and full of spirits, he has returned to his native land."

"Oh, and I shall look upon him once again—once again hear the music of that voice, and repose upon that breast, which is a heaven to me. Margaret, it was cruel to alarm me thus; why do you rob the pleasant and happiest tidings I can hear of any portion of their charms, by telling them in such a tone, and putting upon the telling such a look as that?"

"Because," said Margaret, slowly and distinctly, "you have not heard all."

"But I have heard enough. He is well, and returning to me; there can be little else that would cost me the passing pang of a moment."

"So you think now; but you will find too soon that there is a something else, the pang of which, far from being the passing one of a moment, will sink into the agony of a heart's whole existence. You have not heard all yet, Emily Wyvill!"

"Margaret, you alarm me—an unknown tremor seizes me—what do you mean —what do these fearful words import?—what is that that will cost me so much misery, when I have already been told that he, who has my heart's best adoration is well; this is some hideous jest, Margaret,—it is a cruel one."

"I would it were, Emily Wyvill; the honour of my name—the honour of the ancient family of which I am a scion, is dear to me. It is because I feel that dishonour, contumely, and disgrace, will light upon them, that I now suffer—yes, suffer—"

"Suffer, wherefore; are you not happy?"

"Yes, very happy. Emily, it is now nearly a week since I knew my brother and your husband was about to return to his ancient home—the honoured home of his race—that home, which has yet never been disgraced by one of its members, but which will henceforward become a by-word and a scoff for those who would point a moral or adorn a tale at our expense."

"You speak in riddles, and more than all, you tell me of a cruel act that you have done; you know the joy that the news of my husband's return would impart to me, and yet, by your own showing, you kept it from me."

"I did—I did."

"Was that kind or just, Margaret? nay, to look closer at it, was it wholly correct?"

"You know not of what you speak. Sir Anthony Wyvill wrote to me—wrote an insult to his sister, which she will not readily forgive; that was the communication I received; since then it has deeply rankled in my breast, and I have struggled hard against the necessity which I knew would come of your showing it, but the time has arrived when I must quench the young joy, that but a few minutes since was dancing at your heart. You talked of being desolate, you must be desolate, or—"

"Or what, or what?"

"So degraded as to be far beneath the poorest pity of any honourable mind."

Emily Wyvill trembled, and yet she knew not why. She felt certain that she was upon the threshold of some frightful discovery, which was calculated to blast her future peace. She could not speak for several minutes, but she looked fixedly at Margaret—fixedly and imploringly, as if she would have begged her to tell her at once the dreadful intelligence that hovered upon her lips—at once to crush her with it, rather than suffer her to endure the horrors of conjecture worse than the most frightful reality.

Margaret well translated the look, for, after a moment or two's pause, she said—

" You shall hear all, you shall hear all. I did not make up my resolution to commence a narrative, which I mean to tell you, with any idea of stopping short in its details. You shall hear all, Emily Wyvill, and you may depend on all you do hear."

Emily only made a gesture for her to go on, and then, in a voice wonderfully deep and impressive for a woman, Margaret continued—

" The letter that I had from my brother was a private and confidential one addressed to me. In it he stated that he had formed an acquaintance on the continent with a young and beautiful female, and he thought so poorly of me and of my honour—God in heaven only knows why—as to suppose that I would truckle to become the panderer to a base amour, and assist him in the prosecution of an intrigue at which my soul revolts."

Scarcely had these words left Margaret's lips when Emily sprung to her feet, and confronted her with a steady and earnest gaze.

" 'Tis false," she said; " wickedly, cruelly false. I am not desolate. You have now relieved my heart from the shadow of the burden you had cast upon it."

" I expected this," said Margaret, calmly.

" He prove false—he, the soul of honour—he who would feel a stain upon his bright name worse than a wound—oh! in truth, this is a most monstrous fable !"

" Your feelings do you great honour; they are well worthy of you. It would have been base and contemptible for a wife at once to believe, upon the mere word of any one, so much evil and dishonour of her husband. But do you fancy, Emily Wyvill, that I am a child? Do you think that I have battled with myself as I have upon this subject, but to come to you with a mere bare assertion, destitute of proof ?"

Emily shook perceptibly, but it was only a passing weakness; the blood again encircled her heart in steady currents—her confidence came back to her.

" No, no," she said, " there are no proofs of that which cannot be. You're deceived, Margaret; you're deceived !"

" Do you think, from what you know of me, that I am a likely one to be deceived ?"

" Then take the other alternative—you are deceiving."

" I expected this, too fully expected it. All the bitterness of reproach that can fall upon the bearer of unwelcome intelligence I am prepared for. It is well understood, and quite to be expected; and now I will go on with my narration."

There was something dreadful about this calm manner of Margaret's—a something which terrified Emily, and almost, at moments, deprived of her self-command. She spoke not; and Margaret, after waiting a few short moments in expectation of an answer, resumed the dialogue herself.

" Yes, he wrote to me a letter, broadly avowing this fact; stating, likewise, that it was his earnest desire to bring his mistress hither, and his request to me was, that I should feign to receive her as an old acquaintance and a visitor of mine own, so that you should have no suspicion of the real nature of the intercourse."

" False! all false !" said Emily.

" As you please," said Margaret, and, stepping up, she laid down before her a folded paper—it was a letter, with one part only folded so that it was visible, and, pointing exultingly to the characters there traced, Margaret said,—

" Emily Wyvill, do you know that hand ?"

A mist, for a moment, seemed to float before Emily's eyes, but then it cleared away, and she looked upon the well-known writing of her husband.

" It is his hand," she said.

" It is !" added Margaret. " Read those lines; they contain a description of the personal charms of her who has attracted him and supplanted you in his heart; read, I say, read !"

Emily obeyed, as if the mandate were one that she could not resist, and her eyes wandered over those lines which have already been presented to the reader, as the postscript of the letter which Sir Anthony Wyvill had written to his wife, but which—as we are aware—was intercepted for her own purposes by the bold and mendacious Margaret.

It would have been a study for some painter to have looked upon those two beings, or rather three, that now occupied that apartment, and much would it have puzzled one unacquainted with the story, to have conjectured what impulses could have cast them in such strange positions.

There was Emily—supporting the child with one arm, while the other hand was resting upon that document which contained so dreadful a proof of what Margaret had just stated to her.

And then there was Margaret herself, standing a little apart, and looking upon her victim, noticing every change of her countenance, watching the expression of her eyes, and drinking in with glad delight the assurance that she was beginning at last to believe something of her own dishonour.

But Emily rallied again ; she was not quite subdued, yet she would not be convinced.

"No, no," she said, "it cannot be—this is some frightful juggle—it cannot—cannot be !"

"You want more proof?" said Margaret, calmly.

"No—no—no—no more ! Let me banish the frightful thought from my mind —I will not entertain it. I want no proofs—I want no explanations—it is sufficient for me that I have confidence unbounded."

"'Tis well," said Margaret, "and it shows that he has calculated with amazing skill upon the person he had to deal with. Confidence unbounded is what he requires. But since you reject this mute testimony of the fact which appears to you even in his handwriting, I have another witness yet to produce."

Emily sunk upon a chair, and, covering her face with her hands, she wept.

"I triumph," muttered Margaret, "I triumph !" as she darted from the apartment.

A few moments sufficed to enable her to reach the room in which she had left Adolphus Dacre, who was becoming intolerably impatient at the long delay.

"Come this way," she said to him, abruptly, "follow me, and for your life's sake, remember that which I told you you had to say."

Bewildered he rose up to follow her, and then, before he hardly knew where he was, he found himself in the presence of Emily Wyvill, in that small antique apartment which twice or thrice he had entered during his visits to the Hall.

Emily was still in the position in which Margaret had left her, while the child was in vain endeavouring to attract her attention by its caresses.

"Emily Wyvill," said Margaret, aloud, "I have brought you more testimony."

"Where—where ?" cried Emily, and she looked up impetuously.

"It is here—you know this gentleman ?"

"I hope you are quite well, Lady Wyvill," said Adolphus Dacre. "Charming weather, madam, and charming ladies, as one may say—you take the wit, I hope?"

"Sir ! what do you do here ?" said Emily; "this place is sacred, at present, to matters, which should be kept far from a stranger's eye."

"Oh ! I—I—why, really—charming weather and charming women."

"Speak, Mr. Dacre, and tell Lady Wyvill where you have been lately ?"

"Oh, yes—why, I was sent—good God !"

Margaret thrust some sharp-pointed weapon between two of his ribs, and then she said—

"I beg your pardon, it was an accident—an accident, Mr. Dacre."

"Oh, thank ye, one for the purpose, I should fancy. Why, you see, Lady Wyvill, I was at Portsmouth, and who should I see there but Sir Anthony ? well, of course, I went to pay him my respects, and found him at an hotel, along with a—a—an individual. ' Charming weather,' says she, ' charming ladies,' says I, and no sooner did I say that than some one from behind gives me a kick, enough to dislocate my back-bone."

"And that was Sir Anthony ?" said Margaret.

"Oh, yes ; there's no doubt about that; it was Sir Anthony, fast enough. You see, Lady Wyvill, he didn't like the idea, you understand, of me saying anything so smart, and taking to his—his—a—a—individual—you understand.''

" Do you understand?" whispered Margaret to Emily. " Has this fool, who wants tact to invent the tale he tells, said enough?"

" Take him away !" said Emily, " take him away !"

" Mr. Dacre," said Margaret, " there's the door."

" The door ! Oh, the door ! well, I see the door ! I know there's the door ; that's not a very brilliant remark, nothing equal to me when I was standing at the window with Mrs. Captain Angerstein. ' Charming weather, sir,' says she to me, and then says I, ' madam,' and I bowed and smiled as I said it."

" Mr. Dacre," said Margaret, " when I requested you to observe the door, I meant that your absence would be desirable.''

" ' Charming ladies,' says I, and then all of a sudden, when one least expected it—"

" Mr. Dacre, will you go, sir ?"

" Oh ! go—well, if you insist upon it, I am going—only it's not every day you hear a good thing like that—far from it, very far from it, I should say ; but I know what made him angry ; he didn't at all like the idea, first of all, of me standing at the window with her, at all, and then he didn't like the idea of her saying to me, ' charming weather, sir.' "

Margaret moved two steps towards him with such a threatening gesture that, knowing her rather violent disposition, he thought it prudent to beat an immediate retreat, but still any one who listened to him would have heard him repeating the charming anecdote as he went, for so firm was the hold it had taken of his imagination, that it was doubtful if ever he would be able to find room for anything else half so witty in his sensorium.

And now they were alone, and Margaret, as she turned and looked upon the heart-breaking spectacle before her, began to feel indeed that she had triumphed. Poor Emily sat like one the picture of desolation ; she spoke not—she moved not, and for the first time in her existence unheedful even of the child, who still strove to awaken her to a consciousness of its presence. She looked more like some monument of grief than a living, breathing creature. But not at all awed at the wreck she saw before her was Margaret Wyvill. On the contrary, she had now made so deep a plunge in crime that she rather exulted than otherwise over the ruin she had wrought ; she stood gazing at the fair, young creature with such a malignancy of countenance, that had Emily Wyvill looked up and seen it, even for a moment, her suspicions that she was being made the dupe of some desperate evil purpose must again have been aroused. But she did not so look up—her whole soul was engrossed in the frightful fact which seemed to have been brought before her.

There it was in his own hand-writing—that writing which she knew so well, and which had often in happier days conveyed to her the sentiments of the purest affection—she had conned it over and doated on it too often to mistake it—no imitation could have deceived her—like the voice of one whom she loved well, it seemed to bring upon her soul all the memories of the past, and she was no longer capable of contending with the arch fiend who had thus ensnared her very reason against herself.

Alas, poor Emily ! why do you not make another effort yet—another effort to cast yourself free from the desperate bondage which is slowly but surely creeping over you—believe nothing but that which is consistent with truth and honour, and you may yet be happy.

But, alas ! that was not to be. The darkest page in her history was about being turned.

And now Margaret advanced towards her, and touched her lightly upon the arm —she started as if a serpent had stung her, and turning, she looked in Margaret's face with a shudder.

" And do you think," said Margaret, " that I do not feel every part of this degradation ? Do you think that I do not suffer when the honour of a Wyvill is at stake ? Do you fancy that I am so cold or so callous as not to know that what my brother does dishonourably dishonours me ?"

"Heaven help me!" said Emily.

"Aye, but you must help yourself, or seek in vain for the aid of higher powers you must help yourself, Emily Wyvill, and you must first ask yourself how much you are desirous of enduring."

"How much? Do not I already endure more than sufficient to drive my reason from its throne? and yet you ask me how much I am to endure."

"You do not understand my question. Do you intend receiving with submission and smiles, and a lip-welcome, your husband's mistress?"

Emily looked her in the face for a moment or two in silence; a flush of colour then mantled on her cheeks, as she said—

"Is it possible, then, that you know so little of me as to believe that I could play so despicable a part?"

"It is well I did not think, much as I have heard of woman's endurance, that there breathed one who would stoop so low as that. Are you equal, then, to staying and enduring the wrangle and the storm of angry passions that must surely be called into existence?"

"Oh, no, no! that I could not do. Margaret, Margaret, tell me what I am to do; you have strength of mind, energy of resolution, both of which I want. Direct me in the course which I should pursue, and like a child, for I am little more now, I will follow it."

This was the point, indeed, to which Margaret Wyvill wished to drive her victim if she could once get her to follow her insidious advice, her irretrievable ruin, she knew, was accomplished.

She feigned for a few moments an assurance of the deepest concern; and then she said—

"Listen to me, Emily Wyvill. I will tell you what I would do, were I placed in circumstances such as those which now oppress you: I would not be revenged."

"No, no!" said Emily Wyvill; "no revenge."

"I would not be revenged, then; but I would act in a manner at once dignified and generous: I would leave for ever the house of the man who had so practically shown that he had ceased to love me."

"Yes!" cried Emily, springing to her feet; "that is it."

"I would scorn to be an incumbrance upon him—I would scorn to step between him and his passions; but leave him to do as he pleased and what he pleased: I would not rest another hour beneath the roof of the seducer and the adulterer."

"It is good advice," said Emily; "it is that which, had sufficient reason been left me, I should have shaped, even for myself. It is admirable advice—and it shall be followed. I will not remain here—not another hour—not another hour!"

"Count the time of your stay by minutes," exclaimed Margaret, "and wish each passed away. Take with you your child, and leave it not to the contamination of such a house as this. Let not the caresses of your husband's concubine light upon it."

"I will not—I will not!—such caresses would be contamination—I will not again breathe the air that circles round this spot; but far off will I go, and hide my grief and shame where best I may."

"You're right," said Margaret; "and trust to me for ample means to carry out such project. Believe me, I feel too much for the wrongs which you are enduring not to aid you in setting them at defiance, as much as it is possible for you so to do. You shall want nothing, Emily Wyvill, you nor your child; but oh, do not delay—do not tamper with your own heart, until some weak feeling may come over you, and you may repent of the noble resolution you have formed. If you are to stay, once and for ever stay—but if you are to go, go instantly."

"Yes, I will; but whither, oh, whither, shall I fly?"

"Leave that to me. It is not to be supposed that, in your present state of mind you're capable of making such arrangements, but I will attend to everything."

"You are my friend indeed. Oh, what a dreadful day is this! Horror—horror! Why rather did he not come home and kill me?—that would have been mercy; and

I could have died blessing the hand that dealt the blow!—but now, all is despair: I have no hope—no joy—no energy."

"Pshaw!" said Margaret, "triumph over such a thing as this! I would scorn to allow myself so to be subdued by the sensation of another's guilt; besides, remember you have one to care for who has now no hope but in you—your child."

"True—most true!—I thank you, Margaret, for reminding me of that. Now I am myself again. Come to my arms, thou desolate little one! Alas, alas! that thou shouldst be thrown upon the weakest of thy parents for that support the strongest should render thee! But, my child, for thy sake—and for thine only—will thy unhappy mother battle against the sea of trouble that oppresses her."

"Away, away," said Margaret, "this is trifling."

"I come, I come! Oh, Margaret, you—you—"

Emily suddenly flung her arms about Margaret's neck, and looked her imploringly in the face.

No. 10.

" What mean you ?" said Margaret. " What means this wild embrace ?"

" Margaret, you're not deceiving me."

Margaret was silent, but it was not the silence of compunction, even *that* moved her not. Oh, what a heart must that woman have possessed who could resist such an appeal ; a very fiend must she have been in human shape, or else, at that last moment, must she have shrunk aghast at her own deep iniquity.

" Deceiving you," she said. " If you think that possible, Emily Wyvill, if you have a thought that way tending, remain and witness your own degradation."

" No, no, Margaret, I do not suspect, I cannot ; besides, have you not spoken of your own outraged honour?"

" And you have seen the letter."

" I have, I have ; oh, I dare not doubt ; would that there were room for any. If I could but for one moment believe him innocent ;—if I could but believe it possible that appearances had deceived even you, Margaret, I might yet be happy, but I look forward to the coming future, and all is despair, all darkness and gloom ; I have no hope, no joy, and whither am I to go ? I have no friend or relative ; he took me an orphan and supplied to me the place of father and mother, and all those dear ties which surround the more fortunate of God's creatures, and now he has left me desolate."

" He has ; but trust to me. In your desolation you have found a friend ; you know the narrow defile which separates this valley from the next—that mountain gorge which in happier times you have so often admired for its wild romantic beauties."

" Yes, yes, I know it well."

" There is a house there, kept by a worthy family of the name of Forster. During the time my brother was abroad, it lay in my power to confer upon them some services, which their gratitude has magnified into something greater than they really were. There, until to-morrow morning—for this very night I expect your husband home with her whom he intends shall assume your place in his affections—you may remain, when I will come to you, and find a more fitting asylum, and at a greater distance from this place, every scene of which must for ever now be associated in your mind with the most painful episode of your existence. You will go there, Emily?"

" Yes, oh, yes ! anywhere but here."

" It is well ; remain where you are for a few moments, and I will return to you."

Margaret abruptly left the apartment, for each moment she dreaded that some announcement of the arrival of Sir Anthony Wyvill at the house would disconcert all her schemes. Her orders were wont promptly enough to be obeyed in that household. She desired one of the most confidential of the domestics— one whom she knew she could depend upon—to have a carriage in waiting at a garden gate, and not the main entrance to the Hall. She knew that this would be done instantly, and therefore she once again repaired to the room in which she had left Emily, to see that she did not waver in her resolution to be gone.

She found her kneeling with her head hidden in the cushion of a chair, while the child was weeping and wailing at her side.

" Up, up !" cried Margaret ; " is this firmness, is this resolution ? There will be time enough for tears and prayer too, when you are far enough from here ; or, if you still waver, you can do so yet—you can still stay and receive her who is to be mistress of Wyvill Hall."

" No, no, I am ready," said Emily, " I am quite ready."

" This way, then—come, come, be quick ; here is a shawl, throw it over your head, it will protect you from the cold, and likewise screen the child—this way.— this way. Time will reconcile you to this change ; it is a necessary one, and you will feel, the more you reflect upon it, that it was not only the most dignified but the most generous course you could pursue. If anything can touch his heart sensibly, and make him feel the wrong that he has done you, it will be your leaving his house thus without a word of complaint—without any reproaches, b ⸳ ⸳⸳⸳⸳⸳ and calmly and quietly."

Thus speaking, to lull her victim and prevent her from reasoning, Margaret Wyvill led Emily, who clasped her child to her bosom, through one of the least frequented wings of the mansion, and thence down a flight of steps, into the beautiful grounds of the Hall. She would not let her pause a moment, although Emily looked wistfully round upon those objects which were so dear to her, and pregnant with the most delightful associations. And now that garden-gate was gained, when the dusky form of the carriage, for the night was dark, showed Margaret that her orders had been promptly attended to. She assisted Emily to enter it; and then, whispering to the driver to go at his utmost speed to the Dyke House in the mountain gorge, in a few moments they left Wyvill House far behind them.

———

CHAPTER XI.

THE ARRIVAL OF SIR ANTHONY.—PLEASANT ANTICIPATIONS.—THE DESERTED ROOMS.— THE EXPLANATION, AND ITS CONSEQUENCES.

THE distance from Wyvill Hall to the Dyke House was but short, and with a pair of good horses it could easily be traversed.

We need say nothing here of the family of the Fosters that inhabited the place. From the first chapter of the work the reader knows sufficient of their characteristics; and probably, by some natural affinity between persons of desperate mental tendencies, Margaret had found that these were a family in every way calculated to assist her in any outrage she chose to perpetrate. Her whole anxiety was to lodge Emily safely at the Dyke House, and then to get back to the Hall with what expedition she might. As for poor Emily herself, she was in that state of mental distraction that she scarcely knew whither she was going, or how she was proceeding; the only two palpable sensations she had were, first, that she was flying from dishonour of the most terrific character, and, secondly that her child, now to her the dearest object on earth, was clasped to her breast.

Upon reaching the Dyke House, Margaret herself alighted, and entered alone; she was not absent above five minutes, and, when she returned, she assisted Emily to get from the carriage, and whispered hurriedly to her, "All is arranged; you can wait here with perfect safety and security until the morning, when I will assuredly come to you: and let me implore you now, Emily Wyvill, not to remove yourself from here, nor suffer yourself to be led astray by any wild fancy of doing something better than you have already done. Remember, I beg of you, that by any step you may now take, without my cognizance and knowledge, you may compromise me most fearfully, therefore am I sure that I may feel I have to ask of you not to do so."

"I will not be assured, I will not," said Emily; "I am too incapable of thought now to achieve anything without your aid—believe me, I will attempt nothing, but wait for you with such calmness as I may—"

"That is right; and now, good night! rest with the assurance that you have done a great and a noble action—that you have acted generously and nobly where thousands would have acted vindictively. You have rescued your child from the infamy of being for one moment beneath the same roof with that woman, whose very presence is not only a disgrace to Sir Anthony Wyvill, but to the home of his ancestors likewise."

"Yes, yes; I feel all that."

"You have acted, likewise, temperately, and in a manner which solemn and calm reflection at any time will approve of. You have done nothing violent—nothing reproachful. Farewell, farewell, until to-morrow."

"Farewell," said Emily, and her voice was nearly choked by a sob.

She then passed into the Dyke House, where she was received by the fawning hypocritical Foster, who, with his arms folded across his breast, in a hypocritical drawl, said that, the Lord willing, he would make her comfortable, for she should have Goliath's bedroom, who was providentially just then six weeks in the county gaol for poaching, and consequently wouldn't want it.

"But the Lord of Hosts is good to us," he added, "man proposes and poaches, and the county magistrate disposes."

    *   *   *   *   *   *   *

Margaret Wyvill, before she sprang into the carriage, again turned almost fiercely to the driver.

"Haste, haste!" she said; "and then, when you reach the Hall, name the sum that shall recompense you for using your utmost speed."

"It's a bad road, madam, and the horses —"

"What care I for the horses? Do my bidding, that is all I require of you or the horses either."

"Yes, madam; but I'm a little afraid of my own neck, if we get into a gallop upon a ground like this."

"Your neck? I purchased it a year ago, and paid you your price. What is that?"

They both started; and then the man, as he shaded his eyes with his hands, and looked up at the sky, said in a low tone,—

"I'm much mistaken, or it was thunder, madam; we shall have a rough night yet. Yes, it was; by Heaven, there's a flash—the horses will go mad if they see this. Woa—woa! I'm much mistaken if we reach the Hall without an accident, for the ground is broken and full of hillocks. Will it not please you to stay here until the storm is passed over at least?"

"No, it does not please me; I must to the Hall—aye, though heaven and hell both were to let loose their fiercest elements to wage war against my progress. You shall have abundance of reward; but be quick—on—on!"

Another bewildering flash of lightning, that lit up the whole surrounding landscape for an instant with its lurid blaze, was so immediately followed by an astounding clap of thunder, that the horses reared, and it required all the man's exertions to quiet them. Margaret, however, would not be deterred; she still commanded him to proceed, and he, probably thinking that it would be the safest plan to do so at a quiet pace, acceded, and, as she sprang into the carriage, he mounted the box, and they drove from the Dyke House.

The storm, which now began to rage about them, was one of those sudden tempests peculiar to mountainous districts — the only consolations they bring with them being that they are magnificently grand in their effects while they last, and uniformly of short duration.

The thunder succeeded the lightning so continuously, and peal followed so closely upon peal, that there seemed no cessation of the alarming sounds, and truly, in the words of the poet, might Margaret have exclaimed :—

> "Whence come those thunder-riven clouds?
> Are they from that blue, wide, ethereal expanse
> That forms the glorious arch of heaven and spanneth earth
> With all its radiant beauty? or messengers from hell—
> A nether depth, from whence come all that's evil,
> And whose pestiferous breath, blasting indeed
> The majesty of the great Godhead's power,
> Fills poor humanity with dire dismay!"

They had traversed about half the distance to the Hall, when Margaret became aware, from the waving and uncertain motion of the carriage, that the horses were plunging, and they must be off their right road.

It cannot be said that she felt fear, for we may truly and hones
that sensation was a stranger to her bosom, but it was anger that ca

at being interrupted in anything that she had chosen to plan, or to say that she would do, even by Heaven itself.

She called aloud to the driver, but such was the tempestuous roar of the elements, composed of the rushing winds, amid the deep-mouthed thunder, and now and then a dash of hail and rain, that his hearing her voice was completely out of the question, and not to be thought of for an instant.

The carriage bounded on furiously; the speed was perfectly terrific, but from the oscillation which ensued, she felt certain that they were in no beaten track, and just as a conviction crossed her mind that some frightful accident was perfectly inevitable, she heard from without a wild scream of terror, and in another instan the vehicle was dashed over on its side, and she lay half-stunned amid its ruins.

As she lay incapable of motion, she heard a furious sound, accompanied by a crashing of the panels of the carriage, which convinced her that the horses were making violent efforts to free themselves from the harness that still clung about them. This, in a few seconds, they accomplished; and then she heard their clattering hoofs as they dashed wildly along the road, most likely to plunge down some precipice, and dash themselves to pieces at its base.

Then all was still—the storm had apparently travelled over, leaving behind it a violent rain, which she heard dashing and splashing against the carriage panels, and felt falling upon her face through the broken glass of the window, which was uppermost. By this time she had sufficiently recovered, to be able to think of where she was, and what she had better do. With an energy that, at such a time, few men ever would have possessed, she got out from among the ruins of the carriage, and, with as much speed as ordinary circumstances would permit, she cleared herself from among its dilapidated fragments.

The night, however, was too dark for her to see around her, so that to know precisely what had happened was a matter of impossibility, and she had no resource but to call loudly, as she did, upon the driver, with a hope, even that if he were hurt, he would be sufficiently near at hand to answer her, and tell her where-abouts they were. But in this hope she was mistaken; no voice broke the still-ness, after the echo of her own had died away. With some anxiety she looked around her, and through the dense shower of rain, she saw some lights at a very short distance off, which, from their height and situation, she felt convinced could belong to no place but Wyvill Hall. The more she looked about her, the more the locality seemed to grow into familiarity with her eyes, until she felt quite certain that although, in their headlong career, the horses might have deviated from the path to Wyvill Hall, they had come back to it again, and brought her close to the palings of the path. This was a most welcome discovery, and not caring little, or indeed nothing at all, whether the man who drove her was only wounded or killed, she hastened forward on foot, and made her way through the locality which was so familiar to her, as to enable her to reach the Hall by the nearest possible route from where she was. Margaret Wyvill was one of those personages who turn even accidents to account; and, on her way, she bethought herself that after all this storm, which seemed to interfere so awkwardly with her plans and projects, might be one of the most beneficial things that had occurred to her in regard to them.

"The man may be killed," she said; "and, indeed, it is more probable that he is—if so, I get rid of a dangerous accomplice, for who is to know, except through his instrumentality, that I was in any way accessary to the flight of Lady Wyvill from the Hall? then, will it not look as if she herself had planned the whole affair, hiring this man to take her somewhere, and that he perished on his road home-ward? Yes, yes, it will be far better if he be killed! so, without inquiry, or sending any one to ascertain his fate, I will even leave him as he is, to the chances of the wind and weather."

This was just a resolution consonant to Margaret Wyvill's usual habits and modes of thought; utterly and entirely reckless had she ever been of even the life of any one who stood in the way of the steady march of her projects. What to her was it that any one perished, so long as it was something added to her chance of success in a plan of her choosing? so that she easily reconciled herself to the probable fact of this man having sacrificed his very existence in her service.

And now she was sufficiently near the Hall that she could see the building plainly—for the storm had entirely blown over, and left behind it that almost preternatural clearness of atmosphere, which so frequently follows the wild convulsions of the elements. As quickly as the heavens had become clouded and obscured, had they again recovered their wonted purity and freshness. And, moreover, there was a bracing elasticity in the night-air, which was most grateful to the senses.

But little time had Margaret to congratulate herself upon the events of the night, so far as they had progressed; for, before she could reach a small gate that would lead her on to the lawn immediately in front of the mansion, she heard the sound of carriage-wheels, and a noise and bustle going on at the lodge-entrance, which gave her the strongest reason to believe she was not a minute too soon to meet her brother on his arrival at his ancient home.

"'Tis he, 'tis he," she said; "he has come; but little suspects he the news that is to greet him. This is the most fearful task of all; for he is not quite so puny-minded as his wife was : and, after the reception he gave to Adolphus Dacre, I have my doubts as to how he will receive my intelligence : but I must and will bring conviction home to him. I can smile at his rage, although it will not be politic to do so; and when he declares his disbelief of that which I shall assert to him, I will point to the deserted chamber of his house, and tell him that there is the confirmation of what I relate."

She heard the confused sound of voices, and then the clatter of horses' hoofs upon the hard road-way which led up to the Hall. The flash of flambeaux came across her eyes.

"'Tis he, 'tis he!" she said; "and truly I have timed it well. Now, if yon knave who drove the carriage be but killed, and Emily Wyvill but hold her purpose, as I hold mine, all will be well."

She darted forward with tremendous speed—she had much strength, being as she was of almost masculine form; and, by her intimate acquaintance with the place, she succeeded in gaining a window which opened on to the lawn, and through which she at once passed into one of the principal lower apartments of the building. There were several entrances into this apartment, so that her presence now in the house could excite no surprise. Her footsteps did, indeed, summon one of the servants to see who it was that was walking in that room ; but, when he observed Margaret, he made a rapid exit, for she occasionally, and not in the most gentle manner, rebuked any intrusion upon her privacy. Feeling assured, then, that her absence from the Hall had not even been noticed, she hurried to her own chamber, where she made such necessary changes in her apparel as would destroy all evidence of her having been out of the house; and then she at once descended to the drawing-room, and sat down to a work-table as calmly and composedly as if nothing had occurred. And there she awaited the arrival of her brother and his travelling companion, who had not yet reached the Hall door; for, in order to give effect to beautiful and picturesque scenery in the day-time, the road was purposely made to wind considerably—a circumstance which delayed the progress of the carriage.

And as for you, Sir Anthony Wyvill, if you could but have known the heavy misfortune that awaited you, well might you have wished the arrival of that carriage delayed for ever; for, at each revolution of its wheels, it was bringing you nearer and nearer to a discovery calculated to blast your happiness for a second time, and for a second time to inculcate the opinion, that there was no faith to be put in woman—that she smiled but to betray, and that her vows were indeed written in sand.

"He comes!—he comes!" said Margaret; "soon he will be here, and an interim, which I a little dread, must come. Hush! nearer, nearer, comes the sound—he is close at hand—now, courage, courage! I have yet the most difficult part to perform of any that I have yet attempted."

And Margaret was right : she had indeed a difficult part to perform; she had to meet the injured husband, and to prate to him of his own dishonour; she had to convince one who adored, another with the greatest faith, that that other had deceived him: a hard and ungracious task, even had the allegation been strictly true, but harder still and more full of danger when it was one at which truthfulness might blush, and humanity wonder indeed, at hearing spoken by any created being, bearing the outward form of woman. And during this time that Margaret was waiting with anxious suspense for the arrival of her brother, he was doing his best to calm a natural apprehension which had arisen in the mind of Mrs. Angerstein, with regard to her reception at the Hall; she said she felt how much she must be an intruder, and that she only hoped Lady Wyvill would forgive her for having taken up so much of her husband's attention.

"Oh, you know her not," said Sir Anthony, "or you would not speak of her in such a strain. She is a very pattern of guileless trusting, honour and simplicity; she will receive you as kindly and trustingly as if you were some dear sister returned to her heart, after a long and weary absence."

"I am pleased to think so," said Mrs. Angerstein; "and yet—"

She paused, and Sir Anthony said—

"Nay, finish that which you have to say, and yet—what—?"

"The presage of some coming misfortune seems to hang about my heart; I thought that this would be a happy moment when I reached your home, but I have not endured one of so much anguish since I first heard the news which left me, as I thought, friendless and desolate."

"But you were neither," replied Sir Anthony Wyvill, "and therefore you may well mistrust the feeling which you say, now oppresses you, and makes you fancy that some evil is approaching, when, in reality, all evil that can approach you is over."

"I will strive to think so."

"You may think so: see, here, we are at home! What can you have to dread?"

"True, 'tis foolish of me, I admit, but you can well forgive these womanly fears."

"Nay, there is nothing to forgive, although a little to reprehend. It is the recent storm that has affected your spirits, doubtless—you're unused, perhaps, recently, to these wars of the elements; but you will find our mountainous district at times abounds with them, and we fancy, perhaps perversely, that they do us a world of good."

"No doubt they do, no doubt they do; I know not why they should not—'tis said that such commotions clear the air of noxious vapours, rendering that atmosphere pure, limpid, and transparent, which would otherwise be pregnant with death-dealing odours."

"That is true; but see, even from the carriage-window you may catch a glimpse of the house that I have often painted to you as that in which you should pass many, many a happy hour."

"Yes—yes—I see it now."

"Ah! I will be sworn my Emily is waiting for me, and with anxious expectation listening to each sound, which seems to herald my approach. I should not be surprised if, ere we go much further, she should rush forth to meet us on our way."

"Oh, what a treasure one so fond, so affectionate, and so agreeable, must be to you!"

"A priceless treasure!"

"Aye, most priceless; for, although I have lost that one being who made up my sum of human happiness, still the memory of the past will cling to me, and I may well say with one, o'er whom the tomb has closed its portals,—

'There was a time when, lightsome as the new-born day,
My heart with rapture beating, I beheld
All objects in their sunniest aspect with a joyful light,
Reflected from that dearer sunshine of the heart,
Which knows no shadow, but, like the glory of eternal bliss,
Cloudless dawns upon the soul, and cloudless lives.'

" A pretty sentiment," said Sir Anthony Wyvill, " where learnt you it ?"

" From an unappreciated poet—one who, finding that he must rather write to live than live to write, was compelled to barter the gifts of Heaven to purposes which, in his innermost heart, he viewed with bitterness and deep contempt."

" These things are sad to think upon."

" Yes; but when such a summons comes to aught human, to exert itself to avert a coming evil, the execution of acts must follow, although to do them they seize upon the very soul ; but it is sad to think how poor the great world rates a genius, and leaves him to descend the stream of time unhonoured and forgotten."

And now they had reached the Hall door, and Sir Anthony Wyvill sprang from the carriage ; his hand trembled as he assisted his companion to alight.

" I wonder," he said, " that Emily is not here to meet us ; but she may not have heard of our approach, although he was a fleet runner, who, at the lodge, promised to speed on, and give notice of it, and he had the opportunity of going nearer route than we could."

Mrs. Angerstein did not speak, but she shook like an aspen leaf, for more than ever did she feel assured that some great evil was impending over those whom she would have fain shielded from every harm.   She shook so, and leant so heavily upon Sir Anthony Wyvill's arm, as they entered the hall, that he could not but remark her deep emotion, and felt it necessary for a time to forget his own agitation and fears, for the purpose of comforting and reassuring her.

" Cheer up, cheer up," he said, " all will be well ; there is nothing in this, believe me, there is nothing in this : Emily has not met us, simply because she does not know that we have come."

" Think you so ?" said Mrs. Angerstein, faintly.

" I am certain of it ; something has happened to my messenger which has made him fail in reaching the Hall.   Oh ! well I know what a sense of lasting regret this will be to her, and almost dread taking her so much by surprise as the suddenness of our visit will."

At the sound of the carriage stopping at the entrance of the Hall, several servants had sprung forward, and now crowded round to welcome their master, who was popular with the whole of them, on his return.

He turned to the first who met his eye, and said in agitated tones—

" Where is your mistress ?"

" Above, sir, in the drawing-room, I believe."

" And well?"

" Oh yes, Sir Anthony, quite well, I believe."

" Thank God ! "

" Has no one," said Mrs. Angerstein, " been to the house to say that Colonel Wyvill was coming ?   Let me know that, before I move another step."

The servant shook his head.   " No," he said, " no."

" Then I am happy," said Mrs. Angerstein.   " I breathe again more freely—the calmness of renewed hope regenerates my frame.   It is not on my account, Colonel Wyvill, (she always called him Colonel Wyvill, because she had been accustomed to hear him addressed by that designation,) it is not on my account that she has come not forth to meet you."

" Nay, now," said Sir Anthony, " what pains you take to make yourself unhappy! This is sheer folly.   I cannot—I really cannot, call it by any other name.   Come, come, you hear that she is well—that she knows not of our presence ; it will be a surprise for her to see us—perhaps a shock ; but still it is one which my letter must greatly have prepared her for, and in that letter I told her all—you will recollect I read it to you."

" Yes, all but the postscript.   Why did you make that a mystery ?"

" You have asked me that question before."

" And you have before evaded an answer to it."

" But I will do so no longer.   I did not show you that postscript, because in it I told her that you were beautiful."

" Oh ! do not say so—do not say so."

"Upon my sacred honour, that was the reason—the whole and sole reason. It was an honest statement, and yet I thought that, if I showed it to you, it would look so like a piece of preconcerted flattery, that I could not bring myself to do so."

"I am more than satisfied," said Mrs. Angerstein; "let us come on; I asked for an explanation, and I got it; but little did I expect, believe me, what it would be."

"I know you did not—I know you did not. But come this way; there—lean upon me, and be assured that no one will be more delighted to see you than the Lady Emily Wyvill. Oh, I know her well; I ought to know her well; and she carries every feeling of her heart imprinted on her face, as in an open book, that all who run may read. I know it is ill manners and bad taste to praise, with all the ecstasy of fondness, one female to another's ears, but without the shadow of a compliment I will say that I know you are far above such petty feelings—very—very—above them."

"thank you for that truth—I am above them. It is not egotism; it is not vanity which makes me say I am, but it is because I really am. You could search long for a theme on which it would please me better to dilate than that which teaches you to praise your trusting and beautiful bride."

They reached the head of the stone staircase which led them to the principal drawing-room of Wyvill Hall.

Sir Anthony paused a moment and laid his hand upon his heart as if it would still its tumultuous beatings ere he appeared in the presence of her he loved so well.

"You shrink and tremble," said Mrs. Angerstein.

"Oh, no—no—no—no—I do not. Come, we shall be in her presence in another moment. You will see what joy will beam in her sweet countenance, for she is beautiful—most beautiful. Now—now—how foolish of me to feel these tremors!

He turned the handle of the lock, and in another moment they stepped across the threshold of the apartment.

The room was well-lighted, and a female form was seated at a table, on which her head was resting on her hands, and which visibly shook with the emotion which seemed to be actuating her frame.

"Is that," said Mrs. Angerstein, "is that your wife?"

"No, my sister Margaret. Margaret, where is Emily?"

Margaret sprung to her feet with a shriek; she flew forward and clasped him in her arms, then she sunk to his feet, still holding him in her embrace.

"Brother, brother!" she cried, "remember that you are a man, and bear the ills that Heaven sends you like a brave and gallant one."

She burst into a flood of tears and wept bitterly and hysterically. Oh, what a charming actress was Margaret Wyvill!

Sir Anthony Wyvill stood like a statue : every energy seemed to be suspended, and had he looked upon that fabled Gorgon's head, which turned all who saw it, to the chill-likeness of a marble statue, he would not have been more utterly paralysed both in mind and body.

Mrs. Angerstein tottered backwards until she came to a couch, upon which she sunk half fainting, for she felt that something dreadful must have occurred.

"Speak, speak, sister, speak!" said Sir Anthony, and his voice was strange and altered, as if he were struggling against a thousand choking emotions, that all but denied him utterance—"Speak, oh, speak!"

"Brother, brother, feel it like a man, but bear it like one."

"Feel what?" he shrieked, "bear what?"

"Your deprivation. She is gone—gone from you like a shadow; past away like an exhalation that melts into the air and is seen no more; gone like a flash of that electric light from heaven, which, ere one can say 'behold,' has vanished from mortal sight—gone for ever, in disgrace and in dishonour."

Sir Anthony Wyvill lifted up his hands; he clasped them for a moment above his head, and then they fell powerless by his side as if they were soul-stricken. The heavy perspiration stood upon his brow like the dew of death. He drew his breath in quick and short inspirations, and then, as he tottered aside a pace or two, and sunk into a chair, he said, in a voice which was characteristic of the very ecstasy of anguish—

"She is dead, she is dead!"

"No, no," cried Margaret, "not dead; would to Heaven she were!"

"Not dead? She lives—"

"Aye, but not for thee, for another; one who has consoled the pining beauty in your absence."

"No," cried Sir Anthony Wyvill, and he raised himself up to his full height, "no; accursed be the tongue that thus reviles the fairest workmanship of Heaven. It is not so. Let troops of angels come from out of their starry sphere to tell me she   false, and I will bid them back again to learn a better, holier   that—the truth of trusting beauteous woman's constancy."

" 'Tis well—speak on—this is worthy of you, brother; it is what I k
I expected, what I could have sworn you would have said. You must h

heaped upon proof, there must be no room for the shadow of a doubt to interpose; you must feel as certain of the faithlessness of Emily Wyvill as you do of the sunlight at noon, or you would be a craven-hearted man indeed to stoop to think so meanly of the thing you loved."

Sir Anthony Wyvill clutched the table for support, and turning he faced his sister.

"Margaret," he said, "there are some things which not even our dearest nor nearest relatives dare trifle with. Did you write to me a letter?"

"I did, to Portsmouth; I sent it by a special messenger."

"I did not believe it could be real. On your soul, Margaret, tell me, I implore you, by all your hopes of serenity here, of happiness hereafter, are you really the victim of such a sad delusion?"

"No, I am the victim of no delusion; what I wrote I knew, but I did not write all that I knew. I would not condescend to detail all that I had heard—all that I had seen. But, brother, you're now in your own home. Where should a faithful and a loving wife be but here, here, to meet you?"

"She—she will come—sickness detains her!"

"You know her apartment—seek her there then—or shall I send some servant of your household to announce that you would gladly see its mistress?"

"Do not mock me," cried Sir Anthony, as he seized a massive silver candlestick from the table and walked towards the door, "do not mock me, Margaret, she is —she must be here—I have yet faith—abundant faith in Heaven and in her—to lose it in one would be to lose it in both."

He rushed from the apartment, and Mrs. Angerstein seeing the frantic gesture with which he did so, rose with a half-shriek, crying—

"Oh! bid him stay—bid him stay—he knows not what he does—detain him— speak to him—reason with him—"

"Hold!" said Margaret, stepping between her and the door, "there is no danger, he has only gone to seek his wife from room to room, but he will not find her—shrinking from the knowledge of his coming she has left her home."

"Oh, Heaven, can this be possible?"

"Yes; with her paramour."

"And he so doated on her, thought her so near allied to Heaven, that nothing mortal could even hope to rival her in all her full perfections. Oh! how he cherished her image in his heart! It was his daily, hourly theme, to talk to me of her beauty, her excellence, and all that made her the worshipped being of his soul."

"She was so; but passion claimed its victim. There came one, I know not who or what name, lineage, station, I am alike ignorant of; but with some devilish arts he must have bewitched one whom I thought pure as unsunned snow."

"I tremble!"

"And I have trembled till indignation—till the sense of my brother's wrong— of wasted affection, crushed energies—has again nerved me, and I can only feel what it is to have been deceived."

"He is long gone. Oh, seek him! seek him! you know this house well, and I do not—seek him now, I pray you—my mind misgives me that something fatal may occur to him; with such heart's agony as his the reason holds but little sway."

"Be it so," said Margaret, "you shall accompany me. Oh, you may well believe how I have looked forward to this day with terror. I have a feeling of thankfulness at my heart that it is over."

Margaret took another light from the table, and followed by the trembling Mrs. Angerstein, she left the apartment and proceeded up a flight of stairs, which she was certain she had heard Sir Anthony ascend.

By the time they neared the top they heard the sound of voices in contention, or rather one voice threatening and another pleading.

Surprised at this unexpected sound Margaret rushed forward and entered a private sitting-room, where, to her astonishment, she saw Adolphus Dacre upon his knees and Sir Anthony Wyvill holding him by the throat.

"Villain," said Sir Anthony, "what do you here? I am certain I have seen your face before?"

"Y-yes—oh yes," said Dacre; "but you'll never see it again if you choke me, Sir Anthony. I—I—came to you at Portsmouth; don't you recollect? and brought you a letter—oh, murder! don't hold me so tight—thank God! here's somebody coming—I should have been dead in another minute—'charming weather,' says she, 'charming ladies,' says I; and then all of a sudden, when one least expected it—"

"What do you do here?" said Margaret, stepping up to him, "did I not command you to leave this house?"

"Why—yes—you did, in a manner of speaking, Mistress Margaret, but somehow or other I went up-stairs instead of down."

"Idiot!"

"And then I didn't know which way to turn, and just as I was thinking of it, in comes Sir Anthony, quite furious. Oh, can I believe my eyes! 'charming ladies—charming ladies, madam,' 'charming weather,'says you; 'charming ladies,' says I. 'I hope I see you extremely well?' you recollect, mum, Portsmouth—the hotel, mum—the window—the great kick behind, mum—'charming ladies!'"

Mr. Adolphus Dacre had recognised Mrs. Angerstein, and it is probable that if Margaret had not instantly interfered, he might have received another salutation from the foot of Sir Anthony Wyvill, but she stepped forward, saying—

"Brother, you remember this person when last you were at the Hall; he is a poor creature of limited intellect, of the name of Dacre, and I trusted him, on that account as much as on any other, to bring you the note to Portsmouth—the genuineness of which you doubted, and so, I am sorry to hear, did not treat him with so much courtesy as he deserved. He undertook the journey, solely from good feeling towards you and me."

"I would not believe it for a moment," said Sir Anthony, "and when I saw such a grinning ape had brought me such intelligence, I own that on the impulse of the moment I treated him more roughly than I should have done; but send him away, Margaret,—send him away, we want no witnesses."

"Oh, you're sorry, are you?" said Adolphus. "'Charming ladies,' that's what put you out. How do you do, mum?—I hope you're well, mum?"

"Go," said Margaret, "go at once."

"I'm going. Good evening, all.—Good evening to you, madam; I tear myself away—'charming ladies,' madam, I tear myself away."

Mr. Dacre left the room, and Margaret followed him to the top of the stairs, and inclining her mouth to his ear, she said in a hissing whisper,—

"If you or me leave the hall at once, I will take steps to draw down the vengeance of Sir Anthony Wyvill upon you, and upon you alone."

"Oh, he's angry with me, because when she said it's charming weather, I said—"

"Begone," said Margaret, and she gave him a push that sent him down five or six stairs; "I have neither time or inclination to be tormented by your folly."

"Folly, indeed," said Adolphus Dacre, as he left the Hall; "upon my word, this is the most complimentary family I ever came near; one tells you you are an idiot, and takes hold of you by the throat—another gets you off from strangulation by pronouncing you a fool; and, in the end, nobody seems to see the wit of 'charming ladies' but myself. I know it, though—I can see it with half an eye, I've made an impression upon that charming young widow, and that's what makes Sir Anthony so angry,—'charming weather,' said she, and 'charming ladies,' said I, and that did the business. Ha! ha!—and now I'll go home to dream, as the man in the play says, 'and perchance to sleep,' and while I'm dreaming and sleeping, there's no saying what may come."

Sir Anthony Wyvill had been through most of the apartments of the house and now he sunk into a chair, with the candle in his hand. He tried to speak several times without being able to articulate a sound, and when he did speak all he could say was, "desolation—desolation;" then the candlestick dropped from his nerveless grasp, and with a deep sigh he fell back upon the chair, in a state of insensibility.

"Oh, he's dying—he's dying!" cried Mrs. Angerstein; "help, help! he's surely dying."

Margaret was herself a little alarmed, although her fears did not reach such a climax as Mrs. Angerstein's. She saw that her brother had fainted, but she anticipated nothing further, and a moment's reflection induced her to think it would be better not to call any of the domestics, but for her and Mrs. Angerstein to attend to him alone.

"Do not be alarmed," she said, "he will recover soon; the excitement has produced this effect upon him."

"Heaven help him!" said Mrs. Angerstein.

"Amen," said Margaret; "he has been cruelly used by one whom he trusted."

This was literally true as regarded herself, although she meant it not so to apply.

"I feel," said Mrs. Angerstein, "as if I were in some frightful dream."

"It is too real—it is too real. I do regret he loved her so, but I foresaw all that has occurred to-night; whe he should hear she had left him, you may well guess what I have suffered."

From a bed-room which was immediately adjoining, Margaret procured water, and a little of it sprinkled upon the face of Sir Anthony Wyvill, recovered him."

When he opened his eyes he looked about him in a wild and frantic manner.

"My Emily, my Emily," he said;—" oh, what a dream—a dream of agony, will you forgive me? 1 thought that you were false—you, the very emblem of all that is pure and beautiful."

Mrs. Angerstein wept.

Margaret leant over her brother, and said in calm, firm accents—

"Remember, brother, bethink yourself—are you dreaming still?"

"What is it?" he said; "what has happened? speak to me, Margaret—what as happened? where is Emily? Is it—is it—can it be true? Oh! no, no, no! he has not left me thus!"

"He remembers—'tis well. Brother, feel this deprivation like a man! but ear it like one; and now that I can see by the expression of your countenance hat you can understand me as I speak to you, I will speak on. It is in vain o make an attempt to gloss over this misfortune; better is it at once to know nd to feel all that you are called upon to endure, than by degrees to arrive at the cmé of suffering. She has left you—she whom you doated upon, she whom ou loved beyond all reason—grown weary of your absence—she sought, and found olace in the arms of another."

"Vengeance!" cried Sir Anthony Wyvill, springing to his feet; "I will have uch vengeance that my name shall, to the end of all time, be associated with ome frightful tale, of what a man can do who has been betrayed where most he rusted—who has been dishonoured where most sensibly he would feel dishonour. I swear it, by the great God of Heaven!"

"No! no!" cried Mrs. Angerstein, "swear nothing—oh, swear nothing!"

"Let him," said Margaret; "so shall passion find a vent."

"I swear," continued Sir Anthony Wyvill, "that this circumstance shall point a moral for generations yet unborn. It shall be found how Sir Anthony Wyvill loved, and trusted, and garnered up in one heart all his happiness; it shall be found how he was betrayed, and then shall follow the tale of how he was avenged."

"You have spoken," said Margaret, "and now let me speak. Brother, you have endured much—much more than you ought to have endured in common justice and in common fairness; but you must still remember who and what you are."

"Have I forgotten?"

"Yes, when you talk of vengeance."

"Indeed; and would you have me sit down tamely, and endure this wrong?"

"No, I would not have you sit down tamely and endure any wrong; but there are three things which you must consider, and consider deeply in this affair. The first is that human nature is most prone to err; that principle in too many cases wages a most unequal war with passion. That all are not so graciously blessed by

Heaven with that gigantic power of reflection, even impulse, which enables the chosen few to walk evenly onward in the paths of rectitude and honour, let the allurements to deviation be what they may; let us, along with our condemnation of those who do deep wrong, pity them, that they have become the victims of the false light that has dazzled their perception, and lured them from the glory of those milder beams that come from Heaven's throne, and are eternal."

"What mean you, Margaret?"

"I mean, brother, that you owe something to reflection and something to yourself. To descend from higher considerations to those which are much lower ; I ask you to remember that you once loved her ; I ask you to remember how dear she was to you, as well as that she is human ; and remembering these things, you will be merciful, and that word ' vengeance ' which you have uttered, must be banished from your mind as most unworthy. You must be dignified and generous, rather suffering than inflicting, and not like one whose pettiest passions are inflamed, seek for that vengeance which may be safely left to Heaven."

"Cease, sister—cease, you cannot feel as I can and must feel in such a case as this. My wounded honour calls aloud for redress, and it must have it."

"How, brother, how? what would you do? Would the infliction of some personal pain upon her whom you once loved, now gratify you? No, I am sure it would not. Bethink you again of some better—some nobler course of conduct, than any which should have violence for its basis."

"Margaret, Margaret, do you want to drive me mad?"

"No, no, I want to save you from such a dire calamity. You will be mad, brother, if you do not listen in this affair to more sober counsels than can be expected from your own heart."

"She speaks well," said Mrs. Angerstein, "she speaks well, Sir Anthony Wyvill. Let me, too, implore you to temper your anger with mercy. Oh! reflect duly upon the cup of misery which, in time to come, she who has thus left you must inevitably drain even unto the dregs, and then ask yourself if you think you can add one pang to those which for herself she has prepared?"

"That is well," cried Margaret. "If you wish for the greatest vengeance, brother, you will wait until the sense of it causes you, and make effort to produce it."

"Speak to me no more," he said; "speak to me no more, if you would have me keep my senses. Leave me alone, and let me think."

Margaret beckoned to Mrs. Angerstein to leave the room, which she did following her (Margaret) to another apartment, and then they heard Sir Anthony lock himself in, as if he had thus determined to shut out the whole world while he held some hours of terrible communion with his own thoughts upon the subject that was now never to be absent from his imagination, but in one shape or another was to haunt him while he lived.

"Are you certain," said Mrs. Angerstein, "that no evil is likely to arise from leaving him so long alone?"

"Not the least, not the least; reflection will now come to his aid, and when he emerges from that apartment in which he has now shut himself, to consider the past and arrange the future, be assured that we shall find him in a different and a better tone of mind than when he entered it."

"I sincerely hope so—Oh, could I but have foreseen the desolation that was about to spread itself around his heart, I think I should have shrunk before visiting this house."

"Say not so ; he will now need all the cheering influences that can be brought to bear upon him to keep him from sinking into the deepest melancholy; your presence, therefore, is a blessed chance at such a time, because it may, and indeed must assist, to wean his mind from objects of sudden contemplation."

"If I thought so, I could reconcile myself to reside here, but I fear he will be heart-broken and inaccessible to all ordinary consolations."

For more than two hours did Sir Anthony Wyvill remain alone in the apartment, into which he had locked himself. The nature of the thoughts which oppressed him during that period may well be guessed, although perhaps not in the full intensity with which they swept across his soul. But suddenly now he emerged, and descending to the lower part of the house, he demanded to see Margaret, who at once responded to the summons, and met him in that same parlour where she had carried on the dreadful interview with the mother and the child, when she crushed Emily Wyvill's hopes of happiness for ever. There was a strange look of earnestness upon the face of Sir Anthony, as he motioned Margaret to be seated.

"I have sent for you," he said, "that you should tell me all, disguising nothing, keeping no one particular from me. From the commencement of this affair, even until to night, let me know everything."

"All that I can tell you, brother, you shall know."

"But first let me know the name of him who has thus stepped between me and my happiness."

"That I cannot tell you, I know him not. The information that such a horror was proceeding came late upon me, and then events succeeded each other with a frightful rapidity, that prevented the possibility of my making due inquiry."

"Then you may be mistaken—it is just possible—you may be mistaken."

"Oh, how I wish that I could flatter you or myself, for a single moment, with such a hope; but it is in vain, I cannot. It is all in vain. I have confirmation strong of the frightful fact, and if anything were wanting, would not her flight—for flight it was, from home at such a time as this, have amply supplied it?"

Go on, go on, I will doubt still, and it will be mercy to let me doubt. I have heard and read of hideous misconstructions of circumstances, which have separated the fondest and most attached hearts for years, which, when explained, were but as particles of dust in the balance weighing against affection."

"And can you be so weak as to cling to such a hope as that?"

"But I have no proof, and will not condemn her yet."

"Read," said Margaret, and she immediately laid before him that note which Emily, in the guileless simplicity of her heart, had written at the dictation of Margaret; "read that," she added, "and then tell me if you can yet find a room for doubt."

Sir Anthony Wyvill held it in his trembling hands, and as he perused those lines the transient colour left his cheek, and Margaret saw that her triumph was complete.

"'Tis done," she said to herself, "'tis done. He feels, he knows, that she is guilty!"

"Whence comes this letter?" faltered, Sir Anthony Wyvill.

"I will tell you. One of your own servants, who suspecting, and perhaps knowing, more than he chose to tell, a something that was proceeding inimical to your honour, brought me this note, without a word of explanation. I could see of course that it had been entrusted to that man to deliver. You know her handwriting better than I do; is it, or is it not, a forgery?"

It was a moment or two before Sir Anthony Wyvill answered the question, and then, as he let the note drop from his hands, he said, faintly—

"It is Emily's hand, I do know it too well to be mistaken. It is her hand, and all is lost."

"And now then, brother," exclaimed Margaret, as she hastily repossessed herself of the note, "and now then, brother, this is a matter in which you cannot well advise yourself, nor is it one upon which any injudicious, hasty friend, ought to be permitted to advise you. No; it is one which should only be spoken of, or thought of, by those to whom your honour is as dear, and your reputation as sacred as they can be to yourself. I will advise you, and in so advising, I say at once, do nothing. Let her take her chance, and with a tacit reproach of being permitted by you, without an effort at reclamation, to heap upon herself what misery she pleases, she will feel much more keenly than if you were to take a world of pains to show how much this blow of fate has wrung your heart."

"But my character, my reputation among men, forbids me to adopt such pacific counsels. Margaret, you speak as a woman; I dare not look over that which has occurred in such a way as you propose."

"Say not so; you can do as you please. Who would dare to cast a stigma upon the courage of him who has fought so well and so nobly for his country as you have? Your conduct, as regards courage, is above its criticism—far above it."

"Say no more—say no more. Leave me till to-morrow to think. When did she leave, Margaret?"

"She was here an hour before your arrival. It was the dread of that arrival forced her from the house. Doubtless the idea of meeting you, whom she had bitterly injured, was too much for her."

"And the little one—?"

"She has taken with her."

"And so I am left alone, to mourn the loss of every tie that bound me to the world. Henceforward, what have I to live for—what to struggle for in the great game of existence? I would that I were dead!"

"No, not so, brother; you must live for higher and nobler purposes than to regret the caprices of a wayward woman; and rather should you be pleased now to know that you are not expending your best affections upon one who cauld never have loved you, than bewail her loss."

"Oh, say not so, Margaret—say not so. Some devilish infatuation has taken possession of her; but do not fancy that she loved me not. I, who know her well, could not be mistaken. She did love me, although now, perchance, she loves me not, or strives to make herself believe that she has shaken off a passion she so often swore would be eternal. But I was wrong to trust the keeping of the jewel of my happiness in any hands whatever but mine own. I am now a wiser, although a sadder man. I have paid the frightful penalty of knowledge—knowledge of human nature—by suffering its worst treacheries. Malignant fate has now no arrow in its quiver which it can launch at my heart, with a hope of touching me."

"This despairing feeling will pass away; and, surrounded by those whom you know you can love, and whom you know that you can trust, you will know a pure happiness than that which resulted from the fitful fever of passion."

"Those whom I can trust!" said Sir Anthony Wyvill. "Dare I trust aught human now? No—I will trust no one—I can trust no one."

"Be it so; I am content, provided I can be useful to you, even to share in that general reproach—a reproach which I can forgive, when I know the cause you have for levelling it at human nature."

At this moment, a servant hurried into the apartment and exclaimed—

"A dreadful accident! Robert Earnshaw's killed."

Had any one been watching the countenance of Margaret attentively, an expression of satisfaction would have been observed at that moment to pass over it; for this was the name of the man who had driven her and Emily Wyvill to the Dyke House, and who, she so diabolically and sincerely hoped, had perished in the storm that had ensued on their return.

"Killed?" said Margaret. "In what manner?"

"I can scarcely tell, madam; but one of the men, observing that something had happened upon the cross-road leading from the Hall to the mountain dyke, proceeded there and found one of the carriages upset and nearly dashed to pieces, while, at a few paces from it, Robert Earnshaw lay a corpse."

"Let everything be done," said Margaret, "that is necessary. When will the terrors of this night cease?"

Sir Anthony Wyvill had paid but little attention to what the servant had said. Nothing seemed now much to affect him; and probably, had he been told, at that moment, that his own fortune was jeopardised, or that Wyvill Hall was upon the point of falling about his ears, he would scarcely have made a passing remark upon the news, so completely does one gigantic evil, like one great bodily pain, obliterate a sensation of all others.

Margaret, after a time, now succeeded in persuading her brother to retire to his apartment, and when she found herself once more alone, she fully indulged in all the congratulations which her guilty spirit suggested, upon the success of all her stratagems.

"Success, success," she cried, "abundant success! I am virtually mistress of Wyvill Hall; nothing now can stand between me and all the power I pant for, and have striven to acquire; there is not a circumstance but has fallen out to the advantage of my schemes, and, were I superstitious, I should say that Providence itself had aided me, for else Robert Earnshaw had not been killed so opportunely to assist my projects. He, the only one who could have betrayed that I had a

greater share in the departure of Emily Wyvill from the Hall than it suits my purpose to acknowledge—he is, at the very moment when he might be dangerous, taken from among the living. This is glorious: early in the morning, before any one's astir, I will visit Emily, and take abundant care to remove her far enough off, that she shall hear nothing of what is proceeding at the Hall, and that there shall

No. 12.

not be the remotest chance of any accidental circumstances producing a collision between her and Sir Anthony.

"The Forsters I know well I can depend upon; they are unscrupulous, and upon the plea of having to live as best they may by their exertions, lay themselves out for the perpetration of any villany that may be well paid for. They will not betray me, simply because it is their interest not to do so, and so I have no confidant to dread.

"And as for Adolphus Dacre, he is a creature who, as it were, holds his very being at my will and pleasure. What care I if he be pleased or angry? He is too idiotic to be an object of any moment, although only of late, since these affairs have been in progress, have I been fully aware of that man's mental fatuity."

CHAPTER XIII.

EMILY WYVILL AT THE DYKE HOUSE.—DOUBTS AND FEARS.—THE WALK TO THE HALL AT BREAK OF DAY.

WE will now glance at the beautiful and most treacherously betrayed Emily Wyvill, as she occupies one of those apartments in the Dyke House which had been previously prepared for her use.

To sleep under such circumstances, or even to make the attempt, was completely out of the question, and she sat looking the picture of desolation and despair until the midnight hour was far past.

Nor did the Forsters retire to rest on that eventful night, for they had had their instructions from Margaret Wyvill to look carefully to Emily, and render abortive any attempt she might make to leave the place.

But she knew not that she was thus virtually a prisoner, and now, as the first faint streak of daylight began to make itself visible, she with much more calmness than before was able to review the position in which she stood as regarded her nearest and dearest connections in this world.

The child was sleeping, so that she was enabled to pursue a train of reflection of an undisturbed character, and, as the tears rolled down her cheeks, and now and then a deep sigh spoke most eloquently to the amount of distress which was oppressing her, she over and over again reviewed those circumstances which had compelled her to become an alien from her husband's home.

"Have I been too hasty," she said, "have I left my husband's home upon the slight evidence of the supposed fact which has induced me to do so? Oh, if I did but think that—if I did but suppose for a moment that there was room for a doubt, I should even now rush forth and throw myself into his arms—but that cannot be."

Whenever it so happened that Emily Wyvill began to entertain a doubt as regards the accuracy of the circumstances that had been detailed to her by Margaret, there came before her imagination the dreadful letter, the writing of which she knew well to be in the hand of Sir Anthony.

And then, again, if that were not sufficient, there was the evidence of Adolphus Dacre—a man evidently of too limited an intellect to invent a tale that would look so coherent and exact, as that which he had told.

"And yet," she said, "I try to make assurance doubly sure. Fain, fain would I know by some other piece of evidence yet more palpable to my own senses, the reality of the dreadful circumstances that have made me the outcast I now feel I am."

But then how could she know that without the dreadful humiliation of a personal visit to the Hall, and if she paid that visit, how much better would it have been that she had from the first remained!

Thus tortured by anxieties of the most fearful character, at one moment adopting some resolution, which at another was abandoned, Emily Wyvill passed some more time, until she saw that the objects in the chamber were becoming dimly visible, as the morning light stole in upon them.

The child still slept, and slept so soundly, too, that she could not be certain that it would not awake, and then the idea crossed her mind that if she could but get as far as the Hall, and not enter it, but ascertain from some of the domestics if really Sir Anthony had come home accompanied by any one or not, she might put an end to a doubt of too fearful a character to be allowed to exist, if by any means *it* could be put an end to.

Not knowing in the least that any obstruction would be offered to her, she did not take into her consideration any means for secretly leaving the Dyke House. Probably, had she done so, she would have been foiled instantly; but, as it was, the Forsters never expected that their prisoner would adopt so inartificial a plan of leaving the place as that of merely walking down stairs, opening the front door, and walking into the open air.

In point of fact, Forster and his wife, who were sitting in the lower apartment of the house, heard her ; but they did not for a moment suppose it was Lady Wyvill; on the contrary, they considered that it must be one of their own family, from the free and unrestrained manner in which the movement was made.

And so Emily passed out, and, in the course of five minutes, was beyond even the power of pursuit; for she rushed forward with a rapidity dictated by her anxiety and agitation, rather than by her ordinary powers of locomotion. At any other time the distance was one sufficiently great to have deterred Emily from at all attempting to walk it; but now she reflected not upon that, nor did she glance even at the road she was taking, but, by a kind of instinct proceeded direct onwards, she came within sight of the tall chimneys of Wyvill Hall.

The sight of this, the house in which she had passed so many happy hours, was now exquisitely painful to her, and awoke such a crowd of exciting feelings, that, for a moment, her strength deserted her, and she was compelled to lean against the trunk of an aged tree for support.

"Oh! that I had stayed," she said, "and seen him, and spoken to him! Who knows but I might have weaned him from his infatuation ; and I could have forgiven all—more than all—freely and easily, but to see him smile upon me again, and to remain in joy with him at the old Hall, which I thought had been my resting-place for life!"

The morning light was advancing, and now she dreaded that, ere she reached her destination, the day would have so far advanced that she would be seen by too many persons, and, consequently, be forced into collision with those whom she had taken so peremptory and sudden a step to avoid. This thought revived her again, and she sped forward with great rapidity, until she reached part of the park-paling which surrounded the Hall. This she skirted, until she came to the lodge, where she knew, of course, she should receive the information she required ; inasmuch as the old couple who kept it, and who, she knew, had the warmest attachment towards her, would be able to tell her who had passed through along with Sir Anthony Wyvill.

No one was yet astir on the premises, and it was only after repeated efforts that she could arouse the lodge-keeper and his wife.

But what was the surprise and consternation of these good people to discover that it was their mistress who demanded admission, and who was on the outside, instead of the inside of her own domain.

The lodge-keeper's wife soon ran down stairs and admitted Emily Wyvill; or rather, she would have admitted her; but the latter did not advance a step, and only stood, pale and agitated, at the threshold of the lodge.

"Oh! my lady," said the woman, "what is the matter? What has happened? What can have brought you here?"

"Hush!" said Emily—hush!—"ask me nothing; but answer me, truly and at once, what I shall ask of you."

The old woman looked terrified at the manner in which these words were spoken, and well she might; for Emily looked as different from her usual appearance as any one thing could be from another.

"For your life's sake," said Emily, "answer me. Has Sir Anthony come home?"

"Yes, my lady, yes: certainly, Sir Anthony has come home."

"And—and—he was alone?"

"Why, no—in a manner of speaking, not alone—he had a young lady with him in the carriage."

"Enough," said Emily, "enough. And now, if you have any principle of gratitude for favours and kindnesses which have been in my power to bestow upon you, and which I have freely bestowed, as well you know—let me implore you to keep this visit of mine a secret. Whisper it even, to no one; but let the knowledge of it remain buried in your own breast for ever. Do not ask me for an explanation—for I have none to give. Do not ask me to remain—for I dare not. And now, farewell for ever; and may Heaven's blessing be upon you both!"

The lodge-keeper's wife was so terrified—we may almost say paralysed—with fear and agitation, at the solemnity of this address, that she could make no answer to it; and Emily Wyvill was gone, and had got a considerable distance off, before she recovered sufficiently to feel or to think that she ought to make some effort to know what was wrong, and to induce her mistress to enter the Hall.

It was not to be supposed but that a woman's wit would be sufficient easily to fathom the fact that, somehow or other, the conduct of Emily Wyvill was closely connected with the appearance of the lady who came in the travelling carriage with Sir Anthony. That Emily was doing something hastily, and on the sudden impulse of outraged feelings, she could see; and now, heedless of being but half-dressed, she ran after her, and clinging to her, implored her to listen to her.

"My lady, my lady! what is the meaning of this strangeness? do not thus leave your home, and those who would do all that lies in their power to make you happy—something has happened, my lady—I am certain that something has happened. Let me implore you to remain and see Sir Anthony."

"Hush, hush! do not urge me, for Heaven's sake; you know not what you say."

"Oh! yes—too well, too well! You're young, and have seen but little of this world, although you're a wife and a mother. It is taking a great liberty for me who am but a servant, thus to speak to you, Lady Wyvill; but when I see you wear such an expression as that upon your face, and look so sorrowfully up at the old Hall, as if you thought that in this world you never would look upon it again, I cannot help speaking something of what I feel."

"It is all in vain, it is all in vain! Do not suppose, for a moment, that I misconstrue the kindly motive that urges this remonstrance; it is well meant, but I cannot, I dare not stay!"

"Nay, nay, you're young and wilful, and Heaven only knows but you may have been played upon by some who have more wickedness in their hearts than even you could conceive the existence of."

"You have yourself given me the only proof I want—a proof that I came not for, but which, having now received, leaves no doubt to cling to. Farewell! and it will be for ever. You have spoken truly when you translated the look which I cast upon Wyvill Hall as one which had in it a long and last farewell. You're right; I never shall look upon that once happy home again."

"No, no, do not say so! Have you seen Sir Anthony?"

Emily Wyvill shuddered as she replied, "No, I have not seen him since his return, and I have no wish. Let him, if he can, be happy in the way that he has himself chosen to accomplish that great end of human existence!"

"This is some error; pray explain to me, and I, even I, poor and humble as I am, may be able to set you right."

"You have told me that my husband came not alone to the Hall last night."

"There was a lady with him, but surely she ——"

"Hush! no more—she is his mistress, and hence is it time for the wife to take her last look upon her husband's home."

The old woman shrunk back; for this, to her, was throwing a new and terrific light upon the affair, and Emily spoke so confidently too, as one who had abundant evidence in support of what they uttered.

What that evidence might be, how argumentative and conclusive, the old woman had no means of knowing, and she felt instinctively now that no commonplace general expression of confidence in Sir Anthony Wyvill would be sufficient to counterbalance the strong assertion that had come from the lips of Emily.

And the unhappy Lady Wyvill now waited for no answer. She had made that statement which was at once so humiliating and so conclusive, and she required no answer to the assertion; she looked no more at Wyvill Hall, but with a feeling of such loneliness and depression as none but one placed in similar circumstances could possibly feel, she took her route again towards the Dyke House.

Alas, poor Emily! How near have you been to an attainment of a knowledge of those truths which would have at once rescued you from the unhappy circumstances that you were taught to suppose were clinging around you; but which, in reality, were but the fables of the desperate intellect of Margaret Wyvill! How melancholy a picture dost thou present, Emily, of that worse than folly which surrenders up its own perceptions to the mind of another! Oh! if you had but for one moment looked upon your husband's face, all those air-woven fancies which Margaret Wyvill had engendered in your brain would have vanished, and in the place of such an amount of despair as previously you could have had no perception of the existence, the greatest amount of happiness that human nature could be susceptible of feeling would have been yours.

It was with a strange, bewildered feeling—a feeling which she would have found impossible to describe, that after this, as she thought, confirmation of her worst fears, she walked with tottering steps towards the only house which now enshrined any of her affections, inasmuch as it was the temporary habitation of her child.

How she traversed the distance she knew not. It seemed to her that only some blind instinct led her onward, and not calculation nor reflection.

What was the world to her? Where were now all those prospects of a long life of felicity, which had dawned upon her soul, but to render the gloom that succeeded their departure more terrific and maddening?

And now the clouds began to lower, and another of those frightful storms, one of which had overtaken Margaret on her road homeward from the Dyke House, spent its fury upon the head of the unhappy Emily.

But she heeded little the pelting of that pitiless storm, before which she bowed like a reed. The thought certainly did cross her mind, that both heaven and earth were leagued against her, and she shuddered as she asked herself, in a moment almost of frenzy—

"What have I done?—what have I done, that I should be thus the victim of boundless persecution?"

But soon this state of mind passed away. It was not one natural to her, and so drenched with rain, and weary with battling against the stormy wind that careered in furious gusts down the mountain gorge, she arrived in sight of the Dyke House. She, with a grateful heart, rather thanked Heaven for the good that it had left her, in the companionship of her child, than repined at the trials which, for its own purposes, it fated her to undergo.

CHAPTER XIV.

THE MORNING.—MARGARET'S VISIT TO THE DYKE HOUSE, AND THE DISPOSAL OF EMILY.—THE ILLNESS OF SIR ANTHONY WYVILL.—THE NURSE.

HAVING no notion that she had effected an escape from the Dyke House, Emily Wyvill made no secret of her return, but knocked boldly at the door of the very dwelling she could now enter with any feeling of satisfaction or of eagerness, because within it there slept, as she hoped, that calm sleep which innocence can only know—her babe.

She had not been missed by the family at the Dyke House, and the surprise of Forster, for it was he himself who answered her demand for admission, was immense at seeing her on the exterior of the dwelling.

He quite staggered into the passage, and could hardly believe the evidence of his own eyes.

"Lady Wyvill!" he said, "are you really Lady Wyvill? Why, we—we—we all thought you were up stairs."

"It matters not," she said, "make way—has the child stirred?"

Forster stepped aside, and looked after her with unfeigned astonishment, as she mounted the staircase which led to the room where she had left her infant. For some moments, he was so puzzled that it took him all his strong convictions of the fact, to feel assured that he was awake.

"The Lord willing," he said, "if Mrs. Margaret was to know this, fine watch and ward would she say we'd kept upon our prisoner! Curses on my own folly, for not taking better precaution. By Heaven! this might have been the ruin of us all."

He walked into the lower room, with which the reader is already familiar, and addressing his wife in something of the tone of a discomfited bear, he growled out, as with his thumb he pointed up the staircase—

"She's been out and abroad. Now hark ye, I think you must have known of it, I'm pretty sure of it; but if I were quite sure, I'd twist your neck as you stand. By Heaven! you should not play me such another trick in this world.'

But if Forster was a man of wild, uneven passions, his helpmate was to the full a match for him; and probably, when it came to invective, she was by far his superior.

Confronting him with flashing eyes, she rather yelled than spoke to him—

"You threaten me—you speak of violence to me, Forster—braggart, ruffian, coward as you are—you—you——"

"Beware!" said Forster, stepping back.

But he stepped not far enough, for snatching a half-consumed log of wood from the grate, she hurled it in his face.

He avoided it to some extent, but it struck the side of his head and shoulder covering him with charred wood, and millions of sparks.

For a moment, and for a moment only, a world of furious passions seemed to be awakened in his breast. He drew from a breast pocket, which was concealed within his coat, a clasp knife, which he opened with his teeth, and which, when opened, was so constructed as to keep so, by a spring that converted it into a weapon of the most dangerous character. In fact, it was a poinard when opened, capable of becoming a weapon for offence or defence, that the boldest might shrink from encountering in the hands of a resolute man.

"Yes, yes," shrieked Mrs. Forster, clasping her hands; "yes, Forster, the old story—the knife, the knife—you're nothing without the knife. A bold man then, but a very braggart under other circumstances. But do you think I fear you? Curses! take that—and that—and that!"

As she spoke, she commenced flinging the burning embers upon him at such a rate as not only almost to smother him, but to endanger the safety of the house.

The noise of this riot between the amiable pair succeeded in arousing one of the gigantic sons, who was asleep in the corner of the apartment, who, being sufficiently accustomed to these little matrimonial differences, did not seem much put out of his way on account of it; at the same time that he, in a very systematic manner, set about terminating it. Two strides brought him up to Forster, and, twisting his huge hand in his father's cravat, he pushed him back till he came against the wall with a blow upon the head that would have stunned most persons, and growled out—

"What do you mean, and be damned! Can't you let a fellow have a wink of sleep: bother you both!"

"The Lord willing," said Forster; "this is filial piety. If you don't take your hand off my throat, I'll put this knife into you."

"Bother your knife," said the amiable son, as he laid hold of Forster's wrist and held him as securely as if he had been in a vice. "Come, are you going to be quiet? I believe I shall have to smash both of you some of these days; such people as you shouldn't have children if you can't let 'em sleep o'nights."

Forster procured his release by letting the knife drop, and making a curious gurgling noise in his throat, which intimated to the young savage that he was very nearly at his last gasp.

Mrs. Forster, with a vindictiveness of rage, came forward with a large roasting spit, with which she made divers lounges at Forster; any one of which would have sent him to his account had they taken effect, but the son warded them off, and soon succeeded in disarming his mother, to whom he addressed the gentle remonstrance of—

"Curse you, won't you be quiet? What do you mean by it, eh? Isn't there enough blood spilt here occasionally without any of our own making a mess on the floor? Where's your feelins, both on you? Can't you take pattern by me? Let's have something to drink."

"True," said Forster. "It is possible, wife, that we're both in the wrong; and if the Lord will but look down upon us—"

"Have done with that, Forster," said his wife. "You know I hate it. If you play the hypocrite abroad, you need not bring it home. You accused me of something I know not what, and made me angry. You ought to know better, for you now that I'm mad at times—mad, when I think of the blood that has been here spilt, and breathe it in the very air on the brightest morning that ever shone—mad when, in my dreams, I hear death-shrieks, and know that over again here, in my brain, one of those tragedies is being acted which we have seen."

"Hush, hush! you're mad now to speak of such things."

"It aint safe; crush me if it is!" said the son. "Give us some brandy—a pint brandy and a pint of ale—and make them hot over the fire—just to take the pour out of a fellow's head when he wakes up of a morning. A quart of that and ha'porth of water-cresses, makes as good a breakfast as any one need wish to have. Somehow or other, I havn't much of an appetite lately. I'm a falling off, but I must take a something to keep up the blessed stamina. Let's have no more quarrelling. We ought all of us here to live like doves in a cot."

Mrs. Forster, after giving utterance to the words she had last spoken, crouched down by the fire-side; where, resting her head upon her hands, while rocking herself to and fro, she kept up a low moaning sound, which, sometimes, after one of those fracas with Forster, would last for hours with her—during which, God only knows what agony that benighted creature suffered.

*   *   *   *   *   *

And, while this scene of riot and confusion was occurring below in the Dyke House, how different, how widely different, a one was taking place in that chamber above, which temporarily was devoted to the use of Emily Wyvill. When she reached it, she found that the child was still sleeping; and to all appearance it had not stirred from the posture in which she last had left it.

Oh, how true, how beautiful, how exquisitely true it is, that in the midst of our greatest misfortunes—when the sky of our destinies seems most to lower upon us, when agonies are at the heart, and despair in the brain—if we but look for it in the right quarter, we shall find the germ of some consolation which shall ripen into the most glorious maturity.

Emily Wyvill looked upon herself as abandoned by him who not only had sworn to love her, but who had said he loved her; the gently uttered word was to her stronger than the oath; she had no friend she could name—no human being as kin to her; and yet, with what a holy calm she now knelt by that bedside, and with a gentleness of gesture that disturbed not the slumber of the beautiful and the innocent, she drew the child to her bosom. Oh, there indeed was a glorious recompence—there she had no dread of cold looks—of evil passions—or of jealousies.

"For thee, for thee," she said, "will I yet live; for thee, thou beautiful and best gift that God could make me. Despair shall find no home within the mother's breast while she can look upon the face of such an one as thou art; hope shall beam in every smile that dimples that velvet cheek; and the half-pronounced words of dear affection that come from thy infant lips so sweetly inarticulate, and yet so full of wondrous meaning, shall be the chain yet to hold me to a world I have too much cause to wish had never dawned upon me."

Even at that moment, as if Heaven had wished to send some blessed sign of its watchfulness and care of that poor mourner's heart, the infant smiled.

Those tiny arms—those arms so fragile and beautiful were clasped around her neck—the little fingers wantoned with the tresses of her silken hair, and she was happy—happy despite all. She forgot in that moment of a mother's joy all falsehood, all treachery, all that heart-suffering, which else had lit the fire of destruction in her brain.

"Thank God," she said, "I am recompensed, even now!"

And she was indeed; for amid all the treasures that earth, sea, or air could offer to her, what could cause so glorious a recompense for all evils that could by any human possibility befall her, more than the possession of such a priceless treasure, her child?

Not long had she remained now in this trance of seeming delight, when she heard the sound of horses feet outside the house. In another moment some one tapped at the door of the apartment, and upon her opening it she found that Margaret had been true to her word, and had indeed come the first thing in the morning to visit her.

There was an expression of excitement upon Margaret's countenance, such as seldom wore, for she schooled her features indifferently indeed, and it was not often that they rebelled against the expression she choose they should mean.

She cast a hasty glance around her in the apartment, as if to assure herself that all was as she expected, and then she at once explained the cause of the look of anxiety and excitement she wore, by saying—

"Emily Wyvil, you did a foolish act by going to the Hall."

"I only wished to be assured," said Emily, "that all was as had been represented to me when last I saw you."

"And you doubted?"

"No, Margaret, indeed, I did not doubt you; but when we parted you could not know that Sir Anthony had arrived and brought with him the person you named to me."

"True I couldn't know it, because we can know nothing probably, so speaking until the act is done; but I did know it in so far as expectation almost reached to the full height of belief."

"And yet, Margaret, I could not carry with me into my self-imposed exile from my husband's house the smallest lingering doubt."

"Perhaps you are right, Emily, and I ought not to blame you. We cannot see things with the self-same eyes. But you are satisfied."

"I am convinced, and had but one question to put, and that I put to the people at the lodge-gate. The answer was in the affirmative, and it sounded once the death-knell of my hopes."

"Yes, and well it might. That question was then, I presume, simply as regards the fact of Sir Anthony's arrival, and by whom he was accompanied."

"You are right. But tell me, Margaret, you have seen him, did he seem happy?"

"He wore an anxious and perturbed look when he crossed the threshold of the house, but when he heard that you were gone, it changed to one of exquisite relief."

"Alas, alas!"

"He demanded, and he had an interview with me, but it was such an one as little dreamt off, I told him of the wrong he had done, and when he told me to" you want for nothing, I in your name rejected the proffered sustenance, coming now from so polluted a source."

"You did well."

"I knew that you would say so. 'No:' I said, 'upon the report of that which you have done, and upon a conviction of the fact that you are retiring—accompanied as you are—your wife left your house with her babe.' 'Where is she?' was his question—but it was one that I refused to answer; for well I knew that his object would have been to make an effort, by affected pecuniary generosity, to hide the shame of the act that has but now driven you from your home."

"No," said Emily, "no: I will take nothing of him. Let him be happy if he can with her: she may love him."

"She is beautiful—she is the mistress of Wyvill Hall—but there is yet some plan on foot to still the voice of general reproach. She is not about to stay at the Hall. If you had, through my sought instrumentality, been imposed upon by some well-

No. 13.

constructed tale as to who and what this woman was, she would have stayed; and it might have been long before you discovered the wretched intrigue that was going on before your very eyes."

" Could he have been so base ?"

" He could—and would ; but now, to avoid scandal, she is about to leave the Hall and take up her abode somewhere, no doubt, sufficiently close at hand for the sympathising visits of Sir Anthony."

" Enough, enough, Margaret : I pray you do not speak to me in such a strain as that; I cannot bear it. I know enough for wretchedness—enough for action—and I ask to know no more."

" 'Tis so, indeed, my poor Emily ; and, now, as you are decided, let me sketch for you a plan which shall enable you to live. And, first and foremost, secrecy from Sir Anthony must be your great object."

" A great object, must it be ?"

" Yes: for he told me that although after what had happened he did not expect, even if he knew where you were, to have you back again, he would make an effort to possess himself of the child, which he hoped and trusted would be effectual."

" Oh, no, no !" cried Emily, in alarm, as she clasped her infant closer to her breast; " no, no !—let him exact any sacrifice but that : he shall not—dare not— take from me my only joy."

" If, then, you would preserve to yourself, Emily Wyvill, so dear a consolation amid all your misfortunes, it behoves you to be most cautious that you keep y ur place of abode a secret."

" I will—I will."

" And you must change your name, too."

" Yes, yes—anything—oh ! anything—to avoid even the smallest risk of having this little one torn from me."

" Then you will be saved—I will take care that you want not for means. About twenty miles from here is a village in which resides a woman whom I know. There you will find an asylum, until you can, at your full and complete leisure, find another more suited perchance to your mind."

" If it be a home," sobbed Emily, " where I can be in peace, I shall seek for no other, Margaret ; but I cannot think of throwing a burthen upon you for my support. Have I not health, and strength, and willingness to work ? No, no: leave me to procure a subsistence as best I may.

" But you have no friends but me ?"

" Not one. There was some distant relative in London that my father used to speak of, but I do not even know her name, and therefore never reckoned her as one at all. I am, saving what countenance you may give me, as you say, completely friendless."

" One friend whom you can trust, Emily, is better than a thousand of whom you know nothing except when fortune smiles upon you ; and such a friend is what I hope to prove myself to be to you. If this distant relative you speak of were a man, I should say, make an effort to seek him ; but as it is, I would not advise you to do so."

" I have no wish. If I had made such an effort, it would have been when I was prosperous and happy, and not now, when all I have to tell is a tale of sorrow and deep distress."

" Then you will adopt the course I recommended to you ?"

" Willingly ! Thankfully !"

" The son of the man who keeps this house, then, has been despatched to the village at the other extremity of the Dyke, to hire from the inn that is there a carriage, in which he will take you to the place I have mentioned. Here is a note addressed to the woman, in whose house you will find a refuge ; but, remember, do not in any moment of confidence trust her with your secret."

" Believe me, I will not."

" If you do see a chance of disturbance, such as perhaps neither you nor I dream of, I will write to you, and you shall answer me fearlessly, only being little careful not to write the superscription of your letter in your usual hand-writing, so that, should one, by the merest chance come into the hands of Sir Anthony, he will not recognise it."

" I will be very careful."

" I am sure you will. There is money for your present necessities, for I presume you brought none away from the Hall with you."

"None, none! But, Margaret, there is a box at the Hall; it is locked, and is in my own room. Alas! why do I call it to mind? But that box contains what little remembrances of my whole existence, which from time to time I have wished to keep, and which I set great store by. You will contrive, Margaret, to send it to me?"

" I will."

" A thousand thanks. I will not now repine, but concentrating all the affection my heart is capable of feeling on my little one, I will strive to be even happy."

" Do so; 'tis a noble and a most worthy resolution you have made. Persevere in it, Emily, and you will find that even such an amount of misfortune as that which now comes over you, may yet be borne."

We need not pursue further a dialogue—all hypocrisy on one side, and all trusting innocence on the other. Such a contrast is a painful one; but we will content ourselves with stating that the barbarian son of Forster duly arrived with the vehicle he had been sent for by Margaret, and in another half hour the latter had the satisfaction of seeing the victims of her machinations whirled away at a rapid rate still further from the Hall.

She smiled as she reached Wyvill Hall again, and exclaimed, when she found herself alone—

"Now am I not truly great—for do I not bend the most stubborn circumstances to my purposes? Have I not, indeed, triumphed most wholly and completely? What shall now stand between me and the entire possession of this vast estate? Nothing—nothing! I know enough of my brother to predict that his stay here will be but short."

There can be no doubt but that when Margaret hazarded a full and unqualified prediction upon any subject, she had good grounds for it; so that we may, indeed, expect that Sir Anthony will not remain for long at the old Hall, which he had come to with a hope and expectation of making his permanent dwelling-place.

He had not yet risen when Margaret returned from the Dyke House, and upon repairing to his chamber, which she did, she found, with some alarm, that he presented all the appearance of being seriously indisposed.

The shock which his mind had received on the preceding evening had apparently quite shattered his constitution, and he was in a state of fever and excitement that made medical attendance immediately necessary.

When Margaret, however, prepared to have advice for him, he shook his head, and in a despairing tone, he said—

"No, no, let me die, Margaret—what have I to live for now? The only tie that bound me to the world is snapped asunder. Let me die, and thankful shall I be to Heaven that it has so soon released me from the misery of thought."

"No," said Margaret—"no, this may not be—it must not be! You have yet duties to perform, which will become, in time, pleasures."

She did not hesitate, but sent to the nearest house for medical assistance, and when the practitioner arrived, he at once attributed the illness to mental causes.

In a conversation he had made with Margaret and Mrs. Angerstein, after he had seen his patient, he said—

" In the first place, he ought not to be left alone; but some one who will talk to him, and whose conversation he will like, should sit with him; and in the next place, if this be the locality in which he has received the mental shock that has caused his present illness, he ought to go from it at once, and try the efficacy of change of scene."

Could there be any advice more admirably adapted to suit the views of Margaret than this? Had she dictated to the medical man what she would have liked him to say, that would answer her purposes, she could not have put better words in his mouth than those which he used.

As for the company, she herself and Mrs. Angerstein would accomplish that desideratum ; and, as for the absence from the Hall, why, that was just what she wanted above all other things, because it left her in undisturbed possession of it and almost, if not quite, absolute power.

Mrs. Angerstein at once volunteered to beguile the tedium of Sir Anthony Wyvill's confinement to a sick chamber, and with all the innocence in the world, little dreaming that there was any one there who would be so wicked as to place a misconstruction upon an act which sprung from the purest feelings, she sat down by Sir Anthony's bed-side, and sometimes talked to him, and sometimes read.

Then by covert hints to the servants, Margaret soon succeeded in getting up among them the sort of feeling she wished, and in fully accounting for the absence of the Lady Emily, who, of course, as she hinted, could not be expected to remain in the Hall under such circumstances.

And Margaret managed all this so, because she could not still divest herself of the dread that Emily might, in some hour of reflection, make a resolution to insist upon coming to the Hall.

If, however, upon consideration she should find nothing but a general confirmation of her fears by all the accounts, she must consider the matter to be conclusive, and then, in all likelihood, would abandon any intention of seeing Sir Anthony.

How little did Mrs. Angerstein suspect the part that she was compelled to play in the plots of Margaret ! Had she done so for an instant how her feelings would have revolted against it ; and how short would have been Margaret's guilty reign !

But on the contrary, and far from suspecting Margaret of any bad design, she only saw in her the careful mediator of her brother's anger, one who most properly and judiciously stepped between him and his guilty wife, saying—

" Leave her punishment to Heaven."

If there could have been any character more than another having about it all the semblance of virtue, calculated to win the heart of Mrs. Angerstein, it would be one acting in so generous a manner, and one giving utterance to such lofty and soul-ennobling sentiments.

She felt at the same time that there was a something about the manner of Margaret which forbade the possibility that she should love her ; but that she should always hold her in the highest admiration, she truly and verily believed.

And so did Margaret appear, in the borrowed plumage of virtue, a very phœnix of perfection.

To Emily she was the kind friend, who could not allow her to be so grossly deceived as she might have been—aye, and would have been, but for her ; to Mrs. Angerstein she was the generous mediator for the guilty wife ; and Sir Anthony Wyvill, when the power of thought was about him, felt that she had, as it were,

"Stepped between him and his warring soul,"

preventing him from doing some deed which, perchance, the repentance of a life-time would not have sufficed for.

But is she, in all the excitability of successful vice, happy ? Has she advanced one step towards real contentment ? We shall soon see if the path she has chosen leads to the pleasant results she anticipates or not. But we must not anticipate.

CHAPTER XV.

THE JOURNEY OF EMILY TO LONDON.—THE RELATION'S HOUSE.—A FAMILY RECEPTION·
—THE LITTLE TODDS.

Six days after the events we have related, there lumbered into one of those ancient inn-yards, which are so numerous in the bye places of the good city of London, a four-horse stage coach.

Dust hung upon the wheels, the panels, the passengers, and the luggage, and it was evident, from the most casual examination, that the cumbrous vehicle had traversed many a mile of road, picking up much of the *debris* that lay upon its path.

The passengers smiled sadly as they arrived at their journey's end, they tried to look joyful, but it was a sickly attempt, for they were really too jaded to feel the happiness of having at length achieved a long and wearisome journey.

The usual crowd of loiterers about inn-yards subjected the passengers to the ordeal of a dead stare as they alighted one by one, and as nobody looks very inviting covered with white dust and in a travelling costume, the investigation seemed to give no pleasure whatever to those who were subjected to it.

One old gentleman in particular took especial umbrage, and poked a boy in the ribs with the end of his umbrella, whereupon the boy advised him to poke some one of his own size, and intimated that if he would come down some certain court which the old gentleman had never heard of, he, the boy, would serve him out, but for some occult reason or another, he declined doing so in that locality.

The outside passengers descended first, for they took the precedence of those within as a matter of course, and if both parties had attempted the feat together, the probability is that a lady might have found the broad foot of some outsider on the top of her Leghorn, but after all the whole ceremony was quickly enough conducted, and the elderly stage-coach cleared of its living occupants.

First of all from the interior came a little old gentleman, who, although upon the shadiest side of sixty, evidently considered himself as not much the worse for wear, but on the contrary, assumed a frank gayish air, as if such young fellows as he of course minded nothing.

A corpulent woman followed, to whom he had been doing the agreeable on the journey, and who had accepted all his civilities in the shape of hot negus, tea cake, &c. at the different baiting places in the road, but who now with a monstrous ingratitude evidently intended shuffling him off.

Then emerged a young man of the class which in the present day would have been denominated a gent—which seems to be generally understood now to be anything but a gentleman. Not that we for the life of us can perceive that it is so dreadful and heinous an offence as the very genteel Mr. Albert Smith would make it, to wear straw-coloured kid gloves instead of white.

Truly there is no refinement like that of vulgarity. Theodore Hook became the head of a school, which was aptly enough denominated the silver-fork school, for a considerable period, and we cannot help thinking that the gentleman who has immortalized himself by so accurate a delineation of gents and snobs, that we cannot help thinking he is like the two single gentlemen rolled into one—a Siamesian specimen of the snob and the gent—playing strange tricks before high Heaven to make angels weep and even wonder.

There was an air of fidget about this third occupant of the stage-coach, which betrayed that he had something upon his mind, and that something seemed to have a special reference still to some one within the vehicle, for there he stood bowing and smirking, as only a gent can bow and smirk and doing all those things which in gents' society is considered to be nobby.

And now there emerged from the vehicle, and the gent sprang forward to tender his assistance to a lady, in the real acceptation of the term. A veil only partially concealed her features, which, although pale, were of the loveliest description, and overshadowed, as they were, by a cast of thought which spoke of much suffering; she presented a deeply interesting appearance to those who were sufficiently in the habit of reading the countenance, that table of the mind, to be able to come to the correct conclusion that her sufferings were those of unmerited misfortune and not of guilt.

Closely clasped to her bosom, from whence she would not surrender it, was a sleeping child, and after this we need scarcely tell the reader that in the beautiful traveller by the stage-coach to London he beholds Emily Wyvill, the deceived wife of one who, even at that moment, was mourning her absence with the bitterest and most poignant anguish.

By the advice of Margaret, she had increased as far as possible her distance from Wyvill Hall, and now she arrived in London armed with a letter of introduction to a family of the name of Todd, which very remotely, through some of the female branches, could claim an affinity to that of Wyvill.

We may state that Margaret had sufficiently acted upon the fears of her victim as to induce her to consent to a change of name, and so to the world she would be a Mrs. Freeman, a young woman left with an only child to mourn her melancholy loss.

And in the most touching manner, when consenting to this arrangement Emily had said to Margaret,—

"I do not feel that I am deceiving one human being in wearing widow's weeds. If any one has a right to mourn the loss of one who was all that was dear in some beloved objects, surely I am that one. My husband's affection has gone from me, and although I can breathe a prayer for his happiness and his continued life, yet is to me as one who has gone to the tomb, carrying with him all the fond regrets of her who can know but little joy except in this of memory in the reminiscences of an affection that has passed away for ever."

But what was it to Margaret, stern of purpose as she was? what motive induced Emily to agree to what she proposed, so long as she did agree, and so she had got her off, armed with this letter of introduction and the promise of an annual sum sufficient to meet the exigences of herself and babe.

Now the gent for the whole journey had been extremely attentive as he considered, but really very troublesome to Emily, and she was determined, as the corpulent woman was, to shake him off on the very first opportunity.

But now, as she stood in the inn-yard, she felt that this was more difficult to do than she at first thought, unless there was really a larger amount of gentlemanly feeling in him than she gave him credit for; and she resolved to make that attempt, for which he gave her an immediate opportunity.

"Really, madam," he said, "you seem to be quite a stranger here. If I can be of any service, command me. Say the word—I'm your most humble——"

"I have a request to make of you," said Emily, "which is, that you will cease to importune me with civilities which even my wish to give every one credit for the best of motives, will not permit me to receive."

"Oh, how cruel!" said the gent; but Emily did not wait for any explanation of the cruelty, for she passed on into the coach-office, and accosting a young girl whom she found there, she asked her if she could direct her to Belvidere-place, City-road?

"Yes," said the girl; "but if you're strange here, you'd better give a lad a few pence to show you."

"Pray allow me," said the gent, darting forward and nearly upsetting a boy with a pot of porter, who took care that the larger portion of it should go down the gent's waistcoat, and then insisted upon having it filled up again at his expense.

This created quite a diversion for Emily, who was admitted within the sanctum of the bar, where the gent had no pretensions to follow her, and consequently could only grin like an ape on the outside, and order several strong compounds, as an excuse for staying, which very soon deprived him of all control over the small amount of brains he really possessed.

"I cannot go," said Emily, "until this person has left. I'm really afraid of further annoyance."

"What's that you say, Miss," exclaimed the coachman, who was taking something neat at the bar, "warn't you a part of my inside?—yes, you was now, I looks upon you again—you and the babby;" then, turning to the gent, he added—"I tell you what, young fellow, it's all very fine, if the lady was agreeable, but she isn't; I'm not a going to-have my insides annoyed by nobody; you'd better be off, I'm going upstairs to change my boots, and if you don't walk I shall put you in one of 'em and scrunch you."

During this speech the coachman slowly advanced towards the gent, who, to avoid coming into actual collision, was forced to retreat, but turn which way he could the persevering coachman followed him up, walking on with all the deliberation possible, until he got him fairly out of the place.

We presume, then, that despair seized upon the gent as he walked away, for certainly Emily saw no more of him. She then, after partaking of some slight refreshment, gladly availed herself of the suggestion which had been made to her at the inn, to be shown the way to her place of destination instead of directed.

A lad was procured who preceded her, and still holding the sleeping babe close to her heart, she proceeded to find a home among strangers in the sad belief that she was denied it where most she had a right to look for it. Her reflections during the walk were of the most painful description; the people to whom she was going had been described by Margaret as remarkably decent people, and tolerably well to do, but still such as would not by any means be averse to the reception of a paying guest. But still it was a nervous and uncomfortable thing for a young person like Emily to go to a strange house and announce herself as a Mrs. Freeman, when she knew such was not her name, to a number of persons who might eventually have the means of accusing her of dissimulation. There was but one motive in the whole world that could have moved Emily to practise this deception, and that consisted in what had been told her by Margaret, namely, that he, Sir Anthony Wyvill, had expressed a fixed determination of getting possession of the child, and had said that although he knew the mother was the legal custodian of it until seven years of age, he would take it by force, leaving her to take the expensive remedy, if she had the means of doing so, of an application to the Court of Chancery for its recovery.

Such a statement as this relieved all Emily's scruples at once, and thus, by a change of name, she placed another barrier between her and Sir Anthony Wyvill's affections. Well did Margaret know, and well she might conceive that such a man as Sir Anthony Wyvill would not be content long with the specious line of argumentation which had as yet kept him quiet. It was possible enough that he would agree with her in her idea of leaving Emily to take what course she pleased, but it was highly likely he would be anxious to know what that course was.

The distance was not great, for it was in the City end of that long thoroughfare, which leads from the eastern to the western ends of London, that the Todds resided; and, as these people will figure somewhat in the course of our narrative, we think we owe them, at least, the courtesy of an introduction.

Mrs. Todd was—we begin with Mrs. Todd, both from courtesy and because she was the ruling power—Mrs. Todd was then a lady (they are all ladies) verging upon her grand climacteric; and if the reader knows what that means, we do not, so we hope we've given a very intelligible idea of her age.

Then there was a Miss Selina Todd, who was in the unhappy condition of a young lady, who was supposed by Mr. John Parry to be continually lamenting that the men won't propose.

Then there was Julia Todd, the second daughter, very sly and prettier than her sister; and then there was Master Olinthus Todd, a very promising and precocious youth, who smoked penny havannahs and ogled the gals; and then, of course, there was Mr. Todd—but who cares for Mr. Todd—he had some mysterious employment somewhere, which laid hold of him at nine o'clock in the morning and let him go again about six in the evening, when he generally dropped in to tea, for he took his dinner with him to the aforesaid mysterious employment in a newspaper, and after tea he generally went out, and it was obscurely hinted that he was a very great man indeed in the parlour of the Bullfinch and Patent Mangle round the corner

Now the Todds eked out an income slender as Titania's waist, by constantly occupying a larger house than they required.

This seemed enigmatical, but we can be explanatory in a very few words : they let what Mrs. Todd called the drawing-room floor, and the advertisement which appeared in the *Times*, when that part of the Todd mansion was unoccupied, always stated that—

" A lady and gentleman, having a larger house than they require, are desirous of taking in a single gentleman, and will feel happy to do anything conducive to his comfort that he may propose."

As the reader may imagine, this was a happy effusion of Selina ; the "propose" at the end of it fixes the authorship as indelibly as the letter B to anything in the *Morning Herald* convinces the editor of the *Times* that Lord Brougham must have written it to vex him.

Mrs. Todd was an ignorant woman—one of the old school, as people call it (by-the-by, that old school must have been wretchedly conducted); but Selina Todd had been brought up at Bow, and afterwards finished at Clapham, so that she could write a little titivating Italian hand, play Robin Adair and a bad set of quadrilles on the pianoforte, make silk purses interspersed with beads, and was a good hand at card racks.

Olinthus had the usual boy's education of London—that is, the rudiments of a great number of things, and the realities of nothing; but he was rapidly making up for any deficiency by the glimpses of high life he obtained at the Eagles, and at sixteen years of age he was competent to cry out " bravo, Rouse !" with anybody.

And this was the family among whom Emily Wyvill was to be domesticated. The appearance of the house made her shrink a little, and the embossed card that hung in the window, signifying that something was to let, genteelly furnished, gave her rather a shock.

After a second thought, however, she blamed herself for these misgivings, and, having rewarded her young guide, she then, without luggage, without even a change of raiment, and with only her child to cling to in the wide world, knocked at the door of a stranger.

Margaret had certainly furnished her with pecuniary means, and had advised her, for the sake of rapidity and ease in travelling, to wait until she reached London, before purchasing what she might require.

A servant girl opened the door, and she seemed to have some instinctive feeling that she was addressing a lady, for she dropped a curtsey, and, upon the inquiry for Mrs. Todd being made, she said she believed she was at home, and would run and tell her.

" I have a letter for her," said Emily, " which I would wish her to peruse immediately, and will await her answer."

Emily Wyvill was shown into a parlour, which had more pretensions about it than, from what she saw of the exterior of the house, she could have supposed ; and while Mrs. Todd was with some difficulty reading the letter of Margaret, we will take the privilege of peeping over her shoulder, and stating its contents to the reader.

"DEAR MRS. TODD,—I think it was about three years since I received a letter from you, in which you satisfactorily proved some twenty-fourth cousinship to the Wyvill family ; but it was my painful duty then to inform you, that, living in a distant part of the country, and having no friends whatever of my own, I was unable to lend the hundred pounds, which you stated would be a considerable assistance.

" However, you may very well believe, Mrs. Todd, that I have borne in mind your letter, and that statement of it in particular which let me know you made part of your income up by taking lodgers, and now and then boarders.

" Bearing this then, I say, in mind, I send you a lady, a widow, of the name of

Freeman, a highly respectable person, who is willing to give one hundred pounds per annum, and very little trouble for board and lodging.

"Should this be suitable to you, I shall be very glad of it, as I have a great respect for Mrs. Freeman; but if it be not, I particularly request that you will endeavour to accommodate her until she can communicate with me, as she is unaccustomed to the ways of the world, and I can find out some other asylum for her.

"Believe me to be, Dear Mrs. Todd, your affectionate cousin,

"MARGARET WYVILL.."

"Lor'!" said Mrs. Todd, and she immediately made a dreadful drag at the *papillots* in which her hair was confined. "Lor'! a hundred a year—we never get more than six-and-twenty a-week—a real lady, I'll be bound. Selina, Selina, come here, my dear, I want you directly."

"Lor', ma', can't you get Maria to do your things for you? I'm putting on my chalies, and couldn't stir for the world."

No. 14.

"But my dear," exclaimed Mrs. Todd, rushing into her daughter's room, "here's a letter from the country, with a widow of introduction—a hundred a-year, and, no doubt, extras—beer and tea, washing, of course—table linen too—two pounds ten shillings, as I'm a sinner!"

"Why, what are you talking about?" said Selina; "do fasten my dress, will you, for I expect Miss Bucher here to-night."

"Bother Miss Bucher! Listen to this;" and Mrs. Todd read the letter. "There now, what do you think of that? But I knew something would happen, I mentioned it only this morning. I dreamt of six tenpenny nails being laid in a row, and I knew it meant something; you know, my dear, I always dream of corckscrews before it rains."

"And what do you mean to do?" said Selina.

"What do I mean to do? why the widow, to be sure."

"Well, I don't mind as she's a widow; but it's very awkward to-night if she's a dowdy thing, for I quite counted upon a nice little quadrille—there's Captain Flundergust, Olinthus met him and made acquaintance with him—who knows but he may propose a dance?"

"Well, my dear, if she is a dowdy, what of that? a hundred a year and extras, think of that, and your father need know nothing about it—what is it to him? it's our business, and if we can but get her to take the second-floor front, won't it be charming?"

"Oh! she won't do that, you may depend upon it; widows are deep."

"Well, my dear, I dare say they are. I should think they ought to be; but we can but try. Oh, gracious! here's a N.B. to the letter, what does it say?"

"N.B.—Any questioning of Mrs. Freeman with regard to her family affairs is what she cannot bear, and should it occur I have no doubt she will leave the house immediately."

"Well, I never—'tis well we saw that, Selina! I should have asked her about her husband's last illness, as safe as the bank."

"Well, ma, I think you're keeping her a tolerable long while."

"Oh, gracious! so I am; come down as soon as you can, Selina, for I really shan't know what to say to her—there's a charming affair. Now, if somebody would come and take the drawing-room, I should say it never rained but it poured."

"Ah! dear me," sighed Selina, when she was alone, "it's a very odd thing that no gentleman stays in these drawing-rooms above three weeks; they always tell me their hearts are smitten, and then I never hear any more of 'em. There was Mr. Verditer, the portrait-painter, he said he should never forget me, and gave a week's notice. Then there was Mr. Goldbeater, that used to do the nice dear things for the newspapers—he told me I'd blighted him, and he didn't give any notice at all, but went away and left a fortnight's rent. Ah! me, 'I should like to marry, if that I could find some charming, willing fellow suited to my mind;' but they won't propose—I hate the men. Oh! I shall never forget George Stevenson; I was coming unawares out of the back parlour, and if he wasn't kissing Julia I've got no eyes in my head. I wonder who this Captain Flundergust is? Olinthus said he met him at an hotel; I've looked in the Army List, and the only name I can find at all like it is Smith. Well, well, we shall see. Olinthus said he'd bring him; perhaps he's a dear fellow, with mustachios. Ah! me, after all the fatal hour has, perhaps, come to-night—an elopement—Gretna-Green, in consequence of objections of his family—how very pleasant! And why mayn't it be? but I suppose I must go down and see this wretched widow—I'm sure I shan't like her, I do so hate fidgety old women."

CHAPTER XVI.

THE PARTY AT THE TODDS.—SELINA'S ANGUISH.—JEALOUSY VERSUS AVARICE.

SOMEHOW or another it seemed to be the opinion of both Mrs. Todd and Selina that in the widow lady, who was to pay so liberally for her board, they would find some elderly person who would act as a kind of foil to Miss Selina's attractions.

But what was Mrs. Todd's surprise upon reaching the parlour to find, certainly, one of the most ladylike personages she had ever beheld, seated there with one of the most lovely infants on her lap mortal eye ever looked upon.

Emily rose and bowed, while Mrs. Todd quite lost in the surprise of the moment all the good breeding of which she believed herself to be such a proficient, and could only stare at her new inmate that was to be with speechless amazement.

" I hope, Madam," said Emily, " that the letter I have brought from Miss Wyvill, is satisfactory to you ?"

" Oh, yes, exactly, yes—dear me—you're Mrs. Freeman ?"

Emily inclined her head.

" And—and the little boy is Master Freeman ?"

" A little girl," said Emily; " I am extremely anxious to know if you can accommodate me ?"

" Why, the real fact is, Mrs. Freeman, that I think you say a hundred pounds a year you don't mind giving ?"

" Yes, I believe that is the amount that Miss Margaret Wyvill stated."

" Well, then, I really don't think we can accommodate you sufficiently for that, that is, I mean to say, I can't give you the accommodation you ought to have for that sum."

" Oh, don't make that an objection," said Emily; " I shall be content, amply content, with whatever accommodation you can bestow upon me. With the exception of this little one, parted as I am from all I hold dear, my only hope now is to pass the remainder of my days in serenity."

" Was he a very nice man ?"

" Who, madam ?"

" Mr. Free—oh, I beg your pardon, madam; I really beg your pardon. Of course, madam, it's nothing to me—nothing at all, madam—I'm very sorry I mentioned the gentleman."

" There need be no excuses, madam; of course one's sorrows are not a theme for daily converse, and I shall certainly esteem it as a favour if mine be not mentioned. Can you accommodate me ?"

Mrs. Todd wiped the perspiration from her brow, for she felt, to use an expression of her own, that she had very nearly put her foot in it.

" If you wouldn't object, ma'am, to the second floor front ?"

" Anywhere—anywhere."

" And washing's extra, and coals and soap, and tea and sugar, and candles and blacking, black-lead, the cruet-stand, and Flanders' brick."

" Yes, yes," said Emily, " I understand."

"And beer, and the use of the sheets and table-linen, and wear and tear of the door-mats."

" Anything—anything you please, so that I have peace and comparative comfort."

" Lor', what a jewel of a lodger !" said Mrs. Todd, aside, and then the door opened and Selina glided into the apartment, no doubt intending to surprise the widow, but truly, instead of that, she was herself astonished, for never before had such a vision of beauty crossed her sight.

With an extra pang of anguish Selina Todd felt that she was but a satellite to the moon of Mrs. Freeman's beauty, and then, indeed, there was such an ineffable air of the lady about her—such a tone of high and courtly breeding mingled with the purest gentleness—Selina Todd felt extinguished, petrified—and she could only stammer out a few unmeaning civilities, that were very far from coming from the heart.

" I've arranged it," said Mrs. Todd, " I've arranged it, my dear Selina. My daughter, Mrs. Freeman, my daughter—quite a wild thing—quite worried with proposals from the men."

Selina groaned.

" I ought not to say it before her face, but she's much admired, plays the piano-forte, mem; might have played the harp if she liked, only I did think half-a-guinea a quarter extra was something too much; speaks French and Italian, Mrs. Freeman, I assure you, like a whole barrel of natives, and does everything, as they say on the continent, *comme fo.*"

" Now really, ma, that's too bad," said Selina.

" I'm most happy," said Emily, " to have the chance of the companionship of one so every way accomplished."

Selina made a suitable reply—such an one as the ways of society had taught her —and which certainly meant nothing.

And so the preliminaries might have been supposed to be fairly settled, as regarded the continued residence of Emily Wyvill in the mansion of the Todds. The accommodating manner in which she had put up with the second-floor front, quite won the affections and the warmest admiration of Mrs. Todd, since by such means Emily was paying the highest price for only the amount of accommodation which would have been vouchsafed to any-one who had paid the lowest; and if that was not amiable in the eyes of a lodging-house keeper, we can only wonder what can be.

She made an effort to get leave to be left alone for that evening, and to be not expected to join the company which Selina had broadly stated she expected. But, as there always is among vulgar, fussy people, there were so many pressing solicitations—not one of which was true—for Emily to stay, that, in her quiet, unsophisticated nature, she really believed she was very much wanted, and that it would be the greatest of all disappointments, savouring almost of bad breeding, were she to refuse.

" I shall be but poor company," she said ; " for of late I have become too accustomed to brood over my own thoughts and distresses; but I so much dislike to refuse a courtesy, that if you will pardon the dulness which perhaps may throw a shade over the enjoyment of yourself and your friends, I will make one of the party you propose."

Selina pretended to be quite delighted, although, in reality, a deep sense of mortification came over her, for abundant self-vanity could not blind her to the fact that she was no more to compare to Mrs. Freeman than a camel to a gazelle.

There was an indefinite number of persons which, by the Todd family, and indeed in many families, were always called " the men," and every action of the females of that family had some reference or another to what the men moving in their own circle of acquaintance would think and say ; and hence it was that Selina remarked to her mother—

" I don't know what you think, but it seems to me that this widow's just the sort of creature to attract the men."

" I'm afraid so," said the mother; " but then, after all, you know, my dear, if a lot of men come to the house on her account, she can only take one of them, and some of the remainder may have the taste to—to——"

" Propose," said Selina, and she cast a languishing look in the glass ; " you're right, mamma, as you sometimes are."

Before Mrs. Todd could make a reply to this, a powerful assault on the knocker announced an arrival. Selina flew upstairs to make such changes in costume as might be necessary, and Mrs. Todd followed her to rescue some of her remaining ringlets from the *papillots* in which they were still confined, while Julia, who was not emancipated from short petticoats and white trousers, tripped down the stairs, ready to receive any visitor who might so early have made his appearance.

We need not specify the arrivals. Suffice it to say that, for the first time, Emily Wyvill was introduced to an evening party in London, in what certainly was not the most aristocratic circle.

As is usual in these cases, the young ladies were the most numerous; and a vast amount of giggling and conjecture was there as to whether Mr. So-and-so, or Mr. Somebody-else, might be expected to arrive.

Their things, by which name they call those portions of their apparel which they were not in the habit of wearing in the house, were all huddled upon Selina's bed, so that they made their appearance one by one in the drawing-room in very great style and state indeed. Several young gentlemen then made their appearance in elaborate fancy vests, which would have thrown horses and sows into convulsions, and then they talked small talk.

Oh! the hideous inanity of what is generally considered smart small talk in very ordinary society—the wretched attempts at wit—the ghastly spectres of repartee— the shadow of the shade of imagination. Heaven save us from some grinning ape at an evening party, who thinks he is wonderfully witty, sharp, and epigrammatic

We cannot hope to present a literary picture of the scene; suffice it, that the wit chiefly consisted of the repetition of some unmeaning phrase, with the exception of one gentleman, who acquired a wonderful character for facetiousness by interrupting every one who spoke before they had half got through a sentence.

For example, if any one commenced an observation with, "Did you ever?" the facetious gentleman would be sure to cry out, "No, I never!" and then he shouted "Ha, ha, ha!" as a signal that he had uttered something unusually piquant. And the young ladies said, "He was quite a wretch, that he was, and they wouldn't put up with him, not they, upon any account!" And then he said, "He'd commit suicide," at which they all laughed again.

Then there was another gentleman who was considered a remarkable well-looking young man, because he was fat and florid, and had that coppery hue upon the cheeks which proclaimed a deification of the stomach. This gentleman, probably with a knowledge that any pretensions in another department would be thought but lightly of, relied entirely for his humorous popularity upon the quantity he could eat, and the various mixtures of compound he could drink, without appearing in a great state of physical distress.

But now an alarming assault upon the knocker at the street-door announced an arrival, and Master Olinthus Todd made his appearance, followed by the great hero of the night, Captain Flundergust.

This individual, whose sole commission consisted probably in his moustaches, had one of those smirking, stupid-looking faces, which are enough to make any one doubt the truths of revelation. He evidently relied greatly upon what he considered the fascinations of manner, and those, in his estimation, consisted of a set grin and a constant wriggle of the whole animal system, which, no doubt, he considered would implant an idea in the minds of his observers that he must have been educated in some court or another. But there they were wrong, for it was an alley.

He was duly introduced to the ladies; and then Miss Selina was requested to sing, and the poor piano-forte was compelled to assist in the slaughter of a popular melody. And then several other young ladies displayed their poor proficiency, and Mrs. Todd remarked to fat Mrs. Burk, the linen-draper's wife, that she rather thought everything was going off remarkably well; to which Mrs. Burk cordially assented, since Miss Burk had just perpetrated "Come, live with me and be my love," an invitation which met with so cold a reception that no one thought it worth while to say even, "No, thank you!"

"Mother," said Olinthus, "who is the lady in black?"

"A widow, my dear; she's coming to board and lodge here."

"My eye, you don't mean that? She's an out-and-outer, mother; cus my whiskers if she isn't. I'll just go and ask her if she ll sing a song."

"Oh! you may depend she don't sing, or she'd have sung before now."

"Oh! there's nothing like asking," said Olinthus, and he proceeded up to Emily, whom he addressed, as he considered, in the most fascinating manner—

"Beg pardon, madam; but—I—I—if you'd have the goodness to favour me with a ditty; anything you like, ma'am."

"Sing," said Emily; "you must excuse me, sir."

"Oh, no, no; 'pon soul now, no excuses. Now, ladies, don't you all think really that Mrs. Freeman has a singing face—by Jove, damme!"

There was a general cry of "Oh!" on the part of the ladies at the dreadful oath that had come from Olinthus's lips, and then followed such a chorus of solicitations to Emily to sing, that it amounted quite to a persecution. The shortest way to escape from which, she thought, was to sing, and with her usual amiable feeling, she considered that, after all, she had no right to mix in the festivities and enjoyments of these people, unless she chose to contribute her share, so she walked to the piano-forte, and sat down, to the dismay of Selina, who whispered to her—

"You—you play—do you, Mrs. Freeman?"

"Yes," said Emily, undisguisedly, who was above the petty affectation of denying the possession of an accomplishment, which, from her earliest childhood, had been the delight of many a lonely hour to acquire.

From the first moment that she ran her fingers across the keys, Selina Todd and all the young ladies wished themselves five hundred fathoms under the Rialto, for they found at once that there was a proficient in the art in which they were such tyros.

The very piano-forte itself seemed to brighten up, and emit tones such as no one else had been able to produce from it that evening; and when Emily, in her rich, clear, contralto voice, sang, the influence of sweet sounds showed itself even upon the unpoetic and unimaginative persons who were there assembled.

It was a short ditty, and one which she had learnt in happier days. It brought to her recollection thoughts and feelings, which she did not wish at that time to bring uppermost in her remembrance; but her auditory gained by all that, for such feelings imparted a pathos to the air which no art could have given to it.

When she was done she glided from the instrument, and then the gentlemen began to be eulogistic, and any one of the ladies could have eaten her up entirely, with the smallest quantity of salt.

"Here's a do," said Selina to her mother; "she's come to get a new husband of course, and everybody's sure to propose."

"Chawming, chawming," cried Captain Flundergust; "allow me to thank you, ma'am; quite chawming, chawming. I never was so delighted in all my life."

"Indeed!" thought Selina, "then I'll soon put you down."

"I mean," continued Captain Flundergust, "I never was so delighted, since a chawming serenade I heard in Spain—hem!"

"Really," said Selina; "captain, so you've been in Spain?"

"Haw—yes, delightful country."

"And did really poor General Evans look so bad as people said?"

The captain looked blank as he repeated "General Evans!"

"Yes, the Spanish legion you belonged to, didn't you?"

Captain Flundergust looked amazed, for the guess happened to be a marvellously appropriate one. He certainly had belonged to that illustrious corps, which had spread dismay into the minds of the inhabitants of Westminster before it started; and deep and fervent wishes at its departure, that in all its entirety it was gone for ever.

"I think I've put him down," thought Selina; "the wretch! He won't come here any more, and that's a good job."

"Let's have a dance," said Olinthus. "Come, gents, clear the stage. Ha, ha! that's what I call a clear stage, and no favour."

This wit was very much applauded, and the tables being moved, the astonishing space of about ten feet by six was found available for a quadrille.

Then, at the end of the first figure, Mrs. Todd rushed in with a tray full of lemonade, and frantically invited everybody to take a little of the portable stomach-ache, as it was so uncommonly refreshing.

A bottle of port, too, was tapped—that at 1s. 9d. round the corner, and another of Cape at 1s. 4d. that did duty for sherry.

Captain Flundergust wanted to make out that he was a wonderful judge, and whispered to Olinthus that he hoped the wine wasn't corked, which Mrs. Todd overhearing, turned sharp upon him, and said,—

"She not only hoped it was, but knew it was ; and she'd like to see anybody send her wine that wasn't."

"I beg your pardon, madam," said the captain.

"No offence, sir," said Mrs. Todd ; but she looked, at the same time, as if some piece of dirt had lodged at the extreme end of her nose, and she was trying to jirk it off into somebody else's eye, by a wonderful piece of facial dexterity.

The captain saw that this was the last invite he should ever get to the Todds.

But we need not pursue the amusements of the evening ; we trust we have given a sufficient sketch, although a slight one, of the persons among whom Emily Wyvill was located.

As the acidulated compound which Mrs. Todd found her guests with became exhausted, supper was announced, which consisted of sandwiches, cut into remarkable, triangular pieces, which were washed down by porter. Then there was another song or two, and finally, just about the hour of midnight, the party began to thin in numbers, and several gentlemen gallantly volunteered to see several ladies to their respective domiciles.

Emily retired to the room which had been assigned to her, fatigued, and indeed exhausted—her thoughts reverted painfully to her once happy home—that home which presented so great a contrast to the place which she now inhabited ; and it is not surprising that she should weep herself to sleep as she did, while the infant, unconscious of its mother's wrongs, or of its mother's griefs, slept by her side the calm sleep of innocence.

And now we will leave Emily Wyvill for awhile, since nothing remarkably adventurous is occurring in her career, in order to see what is passing at Wyvill Hall, and to note if the passionate and overbearing Margaret really made herself the happier by the world of mischief she had done.

CHAPTER XVII.

THE PROCEEDINGS AT THE HALL.—THE FRUITLESS INQUIRIES OF SIR ANTHONY WYVILL.—HIS ARRIVAL IN LONDON.

THE shock to Sir Anthony Wyvill's mind had been so great by this supposed defalcation in the affections of his wife, that for some time he might be considered as a mere puppet in the hands of his haughty and ambitious sister. But this, as she herself had predicted, was a state not likely to last long, and she deeply congratulated herself upon the skill with which she had removed Emily far beyond the reach of inquiry. It was about the seventh day after his arrival at his ancestral home, that Sir Anthony Wyvill, looking as if at least a dozen years had been added to his age, requested Margaret to step with him into the library, in order that he might hold a particular conference with her.

"Margaret," he said, "this place has now become hateful to me ; there is not an object which meets my eyes, not a scene I look upon, but what reminds me of her whom I would feign forget but cannot. She has gone from me, but the task of tearing her from my breast is one which, should I succeed in, would break it ; I cannot— I cannot forget her."

"Remember her if you will," said Margaret, "so long as with that remembrance you remember your own honour, and the honour of the race from which you spring."

"Yes," he said. "But there is another circumstance coupled with her memory that is more important still—the child I long to clasp in my arms, and hear it lisp the name of father.   It is, indeed, too much, by one cruel stroke of fortune, to be deprived of all that I can love."

"As you please," said Margaret.   "Of course there are facilities for the discovery of the retreat of Emily.   Embrace them as you will, but do not, let me implore you, be so weak, when you find the destroyer of your honour, as to act in such a manner that the world's derision may assail you, and all who bear your name."

"I understand you," said Sir Anthony.   "You think that my affection would be sufficient to induce me to forgive even what has passed.   You are much mistaken, Margaret.   I suffer, but I can yet be firm."

"What course do you meditate adopting?"

"I will proceed at once to London, and there consult with such legal persons as will not only give me the best advice how to act, but who, from their habits of business, will be able to aid me in discovering the retreat of the unhappy Emily."

"And what then?"

"England has become hateful to me; the continent is in a disturbed position, and I shall soon again be able, amid the din and tumult of war, to lose a recollection of some of the troubles that oppress me.   As before, I will leave to you the management of my estates.   I have little occasion for money, do with it what you will.   I know that you are careful, and a sufficiently good financier to be intrusted with it."

Margaret could scarcely restrain the feeling of joy that pervaded her heart as she thus felt her warmest anticipations realised.   If she could once get her brother upon the continent, it would be easy to persuade Emily that he had gone there, taking with him Mrs. Angerstein, while she could easily continue to keep him there by an occasional account of how Emily was passing the time with her paramour.   q

The very thing she had to dread was some accidental meeting in London and an explanation between Sir Anthony Wyvill and his wife; but that, since Emily had altered her name, was but a remote probability, and one with which she would not torment herself with by contemplating.   She satisfied herself with warmly approving the course he intended to pursue; she advised him to stay but as short a time as possible in London, and promised that, should he leave without being successful in his search for the child, she would continue it and send him authentic information of all that transpired.

Margaret then took occasion to ask him in what manner he intended to provide for Mrs. Angerstein, who was so wholly dependent upon his bounty, and he immediately replied that it was his wish she should have a sufficient sum allowed her out of the rentals of the estate to do what she pleased with, since he could no longer personally offer her a home.

"I did hope," he said, "that she and Emily would have been tenderly and attached companions; but this dream has fled before the cold truth of reality; and I can only as efficiently as possible perform the duty I so solemnly expressed to Captain Angerstein, of protecting his wife, at least, from any extraordinary vicissitudes of fortune."

The grasping avarice of Margaret made her grudge much any stipend being paid to Mrs. Angerstein, but she was politic enough to see that upon that subject her brother was not likely to be moved; so she affected cordially to agree to his proposition, and when he suggested a hundred pounds per annum she praised the liberality which induced him to do so.   Thus far, then, all affairs were settled to her satisfaction; and then she made to him a curious speech, which he was a long time indeed in finding any key to.

"Brother," she said, "I shall be more satisfied of your welfare, and that nothing evil has befallen you, if some one be with you on whom I can depend as a faithful attendant, and as one who likewise will, in case of your being incapacitated to do so, send me an accurate account of your well-doing."

"I scarcely understand," said Sir Anthony Wyvill, "how you are to accomplish such a purpose."

"I will tell you," said Margaret; "since you were away I have taken into the house a youth who calls himself Ratcliffe ; he is a lad about fifteen or sixteen years of age, full of talent and precocity of intellect : will you, to oblige me, take him with you as your personal attendant, for a faithful one I am certain he will make you."

" Indeed !" said Sir Anthony ; " I have seen no such person since I have come home."

" No," said Margaret ; " I have sent him on an errand some days' journey from home, but if you will promise me to have him when you get to London, I will send

him to you, and you will, I am certain, soon find the value of the services of one who will be attached to you from the gratitude he owes to me."

" As you please, Margaret, be it so ; it's a small matter and I will not thwart you in it, and should I dislike your *protegé* I will take care to send him back to you in safety. To-morrow I will start for London, from whence, as a centre of

No. 15.

observation, I am much more likely to find Emily, be she concealed where she may."

In the latter part of that day Sir Anthony sought an interview with Mrs. Angerstein, at which he explained to her how painfully he was situated, and took occasion to mention the provision he wished to make for her.

Her eyes filled with tears as she replied to him.

"Sir Anthony Wyvill, I know that the best thanks and the best expression of gratitude that can be given to kindness such as yours, is freely and unhesitatingly to accept of it with gratitude. I shall receive that sum from you which will save me from destitution. But, Sir Anthony, before you leave here, and before you shut out entirely from your breast her who has so long possessed it, weigh well every circumstance connected with this most singular case."

"I have, too well," said Sir Anthony.

"I know," she continued, "it ill-becomes me even to allude to the circumstances which have left you, as it were, involved, but a strange feeling crosses me at times which I know not how to account for—a feeling which seems to tell me all is not as it should be. I may be wrong, perhaps, very wrong, Sir Anthony Wyvill, but I mistrust——."

"Mistrust whom?"

"I must speak—you will censure me, perhaps discard me from your regard, but I mistrust your sister Margaret."

"You're wrong, Mrs. Angerstein; the honour of her name and of the family from which she springs, are the guiding stars of her existence; that she's proud and haughty, I know, but these are not the qualities that belong to the deceitful or the intriguing: besides, have I not a damning evidence of the actual absence of my wife from her home the moment I approach it? Does she not leave behind her, too, actually a memento of her own shame in her own handwriting? There is no room for doubt; oh Heaven! would there were!"

"I know," said Mrs. Angerstein, "the circumstances are too strong in this case to reason against, I know that well; but I could not forbear saying to you what I have, and I can only hope that you will forgive a candour perchance unpalatable."

"Rest content that you have spoken to me your mind in this affair, which a calculating person would have thought it injudicious so to do, raises you higher in my esteem. It is a painful subject though, Mrs. Angerstein."

"I know that there are feelings that should not be probed too deeply."

"And this is one of them."

"It is, it is, I am sure."

No more passed between them upon the subject; and as Mrs. Angerstein said she preferred settling in London upon the annuity which Sir Anthony so kindly proffered to her acceptance, he could not, but in common courtesy, offer her his society to the metropolis, little dreaming what frightful evil had already accrued from the fact of their most innocent companionship.

Margaret well veiled the expression of her delight when she saw the travelling carriage start from Wyvill Hall, containing her brother and Mrs. Angerstein; she ran from window to window, higher and higher in the house, to catch the last glimpse of the equipage, until at last she stood upon a terrace near the top of the house, which commanded an extensive view of the whole of the Wyvill property; and as the travelling carriage disappeared from her sight, with the remotest gaze, she clasped her hands, and looking proudly about her, exclaiming—

"Success, success! I have conquered! All is mine that I behold around me; Wyvill Hall and its rich dependencies. I am mistress uncontrolled of every thing, who shall tell me that what the world calls simplicity and honesty of purpose will be more successful than subtlety and craft? Have I not with subtlety and craft achieved wonders—have I not by the exercise of these very qualities made myself mistress of the place, and aye, at the very moment too, when the dominion I had held was threatened with the most total destruction?"

With her eyes beaming with unholy gratification—her lip curled with scorn, as if she defied all that was good, or great, or just, which the world contained, she descended from the elevated position in which she stood to assume the most unbounded sway over the entire estate, and to rule it with a full and complete despotism she had not before ventured upon attempting.

But she had yet something to perform. It would seem that she had yet something to do which required some exercise of that subtlety and craft upon which she so much prided herself.

She ordered a travelling carriage to be immediately got ready, and naming a coast town some two-and-twenty miles distant from the hall as the place where she wished to go, she ordered that she should be driven there with the greatest expedition possible.

These commands were given in a tone which showed that she intended to be obeyed and that she would not take the slightest suggestion by way of complaint.

In less than half an hour she was on her journey, and with a smile of continued guilty gratification, she told herself that she was the mistress of circumstances —she flattered herself she could bend everything to her own sovereign will, and she looked forward now to just the career of wild ambitious projects and arbitrary rule which suited her.

Having arrived at the Inn which was her place of destination, she desired to be driven to a particular house which she named, in a bye street, and alighting, she entered and asked a woman for Charles Ratcliffe.

A lad was sent for from some place in the neighbourhood—he was a thin, well-formed youth, of rather a delicate appearance, and he remained closeted with Margaret Wyvill for more than an hour.

When he came out there was a strange look upon his countenance, accompanied with an expression of deep thought—he spoke but little, although he several times seemed upon the point of saying something to Margaret which he still left unsaid.

She took him in the carriage to an inn, and there waited until a stage coach passed that was proceeding to London ; she saw him upon the vehicle, gave him money, bade him adieu with an air of indifference, and then ordered herself to be carried back to Wyvill Hall, where we will leave her to prosecute what schemes of personal aggrandizement she pleases, and take a peep ourselves at Master Charles Ratcliffe, who was seated in deep thought upon the roof of the stage coach.

It was evident that something must have agitated the boy deeply—he clasped his hands, bit his lips, and seemed totally unconscious that he was attracting a good deal of the attention of his fellow passengers.

Then he took from his pocket a written paper, and in a low whispered voice, repeated to himself its contents.

They were as follows :—

" When you reach London you will immediately inquire for a hotel called Redelle's, which is situated by St. James"s, a few minutes walk from the palace— you will there find Sir Anthony Wyvill, and deliver to him the sealed letter with which I have charged you—you will find yourself retained in his service, and it must be your constant endeavour, for reasons which I have before explained to you and which I think you fully appreciate and understand, to make yourself useful to him, as that will be the very means of eventually producing a result which you tell me you so earnestly wish for, and clearing up a mystery which I cannot at present explain to you.

" Once in each month you will transmit to me a letter, containing a sort of diary of every thing that has occurred, and should Sir Anthony Wyvill think or talk of coming home, you will most particularly, although the monthly letter shall not be precisely due, inform me of such circumstance, as it will materially concern your fortunes.

" Believe me to be always your friend, although of course, I cannot perform impossibilities, or I would place you in a very different position to what you at present occupy."   " M. W."

" What can I think ? " said the youth—" the proceedings of this day are enough to drive me mad. I always knew that there was some mystery attendant upon my birth, and the partial enlightenment that I have received to-day upon the subject, has only the more instigated me to wish to know all. She has given me a lettet also to deliver to a Mrs. Freeman—who can that be?—a letter which she says is mos particular; and shall I, who have been brought up well, condescend to become an attendant upon any one? No. I'm proceeding to London, and having money in my pocket, will seek my own fortunes, and as I am bold and resolute, and feel that I am not very scrupulous, it would be a hard case but I should make my way—at all events let them beware that cross me, for by force or fraud I will have revenge."

*   *   *   *

Long before Sir Anthony Wyvill reached London, Mrs. Angerstein, who regarded him with all the affection of a devoted sister, could perceive that his mental anxieties had made deep ravages upon his health.

It was evident too, that he wavered much in his resolutions as to what he was to do; and that in consequence of the great distress which this uprooting as it were, of all his best affections, gave him, he was rapidly becoming an altered man, and losing all that energy and determination of character for which at one time he had been conspicuous.

Now and then he would despond to such a degree that it took all the exertion she was mistress of to rescue him from a state of almost dangerous depression, and then again a wild recklessness of demeanour would come over him, and he would project a course of life full of riot and extravagance.

It was oppressive grief to her to note how grief arising from the loss of the affection of one upon whom he had built all his happiness, should thus unman him; she implored him to think better for the future. She begged of him for the sake of the honourable name he already bore, to live out as he had hitherto done, his span of existence, an honoured and honourable man:—and so they arrived in London —he swayed by a thousand contrary fancies, and she dreading that yet he would perform some extraordinary feat of almost semi-madness, unless upon his arrival in the metropolis, he fell into the most judicious hands.

She doubted much if this would be the case, for well she knew the wild, licentious opinions entertained by many of the military officers whom he named, and who had served with her late husband during the continental war.

And yet with all her wish to instil into him better thoughts and feelings than those which seemed to possess him, she felt how little she, a female, could do in the matter, and how absolutely necessary, both for his character and her own, it was, that she should separate herself from him immediately on their arrival in London.

She had not even the most ordinary plea of relationship to enable her to abide with him, and therefore all she could do was, during the journey, to make to him the most urgent appeals to nerve himself against the misfortune that had come across him that her stock of eloquence furnished her with.

She took up her abode at once in private lodgings, while he proceeded to the hotel which Margaret had mentioned in her note of instructions to Charles Ratcliffe; and as the most ill-judged step he could possibly take, he wrote to a continental acquaintance, rejoicing in the appellation of Major Greathead, whom he readily ascertained on inquiry at the Horse Guards, was in London.

The major was a brave man, and by several acts of daring gallantry had acquired a certain standing among the officers of the British army: but he was neither a discreet nor a right-thinking man, and consequently was the very worst associate that in the present unsettled state of his mind Sir Anthony Wyvill could have had.

It happens with many minds which, under ordinary circumstances, preserve all the ordinary functions respectably enough, that when any great circumstance happens of a disappointing or a depressing character, the ordinary energies become completely prostrated, and like a ship without a rudder, the individual is tossed to and fro at the mercy of the winds and waves of circumstances, and that any individual may assume the command, and almost arbitrarily control the shattered intellect.

This was unhappily the case as regarded Sir Anthony Wyvill. In the usual occurrences of life he was considered a man with quite sufficient energy to meet any circumstances that might arise: but never before had he been so keenly tried—

never before had his best affections been trampled upon, or it would have been dis-covered that he did not possess in an eminent degree that antagonist principle of mind which lifts some men above anything and everything.

There are some intellects so happily constituted that, like a powerful spring, the greater compression to which they are subjected, the greater is their capacity of resistance.

These are the kind of men to meet the rubs of fortune, and to stand up boldly against the shafts of fate—and we must not mistake the affected firmness of mere pride for the real, steady, sternness of mental organization which is as rare as it is desirable.

We certainly tremble for what may be the want of the shock which Sir Anthony Wyvill has experienced.

The major was sufficiently prompt in obeying Sir Anthony Wyvill's summons, for not possessing so much of that needful auxiliary to extravagance—money—as the wealthy baronet, he considered him well worthy of a considerable amount of extra attention.

The major was all hilarity when he arrived, thinking of course that Sir Anthony's arrival in town must have some pleasurable object in view, but the moment he caught sight of his friend's countanance, it was sufficient to convince him that such was not the case, and he put on as serious and sympathizing an aspect as upon the spur of the moment he very well could.

"Why, my dear fellow," he said, "what's the matter? something must have happened to vex you a little; why you look the very shadow of your former self."

"I have reason to look so; sit down, Major Greathead, and give me your candid advice as to the course which I ought to pursue, under the most distressing circumstances."

"Distressing! why you haven't lost your money, have you?"

"Worse—worse!"

"The devil! You don't mean your estates?"

"No. I could have borne all that well enough; you've heard me, Major Greathead, when many miles from home, speak with all the adoration of loving confidence of my wife."

"Oh, yes, yes!—that's uncommonly true; you had a failing that way,—I recollect."

"Do not jest, the subject is too serious a one,—she is faithless—she, whom I would have trusted in preference to an angel from out of Heaven, and she, whose purity I looked upon as something more than mortal, and like the bright sunshine making all things beautiful it beamed upon—she is faithless to me."

"Well, I am deuced sorry, but I understand why you sent for me; you're going to call the fellow out, what sort of a being is he—creditable to turn out with, I hope."

"I know nothing of it, further than that at my approach she left her home, saying, she could not bear to meet me, and hoping that I might be happy without her, and thus were all my fond anticipations crushed at once—thus were all the hopes which had supported me in the battle field, and caused me to encounter privations, toil, and danger, trampled in the dust, and thus twice have the fondest and best feelings of my heart, been made a mockery of, and when I most garnered up my affections, have I been most cruelly deceived."

"Well, it is too bad," said Major Greathead. "Do you think they've got any prime Madeira here?"

"I really don't know, order what you like."

"Well," said the major, as he rung the bell, "you do afflict me, and I must say that if it aint good and the very primest article, I'll soon let them know it; upon my soul, Wyvill, you've made me quite wretched, but its a remarkable fact, that fond as I am of Madeira, there are not half-a-dozen houses in London that I can get it in perfection at; and so, you don't know even who the despoiler of the domestic—Madeira, waiter, of the best quality—hearth is—damn you, let it be cool—you're not aware of the vagabonds name?"

"No; you have all the information that I have. I have come to London to seek more, for I'm not ashamed to confess to you, major, that notwithstanding all my outraged feelings—notwithstanding I feel that my heart has received a blow that it can never recover, I love her still and would fain know what has become of her—she shall not want.

"Upon my soul, that's very generous and high-minded of you, but I tell you what, Wyvill, the attendance is not good in this house. Damn it, man, with your means, what made you come to such a humdrum place; it's by no means one of the crack houses, and never will be. But have you no guess upon the subject?"

"Alas, no!"

"Well, that's very odd. And how do you mean setting about inquiring?"

"I expect that my solicitors, who understand active matters of business better than I do, will be able to suggest some plan of operations that may give me a chance of discovering her place of retreat. I have no revenge to take upon her—Heaven forbid; but he who has robbed me of so much innocence and virtue, must find that my wounded honour requires reparation, when I have discovered him it shall be your friendly task to procure for me that satisfaction which my injuries require."

"Of course, Wyvill, of course; that's viewing the subject in its proper light, find the fellow out; I hope he's a gentleman, and we'll pretty soon bring him into the field. You shall have a pop at him, but how queer and ill you're looking."

"I've been very unwell at Wyvill Hall, and have scarcely had strength to come to London."

"Oh, that must be all imagination, you must come into life, and now that you are in the Metropolis, you must see something of the great world—you owe it to yourself, Wyvill, to shake off as much as possible the cumber of this care; for God's sake, don't let the world look upon you as a milksop, who is always snivelling for the loss of his wife. I have seen you look bold, and cool, and determined, when round shot was playing around you, don't now put on the demure face and surrender to circumstances, because a woman has deserted you."

"I know well, Major Greathead, that this is the language of the world," said Sir Anthony Wyvill, "but I am sufficiently weaned from it now, to care but little for the false constructions it may put upon my feelings."

"But you must recollect you're a soldier and a gentleman, that you have the character of your profession to support as well as your own—that you owe something to your friends."

"Well, well, you shall not find me backward in that species of social hypocrisy which prompts men to hide all the deepest and real feelings, I will not show what agony sits brooding at my heart."

"That's right, old fellow—never say die—you shall come out with me to-night. I know your habits well and without outraging them in any very remarkable degree. I shall be able to show you something of London, which by filling your mind with other images, will better enable you to shake off your mental depression."

"It may be so, and after all, perhaps, that presents itself to me, as the best chance of gaining some intelligence of her, whom I have loved too well."

"Come along then, for this is damned bad Madeira, and I don't feel inclined to stay in this house any longer, that's the fact; come on, I'll take you to my club, where you'll find some of your old campaigning friends, and after that, we'll sup with la Belle Floretta."

"And who may that be?"

"Oh, a French actress, from the Theatre de Varieties, at Paris, she keeps a nice little place, westward, gives recherché supper parties to those who don't object to lose a pound or two afterwards at cards; so the affair pays her very well, so as everybody gets his quid pro quo, and the utmost morality prevails, nobody but a methodist parson would think of objecting to it."

The Major's hilarity failed in producing even the quietest smile upon the countenance of Sir Anthony Wyvill, who, however, did not object to accompany him; thus showing a fatal example of how easily his nature was led for good or for evil, and consequently how much more disastrous the treachery that had been practised towards him was likely to be.

Of course he had about him that sort of instinctive pride which actuates all persons when they have been wounded in their feelings—namely, to avoid as much as possible an exhibition to the unsympathising multitude of how nearly they have been touched, and therefore was it that he went with Major Greathead into society, which under ordinary circumstances he would not have ventured near.

Never had he yet tasted of the fevered up pleasure, which those who call themselves the fine spirits of the age, seem to think it so essential to partake of. And now he felt like one isolated from the world, one who had nothing to care for, nothing to hope for, and therefore with a false philosophy he told himself that he must become a gloomy misanthrope, or catch the fleeting pleasure of the moment to cheat memory of its pangs.

We need not follow Sir Anthony Wyvill and Major Greathead to the haunts of vice they frequented, suffice it that with a burning and throbbing brow in the morning, Sir Anthony found, but too truly, that he had mistaken the road which would lead him to happiness, or even to forgetfulness.

"Oh! Emily, Emily," he exclaimed. "why have you turned my heart aside from the purer joys and the dearer felicities of a happy home. Why have you made me that which your continued love would ever have prevented me from becoming, las! for the first time in my existence I am taught to despise myself, and to look with the bitterness of contempt upon the life that I am leading."

It was at this juncture that a visitor was announced to him, and as the appearance of that visitor is contingent upon some circumstances with which it is necessary the reader should be made acquainted, we feel it necessary to devote a chapter to that object.

CHAPTER XVIII.

RATCLIFF'S ARRIVAL IN LONDON AND INTERVIEW WITH EMILY WYVILL.

THE boy Ratcliff reached the metropolis with the letters that had been entrusted to him by Margaret Wyvill, one of which he was to deliver to Emily, whose address at the Todds he had written down for that purpose, and the other to Sir Anthony, at the quiet hotel, which had been so much stigmatised by Major Greathead as not sufficiently fashionable for such as he to remain at.

This lad although he appeared to enter particularly into the views of Margaret so far as she explained them to him, we have already shown was of an intractable and indomitable spirit, having a disposition ever to do that which was contrary to what he was required to perform.

It is not surprising then that such an individual should engage his mind almost exclusively during the journey with schemes of his own, instead of thinking over the best method of accomplishing the designs of her who had been his protectress.

He proceeded upon his arrival at the metropolis, direct to the mansion of the Todds, when he asked for Emily by the assumed name of Freman, which she had taken up since her residence in London.

She did not hesitate to receive him, and Miss Selina Todd accordingly vacated the parlor where she had been sitting with Emily, in order to allow the interview to be an interrupted one.

At the first glance Ratcliff seemed much struck with the great beauty of Emily, and the tone in which he addressed her was at once deferential and respectful. He presented to her the letter from Margaret, which she eagerly perused, and then finding that it contained nothing of a hopeful character, but only reiterated the old notice not on any account to show herself, but to remain profoundly still and quiet, lest Sir Anthony should make some violent effort to deprive her of the custody of

the child; she laid it down with such deep disappointment in her looks, that Ra
cliffe spoke to her saying—

"Lady, you do not like the letter that you have received, I have another to deliv
which, I hope, will be liked still less."

"Indeed," said Emily, "to whom?"

"To Sir Anthony Wyvill."

"What! Margaret write to him! and yet why should I feel surprised; it ma
be absolutely necessary that she should, she can feel for my wrongs and yet hol
communication with her brother."

"Yes, they are wrongs," said Ratcliffe, "Margaret told me all, and that's why
pity you, and that's why I will not do what I have been required."

"And what is that?"

"To go into the service of Sir Anthony Wyvill. This letter I have I am tol
is to be my recommendation to him. I was instructed to be ever near him, t
watch over him closely, and to communicate even his very thoughts, if possible,
Margaret."

"And you will not?"

"No, I certainly will not, I've money in my pocket, and will be no man's sla
nor woman's either. I mean to push my fortune the best way I can, and if
dont't succeed I can always enlist into the army, that is a resource which will n
fail me."

"Who are you?" said Emily, looking much interested in the question.

A flush of color spread itself slowly over the boy's face and brow, and with mo
of the vehemence of anger than one would have thought him capable of exhibitir
at his age, he cried—

"Who am I? I am nobody—a nameless creature—one cast out into the wi
world as the butt for the reproval of fools more fortunate than himself. Ask me n
who, or what I am. Let it suffice that I will not play the part that Margaret Wyv
has assigned to me. She may find some other, if she can, to do her bidding, I
do none of it. There is the letter, I will not encumber myself with its possessio
another moment—farewell."

As he spoke he flung the letter on the floor, and evidently in a paroxysm
anger he rushed from the place.

"Hold, hold," cried Emily, "stop yet for a moment, I have much to ask you

But he was gone, if her voice did reach him, it stopped not his headlong caree
he had left her and she was alone. No, not quite alone, for there lay at her fe
the letter addressed to her husband, that letter which let her know where he cou
be found, and which was to have introduced one to him who was to play the s
upon his actions for good or for evil.

But even prone as Emily Wyvill was to place the best possible constructi
upon human actions, to give abundant credit, when sometimes, little indeed w
due; she told herself it must be Margaret's sisterly anxiety, notwithstanding
the evil that Sir Anthony had done, which prompted her to send this youth as
safeguard to him.

"It must be so," she said, "she thinks possibly, that there may be a time wh
he will turn aside from the false passion that now blinds his eyes, when rememberi
the happiness that once was his in the quiet serenity of a virtuous home, he m
sigh to be forgiven, and for the return of those days which should have endur
while life itself belonged to us; and then this lad who was to watch his ev
varying mood, would let her know the better impulse that was creeping across l
soul, and she would write to me to forgive him and we should once again
happy."

"Oh! blissful thought, enchanting supposition; but hold—he will not fulfil l
mission, and here at my feet lies the credential that would have placed him in
enviable a condition. What thoughts are these that struggle through my brai
Am I such a creature of romance as to suppose them possible. Oh! what
dream of joy—that youth—fair and almost with the complexion of a girl, youn
and without the appearance of manhood. Let me think, let me think."

Emily Wyvill clasped her face in her hands, and remained for some time in deep rumination.

Before she look up, Selina Todd, hearing that the visitor had left, returned to the apartment again, and seeing Mrs. Freeman in what she called a brown study,

and a letter lying on the floor near to her, she made no noise, but picked it up unseen by Emily,

"Lor!" she exclaimed, as she read the address, "To Sir Anthony Wyvill, Baronet, Brereton's Hotel, London—a baronet—a live baronet!"

"Who speaks?" cried Emily, springing to her feet; "that letter, give it me, it is mine; who has the just right to it but I? It is addressed to my—my—

No. 16,

"What! what!" cried Selina Todd.

Emily became aware of her indiscretion, and sunk back into her seat, as she added—

"It is addressed to one whom I know I am charged with its delivery."

"What do you mean to say you know a real baronet?"

"Yes, yes."

"Well, I'm quite delighted, Mrs. Freeman. Do you know him well enough now, do you think, to ask him here? I'm sure ma wouldn't mind going to a little extra expense and having a nice little party for a real baronet, if it was only to astonish the Greens round the corner. Only think—why we could put it in the *Morning Post*—actually a baronet, and among the fashionable movements of the week we should see announced,—'Mrs. Todd's evening party for such and such a date;' and then the Greens would go into convulsions, and who knows what might happen next? Is he married, Mrs. Freeman? because, if he is not, whose to say—oh, gracious! he might propose. I feel all in a flutter at the very thought. What sort of a being is he—now do tell me, dear Mrs. Freeman? Is he anything else beside a baronet?"

"A colonel in the army," said Emily, "I believe."

"A colonel! oh, that is delightful! You could just hint to him how much pleased we should be for him to come with his cocked hat and feathers. And if that would'nt put Miss Green into hysterics for a fortnight I don't know what would. Now, my dear Mrs. Freeman, do say that you'll do your best."

Emily could keep up no longer; her feelings overpowered her, and taking the letter in her hand, which was addressed to her husband, she retired from the apartment, and sought the retirement of the room which, by the courtesy of the Todds, she could call her own.

Selina was astonished; but she soon, in her own opinion, found a key to the mystery.

"I know it," she said; "I can see it all as plain as possible now. I've been wondering for this day or two that she seemed so indifferent to Olinthus, when she must have observed that he was quite in love with her; but she's after this baronet, that's it, and she's crying with vexation that I've found it out, owing to seeing the address of the letter. I'll just put on my things and run off to Artillery-place and speak to Miss Dickets about it; she'll give me her opinion, and perhaps put me in some way, after all, of letting this Sir Anthony Wyvill know that if he likes he may come here and propose."

Miss Todd remained quiet a few minutes, and then she uttered a deep sigh.

"Ah! me," she said, "there would, indeed, be a go if I were to become a baronet's lady. Oh, gracious! I think I see two embossed cards with the shiny white stuff upon 'em—the what do you call it?—enamelled—I think I see them tied together with a white riband, and one of them Sir Anthony Wyvill, and upon the other Lady Wyvill—Lady Wyvill, Lady—room for my Lady Wyvill's carriage—Lady Wyvill's phaeton stops the way!"

Selina Todd, as she fell into this remarkable reverie, strode towards the door, and fell into the arms of an extraordinary looking boy who came to clean knives and shoes, and who had been polishing the parlour fire-irons, with which he was returning, shouldered like a musket.

The sudden surprise of finding Selina Todd flinging out her arms and apparently rushing at him intent upon an embrace, at the same time that she requested room for an imaginary phaeton, so astonished the boy that down went poker, shovel, and tongs at once, and he bolted into the kitchen as if he had been shot.

"No," he said to the cook, to whom he related the whole affair, "no, I only gets eighteen pence a week and the broken wittals, and if I'm to come any of that any of that sort of thing I'll have a decided riz, and so I'll tell her if she comes that dodge any more."

     *   *   *   *   *   *

Emily has turned the key in the lock of the room door; she has laid the letter before her which is addressed to her husband—strange and romantic thoughts are flitting through her brain, and it is evident that she has resumed the meditative mood which Selina Todd had interrupted. She spoke not, she moved not; but like some rare statue of beauty she gave herself up to intensity of thought.

And oh! in how many different channels did her imagination travel, how many varied and strange ideas took possession of her brain—ideas which, in her more sober and every day moments, would have been considered as the most wildly improbable now assumed the most clear and tangible shapes, and bore almost the aspect of pre-arranged actions that were to move in the regular course of events.

She seemed now as if she saw her whole destiny sketched out before her—as if she were marked out for the performance of certain objects which only now she was beginning to see clearly and distinctly. A secret and strange feeling of joy crept across her as a stranger means presented itself of letting Sir Anthony see and know eventually the real value of the heart he had cast from him.

"Yes," she said, "yes;" and she rose, and with clasped hands paced the apartment. "Yes, that will be a revenge worthy of me. He shall feel what he ha has lost, he shall know what it is to have cast from him a heart which, despite of all, will cling to its first, fond, dearest affection, and when I have convinced him of that much I will leave him to himself again."

She thought for a moment, and then in slow but tuneful accents she continued, " What is to prevent me, armed with this letter of introduction, assuming the place of the wayward boy who cast it from him? surely I have read of such things well authenticated, where the fond, trusting, heroic heart of woman has nerved her to meet a thousand dangers by flood and field for him she loved. I have read how, in ancient times, the young and the beautiful have traversed distant lands, witching the ears of all who met them by plaintive lays of melancholy love, until, perchance, even in some dungeon's depth they have cast themselves into the arms of him whose image they have so dearly cherished. I well remember, although it seems many years since, when my poor father lived, and we were very happy making up a merry Christmas gambol in which I played a page, why now should not I, in the real drama of existence, play more featly a part which Providence seems to have placed within my grasp. And this letter, shall I look at it contents so that I make no mistake, and then re-seal it? No, no; I dare not break open this sacred envelope; it is addressed to another—I ought not, and yet, if ever motive sanctified an act saving of impropriety, mine would sanctify this one. Shall I do so? Heaven guide me!"

She held the letter in her trembling grasp, and then, fearful that the success of her whole scheme might be endangered by her want of knowledge of some particulars therein contained. " I must—I must."

She broke the seal and ran her eye eagerly over the contents of the letter; they were as follows :

" DEAR BROTHER,—The bearer of this will be the lad of whom I spoke to you; he is diligent, intelligent, courageous, and honest, I wish you would make much of him; for I know something of his history, which, when we meet again, and I hope that period is not far distant, I shall be well pleased to relate to you.

After what I stated concerning him before, I need not write at greater length. His name, as I told you, is Ratcliffe, and he has been respectably educated at a school not many miles from Wyvill Hall.

" Believe me to be your affectionate Sister,

" MARGARET WYVILL."

This was amply sufficient to enable Emily to answer any question that might be put to her. She re-sealed the letter, and then seriously determined upon what certainly, at the first glance, appears to be one of the wildest projects that ever entered the brain of a human being.

And yet how strange it is that familiarity with every idea makes us so accustomed to viewing it in all its different phases, that it soon becomes robbed of all its improbabilities, and the mind easily adapts itself to an order of things which, at the first blush, appeared incredible.

Emily, when she had thoroughly, and without the intervention of any further doubts, made up her mind to supply the place of Ratcliffe in his projected attendance upon Sir Anthony Wyvill, turned her whole attention to the means of carrying out her resolution, and carefully securing the letter, lest any prying curiosity of the Todd family should assail it, she counted over her resources, and found that by the liberality of Margaret, she had amply sufficient to purchase all the necessary apparel and means of prosecuting her singular adventure.

The greatest difficulty of all was as to the disposal of her child; and then, indeed, a severe pang crossed her heart, as she thought of the necessity of being separated from so dear an object of her affection.

We do not wish, or intend in any way to enter into a discussion with regard to the different species of affectation natural and required of the human mind—metaphysicians may settle that between themselves—but certain it is, that the love of Emily Wyvill for her husband, notwithstanding her belief that he had so cruelly treated her, rose superior to the instinctive affection, which made the society of her dear little one so great a value.

"My angel!" she said, as she took it in her arms, "you shall be ever near me, though I shall not look upon your sweet face so often. I will find some kind and gentle nurse for you, and as your brother, I will visit you and sit by you many and many an hour, if I can purchase such an indulgence from him who will become my master."

This point settled, she left the child in the care of Julia Todd, who promised to look to it while, for the first time since her arrival in London, Emily Wyvill ventured into the streets of the great city alone.

She had two tasks to perform, the most important being to find a nurse for the child, one whom she could rely, and the next to purchase for herself apparel befitting the change she wished to make in her outward appearance.

Neither of these matters would have presented any difficulty to one conversant with the ways of the world; but that was just what Emily was not. And after walking a short distance, she stood in the bustling thoroughfare of the City-road, undecided which way to turn, or what to do for the accomplishment of her purposes.

The elegant attire and perfectly lady-like appearance were likely enough to attract observations, and she was soon accosted by one of those butterfly gentlemen who consider it great and clever to annoy any respectable female who appears to be unprotected.

And Emily sadly wanted the necessary tact rapidly to get rid of an importunate intruder.

"My lovely creature," was the observation made to her, "how could you think of venturing out alone?"

She quickened her pace, with the hope of distancing the intruder, but that did not succeed; and then, emboldened by her timidity, which convinced him she was not near immediate succour, he said,—

"You may as well take my arm—don't be cruel, now. If you don't do so, you'll look just as if you did, and perhaps worse; for I shall walk by the side of you."

"Sir, why am I made the object of your insult?" said Emily.

"Ha, the beauty's found her tongue! I thought she would, a duck that she is. Now if you're going far, you'd better take me with you; for that's all in my way, you know."

The poor creature laughed at this miserable effort of wit, but his mirth was destined not to be of long duration, for a female, of rather extraordinary personal dimensions, who had overheard what had passed, suddenly laid an umbrella across his shoulders with an energy that made him jump again.

"Take that, you lawyer's clerk," she said. What do you mean by consulting a decent young girl in the street—that's just the werry way my poor Mary Ann was led astray. Ah, you may look—take that !''

The good lady had been to market, and was armed with an enormous bunch of turnips, which she levelled at the head of Emily's unlucky admirer ; and as they were all tied together, he got so entangled among them, that he run off with the vegetable esculents upon his head, looking like some extraordinary production of nature, or as if adorned with some Indian head dress, for the purpose of striking terror into the inhabitants of the City-road.

" D'rat the man," cried the old lady, " he's run off with four-pen'orth of turnips, and my husband's a raving lunatic if he don't have 'em with boiled mutton. Stop thief—stop him, stop him !"

The gay Lothario disappeared round a corner, and as the pedal supporters of the old lady were not made for the chase, she gave up the turnips, congratulating that any great increase of lunacy on the part of her husband, could be put an end to by the purchase of another bunch.

" These lawyers' clerks," she said, " is the scums of nature, miss. They infest the City-road at this time of the evening ; but never you mind, which way is you going ?"

" Lor, marm," said a carter who was passing, " why didn't you run arter the fellow ? Turnips is turnips, you know, in these times"

" I'm very glad to hear it," said the fat lady, " for the last as we had, if you'll believe me, miss, was all strings done up in a tangle ; and my husband's that sort of man, that if so be as you was to go and buy two sticks as he didn't want 'em, he'd be out at the roof of the house, and round the corner, before you could say Jack Robinson. As I often say to him, miss, he's partly a roaring chain, and partly an iron lion, and that is his character."

" I'm obliged to you," said Emily, " for rescuing me from the intrusion of a stranger."

" Ah, to be sure, miss, I don't like to see anybody put upon."

A sudden thought struck Emily, that possibly this woman, from her greater knowledge of the metropolis and its resources, might be able materially to assist her in the object she had in view.

" I ought not," said Emily, " to intrude upon you, and, because you've done me one service, ask me to do another ; but, I wish to find a nurse for a young child, some one who would attend to it with the tenderness and care of a mother. There will be ample remuneration, and the brother of the infant will visit frequently, as the child is most dear to him, and I know that he will exercise a most watchful care over its welfare."

The woman considered for a few moments, and then she said,—

" Well, that is strange ! there's my sister, as was maid in Lord Duberly's family, has had gave to her, by them, a cottage and ten pounds a year; not to be sneezed at in this mortal spear, where it's as difficult to get a living, as nothing in the world, and the very way as she's going to make all ends meet, is by taking a child to nuss.''

" A most fortunate circumstance," said Emly. " Where does she reside ?"

" Oh, you'll easily find her. It's Prudence Cottage, Spring-place, Grove-end, Bennet's-lane, Seven-sisters, Holloway. I likes to be precise."

I'm afraid," said Emily, " I shall never recollect the address, but if you would be so good as to write it down for me, I should esteem it a favour."

" Well, I would, miss, with all the pleasure in life, but somehow, when I was quite young, they forgot to teach me to write, and what with one thing and another since, I havn't had time; but just you tell me where you live, and she shall call upon you to-morrow morning."

" I thank you, heartily," said Emily, as she gave her the required information. " I shall be rejoiced to see her. By what strange accidents sometimes we succeed in accomplishing our wishes, when our greatest exertions would often fail to produce such a result."

"Yes," said the corpulent lady, putting on a philosophical air, "there's wheels within wheels, and no mistake."

Emily now parted from her new friend, congratulating herself that she had so far succeeded in seeing, at all events, a way of providing for her chief care. Her next object was to procure the apparel with which to enact the boy; and, although nothing was more simple than to accomplish this easily, yet, when Emily stood before a tailor's shop, she felt that she had to consider for some time, as to the most eligible mode of setting about it.

At length she entered the shop, and being most obsequiously received by the tradesman, who had the tact to perceive at once that his customer was no ordinary personage, she tendered a card, on which was written the address of Mrs. Todd, and said,—

"I wish you would, by as early an hour as convenient to you to-morrow, to send to this address some boys suits of clothing—one will be selected, and then paid for."

"Certainly, madam, certainly, with great pleasure, madam. Pray, madam, what may be the age of the young gentleman?"

"About fifteen."

"And have you any idea of his height?"

"My height, as nearly as possible."

"Thank you, madam, thank you. Certainly, it would be more convenient, if the young gentleman would come here to be measured. It would be more satisfactory to us, madam, and probably, to you, as an accurate fit could be ensured."

He's not a gentleman," said Emily. "I only wish such clothing as will be suitable for a respectable lad, going into the service of a gentleman."

"Certainly, madam, I understand perfectly. We shall have the honour of waiting upon you to-morrow morning without fail."

Emily left the shop, well pleased that she had thus far succeeded in accomplishing both the objects she had set herself to do. She was not superstitious, but it seemed to her that the facility with which she had succeeded in making all her arrangements, argued well for the success of the enterprise in which she was about to embark.

When she reached again the solitude of her own chamber, she sunk upon her knees by the bed side, and prayed fervently to that Heaven, which perhaps alone could judge and estimate her motives rightly, for support and assistance, in the path of duty which her best affections pointed out to her.

"It may be," she said, "that this course I am about to adopt, will bring with it many and severe trials. It may be, that I may feel myself outraged from time to time in all those feelings which belong to a wife, and to a mother; but, a sense of rectitude, and a steady and unflinching observance of the great object I have in view, shall nerve me to encounter all. And, oh! if it should be permitted me to wean one, who, although deserting me, is still so dear to me, from the evil course he is pursuing, how bright—how beautiful—how glorious will be my reward?

"If when that time shall come, as assuredly it will, when she, who, casting aside morality and social law, for the indulgence of passion, shall desert him for some newer favourite—if then, he is enabled to discover the truth and purity of a wife's affections, surely with a revulsion of feeling engendered by such circumstances, he will turn to me again, and we shall yet be happy, forgetting and forgiving all the past; but still, gathering from it that experience which shall make the blessing of joy still dearer, because adversity has been felt."

These were the thoughts, pure and beautiful, of Emily Wyvill—these were the aspirations which supported her under the cruel circumstances in which she was placed.

We shall perceive then, when she talked of the possibility of her being called upon to endure much that would be repugnant to her feelings, the words were prophetic, for she had to endure very much, indeed—so much, that could she have foreseen it, she might even then have shrunk back upon the threshold of her enterprise

But she did not do so; the more she reflected upon what she had to do, the more the glory of accomplishing it presented itself to her in radiant colours, until in the enthusiasm of the moment she exclaimed,—

"If this suggested course be as my heart seems to tell me that it is an impulse from Heaven, it must and will succeed, and bright, and beautiful, and enduring, will be the sunshine of the heart that is to succeed the anxiety that now reigns within it."

CHAPTER XIX.

EMILY'S CONTINUED ARRANGEMENTS.—THE CONSTERNATION OF MRS. TODDS.—THE REGRETTED THIEF, AND MISS SELINA'S ANXIETY TO PROPOSE.

THAT night was spent by Emily in a state of great mental restlessness—a thousand times did the whole of her past career present itself to her in vivid colours, but then again as her mind reverted to that future which she had planned out for herself, she fancied she could see the various personages who were to figure in it playing the probable parts that would be assigned to them.

At one moment she could see Sir Anthony Wyvill gazing at her with, apparently, a dim recollection of those features which, notwithstanding the period of absence which had moved, he ought to have known so well. She thought, too, that she saw her (the temptress) who had taken him, from his once happy home and all that should have continued dear to him for those unhallowed pleasures which ever leave their deadliest sting behind. She saw herself attending upon them humbly watching every word and action; and heartbroken with the very picture that her fancy had presented to her, she awoke to weep and tremblingly to doubt her own capacity to endure so much.

Then sleep would come again, and images of a similar import would present themselves until the weary night had passed away, and with the early dawn she became more tranquil, enjoying sound and refreshing sleep, which before the bright sun had shone itself above the horizon's verge, she could not hope for.

It was rather late in the morning when Julia Todd aroused her with the information that breakfast was ready, as well as with the further news that some one was waiting to see her.

Full of expectation that this was the person into whose charge she meant to intrust the babe, she hastened to see her, and found to her great satisfaction a woman who was the *beau ideal* of matronly kindness.

There was that quiet thoughtfulness of feature about her that always predisposes people so much in favour of the possessor.

She had likewise abundance of recommendation. She could appeal to all who had known her; and, finally, she invited Emily to come and look at her home ere she intrusted to her so precious a charge as that of an infant, which she saw had been so tenderly nurtured as had been the young creature presented to her observation by Emily Wyvill.

Much pleased with the woman and her manner, Emily at once concluded a bargain with her, bidding her to come at a late hour in the day to take her charge, and telling her that it was the brother of the child, she being its sister, who would be its constant visitor.

There was a something about Emily's manner abstracted and full of thought, while she partook of breakfast with the Todds, which added materially to Selina's opinion concerning the intentions of Emily as respected the real baronet, to whom the letter had been addressed. A great number of oblique inquiries were made on the subject, to all of which, however, Emily turned a deaf ear, or gave an evasive answer, so that the Todds took nothing by their motion.

They were full of curiosity, likewise, to know what business the woman had with her who had called at such an early hour; but as their assurance did not carry them far enough to enable them to ask such a question directly, and of course, as Emily was not inclined to be communicative, they were to their great discomfort foiled again.

But when, at about eleven o'clock, a man called with an immense bag of clothes, and represented himself as a tailor, and asked for Mrs. Freeman, their wonder knew no bounds, and he was cross-questioned with great pertinacity.

Of course, he could say no more than that the lady had called upon him and ordered some clothes for the purpose of fitting a lad who was going into a gentleman's service.

Now this was most aggravating and mysterious, inasmuch as there was no lad there except Olinthus, and he certainly was not going into anybody's service.

It was really aggravating that Mrs Freeman should thus set the wits of the whole Todd family to work, and yet give them no prospect of satisfaction.

It was Julia who brought the intelligence to Mrs Freeman, and her eyes were preternaturally wide open as she said

"On! if you please, Mrs. Freeman, there's a man come, as says he's brought the boy's things; and when I asked him what boy he meant, he didn't know, if you please, Mrs Freeman."

"Thank you—thank you"—said Emily, as quietly as she could, "will you let the servant take whatever he has brought with him up into my apartment, and tell him to wait."

This was done, and much to the wonder of the whole family, Emily was in her own room for a full half an hour, selecting something from the bundle of clothes which the tailor had brought, while he waited in the hall.

Of course, rational persons would not have made any mystery of the transaction: it was quite possible that Emily might have been going to give away a suit of clothes? they could not tell views or inclination she had to be charitable. But the Todd family were not exactly rational people, and consequently they made a wonder of what would have been let go past by others without engaging any extraordinary attention,

And now the bag of clothes was sent down, with a message to the tailor to look over it and charge for what had been abstracted, which he accordingly did, and then departed very well pleased with the transaction, inasmuch in so charging he had consulted his own pocket than the equity of the affair.

But Emily was not disposed to be critical, so long as, without exciting any suspicion, she succeeded in accomplishing her object.

But now, since other feeling was absorbed in the thought that she was spending the last few hours which probably she would be called to do for a long time with her dear child. She knew not what changes or mutations might occur ere again that little creature would be beneath the same roof as herself; and if her recollection at all could be said to have failed her, it was when the dread hour of parting with that fond object of her heart's idolatry approached.

She sat with it clasped to her heart and wept.

" Dear one," said she, " when in the lapse of years you shall be of an age to think, to bear, and understand your mother's sad story, you will not blame her that for a time she left you to a stranger's care, but appreciate the motive which actuated her; although you may have only the memory of her existence to look back upon, you will not blame her, but give a sigh to her sorrows; and be she successful or not in this enterprise, you shall still love her for the motive which urged her to its performance."

And now the hour arrived, and the woman was punctual—her name was Brent, and she and Emily, with the child, left the house of the Todds, and in a hackney carriage proceeded to the elaborate address which Emily feared she should never remember.

Whether or not Mrs. Brent had been over suspicious with regard to the maternity of the child, we cannot say, certain it is Emily's manner was quite sufficient to convince any one that a nearer connection than that of sister subsisted between her and the little creature who was about to be committed to Mr. Brent's care.

But the kind of society in which the old nurse had lived during her life had imparted to her a sort of refinement, which otherwise, probably, she could not have aspired to, and she forebore asking Emily any questions, which might, for aught she knew, be of a very distressing character.

And so conversing upon indifferent matters they reached Prudence Cottage, Emily marking well the way as she went, in order that no difficulty should arise in her visits.

The cottage was a pattern of cottage neatness and beauty. It was small, but quite a little *bijou* as regarded neatness, while its little garden was stocked with the choicest products of floriculture.

Even accustomed as Emily Wyvill was to the stately park of Wyvill Lodge, its undulating lawn and its rich pastures, she was much pleased with the appearance of Mrs. Brent's cottage.

No. 17.

She was thoroughly satisfied with every arrangement she perceived. She placed a sum of money in the woman's hand for immediate exigences, and then came the worst and most dreaded moment of all—the parting with that miniature resem-blance of herself which she had never thought to part with, until the stern law of death had beckoned her to the tomb.

The struggle against feeling was a severe one—the attempt to exhibit a fortitude she could not feel, was agonizing.

She could not speak—she clasped the little creature in her arms—she covered it with kisses, and deep sobs testified the amount of her emotion.

"Take it, take it from me," she at length contrived to utter, "take it from me, and I will go at once."

Mrs. Brent did so, and then Emily walked dejectedly to the door of the cottage ; for an instant she hesitated, and then returned again. Once more she clasped the babe to her breast. There was a murmured blessing hysterically spoken, and then nearly heartbroken at this, the first decisive step in her enterprise, she tore herself from that spot of earth which henceforward would ever be hallowed in her memory, as the one most dear to her remembrance.

*   *   *   *   *   *

She reached what might be now called her temporary home in such a deep de-jection of spirits, that it could not fail to be remarked by the Todds, who got perfectly desperate to know what could possibly be going on.

Emily had, before leaving home, securely hidden the clothing she had purchased, so that what had become of that, became an additional mystery and a great aggra-vation to the whole of the Todds, young and old, and when they saw Emily return with the traces of tears upon her cheek and without the child too, they assembled together in the parlour and started among themselves some of the wildest conjectures, as to what could possibly have happened, as well as to what was going to happen, in connection with the eccentric and most mysterious Mrs. Freeman.

Julia, who had read a great number of romances, was fully of opinion that Mrs. Freeman had been upon an expedition to murder the child, and that mur-dered it was, to all intents and purposes.

"You know, Selina," she said, "such things do happen, for didn't we read of something very like it in that beautiful romance of the 'Blue Goblin ; or, the Blood-spangled Baby?'"

"It aint impossible," said Selina, "and if she has, it's my opinion that she's found out that the baronet she's in love with don't like children."

"I shouldn't think he did," said Olinthus, "ready made."

"Olinthus," screamed his mother, "how dare you talk in that way, but it's getting towards evening now and she'll be down to tea. I'll pretty soon speak to her if nobody else does. I'll know what's going on or I'll know the reason why ! "It's all very well to bring babies here and then take them away again and have people calling upon you from you don't know where, about you don't know what. In my opinion, my dears, she's a mere fortune hunter."

"Yes; and no doubt wants all the men to propose," said Selina.

The tea-table was laid, but no Mrs. Freeman made her appearance and the utmost impatience was manifested by the Todd family consequent thereupon.

"Just you go, Julia," said Mrs. Todd, "and knock at her door and tell her we're waiting !"

"Yes, ma."

Julia went upon her errand, and instead of knocking at Mrs. Freeman's door, she improved upon it by trying to walk in.

Against such a surprise as this, however, Emily had guarded herself by locking the door, so that Julia was compelled to call to her—

"Mrs. Freeman ! Mrs. Freeman ! the tea's ready and we're waiting for you ?"

"Do not do so," said Emily, " I shall not require tea to-day."

"Well, I never !" thought Julia, as she went down stairs, after delivering her message. " I suppose as she's murdered the baby—she's eating of it now to get rid of the body—what a wretch! It puts me in mind of the 'Fiend of the New Beer Shop; or, the Dollop of Coagulated Gore,' that Olinthus took in the other day in numbers."

" Well, it's all very well," said Mrs. Todd, " but I don't like these proceedings at all. Just you, Selina, run up in a friendly kind of way, you know, and tell Mrs. Freeman you've got something to say to her. She can't make any excuse for not letting you in."

" I will," said Selina, " she's writing another letter to that baronet I'll be bound. Gracious me! what if he has proposed? that will be dreadful."

Selina run up stairs full of this amiable resolve and determined not to be said nay to, unless Mrs. Freeman in saying it got quite out of the bounds of ordinary civility, but she soon discovered how fallacious are human intentions.

It will be recollected that the bed-room which had been assigned to Emily was on the second-floor, and consequently two flights of stairs from the parlour had to be ascended before it was reached. Now Selina went up with great expedition, so much so that on what was called the dining-room-landing she paused for a moment to take breath.

" She'll think I'm flurried," was the remark to herself, " if I can't speak without panting."

Suddenly then, the sound of a footstep broke upon her ear, and although it was approaching twilight, the dark shadow of something passing one of the stair-case windows and descending from the second floor was evident to her.

" She's coming," said Selina, " she's actually coming, but that shan't hinder me from asking about the child, oh, dear no. I'll have that secret out of her, and I'll know more about the real baronet too, or she shall give me some very good reason for not knowing. We shall see—we shall see—here she comes.

Selina looked up, terror for a moment took possession of her, for it was a male figure descending the stairs and not a female. A decently attired lad, of apparently some fifteen or sixteen years of age, came rapidly down, carrying a small bundle, and stood for a moment face to face with Selina.

The first discovery which the latter made was, that the lad was remarkably good-looking, and the next, that he looked remarkably frightened. All that she had ever read and heard of the Claude Duvals, the Tom Kings, and the Dick Turpins, and the Captain Hawks, crossed her imagination, but none of them came near the handsomeness of the young burglar whom she had thus considered she had detected in the very act of robbing the house.

" Thieves! thieves!" said Selina, " if you don't stop this moment I'll make a disturbance."

" Let me pass, lady," said a soft musical voice, " and earn my blessings and my thanks."

" No, I can't," said Selina. " Murder! help!" but she pronounced these words in so low and gentle a tone, that nobody could possibly be disturbed by them.

" Oh, forgive me!" said the stranger; " that I have thus made my way into th house of one that is so dear to me. It is love which actuates me, not plunder. 1 am no thief, but one who would dare anything and everything for the dear object of his affections. I am not likewise what I seem."

" Oh, gracious!" said Selina; " I never saw you before; you mean me ot course—who are you—directly? Now don't begin kissing me, for I won't have it. Are you the young gentleman on horseback that looked at me in the City-road, yesterday?"

" Beautiful creature, forgive me, that I have left my own stately home and all those allurements of existence that surround the titled and the wealthy, to accomplish a purpose near and dear to my heart."

" Oh! oh dear!" said Selina; and she sat down upon the stairs. " How romantic? how delightful!—don't, now, don't!"

" Don't what?"

" I—I thought you were going to do something—but I'll scream."

"Farewell! I may go in peace. If your mother or sister were to see me now, what might they not suppose? Be assured that we shall meet again."

"When, oh when, interesting stranger?" said Selina, springing to her feet and seizing his hand, "tell me when you'll come to tea. Don't ask me to meet you at the corner of the Eagle to-morrow evening at seven o'clock precisely—I aint engaged —I'm going out with nobody."

"Then you think that you could love me?"

"Oh! don't I—I'd try. Hush! I hear mama—what is that you say? one kiss and adieu. Oh! what an incident! Farewell! What name shall I call you to my memory's heart? and when the dimness of sensibility awakens visionary tears and clouds, I—I don't know what I'm saying."

"Farewell! one kiss."

The youth imprinted a kiss upon the cheek of Selina, and was graciously forgiven —perhaps the same spirit of christian charity would have been extended to a dozen.

"At seven—at seven," she whispered; "the Eagle at the corner—I mean the corner of the Eagle."

"Yes, beautiful being—and the—"

"Go on, sweet accordion—and then—"

"I'll propose."

"Oh gracious! here comes Julia—little brat—hush—wait a moment—be calm. I'll put on an air of composure and push her into the parlour; when you hear the door shut, slip down stairs and walk into the street. But you've not told me who you are."

"Did you ever hear of the young Viscount Assafœtida?"

"No, no; never shall I forget that name. Now, Miss Julia, I'll let you know what it is to pry into other people's secrets."

Selina rushed down the stairs singing "I've been roaming," in order to impress Julia and the whole family that every thing was perfectly correct and right above stairs—you needn't go up, Julia, Mrs. Freeman's coming down—that's a dear."

"I aint going to Mrs. Freeman; I'm going—"

"Well, did I say you needn't?"

"Ah! but you know—"

This was too much for human endurance. Julia made an effort to step past her, but Selina caught her by two long tails into which her hair had been twisted, and at the end of which a red or blue bow was usually affixed—with the energy of despair, she dragged her into the passage and thence into the parlour.

Julia screamed, for the tails were nearly torn out by the roots; Selina stormed; Mrs. Todd nearly fell into hysterics with alarm; while Olinthus wondered what the deuce it was all about; and then, in the midst of the uproar, bang went the street-door, and Selina sinking upon the couch, exclaimed hysterically—

"Assafœtida is saved!"

"Assy who?" said Olinthus.

"None of your vulgarity," said Selina. "I'm an injured person—but it's always the way in this family—I'm always caught up in this kind of way—but a day will come when it will be different, and you'll all of you be glad of a little condescending notice from a viscountess."

Julia was sobbing and at intervals complaining of the outrageous manner in which her tails had been tugged at; and Olinthus, as he got up and put on his hat, quietly remarked—

"Selina's in one of her tantrums. It was only this morning she frightened Jem almost out of his wits, and made him drop all the fire irons by wanting room for a barouche or phaeton, or something of that sort. I'm going—"

"Then take that with you," said Selina, as she gave him a sound box of the ears that made his eyes flash fire—"take that with you, you poor ill-looking wretch; go and smoke your cigars at three a penny, and make a fool of yourself, do."

CHAPTER XX.

THE INTRODUCTION OF THE DISGUISED EMILY TO SIR ANTHONY.

EMILY WYVILL had probably adopted the only course which, after meeting Selina, could have enabled her to get clear of the house ; had she temporised in the least, and not attacked this lady on her weakest point, she would have been detained probably under suspicion of being a thief, and in order to rescue herself, she would have been compelled to take the Todd family much further into her confidence than she ever intended.

The importance of the object which she had in view had induced her to pause at nothing which should conduce to its success, and therefore her disguise was astonishingly perfect.

Without a murmur she sacrificed the long ringlets of her beautiful hair, and the change that operation effected in her appearance was immense.

Naturally of a slight and well-built form, she set off to advantage the clothing she assumed ; looking, when attired in her male suit, to be some carefully nurtured and promising, handsome lad of about fifteen years of age.

No wonder, then, that she had attracted the admiring eyes of Selina, and obtained so easy a conquest over that young lady's affections.

Certainly Emily's terror until she gained the street was great, for she still feared that something would happen to retard her progress ; but then she was clear of the Todds' house, and was so far successful. It was rather a subject of congratulation to her that she had passed through one ordeal unsuspected.

She had encountered one person who knew her tolerably well, and with whom her disguise had passed muster, so that, putting aside the fright she had experienced, the meeting with Selina gave her a degree of confidence which she otherwise would not have possessed.

She had carefully placed in her pocket the letter of introduction to Sir Anthony Wyvill, which she had sealed again in a manner which tolerably well concealed the fact of its having been once opened.

It was a strange feeling which came over her in the streets now as she walked along in her new attire, and she fancied that every one who passed her looked curiously upon her.

But this feeling was only imaginary and soon wore away. She had to inquire her route once or twice, and each time she gathered fresh confidence in her disguise, from the fact that the people directed her without appearing to entertain the least suspicion that she was other than what she seemed.

The distance was a considerable one to the hotel where Sir Anthony Wyvill was staying, for, although Major Greathead had declared it not to be one of the most aristocratic of those establishments, it was yet situate at the west end of the town, and Emily, being ignorant of the metropolis, had no conception of the distance until she came to walk it, which lay between the City-road and Brereton's Hotel.

And now her heart beat rapidly, and she felt almost all her courage fail her as she entered the street where the house was situate. In vain she tried to rally all her energies, and call them to her aid. She was compelled to pause and lean for some few moments upon some area rails, with the hope that the tumult in her breast would cease, and that she should be able more calmly and collectively to go through the terrible ordeal of the first interview with her husband, for if she escaped detection at that, she felt that her confidence would return and she would be comparatively safe.

She was favoured by its being evening, which, of course, added to her chances of escape ; and, moreover, she considered that her personal appearance was not so fresh probably in the memory of Sir Anthony Wyvill as it might be, considering that he had not seen her for so long a period.

Moreover, grief had done something to alter the expression of that beautiful countenance, which had beamed with so much serenity before that severe blow of fate had occurred, which deprived her of the joy and comfort of her home.

It was thus she tried to reason with herself, and to think that she really ran but little risk in the prosecution of her romantic scheme.

But the reason has but small power in controlling the imagination, and she trembled, harassed by a thousand fears, as she pictured to herself what might really be the consequence of a discovery.

She asked herself, too, if it were not highly probable she would have to encounter the Mrs. Augerstein who had robbed her of all her felicity, and if the interview with Sir Anthony Wyvill was likely to be one of great pain and sadness, how could she hope to control the natural feelings which would rise uppermost in her mind when she should look upon the destroyer of her peace in the person of her rival!

She shrunk, but it was too late to recede; and then, with more of desperation than real resolution, she walked hastily forward and crossed the threshold of the hotel.

A number of waiters were passing to and fro, and for some few moments she remained unnoticed; but then, one observing her situation, stepped up, saying—

"Well, young gentleman, what is it you want?"

Emily's heart beat so tumultuously she could hardly speak, but, after a moment's pause, she contrived to say—

"Is Sir Anthony Wyvill within? I believe he is staying here."

"Oh yes," said the man, "he has apartments here."

"And—and—" added Emily.

"What is it?" said the man.

"Is he alone?"

"I believe he is."

"But I mean staying here alone?"

"Oh yes, to be sure. I shall be going up stairs in a moment, and will tell him some one wants him. What name shall I say?"

"I have a letter of introduction," said Emily, "and he expects me."

"Oh, then, in that case, perhaps you'd better come up at once. He has dined, and I know there's no one with him."

Emily could only assent to this proposition by an inclination of her head, for her heart was really too full to permit her to speak. She followed the waiter up a spacious and handsome staircase, the soft carpet on which felt like snow beneath the feet. There was a quiet and pleasant air of repose about that hotel, which were the very features that so disgusted Major Greathead, who preferred rather the bustling activity of an establishment of a different class.

"I am near him," thought Emily. "I am once again near him—near him who first whispered to my ears welcomely the words of fond affection—near him to whom I have given all my heart, and whom I loved as I loved Heaven itself. God grant that I may prosper in this most perilous enterprise, for I have staked my all of earthly blessings upon the issue! Heaven aid me now."

She paused upon the landing, while, with an air of respectful deference and gratitude, the attendant opened the door of a spacious and elegantly furnished room. She heard a few words uttered, and then a reply in that voice which had ever been such music to her soul, but which now for so long a period of time had not fallen upon her ears.

She gasped again, as she told herself—

"It is his voice, my husband's—the father of my babe—him who promised before Heaven's altar the best of love, but who has left me now to mourn."

"You're to walk in," said the waiter; but Emily stood with clasped hands unconscious of the words, until they were a second time repeated with more emphasis, and then she started like one suddenly awakened from a dream, and entered the apartment.

Sitting upon a sofa near to one of the windows was Sir Anthony Wyvill. He appeared to have been reading, for a book lay reversed and open before him. One lamp, over which was a shade that threw its principal beams downward upon the book, left the rest of the apartment in comparative obscurity, and, as Emily stood, she could be but dimly seen by Sir Anthony Wyvill.

" You wish to see me," he said, " I think I can guess your errand."

That was a trying moment. She pressed her hand upon her heart, as if with that mechanical action she could still the alarming tumult that there reigned, and with great difficulty she uttered the monosyllable, " Yes."

" Who speaks?" cried Sir Anthony Wyvill, springing to his feet, " who speaks?" and he dashed the lamp on one side, fixing his eyes keenly on the countenance of Emily. " Very like," he said, " but paler; how strange! The voice, too. Speak again, my lad; whence come you?"

" I bring a letter, sir, from Mistress Margaret Wyvill."

" No, no," he said, " not so like now; how suddenly the tone seemed to come over me, like some old-remembered and well-loved notes of music! it was very strange; but those accidental resemblances of feature I have often found to carry with them a likeness in manner and in voice likewise."

He broke the seal of the letter, and while Emily stood pale as a marble statue gazing upon him, he hastily perused its contents.

" So," he said, as he laid it down, " you are the lad my sister recommends to me; I trust that you will be as well pleased with your service as I shall endeavour to make it pleasant to you. I like your looks, boy, although I wish both they and your voice had been different; but it is not your fault that you resemble one I wish not to be reminded of."

Emily bowed.

" You'll consider yourself as attached to my service," said Sir Anthony, " but not menially, mark me, with as much personal liberty as I can possibly give you, I wish and hope that I shall be able to make you confidential."

" I hope so, sir."

" Ah! there again, how very strange! Some trick of the voice at times, even upon the turn of a word, brings the memory of all that I have lost back upon me."

" Lost, Sir Anthony!" exclaimed Emily, clasping her hands.

" Peace, peace, boy, peace! Let it be one of your duties to take no notice of me when in these moods. I must have no questions asked, no prying into my affairs. What you may chance to know I will not ask you, but be it much or be it little, keep it secret and prate not of it as you value my protection and esteem. You understand me?"

" I do, sir."

" Are you fatigued, or could you commence your duties this night by delivering a letter for me at a house not far from here?"

" I am at your service, sir, by night or by day, at all times, and in all seasons."

" It is well; wait a moment."

He proceeded to a writing-desk, and she saw him place a bank-note and a letter in an envelope; he sealed it, and then hurriedly wrote an address upon the back.

" The distance is not great," he said, " and probably you, being strange in London, may have some difficulty to find your way, but as it is necessary that you should become acquainted with the town, it is as well you should get over that trouble as quickly as possible."

" Does the letter require an answer, sir?"

" No; you have but to deliver it; but I wish it to go into the lady's own hands."

" The lady?"

" Yes, boy; why do you repeat my words? Mrs. Angerstein is the party to whom it is addressed."

" I obey you, sir," said Emily, and with a shudder she left the room. She walked down the staircase more like some spectre than a living thing; she passed out into the street with the letter in her grasp; the cool evening air played serenely upon her brow, and recovered her to something like consciousness of the present.

"It is true," she sobbed, "it is all true; now I know the worst, and my first sad trial is to be the messenger of illicit passion. Dare I, ought I thus to forget all the majesty of virtue, all a woman's right, all sense of injury, oppression, and deep indignity? No; I owe it to myself, I owe it to honour and to Heaven; the contents of this letter shall be my husband's accusation."

Her hands were upon the seal; but then a sudden revulsion of feeling took place, and the light of indignation, that for a moment had beamed from her eyes, passed away.

"No, no," she said, "I dare not, and will not! Courage, courage! I ought to have expected this. This is one of the assurances of the success, so far, of the plan of conduct I have laid down for myself. I will not shrink; this letter shall be sacred, and it shall reach its destination; with what calmness I may I will look upon the face of her to whom it is addressed."

The name of the street which was upon the back of the letter afforded no information whatever to Emily, stranger as she was, to the metropolis, and she was compelled to go into a shop for the purpose of making an inquiry respecting her route.

She found that the street was but at a very short distance from the hotel, and that became another circumstance that added to what she considered the conclusive evidence she had obtained of the entire truth of all Margaret's statements.

There might have been something like feminine curiosity at work in Emily's heart to see the individual who had supplanted her in the affections of her husband, but, at all events, it was with very different feelings that she knocked at the door of the house in which Mrs. Angerstein resided.

Upon asking for that lady, Emily was informed that she was at home, and that any message would be taken to her; but mindful of what Sir Anthony Wyvill had said, namely, that he wished the letter to be delivered into her own hands, Emily declined the interposition of a third party, saying, that it was necessary she should see Mrs. Angerstein.

Upon this, there was some little delay, which, however, terminated in her being requested to walk into a parlour, when she was informed Mrs. Angerstein would come in a few moments.

Those few moments were trying and anxious ones; but still Emily kept telling herself how necessary it was for the continued success of her enterprise that she should keep herself perfectly calm, and not, even in the presence of her dangerous rival, give way to the slightest feeling which might be prompted by natural jealousy.

"I will look upon her," she said, "as upon a stranger, and she shall look upon my face as upon a mask hiding a world of passion beneath its cold exterior, and displaying but one fixed and equable feeling, and that one not of the description that agitates the heart."

The few moments increased to about five minutes and then Emily heard a light footstep, and the really beautiful Mrs. Angerstein entered the apartment. Probably Emily had not pictured to herself any mental portrait of the lady, but still there was something about the air and manner of Mrs. Angerstein so completely at variance with what she seemed to have expected, that she could only look at her for some moments with a strange kind of wonder, without uttering a word. It seemed to Emily almost impossible that such an ingenuous countenance could belong to a heart so depraved as the circumstances could warrant her in believing it to be. But could she doubt—ah, no—had she not abundant evidence of the dreadful fact, even without that letter she held in her hand, and had she not herself seen Sir Anthony Wyvill place within its enclosure some of the wages of infamy?

"You wish to see me," said Mrs. Angerstein, kindly.

"I have a letter from Sir Anthony Wyvill, madam."

"From Sir Anthony Wyvill? give it me; I hope that he is well. Have you come from him, even now? Is he looking more cheerful?"

"I have come from him within this half-hour, but not having much experience of his state of mind, I know not if he be more cheerful than he has been."

Mrs. Angerstein was reading the letter, and paid but little attention to what Emily said, and as she read she murmured to herself some observations upon the contents of the epistle.

"How kind, how considerate—alas! what would become of me, but for such a friend?—what a noble generosity—I cannot presume to thank him—words would fall so far short of one's real feelings. Will you take him back a note from me?"

"It will be my duty to do so, madam."

"Thank you; I shall not detain you long."

Mrs. Angerstein left the apartment, and Emily sunk into a chair.

"Now," she said, "I have passed through the third ordeal this day, I have parted from my dear little one, I have looked upon the face of him who has forsaken me, and I have talked calmly and respectfully to her, for whose sake he has done me so much bitter wrong; surely, ah, surely, now I can play my part well, and can have but little to dread from what may now ensue; and she is beautiful too,

No. 18.

beautiful beyond all that I had pictured her to be. Alas, how poor a judge am I of human nature; had I met her under different circumstances, I should have thought her, gathering my opinion from her tones and manners, a perfect piece of virtue. Hush, hush!—she comes!—be still, my heart, she comes."

The door opened, and Mrs. Angerstein re-entered the apartment, with a letter in her hand.

"You will give this," she said, "to Sir Anthony Wyvill."

"Emily, as she took the letter, felt something cold touch her hand, a glance showed her that it was a sliver coin, oh, how the rebellious blood flew to her brow, at the thought, that like a lackey, she was to be paid for carrying the written protestations of unhallowed love between her husband and that being, who was the bane of her existence.

The letter and the coin dropped to the floor, while Emily, just for the passing moment forgetting all caution, drew up her slim figure to its utmost height, and gazed steadily upon the countenance of her rival.

"I regret," said Mrs. Angerstein, "that I have committed an error, if you are a friend instead of an attendant upon Sir Anthony Wyvill, I trust you will excuse me, there is the letter, and we will allow the poor reward I would have given you for carrying it, to remain where chance has deposited it."

"Madam," said Emily, "if I were the poorest, humblest hind, that ever obeyed the nod and beck of an imperious master, I would not degrade myself so low as to play the pander to—to—I pray you pardon me—at times I know not what I say; good night—good night."

Mrs. Angerstein, as well she might, had stepped back in amazement, at this sudden, and to her, most unaccountable, burst of indignation, it seemed so utterly uncalled for by the circumstances, to be so gratuitously insulting, that she could not utter a word until it was too late, and she heard the street-door close upon the retreating form of Sir Anthony Wyvill's singular new attendant; and Emily Wyvill, when she got some distance from the house, began much to blame herself, for the foolish precipitancy which certainly much endangered her secret.

"I told myself I would be calm," she said, "and rating my strength of temper by my strength of purpose, I thought it possible that I should be able to look even upon the face of her who had betrayed me and rendered me wretched, with a feigned, if not a real composure."

She found, however, how hard it was to trifle with the feelings, or for any amount of reflection to succeed in overwhelming such agony of thought, as that which could not but be hers.

She hastened back to the hotel, in order to deliver to Sir Anthony Wyvill, the note with which Mrs. Angerstein had charged her, and here we cannot but claim for Emily Wyvill the deepest admiration of our readers, that she abstained from opening either of these epistles, notwithstanding she must have felt the strongest temptation so to do.

"No," she said, when the thought occurred to her, "I will pursue my purpose steadily and perseveringly, adopting no unworthy methods to hasten its success."

With this resolution she reached the hotel, but upon ascending the stairs which led to the sitting apartment of Sir Anthony, she was informed by one of the waiters of the establishment, that a gentleman was with him. Thankful for the intelligence, inasmuch as it gave her some time to calm her purturbed spirits, she walked into the adjoining chamber, and was not aware, until she had done so, that the door of communication being ajar, she was able to overhear some portions of the conversation which ensued. For a moment she hesitated whether to stay or to go, but when she thought of the close affinity between her and Sir Anthony, she sat down to listen to the somewhat strange conversation that was taking place between him and another.

We may as well inform the reader that that other was Major Greathead, the arch-tempter of the heart-stricken Sir Anthony Wyvill, to all sorts of foibles

"And so, Wyvill," he said, "you have not forgotten how you used to be hoaxed and roasted about what we used to call the captain's legacy."

"No," I've not forgotten, but let it rest. It seems as if my first acquaintance with Mrs. Angerstein, was co-existent with my greatest misfortunes."

" Well, well, you must forget all that. I suppose you've heard nothing of your wife ?"

"Nothing whatever, although I long so much to know what has become of her. She keeps her abode most secret. It was cruelty to take away the child. I could have been a father to that little one, although no husband to her."

"Well, damn it, hang care, you know Sir Harry Vane, of whom you won something last evening ?"

" A trifle, I believe, what of him ?"

"Why, he's one of the most mad-headed fools that ever lived. He prides himself on his years, and upon leaving off a better man, as he says, than he begun. Now's he's had a run of ill luck lately, losing to everybody—the merest tyro could beat him—so he's made me swear to ask you to come to-night to let him have his revenge."

" Do with me as you will, for I am sick at heart."

Emily clasped her hands as he asked herself, " and does he, indeed, begin to feel the bitterness of the wrong doing—does he, after so short a time has elapsed, feel that passion can hold no real contest with principle. Oh! those words have given me a radiant hope !"

" Then, that's settled,'" said the Major, " of course you'll win more of him, that will just serve him right, as he's so bent upon it. Have you communicated with your solicitors ?"

" I have."

" Well, then, you may depend they'll do all that's right and proper, much better than you can. You need not trouble about your wife. It was an odd freak her leaving the house when everything seemed so smooth, and you had no suspicions."

" None at all, I expected to find her as before, and anticipated that she would really find pleasure in the company of Mrs. Angerstein."

" Gracious Heaven !" thought Emily, " is this the man to whom I gave my best affection—is this the being whom I thought all openness and candour, who now talks so calmly and coolly of the manner in which he intended to deceive me ?"

" By-the-bye," said the Major, carelessly ; " you've located the widow in London."

" Yes, I've sent a lad, who is in my employ, with money to her this evening. She's the most amiable of women."

" Ha! ha! no doubt, but come, to the club—to the club, and I shall again have the pleasure of seeing you beat Sir Henry. His looks as he sees his gold slipping from him are exquisitely ludicrous."

" Well, well, I yield to you."

They both left the room, and when they had gone Emily covered her face with her hands and sobbed convulsively.

" Oh! what am I to think ?" she said, "what am I to think ? Is there room for hope, or only ampler latitude for despair, and yet, at times, there was in his voice, a certain mournfulness, a touch of feeling, which struck home to my heart, a mild gentleness that more than once tempted me to rush from my concealment, and cast myself into his arms."

Oh! that she had done so.

" And, now—now, he has gone to-night with the gay throng to make the vain endeavour to lose the remembrance of the misery he has inflicted, in the wild excitement of the gaming-table. Oh! Sir Anthony Wyvill is this you—is this you ? Is it possible that one, whom I treasured so in my heart of hearts, should so turn aside from the allegiance of pure affection, and so utterly deceive me ?"

She leaned her hands upon the table near where she sat, and there, alone in the dim light, which poured its way through the narrow opening of the door from the next apartment, she wept long and bitterly.

*　　　*　　　*　　　*　　　*　　　*

It was strange, but, as Sir Anthony Wyvill went with Major Greathead to the gaming-house that night, his heart smote him, and, notwithstanding he knew he was in such uncongenial company, he said, aloud,—

"Emily, Emily, wherefore have you left me? Was not one hour of joy with thee superior, far superior, to all this excitement of existence, which men call life? Give me the calm repose beneath the quiet shadows of thickly clustering trees, and the whispered accents of fond affection, before all this glare and bustle, and but that I think solitude would drive me mad, painting, as 'twould to me, all that I had lost in the memory of the past, I would not seek the oblivion of a moment in such a scene as this."

Such expressions as these were to Major Greathead incomprehensible. He looked aghast while Sir Anthony Wyvill spoke, and, when he ceased, all he could say was,—

"Well, 'pon my soul, my dear fellow, I don't understand you. But have it your own way you know, and don't say that I said you nay. It strikes me, that, what between your wife and the widow, you don't seem to know very well what to be at."

CHAPTER XXI.

THE QUARREL AT THE GAMING-HOUSE.—THE DUEL BY NIGHT IN THE DESERTED
SALOON.

SOME demon of riot and recklessness seemed to have seized upon Sir Anthony Wyvill that night, or else, what was far more probable, the wine, which he was induced to take immediately upon leaving the gaming-house, was far from being of that pure and healthful quality it ought to have been.

It might be that there were potent drugs introduced, which were such foes to reason and reflection, and which filled the veins with such a vicious and mad blood, that the coldest spirit could not resist their influence.

Certain it was that Sir Anthony Wyvill gave way completely to the madness of the hour, and Major Greathead, that wolf in the borrowed skin of some better animal, exulted, now, over the certainty that he had his victim in his grasp.

He was one of those men who would have money for the support of his numerous extravagancies, let that money come from whence it might. There might have been a time when he was a little scrupulous, and had a choice with regard to the means by which he procured his resources, but, if so, that time had long since passed away, and he was quite willing to sacrifice his friend Sir Anthony Wyvill at the shrine of his exhausted exchequer.

Sir Harry Vane, who has been mentioned already, was a *rouè* of the first water, a man honourable by courtesy, but by nothing else, and, if between him and Major Greathead there was not some understanding, that Sir Anthony Wyvill was to be let win at first, in order that he might be drawn on to greater losses afterwards, it is, indeed, a strange thing to us.

And yet these men, in the world's signification and understanding, were most honourable—one holding a high civil rank, and the other a high military; they were men who would have thought it far beneath them to acquire a subsistence by any honest effort of ordinary industry, and yet, strange to say, by some inversion of intellect, they scrupled not to link together to rob one who trusted them.

Sir Anthony Wyvill took more notice on this evening of the scene to which he was introduced than he had done on the preceding occasion, and most truly was it a scene worth noticing.

Those who would affect to say that the English are not an artistical and imaginative people should pause before they make that declaration, and ascertain what can be done when there is a stimulus to such a kind of exertion of the mental faculties. Nothing could exceed the amount of art that was brought into play for the purpose of dazzling the senses and blinding the judgment of those votaries at the gaming table who were brought together in that most splendid mansion.

There, indeed, the monster vice of gaming presented itself in its most alluring and seductive aspect ; the costly mirrors, the superb hangings, the rich carpets that felt like snow beneath the feet, the statuary, and a brilliant light which shed such a lustre over all, were specially designed to take captive the imagination, and by raising against reason that antagonistic power, thereby lure the victim into the meshes of the destroyer.

" This is, indeed, a gorgeous scene," said Sir Anthony Wyvill.

" Yes, yes," said the major ; " it's all very well in its way, I give them credit for getting up these houses."

" What a strange thing it is," said Sir Anthony, after he had glanced round him for a few moments, " what a strange thing it is that all this ingenuity and real talent, in the shape of internal decoation, is rarely if ever exercised except for some illicit purpose."

" Yes, my dear fellow," said the major, " that's the very thing ; I've remarked, over and over again, your virtuous people are the most disagreeable dogs in the world. They have got a fancy that you can't be moral without being uncomfortable at the same time, and they view with as much horror all these costly beauties of art, as they would some cardinal sin."

" There may be some truth, I believe, in what you say."

" Abundance of truth, my good friend, abundance; but behold, as luck will have it, here comes Sir Harry Vane, the very man you seek."

" Nay, I don't seek him."

" Have it your own way, he seeks you; you've won his money, and he's savage, of course you need not do so unless you like, but it's a kind of understood thing in these cases that you are to give him his revenge if he seek it."

" Well, be it so ; I have no occasion to win any man's money, and I should be far better pleased for him to get it back again than in retaining it."

" Now only look," said the major, " what a mistake you fall into; it is not the money but the excitement of the victory or defeat that lends a zest to play; Sir Harry Vane has an immense income, but he don't like to lose for all that."

" As you please, as you please."

They strolled up to a table which was unoccupied, where they were soon joined by Sir Harry Vane, who, after the interchange of a few civilities, declared his satisfaction at seeing Sir Anthony Wyvill again. " Now, sir," he said, " you shall make your own game, it shall be what you please, you have defeated me once, and you shall have an opportunity of doing so again, we will keep this table to ourselves."

" I can assure you," said Sir Anthony Wyvill, " that my reason for coming here to-night is simply because it is considered inconsistent with the sort of under-standing with persons who play, to refuse the loser a chance of recovering his loss."

" Good," said Sir Harry, " be it so ; what say you to cards? I detest the very rattle of dice, besides there may be some little skill exercised, at *ecarté* for instance."

" 'Tis better," said the Major, and he gave a short, dry cough as he spoke.

One of the well dressed, noiseless attendants of the place glided up to the table, and waited for orders.

" Then is it to be cards?" said Sir Harry Vane. " What wine do you take, Sir Anthony ?"

" None at present."

" Oh, poh, poh ! some of the light wines from the banks of the Rhine improve the faculties instead of impairing them, and if there be anything here you can depend upon more than another, it is in getting your wines pure."

" That's a tremendous ——" said the Major, and he coughed again, for which he was rewarded by a kick under the table from Sir Harry Vane, who thought he was going too far in presuming upon the unsuspecting simplicity of Sir Anthony Wyvill.

The cards were brought, and so was the wine, and a richly decorated screen was placed half round the table, which Major Greathead informed Sir Anthony Wyvill, was an understood sign in the house, that the play at that table was strictly private. "You save yourself," he said, "from the annoyance of lookers on a thing which to me is detestable, for after a time you are sure to be made the subject of all kinds of bets."

"A most uncomfortable thing, indeed."

"Very, just taste that wine. I know a case in this very house where a gentleman was playing at cards, and somebody else, a perfect stranger to him, laid a wager upon his success to a very large amount; the gentleman lost, and then, to his great surprise the party who, without his cognizance or sanction, in the least, had backed him, came round and abused him for playing so badly."

"Very good," said Sir Harry Vane, "but I suppose Sir Anthony Wyvill, you don't believe a word the major tells you."

"Now, confound you," said the major, "you want to spoil a good story just because it may not happen to be true."

"Gentlemen, you must settle the question of veracity between you; and now that I taste this wine, it seems so light and sparkling as to justify the eulogium you gave to it."

"All is right then," said Sir Harry Vane; "and now for a cool hour or two of real play."

The major sat a short distance from the table, but sufficiently near to Sir Harry Vane, to be able to communicate with him if he pleased, while his being upon that side, put an end to any suspicion, if such for a moment had entered the mind of Sir Anthony, that by signals he would make his opponent acquainted with the cards he held.

The play went on quietly with varied success, but upon the whole, Sir Harry Vane was certainly losing, notwithstanding Wyvill played with a carelessness that one would have thought likely to produce a very different result.

"You have all the luck, Wyvill," said the major.

"And it is luck," said Sir Anthony; " "I have much more to thank fortune than any skill of my own. I can just play the game, and that's all. By the by one of your dumb waiters here has removed one bottle I was drinking from, and brought another, although I had not taken about three glasses from it."

"Oh, that's always done here; in about half an hour the warm atmosphere, gas lights, and so on, are supposed to vitiate the wine, so they bring you a cool bottle.

"That's attentive, at any rate, play on, Sir Harry."

There can be no doubt but that the first wine that was placed before Sir Anthony Wyvill, was of the best and purest vintage; with regard to the second, it was quite another affair, and a few glasses of it quickly produced a fever of excitement that became manifest in every word he uttered.

"Come, this is merely play," said Sir Harry Vane, "and it is a monstrous bore to be brushing a few pounds to and fro upon the table; let Major Greathead keep an account for us: we can both trust to him, and we can play on credit; when we leave off I can give you my cheque, or you can give me yours for the amount of loss.

"As you please; it's all the same thing, and certainly less trouble."

"A hundred then, on this game, and double stakes every third round."

"That's heavy."

"Not at all, it's only nominal; we shall go on winning and losing, and neither of us will be much the worst in the end."

'True," said Major Greathead, "and nothing makes a man to forget troubles and griefs, as this kind of harmless excitement. Now, gentlemen, I am ready, go on—play away—and I will give you credit, one of you upon one leaf of my pocket book, and the other upon another."

"Heaven knows," said Sir Anthony Wyvill, as he poured himself out some more wine—"heaven knows, I have some need of a means of chasing away grief and trouble; if this will do it it is welcome."

The play now proceeded with much greater rapidity than before, and it was quite evident that the wine was producing all its expected effect upon Sir Anthony Wyvill, he laughed and talked rapidly, but not at all in his usual manner, there was a wild and fevered excitement about him which any one who wished him well would have been grieved to see.

He won and lost with scarce perception which was which, and almost all he knew of the game consisted, now and then, in asking the major how he was getting on, to which the reply was—

"All right, you are both of you in each other's books. I'll be hanged if I can tell you which way the balance goes."

"That's no matter," said Sir Harry Vane. "You don't drink, Sir Anthony?"

"Yes, thank you, as you say, it's no matter, play on."

And they did play on; another hour passed and the resolution to go had each moment become weaker and weaker in the mind of Sir Anthony Wyvill.

"I am sure I'm losing," cried Sir Harry Vane, furiously, "I'll play double or quits, let the balance be on what side it may."

"Agreed. What's the card?"

"A spade."

"Good. There's the queen."

"And there's the king."

"The king! and what's the meaning of that? I hold it in my hand, or there's two kings of spades in one pack."

"What an infernal blunder!" said the major.

There was a dead silence for a few moments, during which the players looked stedfastly at each other, each holding a king of spades in his hand, then Sir Harry Vane spoke in a tone of braggart insolence, and yet sufficiently low, that it did not reach beyond the table at which they sat.

"Sir Anthony Wyvill," he said, "now mark me, I should be infernally sorry to think you meant to cheat, so I'll look over it and we'll begin this game afresh."

"Ah! that's it," cried the major, "that's the way among friends, always begin again when any cross accident happens."

"I beg your pardon, gentlemen," said Sir Anthony Wyvill, "but I can scarcely view this as an accident. How stands the game, major? I'll play no more."

"Why I think you owe Sir Harry somewhere about £2,500."

"Really, and if I had not happened to have noticed the little accident of two kings of spades in one pack of cards, I might have owed him £5,000. I believe that it would be quite correct, Major?"

"Why, yes, in a manner of speaking, I believe it would."

Sir Anthony Wyvill rose, "Hark ye, Sir Harry Vane," he said, "I do not know you sufficiently well to trust to my own judgment in this matter, if some undoubted honourable men will come forward and say they would pay you, under these circumstances, I will, but not otherwise. '

"Not pay!" cried Sir Harry.

"Not pay! exclaimed the major.

"Not unless the condition I have laid down be complied with."

Sir Anthony Wyvill, now that he stood, began to feel the effects of the drugged wine he had partaken of, he reeled slightly and was compelled to hold a chair for support. Sir Harry Vane stepped up to him and spoke in a low hissing whisper—

"By Jove!" he said, "do you mean to tell me, after pocketing all my ready money, that you don't mean to pay your losses?"

"I will not!"

"Under what impression, sir?"

"Hush, hush," whispered the major, "come along, come out of here, we'll manage it elsewhere."

"I'll do no such thing," said Sir Harry Vane, whose countenance was ghastly pale, and who was evidently infuriated at the detection of the fraud he had attempted. "I'll do no such thing. Do you mean to tell me there was an attempt to—to swindle you?"

"I have no objection to call things by their right names. I do think so."

Sir Harry stepped back a moment, and in his desperate anger he snatched from the table a full glass of wine and hurled it, glass and all, into the face of Sir Anthony.

"You shall fight me," he cried, "and sell your life for the amount, if you won't pay it."

This hostile and sudden movement rather confused Sir Anthony for a moment or two, but then springing forward, he grappled with his opponent.

"Part them, gentlemen, part them !" cried the major, "they're incensed, and we shall have bloodshed here if we don't mind."

In an instant the numerous tables were deserted, and Sir Anthony Wyvill was dragged away from his opponent to whom otherwise he would certainly have done some serious injury, for Sir Harry Vane was no match for him.

It was a curious thing to see how little the players in the gambling house, and the officiating persons connected with it, cared for the cause of the quarrel. It seemed quite sufficient for them that there was a dispute which became an annoyance, they paid no attention to the explanation of either party, but, in the course of a few seconds, ejected both into the street, without any ceremony.

Major Greathead now interposed between them. It was no policy of his to be mixed up in a street brawl, although he felt that a severe blow had been given to anything like a continuance of his intimacy with Sir Anthony.

"Gentlemen, gentlemen !" he said, "for Heaven's sake settle your quarrel in another way than this."

"I have done," said Sir Anthony. "I know not how it is that so small an amount of wine has driven me almost mad."

"I will have satisfaction,' said Sir Harry Vane, as he ground his teeth together. "I'll have satisfaction—immediate satisfaction."

"How can you be such a fool ?" whispered the major to him ; "it was your own fault."

"I don't care, I'll have a shot at him, by Jove! He has nearly throttled me. Sir Anthony Wyvill, will you hand me your card, sir ?"

"Nay, now this is great folly," said the major ; "we'll have no fighting."

"It is not for me," remarked Sir Anthony, and he spoke thickly, and with difficulty, "it is not for me to refuse any man satisfaction, I am a soldier, but let it be at once—within the hour, if a convenient spot can be found."

Sir Harry Vane looked at him, and saw what an effect the wine had produced ; he saw, by his flushed countenance and unsteady gait, that he would be an easy victim, and with a tone of exultation, he said,—

"Well, within the hour be it, we'll soon find a fitting place."

CHAPTER XXII.

THE OLD VILLA BY KENSINGTON.—THE DANCING HALL.—THE FIGHT.

In vain did Major Greathead interpose to prevent affairs from taking so serious a turn as they threatened, but now, the passions of both parties were by far too much aroused to allow their being easily quelled.

"Now, listen to me," he said, "put off this affair until to-morrow. Sleep upon it, both of you, or you may take my word for it you will be the worst, whoever comes off the victor. Are you men, or angry children merely ?"

"It's no use talking," said Sir Harry Vane. "He has accepted my challenge. You can come as his friend upon the occasion, and I know where to get somebody to come as mine, and if you don't like that, you can leave it alone altogether."

"Are you, Sir Anthony Wyvill," asked Major Greathead, "as mad as this fellow to fight ?"

"Major Greathead," said Sir Anthony, "this Sir Harry Vane, you will recollect, is your friend and not mine. I am much in the habit of judging people by the company they keep, and yours is not of a choice quality."

"You mean to say then—but no matter, I care not. Since you are determined upon this adventure, you may carry it out. You shall not have to say that you wanted to be shot, and that I baulked you in the matter."

"For want of a better, then, Major Greathead, I am willing to take you as my friend upon this occasion, I presume you will not refuse the office."

"No, since you wish it; and I'll take good care," he added to himself, "that it's the last time you require any such service." Turning to Sir Harry Vane, the Major then added, "Are you still resolved upon this matter?"

"I am. If you and your principal will follow me, you will find, that even unseasonable and strange as this hour seems, I can introduce you to some one who will second me."

No. 19.

"Go on, then—we follow."

The Major and Sir Anthony Wyvill followed Sir Harry Vane, the whole evil of whose nature appeared now to be so thoroughly awakened, that nothing but a personal conflict could appease it in any way. That he thirsted for the blood of Sir Anthony Wyvill, there can be no doubt. Rage and disappointment made up such an amount of anger in his heart, that nothing short of the conflict, he insisted upon, could satisfy him.

As regarded Sir Anthony, there can be no doubt, had he been in full possession of his usual cool and sober judgment, he would have refused unhesitatingly the sudden demand for satisfaction upon a point where he himself was, without question, the injured party; and, indeed, where the offence had been of a nature almost to take his opponent out of the pale of honourable society, and so to deprive him of the right to seek that species of satisfaction which he demanded. But Sir Anthony was not then in possession of his usual faculties. Each moment the effects of the drugged wine he had taken were becoming more apparent, and it was only wonderful to both the Major and Sir Harry that the potent liquid did not exercise a more powerful effect upon him than it had.

Probably for such partial infirmity Sir Anthony had to thank the vigour of an unimpaired constitution, for upon a more weakly frame doubtless the effects would have been most severe; and it was strange to them how, when he did speak, he spoke as if his judgment was unclouded, although such was not really the case.

No conversation took place between the Major and Sir Anthony as they proceeded. The former had his thoughts full of the reflection, that in the event of the death of Wyvill at the hands of Sir Harry Vane certain small and large sums of money which he (Greathead) had borrowed of the baronet, would at once be liquidated by his decease. This was certainly a consideration which the Major thought deserved its due amount of weight in his mind, and so it would have been if pay-day was likely to ever come, and he had not been, by the death of Sir Anthony, getting rid of the goose that laid him golden eggs; for nothing was more unlikely than that the latter should ever ask for a return of that class of favours; and that it was questionable whether, upon reflection, the idea that already seemed to have found a home in the breast of Sir Anthony might not grow into a much stronger shape.

It was quite clear that at present such an idea had crossed even the disordered brain of the attempted-to-be-victimised baronet; so that, upon the whole, perhaps, his death at the hands of Sir Harry Vane was the shortest and most agreeable mode of getting rid of the acquaintance.

As he followed Sir Anthony he could not but remark the unsteady, zigzag manner in which he walked, and the idea of a man in such a state fighting duel with any weapons whatever, was one which would not have been entertained for a moment except by such unprincipled persons as the unhappy Sir Anthony had fallen amongst.

The night was far advanced, indeed it wanted but an hour to the time when the first rays of the morning sun might be expected to appear, when Sir Harry Vane paused at the door of a house in rather a mean street at Westminster.

He turned then to those who were following him, and said,—

"I shall expect to be waited for; the gentleman who will second me resides here, and I may have to rouse him from his slumbers."

He then let himself in with a key which he took from his pocket, leaving Sir Anthony and the Major waiting in the street for his reappearance—a circumstance which the latter entertained some doubt of, for never yet had he seen passion get so much the better of the usual calm and cool effrontery of Sir Harry Vane.

Sir Anthony Wyvill still showed no inclination to speak to his second, but at length, when about ten minutes of uninterrupted silence had ensued, he himself broke it by saying,—

"Sir Anthony, you must still avoid this conflict. I tell you, for your private information, that Sir Harry Vane is an unerring shot; I don't know how you may be in that particular, but you will bear in mind that whatever skill you may have with the pistol detracts in no manner from that which he possesses."

"I care not," was the reply; "the first and the second insult came from him to me. I am a man now with little of anything in this world to live for; he may as well take my life as allow me to continue its possessor when it has become a burthen to me."

"I can well perceive that no interference, but such an one I should be loth to exert, will now suffice to stop this duel—see, he comes!"

The door of the house opened and Sir Harry Vane made his appearance, closely followed by a most singular-looking personage.

He was small and meagre in appearance, and the small countenance that nature had given to him was almost completely hidden in a bush of whiskers and mustachios; there was a swaggering, half-military air about the man, as he bowed to Sir Anthony Wyvill and the Major.

"Very much regret, gentlemen," he said, "very much indeed that these little affairs will occur, but there's no helping them, and when they do they must be settled in a gentlemanly manner."

"Certainly, sir," said the Major; "but there's a difficulty to find a suitable place, unless we go somewhere and wait till sunrise; perhaps, Sir Harry, you will have the kindness to introduce me to your friend?"

"Oh, certainly! I will explain to him who you are, gentlemen, and as to himself, he's a Colonel Mason, in the service of—of— What the deuce are you in the service of, Mason?"

"The Republic of South America."

"Oh, yes, I had forgotten; now, gentlemen, you know each other."

"Then you will permit me," said Colonel Mason, who looked uncommonly like an adventurer of the very lowest class, "you will permit me to suggest, gentlemen, always provided that you really mean to fight, a course of conduct which I always urge upon my friends on such occasions."

"What is it, sir?"

"Certainly not to fight in the open air: you are liable, by doing so, to a thousand contingencies that otherwise would not arise."

"I never heard of a duel in a house," said Sir Anthony.

"Well sir, and gentlemen all, if you don't mind following me, I'll take you to an uninhabited villa, not much above three quarters of an hour's walk from here, in one of the spacious apartments of which there is nothing in the world to prevent your having your quarrel out, and defying any witnesses to anything unpleasant that might occur. Have you any objection?"

"None," said Sir Harry Vane.

"And none on my part,' exclaimed Sir Anthony; "but we have no arms."

"Excuse me," said Colonel Mason, "I have as good a brace of pistols here as ever did good service. Since you're are all agreed, come along!"

The singular being then started off so quickly that it required a sharp walk to keep up with him: it was quite clear he was well acquainted with the way he wished to go, for he never hesitated in the least, but conducted his followers through a number of intricate thoroughfares until he brought them out into the Kensington Road, at a much greater distance from town than they could have supposed, in so short a space of time, they had reached.

"There is a green lane close at hand here; a short distance down it is the house I speak of."

"And you have the right of entrance, I suppose?" said the Major.

"Oh, yes; there are four of us—we can easily break in somehow."

"Break in!"

"Aye, to be sure; how else are we to effect an entrance? You don't suppose I would let you fight in it, if it was my own house. Come, come, that's no difficulty. I've seen the place in better times, and I know there is an apartment in it that will give you a good twenty paces to stand at, if you want as many—there are no neighbours close at hand, so that if any alarm be given by hearing the shots, we shall be off before they can reach us."

"Well, I don't dislike the idea," said the Major.

"It's a good idea, you may depend. If you fight in the open air, you don't know who may be looking on at a distance. I know of a case in which a man, at a quarter of a mile distance, saw through a telescope the whole of the parties to a hostile meeting, and identified them afterwards."

They now turned down the lane, which, when we come to consider its proximity to London, was extremely picturesque, and full of natural beauties ; tall lime-trees formed a hedge-row on either side, and, meeting overhead, formed at night a canopy which prevented the smallest ray of light from penetrating it, while during the day-time, and particularly in the season of warmth and bright sunshine, it created a walk of the most grateful coolness and shade.

At the hour those whose fortunes we are following entered the lane, all was darkness—it looked like the mouth of a cavern, in the profound depths of which there might be many an unseen danger.

"Follow me," cried the self-styled Colonel Mason ; "there's nothing to tumble over, and no ditch—mind you don't pass me, that's all. I have a lantern here, which I will light in a few moments, when we get a little more clear of the high road."

About three minutes' rapid walking took them a considerable distance down the lane, and then the South American Colonel cried "halt," and in another moment the dim blue light of a match was visible, and he fulfilled his promise of lighting a lantern, which, although it shed but a faint ray around, sufficed, when held up, to show a small door-way in a brick wall.

"This is our point of attack," said the Colonel ; "I don't myself see anything in the world to hinder us breaking into this place."

He produced a small steel crow-bar, which with the skill and the use of it must have resulted from practice, he used so as to wrench the door almost from its hinges.

There was now no difficulty whatever in effecting an entrance : the whole party passed onward, and they found themselves in a luxurious although evidently neglected garden. As they trod onwards, following their conductor with the lantern, they were saluted with the fragrance of many sweet flowers which they were treading amongst, for their guide led them without hesitation directly to the house, without heeding the originally-made pathways.

"It seems strange," said Sir Anthony Wyvill, as they reached a raised terrace, which ran round two sides of the mansion ; "it seems strange that such a place as this should be so utterly deserted."

"Not at all," said Colonel Mason ; "it has an evil reputation. Its proprietor, who lived in it nearly alone, a man reputed rich, but of frugal and precarious habits, was found savagely murdered in one of the rooms of the house ; since then, although to let, no one has had the temerity to take it."

After some time spent in fruitless endeavours, an entrance was effected through one of the windows, and, as a distant clock struck five, those men who were so bent upon a deed of destruction, gained the lofty and spacious apartment, to the full so well adapted to their unholy purpose, as Sir Harry Vane's singular second had described it to be.

"Now, gentlemen," said that individual, with alacrity, as he placed the lantern he carried upon a marble chimney-piece, one of which was at each end of the apartment ; "now, gentlemen, we will proceed to business."

He took from his pocket six or eight small pieces of wax candle, and, arranging some of them in a row upon one of the chimney-pieces, he lit them, after which he performed the same operation at the other end of the room."

When that saloon, for such it was, was thus lit up, so that all its extent could be well seen, it showed the remains of great beauty of decoration, although now in the most sadly dilapidated state.

"These candles," said the Major, "will last one hour, and if that won't suffice gentlemen, to allow you to settle your difficulties, you must do it in the dark."

"It will suffice," said Sir Harry Vane, whose anger appeared to be as fully as strong now as it had been originally.

"Very well," said the Colonel, "Sir Anthony's friend and I can retire into this bay window, and there settle the preliminaries of what is to be done."

This they did, while the principals kept far apart from each other, nor attempted to interchange a word.

In a few moments the Major walked up to Sir Anthony Wyvill, and said,—

"It is proposed that, if you make an apology, and pay the two thousand five hundred pounds, this affair should go no further."

"You know it is a mere farce to bring me such a proposition."

"I told him so; but, I believe, it is offered more as a matter of form than anything else."

He then went back to the Colonel, and signified the formal refusal of such conditions, so that there was nothing to impede the carrying out the whole affair, as had originally been intended. It was decided that, without reference to the size of the room, the combatants should stand one at each extremity of it; that the signal to fire should be "one, two, three," uttered by Major Greathead, the word "fire" by the Colonel.

Each party was to load his own pistol, and thus all the arrangements were completed, which were to place, certainly, one of the most valuable of lives, in the person of Sir Anthony Wyvill, against one of the most worthless, in that of his opponent.

Men scarcely think under these circumstances; the excitement of the moment, prevents anything like a rational exercise of the mental powers.

Perchance, as was the case with Sir Anthony Wyvill, the imagination will dwell vividly for an instant upon the remembrance of some one dear and well-loved object, feeling at that moment how inadequate is the cause that is producing the danger of an eternal separation; but, if such thoughts do obtrude themselves, they are quickly chased away by the necessity of immediate action.

For a moment Sir Anthony Wyvill wandered in imagination back to his own once-happy and ancestral home. He could see, so vividly was the picture presented to him by memory, as plainly as though it were before him, that one apartment, with its pleasant aspect, that had been sanctified by becoming the choice of her whom he believed he should never again look upon in life.

Major Greathead marked the abstracted glance, and he saw that the thoughts of Sir Anthony were far away.

He touched him lightly upon the arm, and the baronet started, as if suddenly awakened from a dream.

It said something for even such a man as Major Greathead, that, at that moment, he, either from some really latent horrible feeling, or from the excitement of the moment, gave Sir Anthony the best advice he could.

"Fire low! you don't seem to know what you are about; confound the wine, it has unnerved you!"

Sir Anthony Wyvill seemed about to say something, perchance it was a message of affectionate regret, but if so, the unfitness of the messenger to deliver it must have struck him, for he abstained from speaking, and took his place, confronting his antagonist in peace.

"Gentlemen, are you ready?" said the Major.

"Ready!" said both, and so closely together did they speak, that it sounded but as one voice; there was then a slight pause, during which not the faintest sound came upon their ears. Those four men, for all the indications of the proximity of anything human which met their ears, might have been thousands of miles in some wilderness, untrodden save by their own footsteps.

"One!" said the Major.

Before he could utter another word, although his lips had parted to speak, a crash of glass in the lower part of the mansion fell upon their ears.

Involuntarily, they each assumed an attitude of anxious listening, but all was still again.

"Go on! go on!" cried Sir Harry Vane; "if it be an intruder, he is too late to make us pause; although not too late to reap the consequences of his own folly."

"Two!" said the Major, and then, as if he expected some interruption, he paused, and listened attentively; they all clearly heard a footstep in the house, and after that the slamming of a door, which awakened numberless echoes throughout the empty rooms and lofty staircases.

"We are betrayed!" cried Sir Harry Vane, "some one has dogged our footsteps. Give the word, Major! Let us fire! I have other weapons about me that will soon rid us of a spy!"

"Three!" said the Major; then at that moment it became the Colonel's duty to pronounce the word "fire," a shrieking voice called aloud:

"Sir Anthony! Sir Anthony! do you not know me?"

"Fire!" cried Colonel Mason.

Sir Anthony Wyvill had made a rush to the door, and Sir Harry Vane alone discharged his pistol. With a deep groan, Sir Anthony fell to the floor, and a gush of blood proclaimed the fact that he was seriously wounded.

"Let every one take care of himself," said the Colonel, and opening a side door leading from the apartment, which the others had not noticed, he made a precipitate exit.

Sir Harry and the Major paused a moment, irresolutely; and, then they dashed after him just as the wax candles, which he had reckoned would last an hour, with the exception of one, and that was just expiring, all went out.

CHAPTER XXIII.

THE WOUNDED MAN.—THE MYSTERIOUS ARRIVAL.

That the opponent of Sir Anthony Wyvill, as well as the two very doubtful characters who had acted as seconds, should desert a wounded man, under such circumstances, is more a matter of reprehension than surprise, when we consider the general conduct of those parties; and that such a course was just the one they were likely to pursue.

If they thought at all upon the subject, it was probably to tell themselve that they left a dead man behind them, or one who soon would be, for, if any great effusion of blood ensued from his wound, and he became insensible in consequence, he would probably, from want of the commonest assistance, perish.

In that case, they had certainly nothing to do but to keep each other's counsel, and then they were safe, and this they were likely enough to feel the necessity of doing, inasmuch as the same tale would implicate all.

A few moments after they had left the apartment, the last of the colonel's candles expired, and all was darkness; it was evident that Sir Anthony Wyvill had fainted, either from loss of blood, or from the shock which the system had experienced from the wound he had received.

There was not even the slightest sound of breathing, and he might be dead, but that we hope yet better things of him than he has of late performed.

Nearly half an hour must have elapsed before the room-door was gently opened, and a light cautious footstep crossed its threshold, then a soft feminine voice said—

"Was it a dream, or did I really see him? All is darkness, not a sound breaks the stillness of this deserted house. I have wandered from room to room, but can hear nothing—I have called upon him by name, but he answers me not: and yet the presentiment of some fearful evil presses upon my heart. Sir Anthony,

Sir Anthony, surely, surely I could not have been mistaken, and yet there came no answer to my call. What shall I, what can I do?"

This mysterious personage stepped lightly across the floor of the apartment. Had the footsteps swerved but six inches to the left, they would have struck against the body of Sir Anthony; but as it was, Emily, for it was indeed her, felt as if a strange, suffocating vapour was in the room, and became sensible of the fact, after two or three more steps, that she was treading in something liquid, which seemed to be scattered upon the floor.

She shuddered, and yet she scarce knew why, for she could not see by that dim and uncertain light that what she trod in was blood, any more than she could see there was another occupant of that spacious apartment besides herself.

"The sun will soon rise," she said; "even now, no doubt, 'tis faintly illumining the eastern sky. Less than another hour must solve all my fears and doubts, as regards this house. I will creep into the recess of yonder window, and there wait the coming of the daylight. May Heaven protect him whom I thought I traced hither! I surely saw him in one of these apartments, or grief has driven me distracted."

Believing herself secure in her disguise—that disguise, as it had baffled the eyes of a husband, would surely succeed in doing so as regarded indifferent persons—she sat herself down on the old-fashioned window-seat, which still retained some of its ancient covering of Genoa velvet, and there resolved to wait until the coming dawn should enable her to take an accurate survey of the house, and, one way or another, satisfy her hopes and fears.

* * * * * *

While Emily Wyvill is thus waiting, it is proper that we, in order to bring the various parts of our narrative up to the same point, should briefly detail how it was that she who seemed so far distant from such an adventure, should at length come to be present at its hazardous conclusion.

We left her at Sir Anthony Wyvill's hotel struggling between hope and fear as regarded the consequences of the highly romantic and chivalrous position in which she had placed herself.

She had overheard amply sufficient of what had passed between Major Greathead and her husband, to feel convinced of the dangerous supremacy which the Major was acquiring over him.

And it had so happened that the few words which had passed between them had all been such as tended to confirm the story that had been industriously instilled into Emily's ears by the intriguing Margaret.

It was sad, most sad, that this should be the case; and, from the gush of grief which had immediately succeeded, one would be almost led to believe that she really had almost, unknown to herself, entertained some doubt of the correctness of what had been related to her.

But if we may be allowed the expression, there is always as regards the maturer griefs of the human mind, a species of confirmation to be found beyond that evidence which enables us to say, certainly such-and-such a thing has happened.

Thus it must have been with Emily Wyvill. Facts upon facts had been heaped up to convince her of the dreadful conclusion to which Margaret desired she should come, but still to hear it, as she fancied now she had heard it, actually from the lips of Sir Anthony Wyvill himself, was agony, at the moment, past all endurance.

And hence was it that so sudden and so violent an accession of grief had swept across her soul, engulphing for a time in its gigantic progress all the firmness and constancy of purpose which she had fondly believed herself to possess.

It will be remembered that she had allowed Sir Anthony and the Major to leave the hotel without making any effort to follow them—so that, but for an accident, she would have had no clue whatever to their place of destination.

They had been gone about half an hour from the hotel when one of the waiters came to remove the glasses from which they had been drinking the wine that had excited the critical remarks of the Major.

Emily heard the footstep, and hastily brushing away the tears that else would have borne witness to her deep emotion, she prepared to answer as calmly as she could any remark that might be made to her.

She knew that the position she voluntarily assumed, viz., that of attendant upon Sir Anthony Wyvill, placed her in such a position that she had no right to expect otherwise than that the attendant at the hotel should speak to her familiarly.

"Oh, you are here, are you ?" said the waiter. "They say below that you are going to attend upon Sir Anthony Wyvill. Is that so ?"

"It is so."

"Well, you know your own affairs best, but I should say that you would have got on best as a page, now, to some lady. You are just cut out for that with your pretty girl's-looking face and slim figure : you are out of your element altogether by not being a page.""

"I think I shall prefer the service of Sir Anthony."

"Oh, well, I wouldn't advise you out of it, on any account. I am sure I should be very sorry so to do. He's a nice chap, that Major Greathead, for a small tea-party, aint he ?"

"A tea-party !" said Emily. "Does he go to tea-parties ?"

"Come now—don't you pretend to be so jolly green. Does he go to tea-parties ? What an idea ! But you are in the right, my boy, not to speak about your master or his friends, though, as Wyvill is a decent, civil sort of chap in his way, I must say I am sorry to see him pick up with such a scamp as the Major."

"Is he a very bad man ?"

"Bad ? Why, he's a regular out-and-outer ! Bless your heart, he keeps his opera dancer—and I know, between you and me and the decanter, where they are off to now."

Oh, how Emily longed to ask him where. The words of the question were upon her lips, but she forbore to utter them. "No, no," she said, "I will not—I dare not—I will not ask him one question about my husband."

Perhaps it was this very seeming want of curiosity upon the subject that induced the waiter to become so communicative, but certain it is that, after a pause, he said :—

"Well, you seem a pretty decent kind of lad, and not a fellow with too long a tongue, so I'll tell you where they are off to—I heard the Major say it—they are off to Jimvert's."

"Where is that ?"

"There you come it again, pretending to be so out-and-out-green, as if you know'd nothing. Come, I say, no doubt you've been in London before, I'll be bound, and know what a hell is."

"I have indeed heard," said Emily, "that the gaming-houses with which this great city is infested are so named."

"Ah, there you have it, that's where they're gone. It's in Bury-street, St. James's, not much to look at from the outside, but an out-and-out place in, they tell me. However, I don't know one way or the other—you have it as cheap as I do. I heard the Major say that there was some good company expected to-night at Jimvert's, and that's what makes me know—beyond that I know nothing—but I hear the bell below, so I must cut, none of your nonsense, you know—no peaching—to where the governor's gone."

"No, no, depend upon me."

"Yes, I will—damn it, there's that bell again. I say, my little chap, now that I am here, what's it all about ? Did your governor cut away with somebody else's wife ? or did somebody cut off with his ? I'll be hanged if I can make head or tail of it. Now and then he comes out with a regular growl of some sort or another—what is it ?"

"I can tell you nothing," said Emily; "do not ask me."

Another violent ringing at the bell prevented the waiter from staying to make any remonstrances upon the subject, so that the agonising inquiry was spared to Emily, although it gave her a notion that she might be persecuted upon a subject which, of all others, was the one which she wished least to speak upon.

Now that she was alone she paced the room in silence for a time, and then she spoke with much bitterness of anguish in her tones :—

"A gaming house," she said, "and that is the way he spends his leisure. He whom I thought the greatest and best of all men—oh, what frightful madness

is this that has come over him ! How has he changed from what he was when he became the god of my idolatry—when I loved him for every noble feeling that I saw and knew his mind was full of—when he was to me a creature apart from the rest of human nature, full of glorious impulses, and free from those stains of envy, avarice, and selfishness which beset the ordinary run of mortals.

She sunk into a seat overpowered by the excess of her emotion, and then, as the night darkened around her, and all the loneliness of her situation presented itself in its worst colours, she asked herself what she had yet done, or attempted to do, owards the alleviation of the condition in which she was placed?

No. 20.

"What have I attempted yet?" she said. "I have done nothing but pass the ordeal of his critical examination. I have passed that in safety; and, therefore, am I free to act. Shall I hesitate at least to make an effort to rescue him from one of the frightfullest vices that ever could have spread its snares for his destruction—a vice which is the parent of all vices, inasmuch as it destroys the whole mental fabric?"

The moment this idea had suggested itself to her she felt much of her despondency vanish. Hers was one of those spirits that rise with the occasion—if there be anything to do or anything to suffer, they become equal to the requisition, but listlessness and apathy is destruction.

"Yes," she exclaimed, "I will go, and without disclosing my real character, without giving him the least hint, for that would be giving him a full disclosure of who and what I am. I will endeavour to fulfil that which I have promised, namely, to do him good service. The best that I can now do him is to implore him by all that he holds dear and sacred, never again to set his foot within that house whither he is bound to-night."

With this resolution Emily hastily quitted the hotel, and by dint of inquiry soon found her way to Bury-street, St. James's, where the house was situated, which was then one of the most notorious places for high play in the metropolis.

It is more than probable that in the state of excitement in which she was, and having made a determination to use all the simple eloquence she was mistress of in order to dissuade Sir Anthony from the prosecution of such an evil course, she would have disclosed who she really was.

A most happy consummation would that have been; but, like the fabled Tantalus, the refreshing cup of happiness seemed ever and anon to be at the lips of Emily Wyvill, but to be dashed away again by some untoward event that plunged her once more into the realms of conjecture and despair.

Had she encountered at that moment Sir Anthony, one hour of explanation would have defeated every scheme to their mutual detriment which the prolific brain of Margaret Wyvill ever planned.

And this is the risk that the scheming and intriguing always run: their greatest enemy is the simple, unadorned truth; they know not a moment when in all its majesty it may appear, chasing away the mists of dissimulation and deceit, even as the glorious sunshine unfolds the mystic and mysterious curtain of night, to show to the eyes of those who have been watching its advance all the beauties of earth, air, and water, which for a time have been but objects of chaotic confusion, wanting unity and design.

In the simplicity of her mind Emily thought nothing could be more easy than to go into the house and speak to Sir Anthony Wyvill; but when she tapped at the door she was quite surprised to find only a little oval hole opened into one of the panels of it, at which a portion of a man's face appeared, and a gruff voice said,—

"Who's the king now?"

"What?" said Emily.

"Cuss you!" said the man, and slammed the wicket close again.

Then, and not till then, she became aware that some private signal was required from the frequenters of such places, and that, not being in possession of it, she might in vain seek to obtain an entrance by fair means, and foul ones she was far from being in a position to use, nor would they have answered her purpose if she had.

What was she to do? Her first thought was that she would be exposed to much insult in the public streets, for she quite forgot at the moment her male disguise, which, if it had no other effect, would at least protect her from rudeness.

"I will wait for him," she said, "if it be for many hours ere he come out—I will wait for him! He shall find me here faithfully watching his return, and then I will speak to him, and conjure him never again to visit such a place. I will tell him that I have heard of him in the country, where once he lived happy and respected, and—and—perchance I may move him. Some trifle will oft turn the whole current of thought, and, oh! if I could hear him utter but one word of regret—if he would but tell me he lamented that which he had done—all might be happy yet!"

Elated with this idea, Emily paced to and fro, for more than an hour, before the gaming-house; but although she saw parties enter and come out, there was no Sir Anthony Wyvill, and what with the torture of supposing that he might possibly, have gone somewhere else, or that he was so immersed in the fascination of play that he would not come out for many an hour, she was truly miserable.

At length weary, faint, and exhausted, she sat down upon the door-step of that superb mansion of crime. She did not weep, for she feared, as well as hoped, each moment to have need of all her courage, but the agony of her mind was none the less that it found not the relief of tears.

Unconsciously she had assumed an attitude of deep distress; her hands covered her face, and it is more than likely that the deep-drawn sighs that came from her overburthened heart were occasionally audible to the chance passengers who passed that way.

She was suddenly aroused by feeling something cold touch her hand; she started and looked up. A gentlemanly looking man tendered her a shilling, but when she removed her hands from before her face, and stood up, he seemed to see that her appearance was not indicative of the species of distress he had supposed she was suffering from.

"I beg your pardon, my lad," he said, " I judged only from your attitude, and have offended you, I fear, from a good motive."

"No, sir," said Emily, " I should be worse than harsh, worse than ungrateful to one who meant a kindness, were I to feel offended at such generous sympathy."

The stranger merely bowed and passed on, but he slackened his pace, and in a few moments returned.

"My lad," he said, "I know it's very foolish of me, and unworldly to speak to a stranger in this kind of way, but you were certainly in mental distress, if you are not suffering from that species of evil which made the bounty I offered you acceptable. Look at me, and think if you can trust me. I might aid you."

"And can you, sir, make such an offer to an utter stranger?

" Why, I like your countenance: I own that I have made a mistake or two in my physiognomical deductions, but they have not altogether discouraged me. I like your ingenuous countenance, and will befriend you, if I can."

" I dare not think or speak now; tell me where I can communicate with you, and if I should want a friend, I will believe that in you I have found one whom I can really and truly trust."

The stranger took a case from his pocket and handed one of the cards which it contained to Emily: she read upon it the name of the Honorable George Hargrave, Inner Temple.

Emily placed the card in her bosom, considering it one of the most fortunate circumstances that could happen to her that, at all events, there was some one to whom she could turn, who certainly, from no selfish motives, inasmuch as none could exist under the circumstances, had offered to befriend her.

And this little episode gave her courage to wait another hour or two without repining, until at length she began seriously to suspect that Sir Anthony Wyvill could not be in the house, and she resolved in her mind some means of ascertaining that fact.

The more she thought, however, the greater difficulty she experienced in devising any plan that was likely to succeed in producing that result. Patience seemed to be the only ingredient necessary in the affair, and she resolved to wait until the evening's light should break in upon her, until she gave up the generous task.

Scarcely had she brought her mind to this conclusion when the door of the gaming-house was flung open, and she heard several angry voices from within, and a trampling of feet indicative of some tumult going on.

Terrified, she drew back, and cowered under a neighbouring door-way, when four or five struggling men descended the steps of the gaming-house, leaving three upon the pavement, while the rest again entered the mansion.

She glanced upon these three men for a moment, and then a quick throbbing at the heart, and an increased colour upon her cheek, was sufficiently conclusive of the fact that she had recognised Sir Anthony.

Now indeed was she recompensed for the constancy of purpose with which she had waited—now she felt that she had exerted an amount of patience which, under other circumstances, would always give her great hope.

With difficulty she prevented herself from springing forward and clinging to him, and, perhaps, had it not been for the presence of the two others, in one of whom she was not slow to recognise Major Greathead, although who the other could be baffled her judgment, she might have made some such demonstration.

But soon she became completely absorbed in the contemplation of the violent gestures used by the party, and became convinced that some quarrel was on the *tapis* which, perhaps, Heaven had been good enough to her to make her the instrument of averting the fearful consequences of.

She feared to approach near enough to overhear exactly what was said, but after a time she saw them walk off at a quick rate, and it was necessary for her to exert her utmost speed in order to keep up to the pace with which they travelled.

They seemed not to have the remotest suspicion of being followed by any one, so that she had no difficulty whatever in dogging their footsteps, and, in all probability, so immersed were they in the consideration of their own affairs, that she might have approached quite closely without recognition.

But now, what grieved her most of all, and gave her an exquisite pang of anguish, was to see that Sir Anthony Wyvill was evidently unsteady in his movements, which, we know, was the effect of the drugged wine which he had been compelled to swallow.

Our readers may judge of what a shock it was to such an one as Emily, to find, or fancy she found, that the lowest of vices now were becoming familiar to him whom she had, in her partial imagination, endowed with the highest of virtues.

But still she would not be deterred from those pious exertions which she was resolved should terminate only with her life. Let us hope that she will prove a glorious example of what earnest and true affection is capable of achieving.

The distance that she had to go on foot was far indeed to one who, like Emily Wyvill was unused to toil. She felt severely the fatigues consequent upon the exertions she had to make, and were it not for the indomitable, unconquerable spirit which carried her onwards, she must have sunk before reaching that green lane, of which we have given a brief description.

Up to that point and to some short distance beyond it, Emily had not the least suspicion of what was about to ensue. She could have no thought or idea upon the subject; there was nothing whatever to lead her mind to the fact that anything hostile was intended. If she had thought so, her agony would have been excessive, and probably she would not so easily have permitted Sir Anthony Wyvill and his companions to leave her at the door of the deserted mansion, without the means of herself entering it.

She had watched all the proceedings of breaking open the door in the garden wall, and she fancied that after the party had gone through she should herself be able to make good an entrance by the same channel.

In this, however, she was disappointed, for so judiciously had Colonel Mason applied the small crow-bar he carried, that he had only broken the lock of the door, without injuring it itself, and when the party had got inside he shot a bolt into its socket, which made the door as effectual a barrier as ever against such feeble efforts as Emily Wyvill could direct against it.

Now that Sir Anthony had disappeared from before her eyes, the most alarming apprehensions as to the object which had taken him to that place, arose in her imagination, and more heedless than she had ever been, as to the consequences of a discovery, she looked about distractedly for some means of following him.

With hasty footsteps she traversed the whole length of the garden wall, and finding that it turned at right angles into the open fields, she clambered over a fence and followed it until she came to a huge fir-tree, the spreading and luxuriant branches of which were only controlled in one direction by the wall itself, while many of them stretched forward into the garden of the mansion.

This to her was an opportunity not to be lost : all unused, as we may well suppose she was, to such athletic pastimes, her fears lent her strength, and she clambered from branch to branch of the tree, until her head was above the level of the wall.

It was well at such a moment that she occupied a secure position, both as regarded her feet and hands, for from the place which she had now attained, she could see clearly into the mansion, and everything that was being acted in the large saloon, we have before mentioned, was open to her gaze.

Now she could not mistake for a moment the object of the visit ; the sight of the pistols, which were in the hands of Colonel Mason, was amply sufficient. She was completely riveted by astonishment and terror to the spot where she had taken up her position ; it appeared as if she were doomed to be the spectator of a circumstance in every respect calculated to excite her warmest sympathy, and to call into action all the most distressful feelings of her heart. The glare of light in the large saloon looked greater to her gazing at it from without than it did to those who were actually in the apartment, and she could easily perceive the minutest action of the four persons, one of whom she was so deeply interested in. And so utterly helpless was she, so entirely without the means of stopping or impeding the contest which was about to ensue, that she looked upon the whole affair as some dreadful fatality that had brought her to that spot, giving her the power of observation, but depriving her of the power of action.

She observed, by the energetic movements of the parties, that the preliminaries of the combat were being arranged, and how was she to interpose effectually at the distance which she was situated from the room? Were she to raise her voice to its utmost extent it would be very doubtful if it would reach the ears of those for whom it was intended, and even admitting that they did hear it, would it be understood as a warning, and would it be sufficient to deter them from their purpose ?

A sort of mist seemed to come over the eyes of the affrighted Emily, and she feared for a moment she was about to faint, in which case her fall from the tree, into which she had clambered, would be certain, and probably productive of serious injury.

A powerful mental effort will not unfrequently overcome bodily weakness, and such an effort was at that moment made by Emily Wyvill : the feeling of faintness passed away, and once again she was able to see clearly what was going on in the large saloon, where the combatants were stationed.

Then a sudden thought struck her, that by the aid of the tree she might possibly get into the garden of the mansion, which she saw stretched before her ; it was a most perilous feat for her to perform, but yet, under the circumstances, peril was forgotten, and she dared to attempt that which, at another time, she would have shrunk from a contemplation of.

She was compelled, in the suit of the perilous adventure, to turn her eyes from a contemplation of the house, and to fix her whole attention upon her own movements. Clinging to the boughs of the tree which were above head, she continued to make a slow but steady progress towards the top of the wall, and it was fortunate for her that she had a firm grasp of a wide-spreading bough, that was sufficiently strong to support her.

This bough projected a considerable distance into the garden of the mansion, and had it been placed there purposely to assist Emily Wyvill in her enterprise, it could not have done so more efficiently. She found that as she proceeded her slight weight was sufficient to give the bough a downward inclination; she had but therefore to continue clinging to it, and making a forward movement, to be let down as easily and carefully into the gardens as if she had been placed in the midst by some superhuman power.

She let go the branch, which sprung upwards, released from the weight tha had been appended to it, and dropped lightly upon the ground beneath.

This proceeding of Emily Wyvill's was executed in far less time than it has taken us to describe it, probably not more than two minutes elapsed from the time when first this scheme of effecting an entrance to the gardens crossed her mind and its execution.

She knew and felt that each moment must be precious, and scarcely giving herself time to recover from what to her had been a great physical exertion, she rushed, in as direct a line as she could, towards the mansion.

A few moments sufficed for her to reach some of its windows, but not noticing the raised steps which led to the terrace, she made several fruitless efforts to obtain an entrance through some of the lower windows.

Rendered then almost frantic by delay, the consequences of which, for aught she knew, might be fatal, she defended her hands as well as she could from any fragments of glass, by wrapping a handkerchief around them, and then boldly dashed in one of the panes of glass.

This was the sound which had disturbed the duellists at so critical a moment as we have recorded in our last chapter.

She was now enabled to undo the fastenings of the window: it readily then yielded to her, and in another instant she was beneath the same roof as Sir Anthony Wyvill.

Some strong presentiment, that she was now too late, came across her, and as she had nothing to gain from concealment she called upon his name in her natural voice, as she made her way rapidly up the first staircase that presented itself to her, with the hope that it would conduct her to the large apartment which she had seen from her station in the tree.

"Sir Anthony!" she called aloud, "Sir Anthony, pause a moment, do you not know my voice? It is Emily who calls to you."

Nothing was easier than to get bewildered amid the intricacies of such a house as tha . Had Emily Wyvill, instead of turning to the left, turned to the right, when she reached the top of the staircase, she would at once have found her way to the saloon ; but, unhappily, this was not the case, and she entered the first suite of apartments, which occupied an entire wing of the mansion, and every one of which carried her further away from the spot she sought.

It was when she paused to ask herself if she should persevere or not in the course she was pursuing that the discharge of Sir Harry Vane's pistol smote her ears. That was a dreadful sound to her, inasmuch as it had brought to her mind a full conviction ; but notwithstanding all the exertions she had made—exertions almost incredible for so fragile a being—she was too late to effect any beneficial result.

For a moment she stood like one transformed to stone. Had that pistol-shot sealed her own doom the shock could not have fallen with a heavier blow upon her own heart ; but this apathetic state was not to continue ; she emerged from it with a cry of anguish, such as probably never before had awakened the echoes of that deserted mansion, and then she commenced a wild and desperate search from room to room, with the hope of discovering the spot which might have been fatal to him, for whose preservation she had already gone through so much peril.

Along she thus wandered up and down staircases, and from one apartment to another, without discovering the object of her search; she knew not, but absolute fatigue compelled her to pause in a small room which was quite at the other end of the mansion, and a considerable distance from the apartment she sought.

It would seem as if this room had been inhabited while the rest of the house had been deserted and allowed to go to decay; for, by the dim reflected light that came from the night clouds, Emily could perceive that in it there were several bulky articles of furniture, and finding by the touch that she came across a massive arm-chair, she gladly availed herself of its ample accommodation, and sunk into it overpowered by fatigue and mental disquietude.

"Where is he?" she asked herself; "where can he be hidden, that it seems beyond my power to find him. Surely I have visited every room in this mansion twice over, and in none of them is he. Was that sight which my eyes beheld from the tree a delusion of the senses, or a reality which still eludes me? What a cruel destiny is mine! each effort that I make appears but to cast me still further from the object of my dearest regards."

A strange and profound stillness now reigned within the house, and such, too, was the unusual calmness of the night, that not a leaf stirred upon a tree to remind the attentive ear of the world and all its mult'farious existences.

Emily was far from being superstitious, but at such an hour and in such a place, after all that had happened to agitate her, it cannot be a matter of surprise that unknown fears should creep across her mind.

Her imagination became preternaturally active, and she was painfully and intently listening for sounds—sounds there were none. She became much too nervous and anxious to remain where she was, and she rose from the chair which had afforded her a resting place for a while, determined again to pursue her search throughout the mansion, with the hope of discovering a room answering to the appearance of the one which she had seen from the tree.

She had gained the door of the apartment when, happening to cast her eyes upon the window, she saw some darker object than the mere night clouds without between her and the sky.

She felt the blood retreat with a frightful gush to her heart, for the appearance that met her eyes chimed in but too well with imaginative fears that had so recently possessed her.

A moment's attentive examination convinced her that the dark object she saw at the window was some one carefully attempting by that means to effect an entrance into the house.

Be it whom it might who thus stealthily was approaching, Emily felt that she dreaded the encounter; slowly she glided from the room, and, closing the door, she felt about it for some means of confining the intruder within that small apartment, which she had herself previously ascertained had but one outlet. To her great joy her hand struck upon a key which was in the lock; to turn it was the work of a moment, and then, feeling that she had interposed an obstacle to any immediate pursuit of her, she fled with precipitation along an extensive corridor from which that room opened.

She then paused, and determined to be more systematic in her search throughout the mansion than she had previously been.

There was sufficient faint light to enable her to perceive that many doors opened from each side of the corridor, while at its further end its immense window, which looked towards the east, let in those rays of faint reflected light which herald in the coming day.

Emily, therefore, proceeded to search these rooms, the one after the other, in regular order; not that there was light sufficient in any one of them to enable her to see what its contents might be, but still she felt certain that when she came to so large an apartment as that in which she had seen Sir Anthony Wyvill and his three companions, she could not mistake it.

From her station in the tree she had counted five windows along the extent of that apartment, and as those, at all events, would be visible, although faintly, she continued her search with confident expectation.

Every door to the left of the corridor she found led into apartments each much too small for the object of her search; but it was a great mortification to her, when she endeavoured to go through the same process to her right, to find the first three doors she attempted to open were fast.

It was a matter of no small surprise likewise to her that she could feel no lock or other mode of fastening; and then the idea came across her that these seeming doors were but pannels in the wall, made to represent them for the sake of uniformity in the corridor.

This was almost a convincing proof that she had attained the object of her search; for what could so extensive a wall be but the back of the apartment she so much longed to visit?

By pursuing her investigations a little further, she found that although there were three counterfeit doors on one side and three upon the other, that the centre was a reality, and readily yielded to her touch. The five windows were opposite to her, and then she knew that at length she had reached the saloon she saw from the tree.

CHAPTER XXIV.

THE DREADFUL DISCOVERY OF EMILY IN THE OLD MANSION.

SLOWLY but sweetly came the morn, stealing gently over all objects, and lending, even to the meanest things in nature, a beauty of aspect which really belonged not to them. It fell first upon the tree tops that gentle light coming from the radiant east, and it glanced upon the roofs of the tallest houses, plating them with an appearance of silver; and then, as the glorious orb rose higher and higher in the sky, its rays fell upon the lowliest and humblest cottages, making them look as rich and full of beauty as any proud man's mansion.

And what a world of life was called into existence as those slant rays of the rising sun fell so sweetly upon house, tree, and river!

Myriads of insects shook off the sleep of night to live again in all that abandonment of joy which those strange existences seem to feel from the mere fact that they live!

Birds were awakened likewise from the depths of their leafy coverts, and commenced the busy joys of the day with many a gladsome strain of thrilling and exquisite melody.

The only living thing that awoke to pain and to misery was man himself, the arrogated lord of all this great creation, and those few inferior animals which he has made subservient to his uses and his purposes.

And then, in at the windows of the deserted house, in which a scene so nearly approaching to one of murder had been enacted, there crept light enough to render the various objects visible. Then, and not till then, did a shriek of dismay and horror awaken every echo within the place; and that shriek proclaimed the fact that Emily Wyvill had discovered that, during those long and weary hours, she had been but a few paces separated from what appeared to be her murdered husband.

She forgot, at that awful moment, all necessity of disguise, and all the determination she had made to keep inviolate the secret of who she really was; but, flinging herself by the side of what appeared to be that mangled, blood-stained corse, she cried aloud, with shrieking vehemence,—

"Wyvill, Wyvill, my husband, father of my child, it is your Emily speaks to you! Oh, if there be one spark of life remaining, if there be yet clinging round your heart the warmth of existence, let it reanimate you to her, if it be but one word, that I may know you hear me—when I tell you that as I hope myself for forgiveness in the world which is to come, I forgive and forget all that has passed and live but to be your own faithful and attached Emily. Speak, oh speak! to me, or if that may not be—if envious death has already triumphed over the power of utterance, give me but one glance, or make some gesture that I may understand and feel that you know what I am saying."

We can record the words she thus spoke, but we cannot hope to transfer to paper the frenzied agony with which she uttered them. Vain would it be for us to attempt to depict in language the heart-rending sighs, the broken, half inarticulate voice, and ever and anon the wild exclamatory tone which she used; all this, we say, would be in vain, and we can only ask the reader to imagine for himself a being so oppressed by deep affliction, so agonized by a sight sufficient to stop the very current of her life-blood, that she scarcely knows what frenzied words issued from her lips.

"And is there no response? Can no answer no sign, even be returned for all thi appeal, resulting as it did from the purest and holiest affection that ever graced the heart of a human being ?''

Alas ! no, all was still. Sir Anthony Wyvill had either really, in consequence of the wound he had received, passed through the portals of death, or, such had been the war waged against his life, lapsed into a state of complete insensibility —an insensibility which prevented him from hearing those words uttered by a well-known voice, and from recognizing in the speaker the being whom, of all others, he would most gladly have fixed his eyes upon.

And how strongly in his ears would he have heard them, could those words have sounded that spoke to him of forgiveness, when he thought that he had much to forgive, and that far more appropriately from his lips would have come a declaration that he would forget the past.

No. 21.

But he was in no position to reason upon anything : a temporary oblivion was upon his spirit; the world to him was as nothing ; and, except that his soul only slumbered, and had not actually left its earthly tabernacle, he seemed to have bidden adieu to all the cares and to all the joys of existence.

With clasped hands and a face expressive of that unutterable kind of anguish which no mortal language ever yet found words sufficiently expressive to depict, she knelt gazing upon the face—that face which, each moment, more and more distinct as the light of day increased, she conceived to be dead.

" God of Heaven," she said, " and is this the end of the short but most eventful tragedy of his existence? Is it possible that the bold, brave, generous spirit that once animated this form, has thus taken its departure after such a world of care had been thrown upon my anxious spirit, and all in vain? Oh ! why did I ever love and believe in the fond delusion that I was so surrounded by the majesty of that passion that the evils of existence could as little touch me as could a summer's hail-storm touch the warrior clothed in complete steel? Oh ! sad delusion, that I should have imagined for one moment that I had built my happiness upon so sure a foundation that nothing could topple down the structure Imagination had reared upon such a basis ! "

All the agony of despair took possession of her, and for several moments her attitude proclaimed the most intense grief, until finally crouching down with her head resting in her hands, tears gushed from her eyes, and for many minutes the faint echoes of her deep sobs disturbed the stillness of that lonely place.

But those were blessed tears, inasmuch as they relieved her mind of much of its oppression. As they flowed the fever of her brain seemed to subside, and she was able to think a little more calmly upon the present, while she felt with greater keenness the necessity of making some exertion for the future.

Then, likewise, came the thought that there was just a possibility her husband might not be dead, and even as that idea came across her, she placed her cheek close to the pale lips, with the hope of catching some indication of continued existence.

She thought she felt a slight warmth, as if a faint breath yet lingered around the lips, and when she placed her hand upon his heart, that thought was rendered more positive by the certain evidence of a slight pulsation.

The possibility then, of his recovery became at once the paramount feeling of her mind, and what her duty dictated, which was to procure immediate assistance, she at once commenced carrying into effect.

She rushed rather than walked from the apartment in which she was, and made her way into the garden of the villa : a well-trodden pathway immediately presented itself, and it was one in which she fancied she saw the traces of recent footsteps, so she at once pursued it as the most likely one to lead to the open gate through which she could emerge into the lane.

She was correct in her surmise, and hurrying onward she soon found that she could get clear of the premises without difficulty.

She left the gate swinging violently upon its hinges, and then hastened, with what speed she could exert, to a neighbouring village.

A red lamp, the faint rays from which were most ineffectually struggling with the daylight, proclaimed the residence of some medical practitioner, and she at once rung loudly at the bell which hung by his garden gate.

It did not take Emily many minutes to explain her errand, and, without asking unnecessary questions, the medical man accompanied her at once, for he was an early riser, and already equipped for the open air, towards the secluded villa.

Emily's impatience was so great that it kept her some few paces in advance of the medical man, who thus, if he had been inclined, would have found it a very difficult matter to put many interrogatories to his guide, whom, of course he looked upon as a young lad in a great state of excitement, in consequence of an accident to some one whom he much loved and respected.

They passed on through the garden gate which Emily had left open, and proceeded direct to the apartment where Sir Anthony Wyvill still lay in that seeming trance of death.

"Here! here!" cried Emily, "this way, sir; here lies the object upon which I pray you to exert your skill, and tell me, as quickly as you can, for my life or death hangs upon the answer—tell me if he lives, and if so, if he will recover?"

"As quickly as I can," said the surgeon, "you shall have all the information that you require."

He knelt down by the side of Sir Anthony Wyvill, and made a careful examination of him. By the aid of a small pocket mirror he ascertained that Sir Anthony Wyvill actually breathed, for, upon its being held close to his lips, the pure surface of the glass became moist.

"He lives unquestionably," said the medical man; "he seems badly wounded, and perhaps I ought not to inquire how it happened."

"It was a duel."

"Indeed! a duel in a house, that is rather .rare ; but, however, if that was the case, the less I know of it the better ; and as regards this wounded gentleman, I can do little for him now, being without assistance, and I should recommend that he be removed instantly, with as much care as possible, to his home."

"Yes, yes," said Emily, "he shall be removed at once, and I will send him. He lives, and that is life to me."

"Are you a relative of his?"

"Yes—no—that is, I am in his service; he is Sir Anthony Wyvill, a gentleman in the army; for the most part resident in the country, but now residing at a house in London."

"I dare say, then, that I know the resources of this place better than you do," said the medical man; "and therefore I recommend that you remain with him, while I go to the village again, and procure some conveyance, so that he may be at once taken to his hotel, where I will accompany him, if you please; and in London, any further assistance that is required in his case, can be readily obtained."

Emily was most thankful for this arrangement, and expressed herself so, in a few hurried accents, as the surgeon immediately left for the purpose of carrying his suggestions into execution.

Once more then she was alone with that object of all her dearest cares and fondest anxieties—once more she looked into his face with eyes of tearful tenderness ; and when we recollect that, through the machinations of Margaret Wyvill, Emily believed herself to be injured most vitally, and all her best and dearest hopes crushed by the very person upon whom she now looked with such profound affection, it speaks volumes for the kind and gentle spirit of that most amiable of beings.

While the surgeon was gone, she gave utterance to a brief but earnest prayer for the recovery of her husband—and if ever human aspirations, in the shape of prayer, ascend truly and at once to Heaven, and are received there most graciously, such an unstudied, artless piece of eloquence, as that which flowed from Emily's lips, was certain of such a reception.

A calmer feeling spread itself over her soul, and, after a few moments' pause, she said:

"And who knows but, after all, this very circumstance which I viewed with such feelings of terror and apprehension, and which awakened so many fears in me, may be the indirect means suggested by Heaven for restoring me to happiness! In the long, weary hours that he may now have to pass upon a sick couch, reflection may come to his aid, and his mind will revert back with a sense of deep regret that it ever became weaned from such thoughts, to his early affection. Then at some moment, when I see that his thoughts and feelings have taken such a turn, I will tell him who and what I am; I will tell him that I forgive all ; and will tell him that I am content to blot out from my memory, for the future, all that has passed of a nature so fruitful of grief and of harrowing reflection : who shall say that we may not be happy yet?"

These were blissful reveries indeed, and such as tended materially to enable Emily to recover from the first shock she had received when she became cognizant of the fact of her husband's wounded condition. These thoughts, likewise, tended to withdraw her mind from the feelings of impatience with which she otherwise would have regarded the necessary delay caused by the surgeon having to make arrangements in the village, in order to procure a conveyance for Sir Anthony Wyvill; so that she heard the sound of his footsteps coming again towards the apartment, before she began to think it likely he could have completed his arrangements.

" I have provided a carriage," he said, " and can at once proceed to town with Sir Anthony Wyvill. I am afraid you are too much agitated and anxious to assist me in his removal; I have therefore brought a man with me who can do so more efficiently."

Emily felt that she was but badly supporting her male disguise, by a confession of so much weakness and feminine sensibility; but at the same time, she could not help admitting that she was incapable of being of active assistance in the removal of Sir Anthony.

The surgeon and his assistant succeeded, however, extremely well without her, and Sir Anthony Wyvill, still in a state of perfect insensibility, was placed in a carriage, the driver of which had orders to proceed gently to town, so as to shake the wounded man as little as possible; for if the surgeon apprehended any danger at all, it was in producing more loss of blood from the wound which Sir Anthony had received.

Emily sat by the side of her husband and watched his countenance with the closest attention. She started suddenly, as the surgeon said to her—

" It is very probable that the slight motion of the carriage and the fresh air blowing upon his face, may recover him before we reach town, in which case, as he knows your voice, pray caution him at once against making any exertion or speaking too loud, for such may be attended with great danger."

" I will do so."

" Nothing but extreme quiet in these cases can afford the surgeon any chance of saving the patient's life."

It seemed almost as if the words of the surgeon were prophetic, for scarcely had he done speaking, when, with a deep sigh, Sir Anthony Wyvill opened his eyes and looked in the anxious face of Emily, who was bending over him.

There was silence for a few moments, for he was too weak and confused to speak, and her heart was too full to allow her to utter a word. At length, by an effort, he gathered strength, in low tones, to make himself heard, and he said faintly—

" What has happened—is it a dream ?"

" Hush !" she said, " hush ! you have been wounded, and your safety, nay, your very life, depends upon the repose of both mind and body. Be still, for the sake of others who still love you, if you would abandon so much caution for your own sake."

" Who speaks?" he said. " The tones are familiar to my ears; they remind me of happy days that I shall never see again."

Tears blinded Emily's eyes, and almost choked her utterance, but she contrived to say,—

" Do you not know me ? I am your faithful attendant."

" Oh! yes," he said, " you are the lad sent me by my sister. Now I know you, and a dire recollection of past events, which must have resulted in this my present wounded state, comes across me."

" Beg of him," said the surgeon, " to be still. Not knowing the precise nature of his wound as yet, I am not prepared to say how much danger he may incur from conversation."

" I hear," said Sir Anthony Wyvill, " I will be still."

Scarcely any more words of conversation passed between them ere they reached London, and, to the surprise of the people of the hotel, Sir Anthony Wyvill was carried in and immediately put to bed.

The surgeon despatched a note to one of the most eminent practitioners in London, who immediately attended, and between them they made a careful examination of the wound, and ascertained that, although it might be dangerous in some of its ulterior results, it was certainly not, as regarded itself, a mortal injury.

The eminent surgeon, who had been sent for, turned to Emily, saying,—

" As you are in the service of Sir Anthony Wyvill, you should acquaint his friends as quickly as possible with his condition, because everything depends upon careful nursing in this case. The surgeon can do very little, and it may be that, with the knowledge of such a fact, some member of his family might be induced to attend upon him."

" He put trust in me," said Emily; " and there is no member of his family who could or would attend him by night and by day as I shall; but if it be necessary, all who are interested in his fate shall be made acquainted with his condition, and, I presume, he is in a state to come to a conclusion upon that head himself."

Sir Anthony Wyvill was asked by the surgeon if it was his wish that he should be attended solely by the lad who was in his service, and he replied, at once and unhesitatingly, that it was so, so that the surgeon was satisfied, and left the case in the hands of the original medical man, who had been called in by Emily, and who had nothing now to do but to watch its progress, and counteract, with the utmost resources of his skill, any impediment which might arise to the perfection of a cure.

CHAPTER XXV.

MARGARET AT WYVILL HALL, AND THE REJECTED SUITOR.

AND now that, although we have placed Sir Anthony Wyvill in a painful position, we have surrounded him with every circumstance that is calculated to rescue him from it, we can afford time to take a brief glance at Margaret Wyvill and her proceedings at Wyvill Hall.

She felt herself the complete and uncontrolled mistress of that place, and the only anxiety that came over her occasionally resulted from the fact that she received no communication whatever from London.

This state of suspense, however, did not last long, but it was suceeded by feelings of still greater anxiety.

The communication she received was not from either of the parties she wanted to receive it. Instead of being from Emily, or from the boy whom she had appointed to keep such careful watch and ward over Sir Anthony Wyvill, it was from no other personage than Miss Todd.

This young lady, as may be well supposed, was extremely anxious, in addressing a personage of Margaret Wyvill's presumed distinction, to do so in the most fashionable manner, and having read in some silly novel of high life, as it is called, that, in writing a letter, it was fashionable to leave out sometimes articles and prepositions, she did so with a vengeance.

As her letter was rather on that account a literary curiosity, we transcribe it for the benefit of all concerned, and especially those who think it fashionable, to be silly and mighty genteel, to betray a lamentable and deplorable ignorance of their native language.

The letter ran as follows :—

" DEAR MADAM,—Have done myself the honour of writing—hope—you quite well—as we are present—have strange news—to tell—partly connected with self, partly with lady—and child—recommended by you. Am sorry to say—both disappointed—unexpectedly tea time—and think—some arose from jealousy—of expected attentions of certain Baronet—wish to know if you have any acquaintance —with young nobleman—named Viscount Assafetida—.

" No more at present—have slight head-ache—and remain—

" Yours, very truly,
" JULIA TODD."

Julia considered that this letter was the very height of aristocratic gentilit[y] and she only deeply regretted, after she had sent it off, that she had not, by the a[id] of a French dictionary, interlarded it with some foreign phrases, which she cou[ld] easily have done, and then it would have been a most perfect production.

"I shall have another opportunity, however," she thought, "and then I['ll] take care that the most part of it shall be French and Italian. She will write m[e] an answer, because she will at once presume by my note what a thorough[ly] fashionable person I must be. I should not at all wonder that she knows t[he] Viscount, and can tell me all about him, although, I must confess, I cannot fir[d] his name in Mr. What-do-you-call-'em's Peerage."

The only fact which Margaret Wyvill discovered from this letter, that mad[e] the slightest impression upon her, was that connected with the departure, so sudde[n] and unexpected, of Emily Wyvill from the house of the Todds.

It gave her a severe pang of alarm, and when she came to consider likewise th[at] a considerable time had elapsed, during which she had heard nothing from h[er] young *protegé*, whom she had directed to write to her immediately upon h[er] arrival in London, her uneasiness increased to a great height, and she debate[d] within herself whether or not she should proceed to the metropolis, and inqui[re] personally into the aspect of affairs.

How could she enjoy that which she had endeavoured through so much iniquit[y] to gain possession of, while all these uncertainties were passing upon her mind ?

She could not sleep, or if she did, agitating and frightful dreams disturbed he[r] continual apprehensions haunted her by day, and she felt as if she held thos[e] possessions she had done so much to obtain by the frailest possible tenure, and th[at] she could not know a moment when they might be wrested from her, leaving he[r] completely stranded and covered with odium and contempt.

We may well imagine, then, how such a woman, thus tortured, bore th[e] solicitations and troublesome addresses of such a man as Mr. Adolphus Dacr[e] who, notwithstanding she had given him a formal dismissal, still clung to the hop[e] of inducing her to alter her determination.

He called at the Hall with a pertinacity that drove her almost distracted ; and [at] length she determined to terrify him, if he were susceptible of that feeling, fro[m] attempting to continue his troublesome addresses.

She had passed a couple of hours of extreme restlessness, and was debating i[n] her own mind the propriety of going to London or not, when Mr. Dacre was agai[n] announced, and it required all Margaret's self-command to enable her to control [a] burst of passion at the very mention of his name.

She ordered him, however, to be admitted, for she felt that at that moment [it] was something to have somebody upon whom she could wreak her vengeance, s[o] that when he was admitted she at once commenced upon him in such a furiou[s] strain that he was amazed and terrified.

"Mr. Dacre," she said, "you need not utter one word, for I know what yo[u] come about. There was a time when I thought it the wisest thing a woman coul[d] do, who had ample means of her own, was to marry a fool, because, by bein[g] married, she was placed in such a position in society that she became now important I say, I once thought that, Mr. Dacre, and therefore I singled you out; but I hav[e] altered my mind now, so there is the door."

"The deuce !" said Mr. Dacre, "you don't mean that?"

"I trust I have spoken sufficiently plain, and for the future I shall order m[y] servants to repulse you from the door-step, and for myself, I formally forbid yo[u] setting foot upon my domain."

"Very good," said Mr. Dacre, "I wonder you aint afraid that I'll find out Si[r] Anthony Wyvill and tell him all I know."

"Tell him what?" shrieked Margaret, "I thought you knew nothing?"

"I don't know that. By-the-by, that's a very good joke; and as for not knowin[g] anything, it strikes me very forcibly that after all the row that has taken plac[e] between Sir Anthony Wyvill and his wife, there aint much fault on either side[."]

Now, if I were to go and tell him that Mrs. Wyvill left home just on account of that lady that I saw at the hotel at Portsmouth—"

" You would get kicked again for your pains."

" Well, certainly, he did give me a dreadful kick, and I never could make out what it was for. There was the lady standing by the window, and she said to me in the most natural sort of way in the world, ' Charming weather, sir ;' and I, in my gallant sort of way, with a sort of bow—you know how I can do those kind of things—replied to her, ' Charming ladies—' and then, before I could say another word, Sir Anthony Wyvill gave me that dreadful kick that nearly sent me out of the window."

" If I have heard you tell that anecdote once," said Margaret, passionately, " I have heard it at least one hundred times. Will you leave this house at once, or must I be under the necessity of ordering my servants to turn you out ?"

" Oh, I'll go; I don't care, since you won't have me. There is Miss Grove will be very glad, and perhaps I may come across Sir Anthony Wyvill, and if I do I will tell him a bit of my mind."

" Listen to me, sir, before you leave here : if you attempt in the slightest manner to interfere with me, I have both the means and inclination to heap on you a most severe revenge—a revenge which you little dream of, but which will make you rather wish that you had put your head into a blazing fire than interfered with me."

" Good gracious !" said Mr. Dacre, " what an idea ! I think I see me putting my head into a fire ! A likely thing that I should do so ; I aint quite such a fool as that. Good bye to you, Miss Margaret Wyvill ; I don't intend to trouble you any more, and mind you, this is the last time I will pay you a visit."

Assuming, then, what he considered a very dignified air, Mr. Adolphus Dacre left the place.

Although Margaret in her heart despised this man to a most unprecedented extent, yet, knowing what she had done, she could not look with indifference even upon his threat.

It took her some time to console herself, which she at length did, with the reflection that in all probability by this time Sir Anthony Wyvill had left England for the continent, and consequently, a meeting between him and Mr. Dacre was next to an impossibility.

" I am foolish," she said, " to disturb myself about such a circumstance as the paltry threat of such a man. He can do nothing ; and his mean, cowardly spirit is such that he will attempt nothing ; so I will calm myself, and be at ease as regards him ; but there are other subjects that are of deep importance to me, and which do require careful consideration."

She was silent for a time, and it seemed that during that time the probability of some disastrous circumstances occurring had crossed her mind, for when she spoke again, she said,—

" Well, well, let the worst come to the worst ! I have made up my mind that nothing shall stay me in the career that I have commenced. I have made up my mind thoroughly and entirely that if it be necessary to take a life, and if that life be Sir Anthony Wyvill's, it shall be taken : the Fosters will be the ready tool of any scheme I may find it necessary to undertake, and let that scheme be as dark or as sanguinary as it may, it will but suit them the better, for well I know if there be a house in all England where murder has been committed, that house is the Dyke-house, and the Fosters are the criminals !"

With these observations, Margaret retired from the apartment where she had been sitting, to that more private one which we have before noticed as being one in which she usually locked herself while concocting her most infamous schemes and projects.

Then she felt that, free from interruption, she could resume her wicked plans and schemes, for she had given strict orders to the whole household that, on no pretence or account whatever, was she ever to be disturbed while in this sanctuary.

Then, after a time, she determined that she would not take so precipitate a step as to go to London, until she had something positive instead of negative to induce her to imagine that affairs had gone amiss with her plans and projects.

"After all," she said, "there may be many circumstances that may have induced Emily Wyvill to leave the Todds, and as for my correspondent, the boy, I had my fears from the very first that he was not greatly to be depended upon."

Thus it was that she endeavoured to get over circumstances that really gave her much uneasiness; and, notwithstanding all the delusive arguments by which she sought to make them of no account, they still lay rankling at the bottom of her heart, and at times caused her the most excruciating pangs, lest the fears that suggested themselves should be but too well founded.

Feeling now that more important matters than ever the mental disturbance which Margaret Wyvill is enduring call upon us for attention, we will proceed to the metropolis again, and shortly to the bed-side of Sir Anthony Wyvill; but, before we do so, let us look at a strange scene which is taking place in that house, where, in her capacity of attendant upon Sir Anthony Wyvill, Emily had taken the letter containing money to the captain's widow.

The easy circumstances in which this lady was placed by the munificent generosity of Sir Anthony, will account for the many luxuries with which we find her surrounded. She is seated in an apartment replete with every luxury that can charm the imagination. Pictures of great merit adorn the walls—the rich carpeting yields like snow-flakes to the slightest pressure—and everything in and about the apartment is of the most costly character.

There is but one drawback to the general glitter and apparent joyousness of the scene—that drawback is to be found in the person of the occupant of the magnificent chamber. She is seated at a table, and a book is open before her, but she does not read. She has tried to do so, but her thoughts have travelled away from the page which lies before her to widely different channels.

She sees nothing of the beauty by which she is surrounded: the costly hangings take rich folds in vain for her—the exquisite paintings, so life-like that they seemed to be transcripts of human nature, entirely failed to attract her attention. She is absorbed in her own thoughts, and knows nothing, heeds nothing of surrounding objects.

That those thoughts are of a painful character, and such as produce a great mental struggle, it is not difficult to perceive, for at times her countenance flushes with colour, and then again every particle of life-blood seems to desert it, leaving it so pale and wan that she looks more like a statue than a living being.

Her lips moved as if she would speak, but for a long time she uttered no sound, because she dreads that the first words she must utter will involve a mental confession humiliating to herself, and such as she, with her pure feelings and innocence of heart, may well shrink from.

Our readers will imagine probably for themselves that in this female they see the captain's widow, who most unhappily was forced by the machinations of Margaret Wyvill to play so important a part in the plot which drove Emily from her home.

At length she speaks, and for the first time she utters to herself a truth which her heart has confessed for many a day.

"I cannot, I dare not shrink from the avowal," she said. "It is necessary that I should make it for my own peace and for my own guidance, as well as for the peace and guidance of others. I love him! yes, I love him!"

It was with a half shriek she pronounced these words; and the moment she had done so, although she was alone, a crimson flush of shame suffused her cheeks, and she covered her face with her hands and trembled perceptibly.

But after a time she seemed to take better courage, and again she spoke.

"Where," she said, "is the shame in loving excellence and virtue? I love him because he is that which makes it impossible that my love can ever assume a criminal aspect. It is because I know that he is the soul of honour, and because I feel that he has behaved to me with a delicacy and a kind condescension, I might in vain, in my unprotected state, have hoped for from ordinary men, that I love Sir Anthony Wyvill; and now, because I do love him, I must fly from him. Yes! I must fly while I have the firmness so to do, and before I have so familiarised myself with the idea of loving him, that it shall lose part of its sinfulness, and no longer seem to establish a necessity for our separation."

She remained then in sad reflection for more than an hour, only at times uttering faintly disjointed portions of her thoughts. But at length she came to a fixed determination, and that she gave free utterance to.

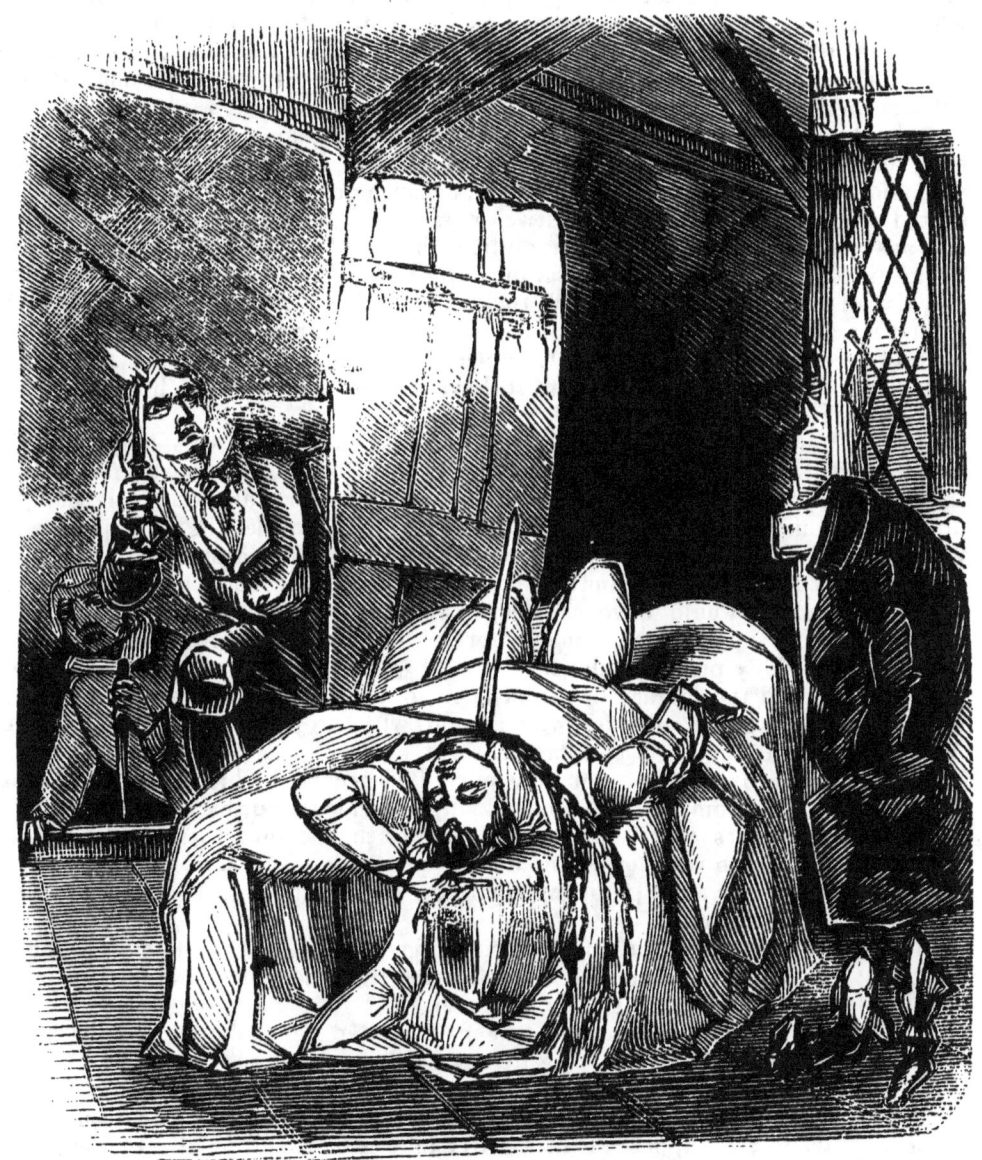

"He seems," she said, "to have abandoned his intention of leaving England, or he would have done so before. Now, I must ascertain from him if such be still his intention or not; if it be, I can keep the secret of my heart while he remains, but if it be not, I must beg of him, in the abundance of his generosity, to allow me to retire to some other land without asking me the reason why I prefer the request."

No. 22.

And now came the anxious question in her mind whether she should see him or write to him. Over and over again she told herself that the former course had many advantages over the latter ; but as often as she had made up her mind to it she trembled and drew back again, full of fear that she should not have courage to conduct such an interview ; so she resolved upon writing to him a letter, which, after many expressions of grateful feeling for all the kindness and protection she had received at his hands, contained the following paragraph :—

" And now, Sir Anthony, after telling you how much I consider myself your debtor already, it will sound strange that I have another request to make of you, which, perchance, you may disapprove of, but which still I must urge again and again until you grant it to me. That request is that, in the first place, you will much reduce the amount you have hitherto given to me for my subsistence, and that you will not think me unkind or ungrateful if, with apparent caprice, I take that sum to a considerable distance off, so far, indeed, that you and I may never meet again. And now, that I have propounded my principal request, I have another boon to ask of you, and that, perchance, you will smile at, because you will say it is what a woman should always ask in common charity as regards her actions. It is, that you will not ask me the reason of my resolution, but will suffer me to carry it out unquestioned, as though I were infallible, and what I determined must be right."

This was the only paragraph in the letter which we need transcribe to the reader, inasmuch as those who have followed us thus far in our narrative must be well aware of what feelings of gratitude actuated the captain's widow, and from a knowledge of her character they must have a fair perception of how she would express such feelings.

She felt much relieved in her heart after she had written this letter, and she was impatient, until she had sent it on its destination ; but when she felt assured that the act was irrevocable, and that it was done past all recal, she had the proud consciousness that she had done her duty, and that, let the consequences be what they might, principle had most completely conquered passion.

Alas! how few can say as much—how very few, under such circumstances as she was placed in, would have shrunk as she shrunk from the very shadow of dishonour? Let us give abundance of praise to the pure spirit that, knowing it stood upon a giddy precipice, down which all was guilty joy and a region of love and romance, had the courage to shrink back to the more sterile regions of colder virtue, and to take the only step which could with propriety be taken to rescue herself from the trammels of temptation.

Little did she dream that a circumstance had occurred which, in lieu of separating her for ever from Sir Anthony Wyvill, was calculated, by awakening all her tenderest sensibilities, to draw still closer the ties that bound them. She did not tell her messenger to wait for an answer to the epistle, because it was not a mere question and answer affair ; but we shall see how that messenger fared in the prosecution of his errand.

He was a boy, something of the young tiger class, and as knowing and as impudent as any man would be, except when he knew he dare not assume a familiar tone, and then he was quite the reverse.

" Well, old fellow," he said, to the first waiter he came near at the hotel ; " well old fellow, what do you bring it in now ?"

" I'll bring it in," said the waiter, " a good box on your ears if you don't be off."

" Will you though? I should like to see you This is a rum sort of house to bring a letter to ; I suppose I had better take it back and let the gentleman go without it."

" Then why didn't you say you had a letter at once? Who is it for ?"

" Let me see—Sir Anthony Wyvill, Bart., &c. &c. I say, old red nose, Bart. is a rum name, aint it ?"

" You young scoundrel, you know as well as I do that Bart. means a M.P. and a Barrownight, and as for the &c. it means that he is very likely to be somut else one of these days, but they don't know what exactly."

" Lor!" said the boy, " you will burst some of these days with all that larning ;

I suppose it was worked into you with some engine, you couldn't have come by it in a natural way."

The waiter was so angry, that, had it not been for the sudden appearance of the landlord of the hotel, who, upon hearing an altercation, came out to see what occasioned it, he would have made some assault upon his juvenile adversary, whom he was no match for in wit whatever he might have been in a fistic argument.

" What do you want, my lad ?" said the landlord.

" I have got a letter," said the boy, " for Sir Anthony Wyvill."

" You can leave it, if you like ; but there can't be any answer to it, and you had better go and tell whoever sent it by you that Sir Anthony Wyvill has been nearly killed, and is lying just now in a very doubtful state as to whether he will recover or not."

" And what am I to do?" said the boy. " I suppose I must leave it."

" There is a young lad here," said the landlord, " who attends upon Sir Anthony, and who can take it or not, as he likes; I will call him down, if you please, to see him."

This arrangement was assented to, and resulted in Emily being called down to receive the note. For a few moments when she reached the hall she looked confused, for she had been weeping in the sick chamber and had scarcely heard the message given to her by the waiter.

" Now, spooney," said the boy, " can't you open your eyes a little wider, and not stand winking and blinking there like an owl in a fit ?"

" What is it—what is it ?" said Emily.

" What is it ? why, it is a letter for your master, to be sure. You are a regular muff, I can see ; I wouldn't give you nothing a week and let you find yourself."

" A letter," said Emily ; " from whom ? Alas ! Sir Anthony Wyvill can read no letters."

" Can't he?" said the boy, mimicking the aspect and voice of Emily. " I'm blowed if it aint enough to make him ill to have such a fellow as you about him."

" Thank you," said Emily ; " he shall have the letter as soon as he is capable of reading it."

" What !" cried the boy, " won't nothing aggravate you ? Just come outside, and I'll polish you off in a minute."

If Emily had considered for a month, she could not have adopted a more intensely aggravating course than that which she quite innocently pursued to the boy, by walking up stairs with the letter in her hand, and not making the least reply.

The fact is, her mind was so intensely occupied upon other matters, that all his insolence and all his defiance, although extremely amusing to the waiters, was quite thrown away upon her ; for what she did hear of it, she really did not appropriate to herself in the least.

" Well," said the boy, " of all the cool chaps that ever I met with, that's the coolest. I'll have it out with him, if ever I meet with him in the street. Only let him come to our house on a message, and I'll soon cook his goose. Curse his assurance !"

The boy walked away in a state of extreme indignation, while Emily went back again to the bed-room of Sir Anthony Wyvill, quite unconscious that in a few short moments she had made an enemy.

She sat down at a table on which a dim light burnt, for it was getting towards evening, and the shutters of the bed-chamber were partially closed, in order to exclude as much as possible the noise of passing urchins. She laid the letter before her, and looked at it attentively ; then she said, in a low voice,—

" Yes, it is from her. This letter is from my great enemy, who, as yet, doubtless knows not what has taken place. Its contents are most likely those of joy and hilaritye ; perchance it breathes those words of tenderness and affection he has so often heard from my lips, and declared his unwillingness to hear those of another. Lie there, then, thou chronicler of passion—thou shall be sacred from my eyes, and it shall be my triumph to deliver thee into his hands myself. Hush! he moves."

"Some drink," said Sir Anthony Wyvill, in a low voice.

With a noiseless step Emily approached a side-table, and, taking from it a drinking vessel, she held it to Sir Anthony's lips, saying, in the disguised tones which she had adopted from the first, —

"Is your wound easier, sir?"

"Not much, my boy," he said, faintly. "I cannot expect it; but when I do recover, be assured that your affection and your devotion shall meet their full reward."

Emily's hand trembled so, that she could scarcely set down the cup, and she murmured to herself,—

"Shall my affection and devotion meet with their full reward?"

"What say you, boy?" asked Sir Anthony.

"I only said, sir, that I would endeavour to do my duty."

"You do more than your duty, Robert. Your mere duty would have been done with a hundredth part of the kindness I have had from you."

"I have watched you when you thought that I was sleeping."

"Watched me, sir."

"Yes, Robert, and not the most skilful actor that ever trod life's stage could have assumed an appearance of so much devoted interest, if he felt it not."

"Still, sir, I say it is my duty; and do I not owe all to you?"

"You owe me a little, but I owe you much, and I say again, Robert, on my honour and my faith in Heaven, your affection and devotion to me shall have their full reward."

Emily clasped her hands as she said fervently,—

"Thank Heaven! Those are blessed words, sir; I pray to Heaven that the day will come when I shall keep you to your word."

"It shall come, Robert, for, even if I die——"

"No, no," she cried—"no, no—recal that word—it is too terrible to think of—you will live, you must live! Heaven in its goodness will preserve a life upon which——"

She paused, and, after a few moments, Sir Anthony spoke, saying,—

"I do not know, Robert, how I have so won your heart. My sister Margaret certainly told me that you would do me good service, but she did not and could not, tell me that I should receive from you the affection you have lavished upon me. I cannot pay you, Robert—I would not insult you by offering you money as wages for such services as you render to me. No, you must be my friend."

"You are too weak, sir, to continue speaking thus. A letter has come for you, sir."

"I cannot read it; open it, Robert, yourself, and send what answer to it you think fit."

He turned his face away, and composed himself to sleep.

"No," said Emily, "no, I could answer any letter but that. It shall remain with its seal unbroken. I cannot, will not, dare not open it; but I will brood over those words that he has uttered, and live upon the remembrance of them, trusting in Heaven that the day will come when my affection and devotion will indeed have their full reward; and surely that reward must consist in the happiness of him whom I love as well as myself. Oh! what a blessed thought it was that induced me thus to place myself with him. If I were not here now that he is suffering, what agony would be mine, and what frantic measures I might resort to, to place myself in a position which I have now obtained without an effort!"

She carefully placed the shade of the lamp, so that none of the bright rays disturbed the sleeper; and then she sat down, with a feeling of greater happiness at her heart than she had experienced for a long time, and fell into a reverie, in which she pictured to herself a future full of happiness and joy.

* * * * * * *

The captain's widow waited impatiently for the return of her messenger, not hat she expected an answer to her epistle, but she wanted to feel assured, by being told of the fact, that Sir Anthony Wyvill had received it.

She had ordered the boy to come to her on his return ; but, as that return was protracted, in consequence of several adventures he met with on the road, her patience was nearly exhausted before he came to her.

" Well," she said, " you delivered the letter ?"

" Certainly, ma'am."

" And you saw Sir Anthony ?"

" No, ma'am, I didn't see the gentleman, because something has happened to him, and he is just upon dead. So you see, ma'am——oh! my eye, if she hasn't fainted—here's a jolly spree !"

The moment she heard the tidings which the boy uttered, the sudden shock was so great, that she had just time to totter to a seat, into which she sunk insensible.

" Ah !" said the boy, as he put his hands into his pockets, and looked on as coolly as possible, " this is what I calls a rummy go. Let me see. I suppose I ought to ring the bell like vengeance. I'm blest if ever I had hold of a bell-rope before, but now I have, I shan't let it go again in a hurry."

By standing ingeniously in the middle of the hearth-rug, he got hold of the bell-ropes, one in each hand, and executed such a peal upon the bell, that the whole house was speedily alarmed ; but, before anybody could come into the room, one of the bell-ropes came away in his hand, and, fearful of the consequences of that feat, he crept under the sofa with it, and there remained concealed from observation, just as, with a wild sort of rush, all the servants in the house came into the apartment.

CHAPTER XXVI.

THE STRANGE MEETING AT THE HOTEL.

WHEN the servants made their way into the apartment, from whence a bell had been rung so violently, that circumstance was sufficiently explained by finding the officer's widow in the state we have described her ; although, how she had rung the bell, and then got to the other end of the room, they could not very well conceive.

Neither was it quite clear what had become of one of the bell-ropes, which, if we may be allowed the expression, was sure to be missing.

However, all other considerations were for some minutes merged in the one of recovering the officer's widow, who, in a few minutes, showed signs of returning animation.

As soon as she was sufficiently recovered to recollect what it was that had produced such a shock upon her, she cried, with frantic eagerness,—

" I must go out at once—let me go—do not surround me—I must leave instantly—give me a shawl or cloak—anything, so that I am permitted to leave at once."

Everybody dissented from this proposition, declaring that she had not strength to do any such thing, and that she ought not to think of it ; while several pretty palpably hinted that they would have no objection at all to know what it was that had caused her to faint.

Finding herself, then, unequal to the task of insisting upon leaving the house at once, she consented to be assisted to her chamber ; but fully resolving in her own mind that she would seize the first opportunity, when she was alone, to equip herself for the streets, and make her way to Sir Anthony Wyvill's hotel.

Only one of the servants accompanied her to her room, for she was quite capable of walking, while the rest remained in the apartment she had left.

" Well." said one, as she sat herself down on the sofa, " I should certainly like very much to know what it was she fainted away about."

" Ah," said another, " there is no saying, and you won't get it out of her neither. You heard how she wanted to go out, and that, do you know, convinces me."

" Of what—of what ?" cried everybody.

" Why, it convinces me that there is some new man in the case."

" Indeed, indeed—you don't say so ?"

" Yes, I do; and I mean to say this too, that I have no patience with people fainting and kicking up disturbances, pretending to have such fine feelings—I say I have no patience with them—now, for my part, let what will happen—Gracious Providence, what is that ?"

The boy under the sofa gave a hideous howl, which half-a-dozen cats, with their tails in a hand-vice, could not have equalled, and then he held her who was sitting upon the sofa tight by the ankle, whilst everybody else ran away as fast as they could.

" I'm the devil," he said, and then the lady fainted, and he thought it high time to decamp, so as, if possible, to conceal his share in the transaction ; and if he kept his secret well, there could be very little doubt that from that time forthwith a strong belief that the devil was actually under that sofa on the occasion in question would prevail in that establishment.

And it did so, to the great detriment of it and the grievous terror of all servants who took service there from time time, and from whom the secret was always religiously kept until they fairly took possession of their places, when they were duly informed that the devil occasionally made that house his head-quarters.

* * * * * * * *

To describe the state of anguish which she who has already made to us such a confession of her affection for Sir Anthony Wyvill was thrown by the intelligence that was brought to her of some serious accident having befallen him, would be impossible. Suffice it to say, she waited in her chamber, enduring the most excruciating agony of suspense, until she had gathered strength sufficient to leave the house.

" Away with all scruples now," she said ; " I will be firm in the rectitude of a good purpose, and, in defiance of all a venomous world may say or do, I will obey the dictates of gratitude and ordinary compassion."

She hastily threw on apparel fitting for the street.

" When I," she said, " was alone and in distress, and deprived by death of him who had been my only protector, Sir Anthony Wyvill did not stop to think what the world would say before he took me by the hand and succoured and consoled me. Shall I, then, desert him now that he is alone, and that death, perhaps, is hovering round his couch ?

" She has left him who ought now to be a ministering angel in his affliction, and so far as tender solicitude and careful watching can supply a wife's place, I will supply hers to him. No stranger shall watch by his bedside, no hireling shall view with indifference those duties that affection alone should perform."

Of course, except by advice, no one had the remotest right to interpose any obstacle to her proceedings, and if she left the house quietly and secretly, it was rather that she wished to avoid the assertion of a right in the face of friendly remonstrances, than that she doubted her ability to do so.

She gained the street, and intending to take advantage of the first hackney carriage she met, she hurried forward in the direction of the hotel, in order, at all events, to lose no time in reaching it.

The distance was short, and, as it turned out, she had to walk the whole of it, and her impatience forced her to walk quickly, so that, when she reached the door of the hotel, she was exhausted, and presented all the appearance of a person in a state of extreme excitement.

She paused a moment on the steps, in order to nerve herself before she should ask for Sir Anthony Wyvill, and then she ascended the steps, and entered the hall of the building.

Oh, with what dread it was that she answered a question that was politely put to her as to her business there ! For a few moments she could not answer it at all, and when she did, the effort to pronounce the name of Sir Anthony Wyvill was so great that she was scarcely equal to it.

" I have come," she said, " to see Sir Anthony Wyvill."

" Are you aware, madam, that he is dangerously ill?"

" I am," she gasped, " I am !"

" I don't know, madam, if he be sleeping or waking."

" It matters little, show me his chamber—I have come to wait upon him therefore I may take my place at once."

" Oh, I beg your pardon ; I was not aware, I thought that the young lad was to attend him."

" To attend the sick is a woman's office, and I have come to fulfil it."

" Certainly, madam; I will show you the way—this way, if you please. If you will follow me, I will take you to his room door."

" Stay yet a moment, and pardon the trouble I am giving you. Can you tell me how he got the hurt ?"

" Why they do say, madam, that it was a duel."

" Gracious Heaven ! now I can guess it all."

The most natural supposition in the world occurred to her, and that was, that Sir Anthony Wyvill had protracted his stay in London for the express purpose of finding out who it was that had weaned his wife's affection from him, and that, having made that discovery, it was in a conflict with that individual that he had fallen.

The reader will perceive what a tremendous entanglement of mistakes and cross purposes had arisen from the vicious planning and plotting of only one individual. It is singular indeed to perceive how these persons were placed in the most strange and awkward relative positions towards each other.

There was Sir Anthony himself mourning with the bitterest feelings the dereliction of duty on the part of Emily ; and there was Emily herself acting in the most heroic and admirable manner from a similar mistake, while she regarded the officer's widow in a light as contrary to the real one as midnight can be to midday.

And all these entanglements were produced by the bad passions of one individual ; but we sincerely hope that that one now stands upon a precipice, the frail edge of which will soon give way beneath her feet, and hurl her to the destruction she so richly merits.

But to return from this digression. The next question which was asked the man of the hotel was an anxious one.

" Do the medical advisers of Sir Anthony Wyvill give hopes of his recovery ?"

" Oh ! yes, madam ; they say he will get well if nothing unusual occurs, and he be kept quiet."

" Thank Heaven for that much!"

She now ascended the stairs with almost a joyful feeling, for her first great apprehension—namely, that Sir Anthony had received his death-wound—had passed away, and when the chamber-door was opened for her, and she glided in, hoping rather that he was sleeping than waking, because, in the former case, she would have more time to collect her scattered thoughts, and to prepare herself for what she should say to him when he should open his eyes, and observe the fact of her presence.

By the dim light that was in the apartment this visitor, whose heart was so full of kindness and of virtue, could not perceive that there was any one in the room watching by the bedside of him who received certainly at the time the best attendance that could be given to him.

She did not perceive the darkly-clothed form of Emily, who was seated close to one of the curtains, and partially hidden by its heavy folds. But Emily saw her, and, with mingled feelings of surprise and indignation, waited her advance into that chamber which she considered so sacred.

The visitor clasped her hands, and stood for a few moments a pace or two within the threshold, as if then her strength had deserted her, and she had lost the power to proceed.

" And is he thus deserted ?" she said—" he who fondly believed himself so

much beloved ?   Alas ! alas ! he now lies beneath a stranger's roof, dependen
upon those who love him not, for that gentle service which only affection ca
render.   Oh ! that it should be so with one so brave, so great, and good !   Surel
envious fate might have surely permit him evils of some less agonizing natur
to test his firmness."

She advanced a few paces farther in the apartment, and then, overcome b
contending emotions, she sank into a seat, and remained for some moments i
silence, gazing towards the bed, where she could see the dim outline of the forn
of him whom she believed to be the victim of another's passion and another'
destitution of principle.

" Woe, woe," she said, " be to her who has wrought all this evil!   Woe be t
her; and although I would not deny the exercise of Heaven's mercy even to her
yet there should be, and there must be, a day of retribution for the guilty hear
that has done so much evil."

" Yes," said Emily, suddenly stepping forward, for she could bear this scen
no longer, " yes, there will come a day of retribution."

The captain's widow gave a faint cry of surprise ; but Emily waved her arr
authoritatively, as she said—

" Hush ! he sleeps, and his sleeping is of more consequence than the awakenin
of the guiltiest heart that ever beat in a human bosom to a consciousness of it
own deep iniquities."

They looked at each other then for some moments in silence, and then th
widow spoke, saying—

" I thought that he was alone."

" Yes," said Emily, " and you thought likewise that pain, although it mad
him silent, would serve to make him wakeful, and therefore was it that you
hurried words fell from your tongue. Begone, begone ! I say, at once, and n
longer profane this chamber with your presence."

" What is the meaning of this language ?   Profane ! say you ?"

" Yes, and a most horrible profanation it is.   Go, go, at once, if there be on
particle of womanly shame left within you. Begone, I say, and force me not t
raise my voice in defence of the insulted majesty of virtue."

" This language, boy, from you to me, is one of those gross, unwarrantable insult
that cannot be endured. I know not, and cannot guess who urges you on to use you
tongue so freely, but your master, boy, shall know of it, and not the most faithful servic
that a pampered domestic can render should excuse such insult.   Leave this plac
at once ; I will watch by the couch of Sir Anthony Wyvill, and such service as h
may require out of this chamber, or that I think you can execute, I will summor
you to do, but take heed that you be more respectful in your manner."

During the time this speech was being uttered to her, Emily's bosom swellec
with such an amount of indignation that nothing but the stern resolution to contro
any violent exhibition of feeling on Sir Anthony Wyvill's account, could have
given her the power to speak in the low tone of reply which she did.

" Woman !" she said, " disgrace to your sex !   The effrontery which produce:
your presence here, and the world of hypocrisy which has enabled you to utter
the words that have fallen from your lips, are clear and transparent.   Remove the
delusion from your mind that you are speaking to one who does not know you
My term of service with Sir Anthony Wyvill has not been so short but that I know
all that has occurred of late to him ; I know all he has lost, and all that he might
have retained to himself, if some better adviser than the mere passion of the
moment had been at hand.   After this declaration of mine, even you might shrink
from looking me in the face, or remaining another moment in this chamber."

" Good Heavens !" replied the officer's widow, " are you mad, or what strange
misconstruction is it that you labour under ?   I cannot say that I misunderstand
the implication that can be drawn from your words, but yet, to me, they can have
no signification.   Tell me who has urged thee on thus to insult me ; or are you so
cunning in evil for your years, and have such a knowledge of iniquity that you
suspect its existence where it has no home ?"

" I suspect nothing," said Emily ; " but I know much that I would have given my very life never to have known. Again, I say, begone, while I have judgment sufficient to repress a rising indignation that may exceed the bounds of prudence, and force me to brand you with terms of infamy I would fain spare myself the pain of uttering, although you well deserve the pang of hearing them."

" I will not begone ; I came here on a great and sacred errand. The unworthy wife of Sir Anthony Wyvill might be addressed as you addressed me."

" Unworthy wife ! Do I dream, or is it possible there can be a human being possessed of such unparalleled effrontery as this ? Unworthy wife !"

" Perhaps I ought not to have uttered the words ; but you say that you know all, and if you do know all you know that I need not retract them. Dismiss from your mind, boy, the base suspicions which, perhaps, a knowledge of human nature, acquired of some bad source, may have implanted in you. Leave me to attend upon Sir Anthony Wyvill. I am better fitted for the task than you can be ; but do

N o. 23.

not force me to make to him a formal complaint of insults received from his servant, that it was as much even as I could do for his sake."

"Not for one moment," said Emily—"no, not for one half moment, will I permit you to arrogate to yourself a duty, which of right, and in the purity of innocence, belongs to me. Once more, I say, begone, and do not let this altercation continue until Sir Anthony Wyvill shall have the pain and the agony of witnessing it. Begone now, and carry with you the loathing and abhorrence which a stricken heart——: enough, enough! I cannot condescend to utter more in such a strain; I will strive even to forgive you, but let me implore you to give me a plea for so doing, by at once leaving the chamber."

"This must be the height of insanity. Boy, you know not what you say, and yet you speak like one so full of feeling, and so deeply impressed with the truth of what he utters, that I cannot feel towards you the indignation that otherwise would find a home in my heart. You judge me harshly, but I dare not now leave, lest by so doing I give a colour to transactions, and a plea for increased suspicion, that I shrink from with horror."

"The excuse," said Emily, "is a paltry one: it is such as might and must rise with the ready impulse of the moment to my lips. I cannot, will not endure what I now suffer. Wyvill, Wyvill, awake—awake! now to the consciousness—no, no! what have I done, what have I done? Oh, agony unspeakable! I have aroused him from that health-giving slumber which they told me was life to him, and to disturb which might be death. Sleep on, sleep on; and, let me endure what I may, my voice shall not be raised above the even current of my breath. Have mercy, Heaven, I have awakened him."

It was so indeed; the sound of her voice broke through the trammels of slumber, and opening his eyes he looked about him in amazement, faintly ejaculating,—

"Speak again, speak again! What tones were those that lingered on my ear? speak again! oh, speak again!"

"It was I that spoke," said Emily, and she altered her voice to that assumed one in which she had of late addressed Sir Anthony Wyvill, and which only occasionally brought upon his mind the reminiscences of gentle and affectionate tones he never thought to hear again.

"You," he said, "you, who spoke?"

"Yes, it was I; be calm, I pray you. There is nothing amiss; sleep on, sleep on!"

Turning aside, she wrung her hands, exclaiming,—

"Heaven help me! Heaven help me!"

Then Sir Anthony Wyvills visitor stepped forward gently to the bed-side, and, in weeping tones, she thus addressed him,—

"Sir Anthony, I have heard, and heard with pain and agony, of the sad accident that has befallen you. Do not, I pray you, tell me now to leave you; I have come with a firm and full resolve to attend upon you. Urged by gratitude, I hope to be able to show, in this sad emergency, that the noble, generous kindness you have bestowed upon me has not been cast upon a barren soil, but that being productive, as it ought to be, of an earnest and a deep desire to repay in some measure the heavy debt I owe, it shapes itself into a wish to attend upon you with such sisterly care and true affection as I may bring to bear upon the task."

She paused, for feeling choked her utterance, and as she looked into his pallid face she fancied that it wore the aspect of coming death, and that soon she should have to mourn his departure from a world, the desolation of which to her had only been made endurable by his kindly consolation.

"This is too much," said Sir Anthony Wyvill, "for me to expect or hope; for it is what I ought not to accept, and yet how noble is it of you to offer."

"Nay," she said, "accept it as it is offered frankly, freely, and at once. Let nothing stand in the way of your entire acquiescence in that which I propose. Did you not, when I was sick, friendless, and destitute, and in a foreign land too, step forward to my relief, heeding not the world's opinion, caring nothing of the misconstruction of the dissolute, and with a noble patience, conscious in the rectitude of your own purpose, pursuing a course as honourable as it was great and noble?"

"You think too much of a poor service."

"Am I not the creature of your bounty? Do not, I pray you, do not prevent me from laying to my heart the pleasing delusion that I am paying at least a small portion of the debt of gratitude I owe you."

"Far be it from me," he said faintly, "to repel the dictates of kindness; I have suffered enough already to pause ere I inflict one pang of unrequited feeling upon another."

During this brief dialogue, Emily had staggered to a seat, where, involved in her own painful reflections, she heard nothing of it, but with an agonized heart, and a brain teeming with wild impulses and images, she trembled with emotion.

But now she rose, and tottering forward to the bed she spoke.

"Sir Anthony Wyvill," she said, "have I forsaken or neglected my trust that you must take another to fill my office? Speak to me, oh speak! Bid me begone at once, and then I may seek in the arms of death the refuge that this world denies me."

"Robert," said Sir Anthony, "what means this emotion—you are strangely agitated."

"I am," she cried—"I am. Choose, Sir Anthony, choose between my faithful, unbought service, the service of an affection you cannot know, and do not now comprehend, and that of this woman."

"Robert, you amaze me—I can scarcely speak, for a strange languor creeps across me; but have I shown myself ungrateful for your services?"

"I will answer all and everything, and I will make a revelation to you I thought not to have made for many a day; but ere I speak you must dismiss this person. Bid her go, taking with her your forgiveness for the evil she has done. Bid her likewise hope for the forgiveness of that other one, whom more deeply than you she has injured, and then I will tell you the meaning of my speech."

"Robert, Robert!" said Sir Anthony, "this is a strange kind of frantic jealousy. You know not what you say. Be patient, and if you have aught to communicate that it concerns me to know, speak freely before this lady, who has and is entitled to my utmost confidence."

"It is enough," said Emily, "it is enough—farewell for ever!"

"No, no, Robert, stay; I have not known you long, but my heart clings to you!"

"Say but those words again," she cried, "and bid this person leave you."

"I will say those words as often as you please, Robert; but not saddled with the condition that I inflict pain upon another ——"

"Whom you love."

"Yes, with such love ——"

Emily stayed to hear no more; but with a cry of anguish, which rung painfully in the ears of Sir Anthony Wyvill, she rushed from the apartment, and pausing not for a moment she gained the street.

The night was dark, but she fled onward, she cared not, knew not whither; but ever and anon she clasped her head in her hands, and uttered that same half shriek of mental anguish which had come from her lips at the moment of her leaving the apartment in which Sir Anthony lay.

"Welcome death," she said, "in any shape! I have now lost hope. The shadow of a suspicion that I might be wrong has passed away before the horrible confirmation of his words. He has owned that he loved her. I heard enough, and it would have driven me mad to have remained to hear with what asseveration he confirmed his passion."

CHAPTER XXVII.

THE CONFERENCE IN THE SICK CHAMBER.

WHEN Emily had left so abruptly, and evidently in such a state of terrible and intense excitement, she left Sir Anthony Wyvill and the Captain's widow so bewildered and astonished by the conduct of the seeming boy, that for some minutes they neither of them spoke.

At length Sir Anthony himself broke the silence by saying—

"Can you understand, or can you afford me any clue to the strange conduct of the lad ?"

"I cannot," she said; "but, from the first moment that I saw him, he has treated me with this marked strangeness of manner—a strangeness I cannot comprehend, because the lad is evidently well-informed and educated, and from his manner must have been gently nurtured."

"It would seem so, and up to this time language will not enable me to describe the tenderness with which he has waited upon me, and the devoted affection which I have received from him."

"It must be that he is one of those jealous tempers that cannot share even affectionate duties with any one !"

"Heaven help him if he go through life with such feelings and such passions ! I cannot but think he will return shortly, when more sober judgment resumes her sway in his mind."

"From your tone I can tell you are suffering from much exhaustion. There are a thousand things I wish to speak to you of; but, I pray you, say no more. Rest, and I will watch by your couch."

"I am indeed faint and weak, and this strange conduct of the boy's has agitated me. I will try to sleep ; but should he return awake me, for I love the youth despite his strangeness, for which there yet may be some reason I know not of."

Sir Anthony Wyvill again endeavoured to seek repose, while she, who little thought who it was that she had displaced from his bedside, sat down in the chair vacated by Emily, and watched him as he slept.

She did not for one moment regret the determination she had made to attend on Sir Anthony Wyvill ; but it was with a feeling of exquisite distress that she found that she was thus, at the very moment when she commenced a course of conduct perfectly consistent with the purest and holiest morality, that she found herself subjected to such opinions as had been expressed.

If this lad, she thought, standing as he does almost upon the threshold of life, draws from my purity of purpose such harsh conclusions, what am I to expect from others who have seen still more of the world and its vices, and consequently become more distrustful ? But this shall not deter me from my duty ; I will not be deterred from doing that which is right for fear others may think it bore the aspect of wrong. Heaven and my own conscience will do me justice.

*　　　*　　　*　　　*

It might be that the agitation he had gone through exercised a baneful influence upon the state of the wounded Sir Anthony Wyvill, or perhaps it was the natural consequence of the serious nature of the injury he had received, but certain it is that on the following morning, when the surgeon called, he at once saw that his patient was much worse.

A state of fever had ensued, which was just what the medical man dreaded, and at times Sir Anthony seemed scarcely collected in the answers he gave to the questions that were put to him.

His new nurse was inexpressibly alarmed at this state of things, for she saw at once, from the countenance of the surgeon, what were his feelings and sensations upon the subject, although, of course, in the immediate presence of his patient, he said nothing but what was of a cheering and hopeful character.

But the captain's widow followed him into another apartment; and then, with a deep earnestness, which showed how much she felt on the occasion, she implored him to tell her the truth.

"Is there danger?" she said. "Oh, tell me, if there be danger?"

"There is danger, madam," was the reply; "but we are not to presume because there is danger that a fatal result must ensue. That would be going too far; and it is hardly to be expected, in an affair of this sort, that there should not arise symptoms occasionally attended with very serious dangerous results."

"Then you do not anticipate the worst?"

"Oh, most certainly not; for although his health has, at present, taken an unfavourable turn, and gives certainly room for anxiety, there is nothing from which we can draw a strikingly unfavourable result."

"Thank Heaven for so much comfort as is contained in these words!"

"I presume I have the honour," said the surgeon, "of speaking to Lady Wyvill?"

"No; but you are speaking to one who will attend to Sir Anthony with sisterly affection."

"Oh, his sister," said the surgeon, jumping to a conclusion, which was scarcely warranted by her words—"I am quite sure, madam, then, that he will receive every attention. The great thing is to keep him serene and quiet; and, by so doing, more will be accomplished towards allaying the present unfavourable symptoms than any of our medicines could hope to do."

"Alas! there are those things upon his mind which almost forbid the possibility of great serenity."

"I regret to hear it, but one might suppose so from the circumstances themselves; and when we consider that it is in a duel he has received his hurt."

"It is so, indeed!"

The surgeon promised to call again in about four hours, and during that interval of time, Sir Anthony Wyvill's solicitor made his appearance, and found the wounded baronet only just sufficiently collected to give directions concerning some money matters, so that ample funds should be placed at the disposal of his kind nurse. But before the lawyer departed, he spoke to him seriously, saying,—

"I cannot disguise from myself that the situation I am in is one of extreme peril, and that I may never rise from this bed a living man."

"Oh, Sir Anthony," said the attorney, "you must not think that. I hope to see you about again as well as ever, shortly."

"It may be so; but since it may be otherwise, it behoves me so to arrange my affairs, that, were I to die, justice would be done where I most wish it."

"Well, sir, as a matter of ordinary precaution, let a man be in as good health as he may, I always recommend him to make a will, if he has anything to leave; and I shall of course be happy to take your instructions on that point."

"When first I came to town, I informed you what my painful errand was, and that my great anxiety consisted in making some provision for her who had left me, and to discover my child."

"You did, sir."

"The painful thought presses upon me that the day will come, when. deserted by her seducer, my wife will awaken to all the horrors of conscience and of destitution. My great wish, then, is to save her from the latter, if I cannot from the former. She shall never want in this world."

"I am sure, sir, that is very kind of you, and not what one man in a thousand would do, under such circumstances."

"Never mind, never mind, say nothing to me upon that head. Continue your search for my child, who of course inherits my estates; but draw me up some deed by which £200 per annum, at my death, may be charged upon my property, for my wife's use, always provided it be proved to the trustees that she is living alone, and is otherwise unprovided for."

"I understand, sir, your object is not to keep her in guilty extravagance?"

"No, it is to provide her with the means of repentance of a better mode of life, so that she shall have no earthly excuse for pursuing the frightful career she has commenced. That is my object, and I would wish you would set about it at once."

"Be assured, sir, I will by to-morrow. I will bring you deeds, with blanks for the names of trustees, and you can execute it at once, so that it will be off your mind; and you will have no anxiety upon that score."

"I thank you, I thank you—that will be a great relief."

This conversation, short as it was, seemed much to exhaust Sir Anthony, and after it he dropped into an uneasy slumber—a slumber which was evidently disturbed by many visions; for deep groans came from his labouring chest, and occasionally he muttered incoherent sentences as he flung his arms to and fro in wild disorder.

These were indications of a mind ill at ease not to be mistaken, and the captain's widow would have at once awakened him if she had not received the most positive orders from the medical man not to do so, although, in all probability, those orders would have been at once altered, could he have seen the state of mental agitation into which the patient was thrown.

And during those weary hours she had ample time for reflection; and the tone of her reflections all took a turn towards the mysterious conduct of the youth who had been attending upon Sir Anthony.

The more she reflected upon what the apparent lad had said, the more she began to feel convinced that it must have reference to some foregone conclusion of which she knew nothing.

When once such a mystery as this was awakened in her heart, it was not at all likely she should rid herself of it; and as she sat brooding over it, it assumed to her mind some of its most gloomy shapes and aspects, and she began to suspect that possibly in the minds of others, as well as of the youth, she might be considered guilty of an amount of iniquity that had never entered into her imagination to suppose any one could be capable of.

Bitter tears came from her eyes as she thus reflected, and she did indeed, as well she might, feel it to be a hard case, that because she had the elevation of mind and the necessary virtue to act, as she was acting, she should be subjected to such frightfully cruel misconstructions.

"But this is ever the way," she said. "Guilt may escape part of the consequences of its deep iniquity, but when did virtue ever escape detraction? It is a hard case, but I saw that it was so; that such a man as Sir Anthony Wyvill could not befriend me as he did, in the depth of my distress, without being subjected to a thousand cruel taunts, some of which, although he knew it not, came to my ears; and now, when feeling as I do the weight of gratitude, which impels me forward to tend his sick couch, I in my turn become the subject of detraction, and to the worst of motives are attributed what surely must be the best of feelings.

There are two courses, either of which many persons, in the situation of this feeling and right-minded woman, would have adopted—the one was to yield to circumstances, and earn for herself the reputation which society chose to give her, and the other was to fly at once from the position which entailed the possibility of so much censure.

But she, with a purity of soul, and a high-minded resolution—such as, indeed, are most rarely to be met with—resisted either of these courses, but choosing a third and more exalted alternative, she persevered in the steady performance of her duty, which surely would win the highest applause and approbation of Heaven, although it might meet the censure of the illiberal among mankind.

Thus was it that she placed herself in an exalted position—a position so full of interest, and one so every way calculated to excite admiration, that we claim for it the highest meed of consideration.

It is not our intention, by thus exalting such a character, to detract for one moment from the many excellencies of Emily Wyvill. No—the tenderness and devotion which she has shown, when she thought she had abundant evidence of the deepest injuries having been inflicted upon her, entitle her to as high an eulogium as can be passed upon any living being.

Oh, how happy might those three persons have been—the joy of whose existence seems now so suddenly to be extirpated—were it not for that serpent in the Eden of their felicity, which had contrived for a time to poison all those delights which should have sprung from the extended intercourse of such congenial spirits.

We mourn most truly and acutely to think hat it should thus be in the power of one vicious disposition to crush so many noble ones, and to cast the cloud of despair over so many of the best feelings of human nature.

But surely this will not last, and a brighter sun will yet shine upon the fortunes of those in whom we feel so deep an interest; but most of all do we dread what will become of poor Emily, who left the hotel in such utter abandonment of all hope, and who deserved so much happier a fate than that to which she may be hurrying.

But it becomes necessary now that we turn our attention more closely to the proceedings at the Dyke-house—proceedings which will sufficiently mark the desperate characters of those who inhabit that lonely mansion, while they, at the same time, show what frightful associates Margaret Wyvill scrupled not to make.

CHAPTER XXVIII.

A SCENE OF HORROR AT THE DYKE-HOUSE.

THAT building, which was called the Dyke-house, and which stood in the romantic dell, uniting two valleys, in one of which was situated the estates of the Wyvill family, had been, within the memory of some of the inhabitants of the spot, completely deserted.

The winter storms too, as well as those which in the height of the vernal season produced sometimes havoc and destruction for miles round, had made such assaults upon the old building, that it was considered positively unsafe as a human habitation.

Great was the surprise, then, when the Foster family took possession of it, despite its crazy appearance, and announced their intention of residing there permanently. They mended the rents in the walls, and with great labour and perseverance repaired the roof, giving the old building a much more habitable character, and as, whoever at one time had been the owner of the property, appeared for a long time to have abandoned it, no one had authority, or perhaps inclination, to disturb them.

In a short time they converted the place into a rude house for entertainment of travellers, and although there was a suspicion upon the public mind of the neighbourhood that all was not right, people could scarcely imagine such an amount of depravity as characterised that most atrocious family.

It was considered rather an advantage than otherwise that there was an inhabited house in that mountain pass, where travellers, or such of the inhabitants of the vicinity who happened to have been out on fishing or shooting excursions, might find refuge on the occasion of any of those tremendous storms, to which a mountainous region is peculiarly subjected.

Of course it was soon found that the Fosters were not the most polished people in the world, and then after a time there began to be strange stories concerning people who had entered the mountain pass, at one end or the other of it, with the intention of proceeding to the neighbouring valley, but who had never reached their destination.

These stories, however, were of a very vague nature, and not such as to constitute anything like good grounds of accusation against the Fosters, and as these persons who had disappeared were strangers to the locality, no great disturbance was made about the matter, nor did it seem fair to accuse the Fosters of any crime upon such uncertain evidence.

But we, who have it in our power, from authentic records, to lay bare the system of iniquity pursued at that house, now proceed to do so, in a case, which for its heartless and cold-blooded details will scarcely find a parallel, except it be in that atrocious murder, some of the particulars of which we commenced this work by recording, and the consequences of which have yet to show themselves to be fulfilled, when we still have a hope that retributive justice will be dealt out to that family of murderers.

*　　　*　　　*　　　*　　　*

One evening the sun sank with a strange and a lurid aspect, as a traveller entered the mountain pass, from the valley in which the Wyvill estates were situated. It was a complete gorge, and though not so high as the mountainous elevations around, yet it was high enough to give him a wide range of horizon, broken every here and there, at less or greater distances, by the rugged peaks of some of the hills in the neighbourhood, and were within the ken of his vision, and which, as he was sitting, gave the traveller an extensive range.

Then again, when for a moment his eyes quitted the glories of the sun-set, and the rugged and elevated landscape, he cast a glance upon the prospect below his feet, and there, extending out before him, he beheld one of those

' Welsh vales, 'mid mountains high,'

which gladden the heart of a traveller who has passed over many miles of rugged and uneven paths and roads, and where he had met with but little to interest a traveller, or any one whose chief object consisted at the moment in his desire to meet with some place in which he could repose in safety during the night.

It is difficult at all times, after dark, to obtain lodgings in the country. Solitary alehouses are fearful of admitting a stranger under their roof, lest they be imposed upon, and harbour some character that will punish them, at least for their indiscretion as they would call it.

The traveller looked down upon the valley as its recesses were darkening each moment around, and the shadows of the surrounding hills were growing longer and longer, and more intense in their darkness.

Great was the traveller's relief as he bent his eyes in earnest gaze to ascertain his proximity to some house, where he might hope to obtain food and rest: he could not expect any great deal, but that much he earnestly longed for.

Below him, in a rocky nook, at a considerable elevation, he perceived the white smoke of a solitary cabin or house, in which some civilized human beings resided, at least he hoped so.

There could be none so churlish who would not give that much, where payment was ready for whatever they did, and very few anywhere there who would refuse. The Welsh peasantry are not insensible to the charms of money, and will grant anything in the shape of accommodation they have for travellers' payment.

The valley below was one of great beauty, and even when evening threw a great part of it into shade it was an object of some interest to the traveller.

On either hand the elevated region rose abruptly, and the peaks of hills and mountains were seen in the glowing sun-set in the west, as their dark and rugged points jutted up into the golden light.

As the traveller looked down below he searched among the pastures and corn-fields for the town or hamlet that might be considered the centre of the spot, but he could not well see it.

In the distance he thought he could discern the smoke of some houses, but the darkness below was increasing, and rendered objects uncertain.

"At all events, night will be advanced, and I shall have to wander on or take the shelter of some rocky nook or projection—in either case, it will not be the most pleasing mode of passing the night."

Again he looked towards the wreath of smoke he had once before seen, and then it came up afresh as if new fuel had been heaped upon the moss.

"At least I shall get there within half-an-hour, and if I can obtain but shelter and food I must be satisfied,—the accommodation of richer provinces I must not count upon, for it would be unlooked for here, save once, in distant periods."

The sun now became darkened by a heavy mass of clouds, which suddenly interposed between that luminary and the earth, robbing the traveller of his rays, but gilding itself by the golden light, and at the same time changing them to a deep blood-red hue, deepening occasionally into black.

By degrees this bank of clouds, which at first was broken here and there, and permitted the sun-light to pass through, became darker and darker; at the same time there were evident signs of a storm brewing; the wind had almost ceased, though it was but for a short time; but there were other signs.

The clouds bore not the appearance of a bank of night clouds which sometimes come up as the sun sinks, but had that full, heavy, low appearance that usually denote a sudden and violent storm.

These signs were not lost upon the traveller, who was by no means desirous of passing a night on the rocky road, or even in facing a storm in such a position, which he knew sometimes becomes dangerous from its extreme violence, and at the exposed situation rendered it liable to be swept by the strong and fierce currents

No. 24.

of wind that accompanied storms in elevated regions; and moreover, the mountain torrents not unfrequently rush across the road carrying all before them and hurrying them to destruction.

No man can stem one of those mountain torrents which suddenly burst over some rock and sweep man or beast away that happens to cross the furious gush of water.

The traveller still progressed, and push on as well and as rapidly as his rugged pathway would let him—it could not be called a road—and at the same time mutterings of the storm reached his ear.

"Ay, ay, there it comes! I thought as much. How sudden! But the peaks of those hills hid the mass of clouds for some time until they came up to them and showed itself. I wish I were under some shelter. These mountain storms are furious!"

He wrapped his cloak around him and slouched his hat down over his eyes as though he expected to be at once assailed by the angry elements.

Suddenly a bright and vivid flash of forked lightning shot from the heavens, so bright and so jagged that it seemed to play about in different directions, but at length it struck an aged tree by the way-side and hurled it into the road.

It was scarce a hundred and fifty yards before the traveller, and so vivid was the flash that he saw not what was done! On the contrary, he lost the use of his sight for more than a minute, and he put his hands before his eyes.

The tree was struck in two: while one portion lay burning in the road the other threw a bright light over the road, for the stump flared up with a strong flame like a signal fire!

This had scarce been done, before a crashing report came down upon the ears of the traveller, as though it would burst the very drums of his ears.

Crash it went, and then it rolled along the heavens, reverberating with deafening sounds; while the hills around caused a fresh accession of sounds, which seemed as though they would never cease.

Then came a few pattering drops of rain down, as the thunder-claps burst over head which increased every moment, until it suddenly came down as though a deluge had burst over head; and torrents of water fell, that it darkened the air, and nothing could be seen a yard or two beyond the spot on which he stood; but it was no time to pause, so he pushed on as rapidly as the nature of the ground and the storm would permit.

Now that the storm was right over him, he felt the wind, which now swept up the valley in the course of the storm—it was fierce and violent; no sounds could be heard but those accompanying the storm.

He pushed on as well as he was able, until he came to the house, at which he knocked for admission.

The wind howled round the house, and came rushing along with a mighty sound, as though there were no forces that could resist it. The thunder too, rolled around and appeared to shake the very centre of the earth. The traveller felt sorely apprehensive of his own safety.

It was true the house was built under the projecting shelter of a rocky projection; indeed, it seemed as though it was partially let into the rock, and he here escaped some of the fierceness of the wind.

However, it was some minutes before any one could hear from within, the noise without being so great; and besides, not far from the house was a large dyke, which carried off any surplus of water in the winter, and acted as a sort of reservoir in the summer; and now the water began to collect and run over the dams or weirs, and increased the noise and confusion.

At length the door was opened by an elderly woman, who shaded her eyes to look at the stranger, who, without waiting for question or answer, entered the kitchen, and walked up to the fire.

"My good people," he said, "the strength of the storm must excuse my intrusion; but if you can give me shelter for the night, I will repay you."

There were three other persons present besides the old woman : an aged man, and two young men—all evidently of one family.

"You are welcome, stranger," said the elderly man, whose harsh voice and grim features were no recommendation to him ; but among the peasantry of Wales—men who are exposed to all weathers and hard work—there are some whose natural physiognomy is hardly an index to their nature, which, however, may be rough, but kindly.

"What house is this ?" inquired the stranger.

"The Dyke-house."

"A house for public entertainment?"

"Yes," replied the man, laconically.

"Then I shall be less fearful of disturbing you. If you will permit me to sit near the fire to dry myself, I should be glad."

"There is a chair, stranger," said one of the young men, rising, and offering his seat.

"Thank you, thank you. The storm rages fierce and violent without—it is terrific."

"The storms are strong here sometimes, and they last longer than may be thought, considering the violence with which they rise."

"I had no idea of this, though I have seen many ; but I hardly expected it as the sun went down. It was beautiful until the storm clouds came up beneath the sun in the west."

"Ay, they come up from the sea."

"Did you come from below ?" inquired the old man, who appeared to be the father of the two young men, and the husband of the old woman ; and, as he spoke, he nodded his head in the direction of the valley, which the stranger had seen.

"No, I was travelling towards it; I came from above, and, when there, saw the sun set fine enough; but, before he vanished, the clouds came up."

"Ay, you saw more of it there than we saw here : the thunder was the first we heard of it, and it seemed to rock the house."

"It was dreadful, certainly. I am sure I cannot even remember hearing it burst more terrifically. It seemed to fill the whole air with crashing and overwhelming sounds, so as to cause the very air to become tumultuous, as if vibrating with the force of the concussion."

"Oh, I dare say it's bad enough, though I have heard it worse than this when I have been on the summit of Snowdon," said the old man.

"Have you been there?" inquired the stranger.

"I have."

"Let me have what your house affords," said the stranger ; "I am weary and hungry."

"Here, wife," said the elderly man, "see what you have in the larder; we don't usually have much, for visitors are not many in these parts ; but we can accommodate you with something."

"That will be sufficient. I shall easily be satisfied, for I am persuaded I can eat anything short of an inch-board, or drink water, and I could do the last, if required ; but I'd rather have anything else."

"We shan't tax you so hardly as that," said the man, "for we have some ale you will say is worth drinking ; we keep that good."

"It will do me good now then," remarked the stranger, "for I am cold with the wet. How the wind blows and roars in the chimney !"

"Yes; we hear a little of it here."

The old man arose and left the kitchen, and went backwards, having taken down a metal tankard, which appeared but a rarity, for there were but two visible ; at the same time the old woman spread a white but coarse cloth on the table, on which she placed a plate and some other utensils, and some bread.

She then went to the larder and brought out something in the shape of a pie, meat there was in it, and placed it before him, saying—

"There—it may not be such as you have been used to, and yet you will find it good and wholesome."

"I doubt not, my good woman," said the traveller; "and I must admit it seems so—besides, the best sauce to one's food is a good appetite."

So saying the stranger began to he'p himself to the meat-pie, which was exceedingly good, quite a treasure to him in it's way; at the same time the elder man brought him the jug of ale.

"There," he said, "you will find that will do you good, and will make you warm."

The stranger took the ale, of which he drank a copious draught, and set the jug down with evident satisfaction to himself.

"Well," he said, "I am disappointed."

"Disappointed!" said the old man, with a disagrecable expression of countenance.

"Yes, it is altogether better than I could have believed it would be. Say what you will, you have good ale—very good ale,—and it throws me out in great warmth all over. I am quite comfortable."

The stranger had eaten a hearty meal before he made any attempt to inquire into the nature of the meat he was eating of, and then he said, as he laid down his knife and fork—

"I have eaten hearty, but I cannot tell precisely what it is I have been eating; there is too much flavour for lamb, and the meat does not cut like mutton."

"It is neither,'" said the landlord.

"What can it be then?" inquired the stranger very quietly, and with some reluetance.

"Goat's flesh," said the landlord.

"Goat's flesh, eh?" said the stranger; "well, I thought goat's flesh was rank."

"I never found it so; but that is the flesh of a kid. It was fed upon the mountains, and hence it is that the flavour is much finer than that which it would have if fed as they are in some places; the fragrant herbs and shrubs they eat here may not afford such nourishment as they could get in some places, and their growth is not so large, but they are better to my mind."

"Well, from what I have seen and tasted, I am of your opinion too."

Thus the time passed until the traveller had sat for more than an hour after his supper and had drank his ale, and then he said, turning to the old woman—

"I am very weary; can I have the accommodation of a bed for the night?"

"Yes," said the woman, "you can. It is small, but bigger men have slept in it than you are."

"Then, my good woman, it will do for me, well enough; I can accommodate myself to circumstances well enough—so, when you can show me the way, I shall be glad."

"You can come at once," said the old woman, who arose and took a small candle, which she lighted and placed in a curiously-constructed nondescript kind of candlestick, which was evidently a luxury not often used.

The traveller rose and followed the old woman, wishing a good night to the three men.

"This is your room," she said, as she opened the door. "It is small, but it is the only one we have for travellers; the bed, too, is small, but enough for one, and no more."

"I see it will do very well for me—ay, it is sacking—that will make it soft: thank you, good night."

"I wish you good night," said the woman, as she left the room, and then returning suddenly she said, "at what time would you rise?"

"As soon as you rise yourself, or as soon as I can get breakfast, I shall not go without that, so that must rule the time you awake me—however, the sooner the better."

The old woman left the room, and the traveller began to survey his sleeping apartment, as though he had not the most comfortable suspicions as to what might be the character of his host.

The room was a moderate sized one, with little or nothing but bare walls, and a lattice window ; there was one chair and a table ; upon the latter he placed the candlestick, and examined the flooring.

All was correct: the bed was small, but not very ; it was large enough for one person, and but slackly laced up, so the person when reposing in sleep was sure to lay in the centre of the bed.

" Well," thought the traveller, " I am better fed and lodged than I had any hope of. How the wind roars, and the rain falls in torrents !"

He soon threw himself upon the bed, after having in vain endeavoured to pierce the darkness of the night from the window, and then soon fell asleep.

*   *   *   *   *

The old woman returned, and sat down by the fire for some minutes without speaking, nor did any one of them do so, they were silent and moody.

" Did he seem quiet ?" asked the old man.

" Yes, quite ; he has no fear, but appears comfortable, and will soon be fast asleep."

" That is all right."

" I think he has plenty of what we want," said one of the young men.

" Ay, money."

" That is it ; he had a heavy purse, I am sure it was plain enough to me."

" Ay, and I saw it too : besides, when a man talks about paying, you are sure he has got money."

" Yes," said the old woman, " his clothes are too fine for a poor person, but he wants to be called early, and will have an early breakfast."

" I am afraid he will not find appetite enough," said the man—"he will find another matter to attend to before to-morrow."

" When will you do it ?"

" In his first sleep."

" And not wait till midnight?"

" No ; there can be no need. His first sleep will be the heaviest, and that will be the safest for us all. If he should jump up at the first prick we can easily dispatch him by other means."

" There will be no need of that, the ale is strong, and he is tired."

" Go and listen if he be asleep."

The woman arose and went backwards to the bed-room of the stranger, at whose door she listened for some time, and could distinctly hear him snore. She returned to the fire, where the three men were seated waiting her return.

" Well ?" said the man.

" He sleeps," replied the woman, " and sound and loud too, for he snores."

" That will do ; we will give him half an hour, but we will get all ready."

So saying, he arose and took out of a cupboard a hammer and chisel and some nails, which he placed beside the fire-place, and then taking the only other light there was, he said, " Come boys, come."

The two young men arose and followed their father, who opened a door in a passage and went below, followed by them, and then they all went down some steps until they got into a room below.

It seemed as if hewn out of the rock, but in the middle of the room was what appeared to be a very strong chest.

Taking a couple of iron handles from a corner they fitted them on to axles in either side of the chest, and then dropping some oil on certain parts they slowly turned the handles.

Quietly and without making any noise there arose from the top of the box, as if it were piercing the lid, a sharp sword-like point of polished steel—very sharp and pointed—and which rose up gradually to a great height, when it reached the low ceiling, and then it fitted itself to one of the chinks, between which it gradually passed until it met with an impediment above.

There was a pause, and then two of them took the handles, while the third placed the door open and gave the signal. The handles were at once turned round softly, and then, after some of the impediments had given way, they used their force, turned the handles with great rapidity, and the sword point went up quickly through the bed and the body of the sleeper.

A deep groan and a stifled scream was all that was heard, and then there was a dead silence; some struggles might be seen by the shaking of the spindle; but when that ceased, the man said—

"That will do, boys."

They immediately left the handles, and, taking the candle, the whole party had left the room, and hastened above stairs to the room above, where the traveller lay a corpse in the bed he had fallen asleep.

They forced open the door, which was easily done, for the lock gave way in a suspicious manner, and there lay the traveller weltering in his own blood.

"Out with 'em," said the landlord. "But see he has not put his purse under the pillow."

They felt, but there was nothing there; the clothes were immediately searched, and all was taken out and placed on one side, and the remainder were thrown upon the corpse, as being dangerous to keep.

"There, boys," said Foster, "roll him up tight and bring him down, while I go and open the door."

He left the room, and, going to the kitchen, he tore down some boards, which discovered a kind of apartment, in which the sons placed the body.

The apartment appeared to be hewn out of the solid rock, and was but of small dimensions : there was, too, some smell in it that was altogether suspicious. However, they did not remain in this place many minutes, and, when they came out, they carefully secured the entrance, and nailed up the boards again; and then their attention was directed to an examination of the plunder, and to efface all marks of the deed of blood they had committed.

CHAPTER XXIX.

THE PROGRESS OF SIR ANTHONY WYVILL, AND THE LETTER.

We left Sir Anthony Wyvill in a most precarious position, inasmuch as the nature of his wound had begun to call forth the most serious apprehensions, and it is with pain that we record those apprehensions as having increased, instead of diminished, in the course of the next few days.

Notwithstanding all the care and attention that was lavished upon him, and they were very great indeed, the feverish symptoms that had attacked him, and had excited the apprehension of his medical advisers, increased in intensity, and by the third day after the captain's widow had taken up her post as attendant upon him, his situation became critical in the extreme, and she began to fear indeed that nothing could prevent the calamitous result of death occurring.

We may well imagine into what a state of terror-stricken anguish she, who watched every turn of his countenance, was thrown, when the surgeon took her aside, and said to her :—

"I feel that I ought not to conceal from you the fact, that unless a favourable change ensues in the course of the forthcoming night, I can give you but little hopes indeed of an ultimate recovery."

Tears gushed to her eyes, and sobs for a few moments choked her utterance.

"Alas, alas!" she said, "and has it come to this ? Is this indeed to be the end of one so full of generosity and nobleness ? Can nothing more be done to afford him a chance of life?"

"All that can, with any propriety or chance of success be attempted, shall be so ; but I cannot promise you with certainty a result satisfactory to your wishes. Do not, however, absolutely despair. Life is not so frail a possession as people imagine it, and I have known a person, in a much more dangerous crisis than Sir Anthony Wyvill is now in, entirely recover from an effort of nature, even without the physician's aid."

" I thank you for giving me so much hope."

" I will leave a medicine with you, which I wish you to give him, should he awaken, and appear to be cool and collected ; but if he continue in his present feverish condition, it will be useless, utterly useless."

" He falls into an uneasy slumber generally at sun-set, at least such has been his practice for the last three nights ; but he awakens about midnight, and then commences raving wildly of the past until the dawn of morning."

" Doubtless but those symptoms now have reached to a crisis, and they must terminate to-night in a recovery, or in a remarkable change for the worst."

The surgeon handed the medicine to her, and then, with renewed expressions of his hopes and wishes for a favourable result, he left her, and she sat herself down sadly by the bedside of Sir Anthony.

He was not yet sleeping, and as he fixed his hollow sunken eyes upon her, and compressed together his parched lips, he spoke at times rationally, and then again with all the incoherence of a mind oppressed with fever.

" Has no one come ?" he said. " Have you heard nothing of her ? Speak to me, and tell me where my child is."

" Oh, be calm, I pray you to be calm !"

" She might have left me herself—she might have gone from me, making me feel that I had based the airy structure of my happiness upon sand ; but she should not, she need not have taken with her the innocent child, who might have been some solace to me."

" In truth she need not," said his weeping nurse.

" Where is Robert ?" he said, after a pause. " I want to see Robert. Bid him come to my bed-side—I would feign speak with him."

" Do you not remember he left you ?"

" Robert left me ! He left me ! Oh, no, he loved me too well, and I him. He did not leave me, he could not. Some one sent him away from me."

" No, in truth he left you of his own free will. Do you not remember ?"

" That matters little. It is my child I want—my beautiful child. Why did she take that with her ? She should not—no, she should not have taken it."

" Will you not try to compose yourself to sleep ?"

" To sleep, to sleep ! how can I sleep, with such a demon glaring upon me ? Look ! do you not see his eyes ? I must close mine in order to avoid the frightful glare. I will seem to sleep, if I cannot in reality do so."

He closed his eyes, and after a few moments the same sort of uneasy slumber that on the preceding evenings had characterised him, crept over him, and all was still, save now and then when he moaned, and uttered disjointed sentences, flinging his arms to and fro in wild disorder, and calling upon Emily to bring back his child, which now seemed his prevalent idea.

It was a sad and weary watch that that gentle-hearted being kept at his bedside. Her feelings were at one moment buoyed up by hope, and at another she would sink into an abyss of despair, from which she would in vain seek to rescue her imagination.

And thus hour after hour crept along, until the sound of footsteps and the distant murmur of voices in the house became still, and she could hear nothing but the deep inspirations of the troubled sleeper, and the beating of her own heart.

It wanted but a quarter of an hour of midnight, and she had just risen to place the lamp in a more favourable position, so that she might look upon the face of the sleeper, when she thought she heard a footstep, and the door of the room slowly opened at the same moment.

So strange and silent was the movement that, for a few moments, she continued gazing at the entrance, while a feeling of horror crept over her, and the blood rushed back to her heart with a frightful gush, as she asked herself if she was not about to behold something strange and supernatural—something that would forbode the coming death!

Then in the dim light from the night-lamp that burnt in the apartment she saw a figure move, and make its way with a strange staggering sort of movement towards the bed on which Sir Anthony Wyvill lay. She could not move, for terror paralysed her limbs. She could not speak, although she strove to do so, for intense fear prevented her.

Slowly the figure advanced, and she saw that it was enveloped in a cloak; it stooped over the slumbering form, and imprinted a kiss upon the fevered brow of the sleeper.

"Farewell!" said the strange intruder, in a deep and hollow voice. "Husband once so dear, farewell for ever!"

These words broke the spell which bound up all the faculties of the widow, and she sprung forward, crying—

"Stop, Emily Wyvill, stop, for the love of Heaven, if it indeed be you!"

She was too late; the figure had darted down the staircase like a beam of light, and was gone. When she turned again and looked upon the couch she saw that the eyes of Sir Anthony Wyvill were open, and that he was looking intently on her.

"I have destroyed him," she said—"I have destroyed him. May Heaven forgive me! for in the suddenness of my exclamation I have awakened him from that sleep it was so important he should not be aroused from."

"What mean you?" said Sir Anthony, quite calmly.

"He will live! he will live! Oh! speak again, and speak in that calm collected voice. Tell me that the fever has left your blood, and that I have not destroyed you?"

"I am much better," he said faintly, "I am much better, and could sleep again. I could sleep for ever with such a blessed dream hovering around my couch."

"A dream!"

"Yes; such a dream of happiness as I may never know again. I thought that she, my long-lost Emily, came to me, and hand-in-hand with her was a radiant angel, who, pointing to the sky, said that not more true or loveable was heaven than she. Then I fancied that my Emily stooped and kissed my brow, and then, as if by magic, I awakened with the fever that has raged in my veins so long, all departed as it is now."

The kind nurse thought of the medicine which had been left to be used on such an occasion, and while tears of pleasurable feeling coursed each other down her cheeks, she presented to him the draught.

He took it on the instant, and then sinking back he merely uttered the words—

"Much happier!" and sank into a profound, and what seemed to be a healthful slumber, such as had not visited his eyelids for many a day.

The crisis was passed, and it had passed favourably. Then she who had waited for it with such intense anxiety felt all that sudden revulsion of feeling which such circumstances were calculated to produce, and reclining her head upon the table near which she sat, she found relief in abundance of tears.

When she had recovered herself sufficiently to reflect more calmly upon what had occurred, it became a serious question with her whether or not she should report to Sir Anthony Wyvill, upon his awaking, the strange visit that had been made to him, and which either had produced, or had chimed in so wonderfully well with the dream that had disturbed him; at the same time, it brought with it such great consolation and such sensations of pleasurable delight.

She could have no motive in the world for not informing Sir Anthony Wyvill of what had occurred, except some feeling that it would be unfavourable to his peace of mind; but as now, upon more mature reflection, she considered that such would not be the case, she determined, the moment he awakened, and was in a fit state to listen to such a communication, that he should have it made to him.

And now that we have so far carried Sir Anthony Wyvill through his great danger, and placed him in a position which, we trust, will soon result in his complete recovery, we will draw our attention to Emily Wyvill, concerning whose situation we have not been unmindful, although we dreaded depicting the agonised feelings which must have been hers when she left the hotel, fancying that all her devotion and tenderness had been scattered to the winds.

CHAPTER XXX.

FOLLOWS THE FORTUNES OF EMILY WYVILL.

The few chance passengers which Emily encountered when she left the hotel shrunk from her, for her manner was so frenzied and strange, that they might well suppose her to be some maniac who had got loose from a wholesome restraint, and to attract whose attention might be mischievous.

No. 25.

She rushed onward, she cared not, knew not whither, until absolute exhaustion induced her to pause, and then she found that she had reached the outskirts of London, and was on a country road, with open meadows upon one side, and here and there detached houses on the other.

She leant upon a stile for some moments, until she heard the sound of approaching footsteps and men's voices in apparently boisterous and drunken altercation.

Alarmed lest they should interfere with her, and feeling that in her present state of mind she was quite incapable of making the least effort to return such an answer to anything they might say as to induce them to continue on their way without disturbing her, she clambered the hedge, intending to conceal herself in the meadow until they had passed on.

There was an aged tree, an elm of gigantic height and proportion, and its twisted and gnarled root, as in many cases it projected from the ground, presented to her a seat, so that even when the brawling boisterous men had passed by, she sat there still, reflecting deeply upon her situation.

She was hardly yet calm and cool enough to reflect upon what she was about with the requisite degree of careful judgment, and for a time nothing but confused images of despair and death floated through her imagination.

Had it not then been for one recollection, she might, in the despair of her heart have done some dreadful deed which there would be no recalling, but that recollection saved her; and our readers, no doubt, can well fancy it was no other than a thought of her child, which, if she were to leave, might encounter a world of trouble by being dependent upon the precarious affection of one who had shown no constancy to her whom he had sworn to love.

"I will live," she said; "but my dream of restoration to the joy that once was mine has passed away for ever; it never can return. I have heard from his own lips that he loves her, and to hear more would be agony indeed."

But then came the anxious thought of what she would do; for to be dependent upon Margaret Wyvill was a thing she now determined should not be. Youth is ever sanguine, and Emily fondly fancied that surely, with industry, the will to achieve a subsistence could not fail.

Little did she dream of the great struggle for existence in such a country as England, when she imagined that will and capacity were certain of success. If she had known what a very short experience taught her, her thoughts upon that occasion would have taken a much more serious and sombre view than they did, and she would earlier have her resolution, which at length she was forced to make.

But we will not anticipate, for Heaven knows, as regards the misfortunes of Emily Wyvill, sufficient for the day was the evil thereof.

"Such few accomplishments," she said, "as I can call to my aid, I will now make subservient to procuring the means whereby to live. I am in London, the great emporium of the arts and of commerce. For my child's sake, I must shake off the deep depression of my spirits, and endeavour to accomplish something which shall place it above the reach of want."

It cannot be said that Emily doubted Sir Anthony Wyvill's wish to support the child; but her repugnance that it should associate with that person, whom she considered she had had abundance of evidence had deprived her of her husband's affections was far too repugnant to her feelings for her to entertain for a moment.

"No," she said, "no; better with me in poverty, provided such poverty descends not to actual want, than surrounded with all the luxuries of Wyvill Hall."

She found, upon examining the contents of her pocket, that she had money sufficient to last her probably for some weeks with care, so that she was in no danger of immediate want, and this was a gratifying conviction, because it enabled her to hover round the hotel, and ascertain the actual position of Sir Anthony Wyvill, and and how his recovery from the wound proceeded.

The effort that she made to withdraw her mind from what was painful to contemplate, and to fix it instead upon what she considered it was her duty to attempt to accomplish, was a great and heroic one, deserving of the highest amount of praise.

It was an effort that few, indeed, situated as she was, would have attempted to m ke; and, no doubt, even she, without the stimulus of a mother's love, would never have ventured it.

She sat there until the dawn of morning, revolving in her mind all the steps which it would be necessary for her to take, and then, as the soft night of the young day stole gently around her, she proceeded towards London again, to carry her plans into execution.

She purchased a hat instead of a cap which vastly altered her appearance, and then enveloping her slender form in a cloak, which she likewise purchased, she felt that she might, without fear of detection, make inquiries concerning the progress of Sir Anthony Wyvill to what she hoped was approaching convalescence.

By the time she had completed these arrangements, the bustle of the day in London had fairly commenced, and the remainder of the daylight she appropriated to visiting her child, which, it will be remembered, she was to do in the capacity of its brother.

Then she lingered listening to the innocent prattle of that young creature, who knew, as yet, nothing of those deeply anxious and absorbing cares that made its mother's breast so heavy, until the solemn and beautiful shades of evening once again began to show themselves.

She then left it, after imprinting many a kiss upon its soft cheek, and proceeded again to London to seek some temporary place of abode, near to the hotel, where she could for a time remain, until she no longer had any motive for so doing, in consequence of Sir Anthony being completely recovered.

There it was that, by encountering one of the waiters, she learned with inexpressible agony, that the unfavourable symptoms were increasing, and her anxiety reached a point which, more than once, was nearly sufficient to induce her to seek his presence, and proclaim who she really was, claiming her right, in that hour of affliction, to attend upon him in preference to her who now arrogated to herself that office.

But she restrained the impulse; how happy would she have been had she yielded to it, but it was one of Emily's misfortunes that her very virtues and her strength of mind arrayed themselves against her happiness.

Had she, in any one instance, given way and allowed feeling to get by far the better of her judgment and the conscious pride of innocence, she would have escaped many of the evils that had surrounded her.

But thus it is ever that villany may always calculate upon a certain extent of success from the working of the very high and noble qualities it opposes.

The next night Emily lingered around the spot, until the same man came out of the hotel whom she had before questioned.

" Will you tell me," she said, eagerly, "how Sir Anthony Wyvill is?"

" Rather worse, I believe," was the reply, and Emily's heart sank within her as she heard it. " Worse " she thought, " and I not there.'

" Pray tell me is he still attended by any one?"

" Yes, there is a lady, we don't know who she is, or what she is, nor where the deuce she came from, but it seems all right, so it's no business of ours; he is pleased and she is pleased, and I must say she don't mind what trouble she takes, but sits up with him all night."

" I thank you," said Emily, faintly; "will you to-morrow, at this hour, meet me here and tell me how he is, I am deeply interested—I do not wish to trouble you for nothing, and you shall name your own reward."

" As to reward, I don't think we shall want any reward. I'll let you know—you see it's a friend of mine that keeps the public-house—I don't go there to drink, because there is always enough to be had at the hotel, but, however, I shall be just popping out about this time, and then you may depend I will manage to let you know."

" A thousand thanks," said Emily, " I shall be much beholden to you if you will do so."

It is astonishing how a small alteration in costume will produce a remarkable effect, and the transition of Emily from the boy to the young man, which her dress and her adoption of the hat and cloak gave her, was so perfect, that the waiter at the hotel, although he had often seen her in her former character, had really no idea that he was addressing the same person who had been the attendant upon Sir Anthony Wyvill.

He kept his word on the next evening, and Emily again addressed him most eagerly.

"Is he better—is he better?" she exclaimed. "Tell me—oh, tell me that those symptoms which presented themselves have passed away, and that he is better."

"I am sorry," said the waiter, "that I cannot do so, because I see that you are deeply interested in him, and I fear it will be a great shock to you to hear that he is worse."

Poor Emily was struck speechless, and, with clasped hands and uplifted eyes, she looked in the face of the man as if she thought it possible there to gather some contradiction of the words he uttered ; but that hope was in vain ; she saw nothing to induce her to entertain the smallest doubt of his veracity, and once more she could have forgotten and forgiven all, could she but have placed herself by the side of her husband.

She could scarcely murmur her thanks to the waiter, and then feeling she must adopt some course, and that, be it what it might, was one which required earnest and careful thought; she retired to the little apartment she had taken for her own use in the immediate neighbourhood, and flinging herself into a chair, she sat for a considerable time immovable as a statue, and endeavouring to reflect calmly upon a subject which set all calmness at defiance.

But in her reflections she started with what might be called a proposition, and that was, that she must see Sir Anthony Wyvill again. This was a fixed idea and the only thing she had to consider was, the best and most eligible mode of carrying it out.

But time waited not for the termination of her resolves. The evening deepened into the still night, until at last she felt that she was rapidly approaching the midnight hour, but as yet she had come to no decision which deserved the name of such.

"I must and will see him," she exclaimed, "no one shall prevent me ; and although I cannot remain with him while that woman holds her occupation in his chamber, I must look upon his face again if it be but to bid him a long and a last farewell."

She wrapped the cloak about her, and went into the streets taking her way with anxious and hurried footsteps towards the hotel, at the door of which she paused to ask herself what she should say as an excuse for seeking the chamber of the invalid.

She felt then that if anything was to be done effectually it must be done by boldness and decision, and that any faltering or appearance of doubt upon her part would at once defeat her object.

She accordingly entered the hall of the hotel, and walked leisurely towards the staircase, until, as she fully expected she should be, she was stopped by one of the establishment, who said,—

"Do you want any one, sir."

"You need not trouble yourself," she said, " I know the way, I have merely come to see if any change has taken place in Sir Anthony Wyvill since I was here last.

"Oh, I beg your pardon, sir, certainly, certainly."

"Who was that," said the master of the hotel to the waiter.

"Oh, only one of the doctering people come to see Sir Anthony."

"Very well, but you might have shown the gentleman up."

Emily felt like a person walking in a dream as she slowly ascended the staircase which led to Sir Anthony Wyvill's apartment. No one knew better than she the road to it, for during his stay at the hotel she had ascended and descended that staircase many a time and oft.

Now she paused at the very door itself, and listened intently, in an endeavour to catch some sound from within the apartment which should give her better hopes. But as we are aware that was the period at which Sir Anthony Wyvill slept, and at which so many sad and painful thoughts had swept across the mind of his attendant nurse, and hearing nothing, and feeling that each moment she delayed was making her less capable with firmness to go through that which she ought to do, she gently opened the door and, made her appearance in the chamber in the manner we have before recorded.

She scarcely knew what she did, and the words that came from her lips were far more those of impulse than of reflection.

Not above five minutes elapsed when she found herself again in the open street. She had seen Sir Anthony Wyvill, and it might be that she had seen him for the last time in this world. She felt almost incapable of movement, and a heavy feeling came over her, coupled with a dreadful apprehension that some deadly sickness was creeping over her. She made the best of her way to her humble lodging, and when she reached it, she sank exhausted upon the bed, as she said to herself faintly,—

"Surely, surely, these are the premonitory symptoms of death.''

Nothing now but some powerful impulse—some extraordinary feeling that would enable the mind to overcome the body's weakness—could have roused her to the task she undertook.

"Sir Anthony," she cried, "may yet live; but I feel as if the cold hand of death was already placed upon my heart. A favourable change may in a few days produce in him every hope of recovery, while I may linger here desolate and alone, with death stealing over me, and each moment robbing me of the power of action. What, oh, what is to become of that dear little one, who has no other friend on earth than myself. Dare, ought I to keep any longer the secret of its place of concealment from Sir Anthony Wyvill. The feelings of a father will prompt him to extend to it the hand of affection although I am deserted."

She rose even as she spoke, and drawing writing materials towards her, she sat down with the determination of addressing a letter to her husband, forgiving all that had passed, but imploring him, as she considered that her own end was approaching, to play a father's part towards the child.

She wrote as follows :—

"To Sir Anthony Wyvill :

"Without the name which is appended to these lines, you can be at no loss to discover the hand that writes them; they are only written in the extremity of sadness, and in the belief that in the grave I shall soon succeed in finding that oblivion to sorrow which this world can never afford me.

"You are now upon a bed of sickness, and they tell me that your situation is one of peril and of danger, but still the powers of life may triumph in your more hardy and robust frame, while in mine they sink to rest for ever.

"Anthony, I think that I am dying, and therefore is it that I write to you that you may know where to find your child, which otherwise would be destitute. On the scrap of paper which is here inclosed, you will find written the name it goes by, and the address of the female who has charge of it. Be to that dear little one, I pray you, both mother and father, and then she who, in sadness and sorrow, rather than in anger, writes to you, will die forgiving and content. The time has passed away when some bitterness of feeling might have characterised a commission from me to you, and now grief, with no small portion of despair, is all that I can feel.

"The time has passed away when some littleness of feeling might have characterised a commission from me to you, and now grief, with no small portion of despair, is all that I can get.

"I do not regret leaving this world, because, whatever apparent joy it may now present to me, would be so tinctured by sad remembrances of the past that every particle of happiness would be clouded and made to assume an aspect not its own.

"It is fitting that at such a moment as this, and along with such a letter, I should state briefly how I have disposed of myself from the time that I left Wyvill Hall, friendless, and with such a desolation of my heart that I could have blessed any hand that had been raised against my life.

"From the moment that I was informed by Margaret, your sister, that you had written to her, asking her to aid you in concealing an intrigue which you wished to carry on even beneath your own roof, I felt as if my doom was fixed.

"And yet I doubted ; a throng of old affections clung to me making me think it surely impossible that you, whom I had enshrined in my heart as something more than mortal, could thus deceive me.

"I waited for more evidence, and I got it. A Mr. Adolphus Dacre declared that he had seen you at the hotel at Portsmouth with the new object of your affections, and that you were rapidly approaching Wyvill Hall.

"I dared not trust myself to meet you; it was sufficient for me that I had lost your affections, and after leaving for you, hastily, a note, dictated by Margaret, and containing I know not what, I left the Hall with my child in my arms, and from that time to this have been a sad and solitary wanderer.

"And then arose the hope—n hope breaking like sunshine through the storm cloud of my destiny—that I might wean you back again to love, to honour, and to happiness.

"Disguised as a boy I have attended upon you ; and there are times when I have seen you start at some sudden tone of my voice or expression of my face, and I feared my secret would be discovered.

"But it was not. Perchance your mind was too full of another, that other whom you pressed, and who, but a short time since, chased me from your bedside, and herself usurped the place of right belonging to me.

"Farewell ! farewell for ever!   It is better that we should never meet again.

"EMILY WYVILL."

Having wafered a scrap of paper within the letter, on which was the address of the woman who had the child to nurse, Emily folded it and sealed it, addressing it to Sir Anthony Wyvill, at the hotel, where he was staying.

It seemed as if this was the last effort she could make previously to great indisposition ensuing ; for, when the people of the house where she lived, being surprised at her nonappearance in the morning, went to her room, they found her quite insensible.

The nearest medical practitioner was at once sent for.   This was a physician, of the name of Hammerton, a man who had the character of being very eccentric and of harsh, repulsive manners ; but those were but the rough asperities that hid the diamond polish beneath.   He made some inquiries concerning Emily, and then he was shown the letter which lay upon the table, addressed to Sir An hony Wyvill.

He directed that this should be immediately taken to its address ; but the answer that was brought back was to the effect that Sir Anthony was not in a state to read it, and that it was left in the hands of the hotel-keeper, and would be given to him in the event of his recovery, a fact which was extremely doubtful.

"Well," said the physician, " I shall attend upon this young person ; and as that can be done with greater effect at my own house than here, I shall speak to Mrs. Hammerton to come and take immediate steps for her removal."

In about a couple of hours the eccentric physician returned, accompanied by his wife, who at the first sight of Emily was so prepossessed in her favour, that she not only acceded to, but warmly eulogised the plan of bringing her to their house.

The sufferer was carefully placed in the carriage of the doctor, who was quite wealthy enough to do such an act of kindness and genuine philanthropy as that which he was about.

Emily had been restored to consciousness ; but from her deeply dejected manner, the physician drew a just enough conclusion that the mind had more to do than the body with the state she was in ; but he forebore questioning her, and likewise strictly enjoined his wife not to do so.

"Win her confidence," he said, " if you can ; but do not ask for it.   When she feels inclined, she will tell you who and what she is, but not before."

CHAPTER XXXI.

THE RECOVERY OF SIR ANTHONY WYVILL.

THE composing draught which the surgeon had left to be given to Sir Anthony in case he awoke from the fever, which was so much to be dreaded, did its duty, and sent him into a profound and peaceful slumber, which lasted until the sun had risen high in the heavens on the following morning.

Before he awakened, his medical attendant had called upon him, and being extremely anxious concerning the case, he resolved to wait until the sleep should leave him.

It was during this time, and before Sir Anthony Wyvill opened his eyes, that a messenger came with a letter—the letter from Emily—but of course there was nothing about its exterior to indicate the deeply interesting nature of its contents.

It was the physician who sent back the message that Sir Anthony was not in a fit state to read letters; and when the messenger had left, he turned to the captain's widow, and said, earnestly,—

"Place this letter, as well as any others that may come for him, aside, and do not let him see them on any account. His life is now the first consideration, and any agitation or perplexity concerning business might again endanger it. Let me beg of you, therefore, to be particular that he sees no visitors and reads no letters."

This was promised as a matter of course, and so it was that Emily's epistle was put on one side. In opening a drawer, in which she proposed laying it, the widow found her own epistle unopened, and as now it had lost its immediate object, she thought of destroying it, but she did not do so, for she said with a sigh,—

"He will recover soon, and then again I shall require to throw myself upon the same kind consolation I invoked in this epistle; so that I will leave it, and when I am permitted to do so, place it myself in his hands, so that he may himself judge of the feelings which actuated me, and at once be induced to grant my request."

At that moment Sir Anthony Wyvill gently moved in his bed and opened his eyes. The surgeon immediately spoke to him in a low voice, saying,—

"You are decidedly better. The fever has left you, and your ultimate perfect recovery will entirely depend upon the state of quiet and repose in which you keep yourself. Let me beg of you not even to converse much, and not at all upon any agitating topic."

"I thank you," said Sir Anthony, but he spoke very faintly. "I will attend to such good advice. Where is Robert, has he returned?"

He was informed that he had not, and the surgeon shook his head as he said,—

"Indeed you must not agitate yourself about the fate of any one at present. Remember that the sooner you are restored to health, the sooner, of course, you will be able to mingle in the business concerns of life; and that you will positively save time by weaning yourself at present from everything that can disturb you in any way."

"I will, I will; and perchance I may hear something from the lad, who has so unaccountably left me. It was cruel of him to do so—very cruel."

"You must," whispered the surgeon to the captain's widow, "you must endeavour to wean him altogether from this subject, or to get some news of the young man of a satisfactory or conclusive nature."

"I have no means," she replied, "of doing so; but should anything arise, I will first take your opinion, and then communicate it to Sir Anthony."

"Do so; because if the information be of an agitating nature, I shall not be able to give you anything like a warranty that it may not produce a very serious effect upon Sir Anthony."

* * * * * *

While this conversation was proceeding at the hotel, the doctor's wife sat by the bed-side of Emily Wyvill, endeavouring, by such means as were in her power, to draw the young and beautiful creature into her confidence, and induce her to confide her sorrows to a sympathetic breast."

" I am far from seeking," she said, " to intrude upon you ; on the contrary, bear in mind, most distinctly, that we do not consider, because it has been in our power to offer you some kindness, that we are intitled to exact from you your history in return ; I beg that you will not, for one moment, fancy such a thing; but in almost all the concerns of life, those who are willing to aid and assist others may generally manage to do so, and when you consider that you are so young, and that you must be inexperienced, in consequence, of the world's ways, you ought scarcely to shrink from claiming the assistance of those who know more of general society than yourself, and who are so very willing to render it.''

" Alas !" said Emily, " the story of my distresses is too painful an one for me to inflict upon you. I feel that I ought not to do so, and that I ought rather to bury within the recesses of my own bosom, those circumstances and events which can only give pain to those who would sympathise with me, but would find its impossible to alleviate my sufferings."

" There, perhaps, you judge wrongly. The heart makes much of its own misery by taking so strong a view of its own misfortunes, that it teaches itself to believe those things to be impossible, which really are quite readily within the means of accomplishing."

" Oh, if I could but think so ! But our opinions may change and feelings may alter, but stern and stubborn facts remain the same always, presenting no change whatever."

" It may be so ; and yet those facts, in their results, may surely be much changed, if in no other way."

" Most true; and do not suppose, because I thus plead for the completing of my misfortunes, that it is because I do not wish to make a confidence, for I will do so ; but I would have you wait until to-morrow, ere I speak so freely, for my mind at present is too much oppressed with many sad thoughts and fancies, to enable me to do so."

" Until to-morrow be it then. Heaven forbid that I should press you in a matter which concerns yourself so nearly. Use entirely your own discretion ; and telling us or telling us not, always still believe that you are with those who have the warmest desire to befriend you."

" That I know and feel convinced of. But yet spare me until to-morrow, when I shall have sufficient courage to tell you all—perhaps now I should have at once, but that I dread—'

" Dread what?"

" That you might advise me to some course which I wish not to pursue. I have rights which I do not wish to urge, and have endured injuries which I do not wish to resent—humiliations which I have no desire to hear even talked of."

" Be assured that nothing shall be done, or attempted to be done, without your entire concurrence ; but the only thing in all the world which induces me to say that I am pleased with the promise of confidence at some future time that you have made to me is that I think, and my husband thinks so likewise, that we may see some evident way of being of service to you."

" Of that I am assured ; your generous kindness to me, who am completely unknown to you, is such as to lead me to no other possible conclusion. I am full of deep anxiety on account of one who, perchance, is far from suspecting the feeling that there is one thing I should like done."

" You have but to name it and we will see that it is executed."

" I dread inquiry concerning me, and if you can find some one who will go to the hotel—but I forgot you do not know of what I am talking—what I wish is, that some one would go to the hotel, of which I will give you the name and direction, and say that Robert is no more."

" Robert ? Robert who ?"

"The simple name of Robert will suffice—it contains all the information required."

"You forget that when my husband was sent for to the house where you resided, he saw a letter on the table in your apartment addressed to a Sir Anthony Wyvill, that was sent by his direction to the hotel to which it was directed. Was it the same?"

"It was—it was. I had not forgotten that letter, although I had forgotten, at the moment, the means by which it reached its destination. What I wish is, that some one should go to that hotel, and ask how Sir Anthony Wyvill is, and say that Robert is no more, for—"

"You pause."

"Yes—yes; I was going to say that I was certain Robert soon will be no more.'

'"There is much mystery here, my dear girl. Let me pray you to pause before No. 26.

you act in any manner impulsively, that may exercise an injurious effect upon your future fate. Of course I cannot advise you, but I implore you to be cautious what you do."

These words were spoken with such evident kindly feeling that they made a deep impression upon Emily, and after a silence of about a minute's duration, she said,—

"Madam, it would be treason against the kindness which you have exhibited towards me, were I to hesitate another moment in making the confidence I did think of delaying yet awhile. You shall know all my unhappy history."

"I shall listen with pleasure. But tell me first, will you permit my husband to be a sharer in your confidence?"

"Most certainly—most certainly. Is he not entitled to it by every reason that can possibly be urged? and believe me, too, that it is with no small amount of pleasurable pride that I tell you, the secret of my heart is not a guilty one; I have suffered, but I have inflicted no suffering; I have been made a victim, but I have myself made no victims; my story is a sad one, because it is one of pain to the best feelings of human nature; and it is one that I grieve to inflict upon any person."

"It will be no infliction, but, on the contrary, a source of hope, and ultimately of pleasure, to me, to think that by your making an unreserved communication to me, you will find, perhaps, that your position is not so bad as you have pictured it to yourself. Remember, how frequent a mistake it is, on the part of all persons, to exaggerate, without at all meaning to do so, their own sorrows."

"I know that such is the case, and now, if it so pleases you, you shall listen to a recital which I think will command your sympathies, while I am sure it will ease my heart to tell it."

Emily Wyvill then without further preface, and in the most simply eloquent and artless manner, related those particulars of her life with which the reader is already well acquainted. She told how her affection for Sir Anthony had grown into a kind of devotion—a feeling only second, if indeed it was that, to her love of Heaven. She told how she had waited, and watched for his return, and then how sadly and how cruelly all her fondest, dearest hopes had been blasted.

Lastly, too, she related how she had watched by him, and tended upon him when he knew her not; and the incredible manner in which she had succeeded in discovering him at the deserted house where that sanguinary duel had been fought.

But when she came to tell how she was watching by his bedside, when the one person of all others whom she most dreaded to see, came to usurp her place, her voice faltered, and she could scarcely proceed with the eventful narrative.

"Do not," said the physician's wife, "dwell upon any portion of your story that gives you much pain, I pray you. Let those facts be briefly stated; and if you dwell at all upon any portion of your story, let it be upon some that will give you pleasure."

"I thank you, but it is proper that you should know all, in order that you may feel that she in whom you have taken so kindly an interest is not wholly undeserving of such generous sympathy."

When Emily had concluded her melancholy recital she wept abundantly, for the fact of having thus for the first time put into language the dreadful events of the last few months, seemed to have awakened all her sensibilities, and to have unlocked that fount of tears which else would have remained sealed for many a day.

And the kind friend who had listened to her was not sorry to see those tears flow, because they gave a kind of assistance to her, and a calmness of mind would ensue after them, that she would be well pleased to see in the aspect of her *protege*. The physician's wife, therefore, made no effort to check them; but after speaking to Emily some words of encouragement and hope of better times, she left the room to seek her husband and recount to him, according to the permission she had received from Emily so to do, the eventful story that had just been told to her.

It was a source of great gratification to Dr. Hammerton to find that he had not been deceived in Emily Wyvill, and that in befriending her he had befriended one who was sinned against, instead of herself sinning.

"I am much pleased," he said, "that Lady Wyvill has fallen into our hands, and I hope that we shall be able most materially to alleviate the distresses of her condition. She must, of course, be persuaded to insist upon some maintenance from her husband, because that it is her undoubted right."

"It is, but it is one of those rights which you will never be able to persuade her to exercise."

"Think you not?"

"I am certain of it; indeed, she hinted as much to me. Her pride of conscious innocence is so strong within her, that she revolts from even getting a common subsistence from the man who has treated her in so heartless a manner. One could almost forgive all the conduct of Sir Anthony Wyvill but the attempt he made to induce his sister to connive at the actual residence under the same roof with his wife of her greatest enemy, and his own greatest enemy, as most assuredly he will himself in time discover."

"We must be completely guided in what we do, then, by Lady Wyvill herself. If she proposes anything, I shall consider that her feelings and wishes have first of all to be consulted; and if she will indulge me now with an audience, I should be glad to speak to her at once upon the subject."

"That of course she will do, and at once too, for her feeling of gratitude towards you is so strong, that she expresses it in the most fervent terms."

In a few minutes more the physician was with Emily, and in the interim she appeared to have formed a determination, for she said to him,—

"It is not likely that I shall resume again the unfeminine attire that I have worn; and as Robert, the attendant upon Sir Anthony Wyvill, will appear no more, unless some new and strange circumstances call him again into existence, I wish to prevent my being harassed by being searched for, perchance that Sir Anthony should think I am no more."

The physician was silent for a few moments, and then he said,—

"The more I reflect upon what you propose, the more I like it. If anything can have any tendency to awaken better feelings in your husband's breast, it will be the notion that you are no more; and it will be the only punishment, probably, that you would be willing to inflict upon him for his conduct towards you. Suppose I take care that if he recovers at the hotel he receives intelligence of your death. You say, that in the letter you have despatched to him, you have made him acquainted with where to find your child."

"Yes, let it be so; and then perchance I may be able to watch unobserved what course he takes as regards the dear little one, and note if any regret for me mingles with his existence."

This course, then, may be considered to have been completely decided upon; and Emily, feeling fatigued, was recommended by Dr. Hammerton to seek some rest at once, which she did with a feeling of greater serenity than she could call hers for a considerable time, for she did not feel quite so lonely and desolate as she had done, and a sort of feeling came over her that some favourable change was about to take place in her fortunes.

Let us hope that imagination is a true prophet.

CHAPTER XXXII.

THE REVENGE OF MR. ADOLPHUS DACRE, AND ITS CONSEQUENCES.

WHEN Adolphus Dacre hinted to Margaret Wyvill that he might possibly be revenged upon her for jilting him as she had done, it was not altogether such a very idle threat as the lady evidently at the time believed, or affected to believe it to be.

His was just the petty sort of mind to be pleased with retaliation, and the more especially that sort of retaliation which involved in itself no personal danger or consequences. If it had, Mr. Adolphus Dacre would have been the man of all others, as our readers may very well suppose, to steer extremely clear of such an affair.

But, as it was, he turned over in his small intellect the whole affair, with a view of hitting upon the best means of preventing Margaret from having altogether a good laugh at his expense.

The imagination, however, of Adolphus Dacre was hardly active enough to furnish him with any hint of a sufficiently practical nature for him to go upon; and after cudgelling his brains in vain for a time, he made up his mind, if the curious collection of odd thoughts and feelings which made up

"The book and volume of his brain"

could be so called, to consult some one else.

"Yes," he said, "I will take the advice of somebody that's in the habit of such things. I won't altogether trust to myself, but I'll find out some clever fellow who will be able to tell me what to do, and who as well may, perhaps, if anything should chance to go wrong, give me a helping hand in the way of assisting me out of the mire if I should get into it.

Probably Mr. Dacre had yet a vivid idea of the kick he had received from Sir Anthony Wyvill, and thought that if he could get somebody else to stand between him and such misadventures, it would be just as well, if not a great deal better.

The reader, however, will scarcely be prepared to hear that the person to whom he thought he would apply for advice was actually old Foster of the Dyke House! But such was the fact. We do not mean to say that he so applied because he had any erroneous idea respecting the pleasantness of a companionship with such a man as Foster, but because he certainly did think him a wonderfully clever man, and had heard that on more than one occasion people had taken his advice to advantage.

"I remember perfectly well," said Adolphus, as he placed his finger on the side of his head, as if by such a mode of manipulation, he called into exercise some dormant faculty of perception —"I remember perfectly well that when Farmer Llewellin lost his great he-goat, he went to old Foster, who, for five shillings, found it again for him in an hour or two; and why should not he be able to put me up to some way of being revenged on Mistress Margaret Wyvill. I don't like being jilted, I can tell her. She may say what she likes, and have her own way as long as she likes, but she ought not to have promised to have me and then tell me I'm too stupid."

How then was it that Adolphus Dacre quite lashed himself into as great a rage as he was capable of getting into at all against Margaret? But he little suspected the real character of the man to whom he was going for advice, or the Dyke House would indeed have waited long before his shadow darkened its door.

It was towards the evening hour that Adolphus made his way to Foster's house, for he had certainly a dim sort of idea that it was not the most respectable place in the world to be seen making a morning call at, whatever might be his notions of the great sagacity of Foster, and the great use he was likely to be of to him.

When he reached the Dyke House he was rather surprised to find that the door was very closely shut indeed, which was far from being usually the case, because it was the aim of the Fosters, and naturally enough too, whatever might be the roughness of their manners, to make the place as inviting as possible to strangers.

He knocked; and if we say that he did not expect to meet with the most gentle and inviting reception, yet we can with equal truth assert that he did not expect the odd sort of snubbing welcome that he really did get.

Scarcely had his hand left the door, at which he had executed rather a tremulous rap, than it was flung wide open, and Foster himself appeared, exclaiming,—

"Who the devil is this?"

Adolphus Dacre started back amazed, and then he said,—

"Don't you know me?"

"Oh! it's you, is it, Mr. Dacre! Well, what do you want."

"Perhaps I want one thing and perhaps I want another, Foster, and I must say that when one comes to consider all things, your reception of me is scarcely civil."

"Bah! I was busy. Elspeth, is all right?"

"All right," said Mrs. Foster, from within the long low-roofed room we have before mentioned. "All right. Let him come in, be he whom he may."

"Don't you hear?" said Foster, to the hesitating Adolphus,—"don't you hear you can come in, stupid? Don't stand gaping there, keeping me waiting with the door in my hand all night. If you are coming, come at once."

Thus gently and kindly admonished, poor Adolphus made speed and entered the Dyke House, not exactly knowing whether he ought not in preference to run away or not. But as he had come so far for advice, he did think it a pity to go away now without it; so useful a commodity too as it was.

Accordingly he entered that room which we were, on a former occasion, at some pains to describe, and having accepted a seat which was offered to him by Mrs. Foster, he proceeded to say something on the subject of his errand.

"Mr. Foster," he began, "people give you credit for being a a man of great good sense and sound discretion."

"Oh! do they?" said Foster.

"Yes, they do, I can assure you, and I have heard a few little anecdotes of you, that make me think,——"

"Think what?" cried Foster, furiously.

"Ah! think what," shouted one of the idle, hulking sons, springing from a remote corner into which he had retreated. "Think what? Speak out, or you are a dead man."

"Good God! what do you all mean?" cried Adolphus, jumping up and holding the stool upon which he had been sitting in an attitude of defence. "Have you all gone mad? Come, come, keep off—keep off—I won't be bitten by anybody."

"Hush, hush!" said old Foster. "Excuse us, Mr. Dacre—we—we—that is my wife and little boy here, you see, have been a little vexed, that's all."

"Little boy! Do you call that great hulking fellow your hear boy? Why, he is six feet two in his stocking soles if he is a bit, and if you have been vexed, that's no reason why you should fly down my throat. I did not vex you!"

"Right," said old Foster, "quite right—quite right, sir. You hear what the gentlemen says, Elspeth. If you have been vexed, he did not vex you; don't you hear?"

"I did not say he had," screamed Mrs. Foster. "It was yourself that made the disturbance. Don't try to put it off upon me, for I won't have it. I tell you I won't have it, so don't try it. Say what you like, and do what you like, as regards yourself, and bring yourself to the gallows, if you like. What is it to me?"

Foster glared at his wife like an enraged tiger.

"Who asked your opinion?" he cried.

"You be bothered," shouted the little boy, "and there seemed every probability of this amiable family having a general fight, for the edification and amusement of their visitor."

"Really now," said Adolphus Dacre, who had a dim presentiment that by such a family riot, he might, by general consent, be made to suffer severely to being beaten by the whole of them—"really now, I don't know what you have all got to quarrel about, but it strikes me, that you had much better leave off that sort of thing, you see."

" Come this way," said Foster, snatching up a light. " Come this way Mr. Dacre. Let them eat each other, if they like. You can tell me quietly what you came about."

This was just what Adolphus was panting to do, and he accordingly followed Foster from the room below, up the intricate staircase, to that above, in which was the large old fashioned unwieldy looking bed.

" Well now," said Foster, " what is it?"

" Don't you think, there's an odd kind of a smell here ?"

" No !"

" Oh! well, I don't mean to swear there is, if you say there is not. It only struck me, you know—so I made the remark."

" Very well ! Good night then."

" But you will hear what I have to say, won't you, after I have come all this way to say it. Come now, Foster—come now."

" Why, you have just said it, have you not ? You remarked, that there was an odd smell here. Was not that what you came to say ?"

" Upon my life, that's good ! Why, you don't mean to tell me, Foster, that you thought I came all this way to tell you there was an odd smell in your room. Oh dear no ! I want your advice about quite another affair, I can tell you. It's just this—Margaret Wyvill, you see——"

" What of her ?"

" Well, well, don't get in such a passion. Come now, Foster, you are certainly the most violent man I ever knew in all my life. You must know, that there was a sort of engagement between me and Margaret Wyvill. She was to have me, and in consequence, I ran here, and ran there, and made myself uncommonly agreeable, and now she won't have me."

" You don't expect I can persuade her, do you?"

Oh, no, no ! But then, I—I want to to serve her out in some way, at all events. I don't like putting up with things quite at if I was a stock or a stone."

" Oh! you want revenge."

" Well ! you may call it revenge if you like, though it is a strange term to apply to it. But still I don't like, as I say, to be treated in this sort of manner, and be quite laughed at. It aint pleasant, by any means, I can tell you, Mr. Foster, and I won't put up with it. What I want is, your advice what I should do in the transaction."

Oh, it's all a matter of price, you know."

" What do you mean ?"

" Why, I say, it all depends upon what you choose to give. If you will pay enough, she shall marry you whether she likes it or not."

" You really astonish me, Foster. You don't mean to tell me that you can make Margaret Wyvill marry me, whether she likes or not ? Come now, that is going a little too far, you know. I cannot exactly believe that, Foster ; but I do think you can put me up to some way of making her feel that I am not to be treated in that sort of manner with impunity, you know."

Foster was silent for some few moments, and then he said,—

" If I have the power, Mr. Dacre, to make Margaret Wyvill wed you if I please, I would not advise you to call it into existence, for that woman is one of the most dangerous—excepting always my wife—that ever I come near ; but I can tell you how you may have ample vengeance upon her in a manner that cannot fail."

" That's what I want to know."

" Well, then, you have only to go London and find out Sir Anthony."

" Oh ! and be kicked again."

" No ; you will not be kicked this time. Go and find him out, and tell him that you believe his wife, Emily, is quite innocent ; and that when she left his house, she did so from a conviction that he was guilty in bringing home the lady who accompanied him. But you must not say I told you."

"Certainly not. But how shall I make him believe all that? I confess, I thought of it before; for, between you and me and the post, I do think that Mistress Margaret has managed all that affair to suit herself, do you know."

"Never mind whether he believes it or not. You will set him about inquiring into it, and that will be sufficient to annoy Margaret. And now be off with you, and I don't want anything for the advice I have given you, but your silence as to whence it came from—for, mark me, Mr. Dacre, as sure as you are a living man, if you mention my name in the transaction, you will find something very uncomfortable happen to you."

"Honour," said Adolphus Dacre, laying his hand upon his waistcoat just above his stomach—"honour bright, you know. You may depend upon me, Foster, and I like your advice do you know, because, to do what you command was partly an idea of my own. I will go to London, and find out Sir Anthony Wyvill, and he shall apologise to me yet for the kick he gave me when I saw him at Portsmouth. I was standing at the window, and there was the lady, so she said to me,— 'Charming weather, sir,' said she; and I, with a sort of bow and a smile, replied to her,—'Yes, madam, and there are charming ladies too.' You see the point, Foster—charming weather and charming ladies—you see it?"

"Oh! I see it."

"It was good now, wasn't it? and only fancy what a thing, just as you happen to be smiling, and fancy you are doing something uncommonly well, to get a kick behind, that's enough to send you through a window, quite into the street. How should you have liked it?"

"Liked it?—liked it? You put up with that, and did not take his life!"

"I put down with it, for it knocked me down, I can tell you; but I came away, you see, to think upon what I had better do; not that I put up with it at all—oh dear no. I believe you, I have a spirit, Mr. Foster; and it's rather a dangerous thing for anybody to touch me, only I am not hasty."

"Oh! I suppose you are one of those who think it's wise to run away, so that you may live to fight another day. But, I'm busy; you have had my advice, and you may act upon it or not, as you think proper."

"Oh! well, I suppose that's as good as to say, the sooner I'm off the better. I'm going, and of course I'm very much obliged—though I did think of the same thing before myself—which shows, says you, that two people may think alike; so, good evening."

"Good evening—be off."

Adolphus Dacre left the Dyke House, not over satisfied with his visit; and yet not knowing exactly that Foster was in a position to give him any other advise than he had, and being still doubtful if he dared carry it out.

"Let me consider," he said; "she said, if I attempted to interfere with her, in any way, she would find me out if I was in the bowels of the earth; and I believe she would, if she had to scrape away all the ground with her very nails; she is such a violent, dreadful sort of female. I must consider how to do it."

Mr. Adolphus Dacre was extremely anxious to carry out his plan of revenge if he could do so, without endangering his own safety, and at last, he hit upon the coward's resource, namely, an anonymous letter, which he thought would be the best thing in the world to send to Sir Anthony, because he could say so much more in it than by any other mode or plan of operation that could possibly suggest itself.

"Besides," reasoned Adolphus, "if he should get into one of his rages, he may kick the letter as long as he likes, but he shan't kick me, for he won't have an opportunity; and I'll put at the end of the letter, what so many of the letters in the County Chronicle have put after them—"A Constant Reader." That's what I call a good idea, I may say, a capital idea, and I'll set about it directly—I will."

With this resolution in his mind, Adolphus Dacre went home to carry it out. After some labour, for the powers of composition of Mr. Adolphus Dacre were by no means great he succeeded in producing the following epistle:—

" SIR,—This comes, as I hope it will come duly to hand, to let you know that I
have my suspicions. ' What are they ?' you will say. ' Listen,' says I ; ' I
will,' says you.

" In the first place, then, how came you to bring anybody home to Wyvill Hall,
when you had a lawful wife. In the second place, you ought not to have done
any such thing ; and in the third place, it was decidedly wrong.

" You know, or you ought to know, that your wife left Wyvill Hall on account
of your bringing a lady ; but, from all I have heard among the servants, they
don't think there was anything improper, which of course surprises me, and I attribute it all to Margaret. You ought to be ashamed of yourself!

" Don't be fancying this letter comes from anybody you know, because it don't,
or anybody who is angry at having had a severe kick, because it don't. And hoping
you and Margaret, your sister, may be as uncomfortable as possible for the remainder of your days,

" I remain, your most obedient servant,

" To Sir Anthony Wyvill.   " A CONSTANT READER."

This epistle, Adolphus thought was the very thing ; and he went himself to
post it in the town, that was some short distance off, so as to ensure its being delivered early, and that no one should have the impertinence to open it except
the Secretary of State.

Alas! poor Sir Anthony Wyvill, how strangely circumstances were now all
conspiring to convince you of the innocence of her whom you mourned as guilty,
and to show you the treasure you had lost.

It so happened that on the very day that Adolphus Dacre was writing his
epistle, the old couple who lived in the Lodge held a long and serious consultation over the circumstances, so far as they knew them, which had accompanied the withdrawal from her home of Emily Wyvill.

The gentle manners and the kind and considerate behaviour of the Lady
Wyvill had won the hearts of all on the estate, and none more so than those of the
old couple who kept the Lodge. Probably too, when the gentle will of the
Lady Wyvill came to be contrasted with the harsh and tyrannical sway of Margaret, it presented itself in the pleasantest colours, and from the time that Emily
had come to the Lodge from the Dyke House, to ascertain the fact of Sir
Anthony Wyvill having actually brought a female home with him, they had
always felt a disagreeable impression that she was in some way ill used."

" I tell you what it is, husband," said the old woman ; " I should not have
dreamt last night of white mice, if something had not been amiss."

" But what's amiss ?"

" How can I tell exactly? That's the beauty of a dream, that it does for anything, but to my mind it means something about poor Lady Emily."

" What makes you think that, wife ?"

" I not only think that," said the woman, evading the direct question,—" I not
only think that, but I think, that if you were half a man, you ought to let Sir
Anthony know that his poor wife came to the Lodge to inquire after him with
tears in her eyes, poor thing.".

The old Lodge-keeper was silent for a time, and then he said,—

" Wife, I'll tell you what happened only the other day, which set me thinking."

" What was it, Goodman ? You never told me anything had happened at all."

" No, I know I did not—I know I never mentioned it, and the reason, wife, that
I did not, was, that it made so deep an impression upon me, that I could not make
up my mind what to think about it ; and I did not like to speak lightly upon a
matter of so much importance."

" Importance ! What was it ?"

" Just this,—A gentleman on horseback stopped at the Lodge to inquire his way
somewhere, and when I had told him, he asked me whose estate this was, and
when I mentioned the name of Sir Anthony he said at once,—

" Oh, that is General Wyvill, you mean, whose wife went away with some one."

"No, sir," said I, "it's General Wyvill who went away with some one, and not Lady Wyvill, who is, poor young thing, as innocent as the day; and then he said, —'You very much surprise me, for I heard quite different, and was told in London that Sir Anthony Wyvill was quite cut up at the conduct of his wife, and was living alone at an hotel.'"

"With that he rode away, and I have been thinking ever since, do you know, that there is something wrong in the whole affair."

"You may depend there is."

"Then what ought we to do?"

"Why, put it right, to be sure. How can you ask such a question? You quite surprise me, goodman.

"And you quite surprise me, goodwife, when you say put it right. How are we to put it right? That's the question. How is it to be put right? Tell me that."

No. 27.

" You ought to write a letter to Sir Anthony."

" A letter ? Why, I declare I haven't wrote a letter, since i don't know when. I almost think that I forget how, do you know, wife ; but I'll try, and that at once, too, for 1 don't see why, poor and humble though we be, we should not try and do something to better ourselves, which it will do if we succeed in bringing poor Lady Emily back again,—bless her sweet eyes : none of the poor folk ever wanted for anything while she was on the estate."

These honest but poor and ignorant people then laid their heads together, and after much turmoil and trouble succeeded in producing an epistle which will appear in its proper place, as we continue our narrative.

CHAPTER XXXIII.

SIR ANTHONY WYVILL RECOVERS SUFFICIENTLY TO READ HIS LETTERS AND MAKE SOME INQUIRIES.

From the moment that the remarkable change took place in Sir Anthony's illness, which we have recorded, he continued to mend, to the inexpressible joy of the captain's widow, who found some reward for her noble and generous devotion in the amended state of him, to whom she was under such numerous and deep obligations.

About two days and two nights more made a wonderful difference in him, and the medical man declared that the cure of his wound was proceeding now so favourably and so rapidly, that there was no longer a fear of anything in the shape of a relapse.

This was as pleasant intelligence to Sir Anthony, as it was to any one else, and he having brought his thoughts back to the world and its many concerns, deeply in his own mind revolved the various occurrences that had happened to him and the peculiar situation in which he was placed.

It was towards evening that, turning in his bed, he spoke in a low but kind voice to her who had stepped forward to tend upon him, saying,—

" It is quite impossible that I can ever hope sufficiently to thank you for all that you have done for me, but at the same time I now feel that in common justice to you and to your position, I ought to dispense with your generous services— services which a bad and a censorious world may place a misconstruction upon that would cut me to the soul to think of."

She wept as she heard him utter these words, because she fully and entirely felt their truth, but her heart was too full to enable her to reply to them.

" Do not," he added, " mistake for one moment, and fancy that I have no appreciation of the great and noble feeling which has actuated you on this occasion. I have, I assure you, the highest sense of these qualities—such a sense of them indeed as defies all language to give utterance to ; and must, with this expression of my perfect admiration of the self-devotion which you have exhibited, leave you to imagine all the rest."

" I can imagine all that you think," she replied, sadly, " although for my own part I do, and must repudiate all such praises. What have I done, that should for one moment make me deserving of them ?"

" You have done much to make you amply deserving of them ; you have done wonders—great wonders, I am sure, such as ninety-nine women out of a hundred would shrink from ; for have you not done what you considered right in the face of what you knew would be censure and detraction ?"

She wept again, for she felt the full truth of the words he uttered.

" By so doing," he continued, "you have achieved such a victory as seldom falls to the lot of any individual, and few indeed are there who would have courage sufficient to make the effort in the least."

"I am rewarded,—I am fully rewarded, to see you better ; and if I might speak at all on such a theme, I must say, that it is common gratitude only, that I ought to lay claim to, for what amount of service can I possibly have it in my power to render to you that can at all compare with that which you have rendered to me."

"But the consequences to me were nothing."

"The consequences to me are nothing, for I can afford to look into my own heart, and then to despise them utterly and wholly."

"You are one of a thousand. I have thought over this occurrence, and came to a strange conclusion as regards it ; I mean the wound that I have received. I am certain that it has saved me."

"Saved you? From whom and from what?"

"From myself, and from destruction. Listen to me :—When I came to London, I was in that state of mind from despairing thoughts, and from having all my happiness so completely destroyed in the home which I fondly thought would, while I lived, be such a haven of felicity to me, that I was lost to all self-control ; I was not master of myself, and fell into the hands of whoever would take the trouble to assume a mastery over me."

"And those were bad hands?"

"They were indeed ! I had commenced the steep descent of vice. That precipice which I had all my life regarded with horror, was yawning before me—I was beginning to become a gambler."

"But Heaven averted such a fate ?"

"It did, and this wound, with its contingent circumstances, and its consequent illness, that has given me so many hours of calm reflection, has saved me. It has at once separated me from the evil associates who were taking my judgment prisoner, and, by throwing me back upon my own thoughts, has awakened me to what is yet my duty, and what I owe to my name and to my former good reputation."

"Oh, what joy it is to me to hear you speak thus !"

"Yes, it has awakened all of the better nature that is within me, and made me know myself. I shall never again be so abandoned by reflection as to fall into the grievous errors that were beginning to have an effect upon me. I shall now soon, I hope, be able to devote some time to a discovery of where she, who still holds a place in my heart, is hidden."

"And your child ?"

"Yes, and my child,—that child who as yet has had so few of a father's caresses. I shall yearn to see it, and to find that at least I have a chance of making one living thing love me for my own sake alone."

These words were very far from being intended as such, and yet they sounded almost like a reproach to her who was listening to them. But such affection as hers is ever extremely'sensitive, and hence it was that she looked aside and wept again to think that she was so completely as she was denied the privilege of answering them. There ensued a silence of some few minutes' duration ; after which Sir Anthony said,—

"And in the midst of all troubles and of all congratulations it is very strange how the image of that young boy will perpetually come back to my mind, bringing with it the saddest feelings of deep regret at his absence, and torturing my mind with conjectures as to its possible or probable course, for Heaven knows I was always kind to the youth, because I loved him."

"I do believe he thought highly of you, sir, and loved you, but he had, unhappily, one of those strange, jealous dispositions which look with great dissatisfaction upon any interference between them and their idol, and that he thought I was so interfering was evident from his words and manners."

"It would seem so."

"It must be so. I saw his eyes flash with a strange sort of fire when I came to your bedside, and avowed my intentions of making an effort to show that I was grateful."

" It was strange ; for I have seen him watching me with such a tender, melancholy interest, that I could not have thought any circumstances of mere jealousy would have induced him to leave me. But he is gone, and the pang that his going has cost me reminds me more of the pang that I felt when I heard that Emily was faithless, than anything I am now likely in this world to feel."

" Perchance he will return."

" Heaven send he may! He was a gentle boy."

" I can well and easily perceive that, from some hidden cause unknown to me, he has a great hatred of me. That he did not scruple to express when he brought to me the letter that you so kindly sent to me. But I could well forgive it on account of his attachment to you."

" Indeed ! I knew not of that."

" Nor should I have mentioned it, had we not been speculating on the causes of his leaving you."

" That is the strangest of all to my mind, for boys seldom take up these kind of jealousies of the other sex. But I will hope that when I am strong enough to get out and about, I shall be able to get some news of him, for I am most anxious concerning him."

" And now then, Sir Anthony Wyvill, I think that having thus far seen you, as it were, on the road to convalesence, I may leave you."

" You will take with you my best wishes, and my most sincere and heartfelt friendship."

" That thought shall be a great consolation to me ; and I trust that you will not think that I can ever forget what I owe to you when I am far away."

" Far away !"

" Yes ; I was thinking that—that I should like to live abroad somewhere, in some quiet part—perhaps in Switzerland—where I could, for a very small sum indeed, pass the remainder of my days in the calm serenity of some mountain home, looking upon the beauties of inanimate nature, and in a contemplation of them finding a solace for the sad memories of the past. I hope that you do not disapprove of my scheme."

Sir Anthony was silent for some few moments, and then he said, in a voice of deep feeling and emotion,—

" I know well that, although I can and do feel for you all the affection of a sister, the usages of the world forbids that you should reside under the same roof with me. Of that I am well aware, and I feel that I ought, of all persons, to be the last to hint at such an arrangement that might be to you a source of future annoyance ; but I did hope that you would continue to be my friend and adviser, which at so great a distance you cannot be."

" Do you purpose remaining in England, Sir Anthony ?"

" I do now, if I continue in my present mind. I have the duties of a father to perform to that babe which, at least, Emily might have left to me. She should not have taken the child with her—indeed she should not—that was the unkindest thing of all ! If she no longer loved me herself, why should she seek to deprive me of the love of that little one."

This was a point in the supposed bad conduct of Lady Wyvill upon which the captain's widow felt to the full as strongly as he (Sir Anthony) could do ; but it was one on which she did not like to speak, on the very account that she did feel so strongly upon it, and that she feared the making use of some expressions—however he might admit the truth of them—would give him great pain to hear used ; so she was silent, and, after a slight pause, he continued,—

" Have you quite made up your mind to the course you mention ?"

" I—I think I have."

" Then you have some doubts. Give, let me pray you, to friendship the advantage of those doubts, and let me hope that, for a time, you will forego your intention."

" I cannot say no to such a request from you, and for one month, at the end of which time I hope to see your health thoroughly re-established, I will leave, if I have your consent so to do. I am the creature of your bounty now ; and although your noble generosity makes such a circumstance as little felt as it is at all possible to be, yet I have a hope that by an exercise of those acquirements which were given to me in order to pass a happy leisure with, I may be able to take a burden off you which you ought not on any account to bear."

"Why will you pain me by talking upon such a subject? How can you call a burden that which in reality is not one, and never can be? I do not like to speak on such a theme, but it costs me no effort to provide for you—however, it would cost me pain not to do so. You know my fortune is ample, and therefore, there is little deserving of commendation in spending a small portion of it in such a way."

"I will say no more on such a theme," she replied, "although you may well conceive it to be one that is likely to be uppermost in my mind. Will you forgive the annoyance I have caused you?"

"Rather, will you forgive me?"

"There again," she said, "speaks the generosity that will not blame another."

"I think," he said, suddenly, "I heard something of some letter or letters having been brought for me when I was not in a fit state to read them."

"Yes," she replied, "there were some, and I placed them away under lock and key by order of your medical adviser."

"No doubt it was wise to keep them from me while I was in such a state, I was hovering between life and death, and I recollect my great anxiety was so to dispose of my property, that Emily, if she repented of the step she had taken, should not be exposed to any of the horrors of want ; and if she really chose to follow a different course, and to endeavour in any manner to atone for what she had been doing she, should have a full and ample opportunity of so doing, and in some retirement perchance, far removed from the eye of ordinary observation, she might prepare herself for that heaven which, erring creature as she is, I can still hope, will expand its gates to receive her."

"How few indeed in such a situation as yours would utter such a sentiment."

We cannot but echo the sentiment of the captain's widow. There are indeed few, very few, who, situated as Sir Anthony Wyvill was, would have dreamt of giving utterance to a sentiment which, to the smallest extent implied pity for one who had caused him so much misery.

But he was a man of a thousand, and did not look upon human nature with those jaundiced prejudices, that many persons take a pleasure in regarding it with. And now that that temporary hallucination of intellect, for we can really call it nothing else, which had come across him when first he came to London, and found himself so desolate and forlorn, had passed away, all the higher and better feelings of his nature returned to him, and he became what he once was, a man of fair and energetic resolves, and of active intellect.

There was one thing, too, that he considered, which had all its effect upon such a mind, and in so considering it, he only carried out a principle which had been instilled into him in early youth, and which was one of the most valuable any person could possess.

It was simply this, that the honour of every one is in his own keeping, and that the conduct of no one can possibly affect it.

This was a feeling which effectually prevented that amount of soreness which many husbands would have felt upon being situated as he was, and never for one moment had he considered that the departure of Emily from her home in any way brought disgrace upon him, however it might affect his happiness ; and thus was it that he was enabled to talk with a calmness and a philosophy upon a subject which drives so many persons nearly to the verge of distraction.

And this distracted feeling wholly and solely arises from a foolish notion that the finger of scorn can be justly pointed at any one individual for the acts of another. It is high time that such a feeling was uprooted from the minds of all persons, for a more glaringly unjust one, or one more illogical, even to the verge of silliness, could not have been found. It produces more mischief than people who do not inquire closely can possibly imagine. Why should the vicious and the dissolute hold out, as if even the tenour of their own evil conduct to the virtuous and the good. Is. it not monstrous that one bad member of a family should, from this foolish notion of society, be given the satisfaction of thinking that he has it in his power to bring disgrace upon persons of spotless honour, when, in reality, it is no such thing, and the only power of that nature he possesses is to bring disgrace and all its attendant consequences upon himself.

Such expression as a wife disgracing her husband and bringing dishonour upon his roof, or a son or daughter doing the same by his or her parents, should be entirely expunged from our language, not that evil doers should be made to feel that those worst consequences of their acts centre entirely in themselves, but have no power to touch the credit, the fair fame, or the honour of the meanest living creature that ever drew the breath of life.

We have been led into this digression in consequence of the expression of pity, rather than of anger, which Sir Anthony Wyvill from time to time used, as regards his wife's expressions, that we would not for a moment have supposed to result from weakness, or a deficient sense of what was really due to himself.

And the captain's widow was well aware, from what he had said at different times, that such was the just view he took of the peculiar circumstances in which he was placed.

Reverting then to the subject of the letters, she said,—

"Do you really think you are sufficiently recovered to chance the fact of there being agitating tidings in any of those epistles."

"Most certainly," he said, "and besides, what can agitate me now—do I not know the worst that fate can inflict upon me? I almost doubt if evil fortune has yet another arrow in her quiver with so barbed a point as that which she has already launched at my devoted heart. May I ask you the favour of reading those letters to me, and when I find, as most likely I shall do, that their contents are of little importance, I shall at all events be free from the anxiety of supposing that any one of them might be otherwise."

"I will read them to you with pleasure. It is a grateful task, and far from being one from which I shrink. Here is one letter that only came to-day, it seems but a note of inquiry, and is dated from the United Service Club."

"What name has it?"

"Franklin Bell."

"I know him well, a fellow soldier. I must answer him at leisure."

"There is another likewise, marked, 'On His Majesty Service,' and dated from the Horse Guards. It is a request to know if you are inclined again for active service, and if so, offering you the command of a division of the army now in Spain, and acting in conjunction with Lord Wellesley."

"That will bear consideration, lay it aside."

"Here then is an extraordinary epistle, at least it seems so, for it has gone from place to place, in search of you, and has reached here at last, after several directions have been marked upon it. It must be some mistake altogether, and how your name got upon the back of it I cannot think, for it is signed at the bottom, 'A Constant Reader.'"

"'A Constant Reader;' that must be intended for some newspaper. What is it all about?"

She read it to him, and as our readers are already aware that this was Mr. Adolphus Dacre's letter, with which he thought he should be able to achieve some revenge, at least against Margaret Wyvill, we need not recapitulate it, but safely leave to our readers to consider and imagine for themselves the unbounded astonishment with which it was listened to by Sir Anthony.

When it was concluded he and his exemplary nurse looked at each other in astonishment for several minutes, and then he said,—

"Good Heaven! what can be the meaning of this? Have my misfortunes become such a mere jest, that the most ignorant think it safe to write to me in such a strain, or is it possible that this means something beyond what its foolish writer has had power to express? Who can it possibly come from?"

"If you have no means of guessing, I would hazard a conjecture which has occurred to my mind in consequence of an allusion to a circumstance you cannot have forgotten. You remember a man coming to the inn at Portsmouth, who made some silly remarks to me?"

"I do. He brought to me Margaret's letter, containing the first intimation of the faithlessness of Emily, and in my indignation and non-belief of that circumstance, I was foolish enough to assault him. This letter must come from him, and if so, his name is Adolphus Dacre, and during my brief stay at Wyvill Hall, I was told that he considered himself a suitor of Margaret's. What am I to think of this epistle? Does it really merit any attention, or is it but a splenetic ebullition of wrath against Margaret for some slight she has put upon him?"

"Anything, Sir Anthony Wyvill; let it come from whom it may, anything which implies the slightest doubt of your wife's guilt deserves the deepest and most profound attention."

"It does—it does; I thank you for those words. There is little in the letter but a vague accusation against Margaret, without proof; but I will sit up and write to this man by return of post, requesting him to come to London at my charge and expense, and assuring him of a kind reception if he has anything to say to me upon the subject of his note."

Thus it will be seen how very easily Mr. Adolphus Dacre's secret was discovered, and that with all his cleverness, and all the tact he thought he possessed, he was like a donkey who could not open his mouth without people knowing by the first bray he uttered who and what he was.

The style of the epistle was too like his style of conversation to be mistaken, and Sir Anthony Wyvill, after it had been suggested to him, felt no more doubt regarding the authorship of the letter signed "A Constant Reader," than he did of his own existence.

"Yes," he said, "I will write to him before post time, if I have strength sufficient to rise and do so; and if not, I will get you to be so kind as to do so for me. It shall not be said that anything was lost for want of inquiry."

"What if, after all, she should be innocent?"

"Oh Heavens! I dare not trust myself enough to think of such a supposition. It is true that I have heard and read of such deep-laid and dexterously carried out plots to prove the innocent guilty, that the most unwilling mind has been compelled to yield credence to the supposed fact; but alas! although it is not impossible that I and she, who was so dear to me, may have been made the victims of some diabolical plot, the probability of such a thing is so extremely weak, that I cannot bring myself to lend attention to it for a moment. No, no, it cannot be; a moment's thought brings too many frightful proofs of that which I would give all I possess in the world to be able to disprove, but I shrink in terror from the investigation."

"It may be so—I cannot say but it is so; but, Sir Anthony Wyvill, listen to me. This letter, coming as it does from a man of the most ordinary and weak capacity, may be considered in its opinions as a fair enough exposition of what others think."

"You allude to the injurious expressions concerning yourself in it; but banish them, I pray you, from your mind; think nothing of them; they shall all be retracted."

"For my own sake, I do think nothing of them; and, strong in the consciousness of rectitude, I can and do defy such puny attacks. "But oh! Sir Anthony, what if some busy tongues carried to your wife the news that you were associating with me guiltily, convincing, by seeming proofs, your wife of such a fact, and awakening, as such intelligence surely would, the most agonised feelings in her bosom."

"No, no, no!" cried Sir Anthony Wyvill, "I cannot think that—I dare not think it: it would drive me mad to think it for a moment. She ought not—would not believe anything evil of me upon such mere gossiping, hearsay evidence. No, no, it cannot be!"

"But, Sir Anthony, you forget that this subject was one which is likely to prey largely upon the imagination."

"No, she would have time to reason—to call reflection to her aid."

"There are matters upon which the more we attempt to reason and call reflection to our aid, the less capable are we of arriving at a correct conclusion, and the more likely are we to be swayed by imagination. This is essentially one of those subjects. Do not merely, therefore, Sir Anthony Wyvill, blame your wife if she failed to bring to bear upon it a power of reasoning that no one can bring to bear upon matters closely connected with the feelings. Perchance it is because I am a woman that I feel strongly upon such a point, and can imagine such a set of circumstances as would produce all that has been produced, and yet leave your wife as innocent as it is possible for any human being to be. Reflect, and reflect deeply, upon what you now know; and ask yourself if you can find anything among recent circumstances which shall enable you to imagine for a moment aught favourable to your lady."

"Speak no more—speak no more! Your words are full of hope, and yet full of torture. Oh! if Emily indeed be innocent, what a world of suffering must she not have endured; such a thought of itself is enough to drive me to the confines of insanity."

"Now I regret that these letters have been read to you. Let me read no more. There is another here, but it is better left alone. I have not opened it, and let it rest until the morrow."

"No, no, let me know all at once, the epistle you would keep back may be an indifferent one, upon some common place and ordinary subject. If so it can do no harm for you to read it. But be it what it may, it cannot awaken more fears and more dreadful anxieties than at present find a home within my heart. Let me hear it—let me hear it."

"Of course at your pleasure, Sir Anthony, I open it."

She did so, but when she cast her eye to the bottom of the page she could not, if her life had depended upon it, suppress a sudden exclamation of surprise.

"What is that—what is that?" exclaimed Sir Anthony. "Speak to me, keep me not in suspense, but tell me, for the love of Heaven, who is that letter from?"

"From your wife."

"From Emily! good God, is this possible?"

"Hush! be calm; I will read each word of it to you. I pray you to compose yourself, for the contents of this sheet of paper must resolve all your doubts. You will either be as you were, or you will know again the right road to happiness which, for a short time, you have missed."

"Read—read—read," was all he said.

Then, with an agitated voice and trembling tones, she read to him that letter which the reader is already acquainted with—that letter in which Emily detailed all she had suffered, and all she feared that she knew to be the causes of such suffering—that letter which exposed to the full the hideous perfidy of Margaret Wyvill—that letter which implored him to take the charge of his child, which opened his eyes to the whole of the circumstances that had passed with such frightful rapidity, and which at once removed the veil of mystery which was enveloped around much which had become the subject of conjecture, and supplied every wanting link in the chain of circumstances that surrounded him.

Then he heard how, disguised, she had attended him so faithfully, and then he heard that she was lying at the point of death as she supposed, and that her last words would be a blessing and a forgiveness to him for the supposed evil that he had inflicted upon her.

And she who was reading this epistle paused not until she came to its last word, and then the paper dropped from her hands, and she wept bitterly, and in a voice interrupted by sobs, she exclaimed,—"And I have been the innocent cause of all this misery. Oh, why did I not die upon the same field of slaughter upon which my husband lay, rather than live to endure this sad amount of misery—the worst misery of all since it is the misery of having been a pestilence and a blight when I would feign have been a blessing, if I had had the power."

She sobbed bitterly for several moments, and then, being suprised that Sir Anthony Wyvill said nothing, she spoke to him again in a voice of anguish, saying,—" Sir Anthony Wyvill, can you ever again look upon me with eyes of ordinary friendship or indifference, even when you consider what a great foe I have been to your happiness, when you consider that but for me, Margaret would have wanted a point on which to turn her machinations? Speak to me, Sir Anthony Wyvill, and tell me you do not hate me."

Still he said nothing to her, and, overcome with grief and despair, she flung herself upon her knees, at the bedside, and looked in his face.

Then it was that she saw how little adapted he was, in the state of weakness to which he was reduced, to withstand violent emotions. Then it was that she saw the real reason why he answered her not—he had fainted, and lay alike insensible to joy or to sorrow.

*　　　　*　　　　*

A shriek of dismay burst from her lips, and, although she did not absolutely lapse into insensibility, she let her face drop upon the side of the bed, and felt all

No. 28.

that confusion of mental emotion which ensues as a reaction from a strong excite-ment, and which, in a weaker m_ntal constitution, must have produced total insensibility.

She had not remained in this state more than two minutes when the door of the apartment slowly opened, and a female figure attired in a riding habit, which was covered with dust, and showed evident symptoms that its wearer had ridden far, appeared upon the threshold of the apartment.

She started upon perceiving the group before her, and seemed to be upon the point of retiring at once from the room, but upon second thoughts she advanced, and then her eye fell at once upon the open letter of Emily Wyvill's that fell upon the floor on the spot where it had fallen from the hands of the captain's widow after her perusal of it to Sir Anthony Wyvill.

This female gave but one glance at the writing, and then without waiting another instant she crushed it up together in her hands and darted from the apartment. She descended the staircase with great rapidity, and crossing the hall with rushing footsteps, she gained the street, at the corner of which was a groom in handsome livery mounted on a horse which he had evidently ridden far, and holding another by the bridle, on which was a lady's side-saddle.

This individual, who had made so abrupt a visit to the chamber of Sir Anthony Wyvill, made her way now direct to the horses, and the groom instantly alighting assisted her to mount, she then, and not till then, thrust into her bosom the crumpled letter from Emily Wyvill which she had found in the apartment of Sir Anthony, and turning her horse's head in another direction, she made her way with great speed from the street in which the hotel was situated.

The groom put spurs to his steed and galloped up to her side.

"I beg pardon, madam," he said, "but it's impossible the horses can do it back again; they are nearly knocked up already, and in another dozen miles home-ward they will drop upon the road."

"Let them drop," was the brief reply.

"Well, but, madam——"

"Peace, peace, I say, it is your duty to follow, and do so without remark, while it is my pleasure to lead."

CHAPTER XXXIV.

THE RECOVERY OF THE CHILD, AND THE ARRIVAL OF MARGARET WYVILL IN LONDON.—HER OPPORTUNE DISCOVERY.

MARGARET was getting more and more uneasy every hour. She lived in a fever of continued apprehension, and it seemed to her, as if the gigantic shadow of some evil of immense magnitude had already touched her, and was slowly but surely casting the gloom of its pursuer over all her hopes and anticipations.

By day, or by night, she knew no peace, but she started at every slight sound, and if from that chamber which she devoted to her own peculiar use, and which commanded a view of the lodge-gates of Wyvill Hall, she saw a carriage or a horseman approach them that she did not know, her apprehension became intense, and until the chance tourist had passed away, she knew no peace, and even then her heart did not cease to beat with increased vehemence for a considerable period afterwards.

This was a miserable state of things for the clever, designing, artful Margaret Wyvill. It was a state of things which she did not expect, after the great tact, which she considered she had managed everything, and the great success which had crowned her exertions, to make herself uncontrolled mistress of Wyvill Hall.

Even she began to find out the disagreeable truth, which the base, the unscru-pulous, and the intriguing always do find out, and it is well they should, viz., that success in their plans and projects by no means makes happiness or contentment, or even ordinary serenity, a certain possession.

And at night she suffered more than in the day, for she was necessarily more by herself, and there were fewer objects to distract her attention from a miserable communion with her own thoughts.

She was likewise, in some manner, impressed with an idea that, if danger came to her, in consequence of an exposure of her plans, and the manner in which she had acted, it would come after sunset, because Sir Anthony, or whoever should come from London to Wyvill Hall to be her accuser, would most probably so arrange as to travel by daylight, and so of course arrive at the day's termination.

Then again, although she had treated the threat of Adolphus Dacre but slightly, she could not banish it altogether from her thoughts.

And the fact, that he knew very little, and had not the capacity to surmise much, was really but a small amount of consolation, because what she dreaded was inquiry, and nothing else.

Her safety consisted in the fact, as long as she could keep it up, of Sir Anthony Wyvill having no doubt whatever concerning the infidelity of his wife. The moment he began to doubt that fact, and consequently to institute a diligent inquiry, she stood in the most imminent danger, and she could notbut be aware how very small a circumstance would be sufficient to create that doubt, and consequently to produce that inquiry.

This was what tormented her each moment of her existence, and made her feel all that dread and terror, which such as she must always feel at a discovery of the truth—that sacred immutable truth, which is the friend of the innocent and the just, but the direst foe that such persons as Margaret Wyvill can possibly have, and really what they must live in continual dread of, and what must poison every one of their enjoyments.

She made it her special business to watch the proceedings of Adolphus Dacre as much as she could, but as her prudence prevented her taking any one into her confidence, her opportunities of doing so were but very small indeed, and it was by the merest accident in the world she discovered he had written a letter to Sir Anthony Wyvill. She did discover it though, and it gave her such a shock as she had not experienced for many a day.

Surprised and irritated that she had no communication from the lad she had sent to London as a spy upon the proceedings of Sir Anthony Wyvill, and through whom to procure information formed certainly a most essential part of her schemes, she wrote to him at the hotel where she knew Sir Anthony would be staying, urging him in every possible way, by threats as well as by entreaties, to write to her immediately, and let her know the state of affairs in London.

Heaven only knows where her *protege* had gone, after he had surrendered the letter of introduction to Emily, and had declined himself to taking service with Sir Anthony Wyvill, but certain it is he must have given up all idea whatever of keeping terms with Margaret by the manner in which he behaved towards her.

Being anxious that no one but herself should know that she was communicating with any such person, she, after writing her letter, resolved upon proceeding to the market town to post it herself, and it was by this accidental circumstance that she became acquainted with the fact that Mr. Dacre was not quite so innocuous a person as he seemed to be, and that, fool as he was, he might possibly be exceedingly dangerous.

Upon reaching the post office, she was received with all that distinguished consideration that country post-masters and mistresses never hesitate to bestow upon persons of ample means in their respective neighbourhoods, and among other gossip she was informed, in quite a natural, off-handed manner, that Mr. Dacre had, a few days before, posted a letter to London, addressed to Sir Anthony Wyvill.

This news was more than sufficient to arouse all Margaret's fears to a pitch of perfect agony, and it was with difficulty she suppressed her emotion in the actual presence of the post-mistress. She did contrive, however, to do so, and getting home as quickly as she could, she shut herself up in her own private apartment, to think over those circumstances which seemed to be accumulating about her, and aiming at her destruction.

After much reflection she resolved upon waiting until she saw whether by the next post or not she got a reply to her own letter, that she had just sent to London ; and if she got one she could be guided by what it related to her, but if she did not, she determined upon herself taking a journey to the metropolis, and ascertaining how matters stood.

The fever of impatience with which she now waited exceeds all description.

At one moment she thought she would send for Adolphus Dacre, and make some overtures to him, just for the mere purpose of getting from him what he had written, so that she might be able to judge of the amount of danger ; but, upon further reflection, she rejected this course as replete with both danger and difficulty, and made up her mind to wait, irksome as that waiting was, until the post should arrive.

It came at last, but it did not bring with it the smallest alleviation of her anxieties, for no letter appeared for her.

Then it was that she made up her mind upon a bold and vigorous course, which was to proceed to London at once, and ascertain the truth regarding the various objects of her anxiety.

First of all was she most anxious to know what Emily was about, and where she had gone, when she had left the Todds, so strangely and so mysteriously. Then she was anxious to discover why it was that the lad whom she had so pressed into the service of Sir Anthony Wyvill, forgot so completely all his promises and obligations to her as not to take the least notice of what she had requested him to do so particularly.

And last, although not least, was she anxious to know what Sir Anthony Wyvill himself was about, since she had not heard from him for so long, and all these together formed abundant reasons, to her mind, why she should proceed to London at once, and judge for herself the position of affairs.

She was a good horsewoman, for it was an exercise in which she took much delight, so after some consultation as to her mode of proceeding towards the metropolis, she made up her mind to ride thither upon horseback, taking with her one groom upon whom she could depend, and only baiting upon the journey as often as might be absolutely necessary for her own refreshment, and to give the horses some rest.

She cared not, so long as she reached London, whether the cattle were completely knocked up or not, for she knew that there she could procure more for money, and of that commodity Margaret was really now no niggard.

The groom was amazed at the intense anxiety of his mistress to reach London, but Margaret Wyvill kept those servants who were under her control much too strictly to allow them to make any remarks upon what she chose to say or do, and it must be upon a very special occasion indeed upon which the slightest remonstrance or suggestion was ever made to her.

The first stage she made was an unusually long one ; such a long one, indeed, that the groom, notwithstanding his habitual respect for Margaret, felt very much inclined to speak about it, for if any thing came between him and his wits completely, it was what he considered was over-working a horse, and right glad was he when Margaret at length drew rein at a road-side inn, and alighted ; for the tired horses, for the last half hour had been evidently showing symptoms of being jaded, and wishing for both rest and refreshment.

"I shall wait here one hour," she said to the groom.

"Yes, madam," he said, but he thought to himself—

"One hour! what a remarkably long time to rest a horse in, after he has come twenty-five miles. They ought to have four hours' rest at the very least, and I have half a mind to tell her so ; but I suppose if I do she will get into one of her confounded passions, and there will be no such thing as getting in a word, so I had better say nothing."

The groom certainly adopted the most prudent course as regarded Margaret Wyvill, fo he held his tongue—not that he knew there was any special danger in speaking to her at that junction, although there really was, for, as the reader may well imagine, she was in no mood just then to be questioned by any one.

She galloped on, quite heedless each moment of the increasing symptoms of distress exhibited by the horse, who certainly had already done more than ought to be expected from the animal, and he therefore now began most unequivocally to show that fact.

But let us pause for one instant, to consider what really must have been the desperate state of mind of Margaret Wyvill now.

If ever all her ingenuity and all that capacity for plotting and planning successfully which she possessed required to be called into vivid action, it did at the present moment, when her affairs had taken such an extraordinary turn, and she had so unexpectedly become defeated after so very short and transient a success.

But the very fact of her plans and plots were laid with such consummate art and skill that one was merely adjusted to the other, and there was such a dependence of each upon each, that she was distinctly at the mercy of any little cross accident that might occur.

She was a woman who fully felt this to be a state of things that was inevitable under the circumstances of the case; but she had certainly hoped that time would do something for her, and it would have done so, if Sir Anthony Wyvill had but carried out his original intention of proceeding to the continent, and then if, at the same time, she could have kept Emily's mind amused, so that she made no effort to reach Sir Anthony, or to demand or come to anything in the shape of an explanation, she would have done very well, and a separation which she had contrived really with such great skill and tact might have been rendered complete and lasting.

And any ordinary reasoner upon the subject would have naturally thought that after Sir Anthony had fairly left Wyvill Hall for London, and after Emily had become actually domiciliated with the Todds, a long career of triumph and of power awaited her; but she had to do with people whose mental characteristics she was not wholly aware of.

Who could have supposed it possible that Emily Wyvill, so gentle, so confiding, and so retiring a character, as she was, could have for one moment adopted the course she did, and placed herself in so strange a position as her husband's attendant.

And who would have supposed that Sir Anthony Wyvill, instead of, as he had said he would, proceeding at once to the continent, and endeavouring to forget the causes of his deep mental anxiety in the alarms and dangers of war, should actually remain in London to mix himself up with the ordinary frivolities and vices such as in his greenest youth he had never shown any disposition for.

We say, who could have supposed this possible of such a man, and it can only be at all reconciled to reason by the known fact that there are many minds which, under the pressure of a great shock, lose their equanimity completely, and adopt modes of action totally at variance with what ordinarily characterised them. Sometimes misfortune brings out the bright and strong portion of a person's character; but at other times it brings out the portions that are the weakest, and seems to destroy that energy and determination which otherwise occupies so large a portion of the intellect.

So it was with Sir Anthony Wyvill, for although no ordinary circumstances would have affected him, yet when he became touched so nearly in his affections, the shock was too much for him to withstand, and he felt himself compelled to give way to it at once. His only resource then was, since he could not boldly meet his misfortunes, to endeavour to withdraw his mind as much as possible from a too close contemplation of them; and this he might have done certainly better, if he had had the good fortune to fall into better hands than those into which he had fallen. The major, who had behaved in such a manner towards him, and to some extent victimised him, although not to the extent which he expected, was just about the worst associate that he could possibly have fallen in with.

As a man he was destitute of the most common and ordinary impulses of principle, and one who, when he found that his victim was no longer to be fleeced at pleasure, was quite content that he should be murdered, under the pretence of honourable treatment, in a duel.

That Sir Anthony Wyvill did not actually come by his death in this manner was evidently no fault of the major's, for there was every disposition to destroy him, and had he actually died of the wound which he had received, how delighted would Margaret Wyvill have been at such a catastrophe, and how well pleased would she have been to have amply rewarded whoever brought her such a gratifying intelligence.

But now in ignorance as she was, an ignorance of the most complete character as regarded the nature of Sir Anthony Wyvill's illness, she found herself lost in a complete sea of conjecture, and she would have given no small sum to any one who could have informed her of all the particulars which are so well known to the reader—particulars which to her would have been most important, and which certainly would have enabled her to act with greater certainty and precision than she otherwise would.

The contents of the letter which she had picked up in Sir Anthony's apartment certainly rather surprised her, and while much of it was certainly ambiguous in consequence of her want of knowledge of preceding circumstances, she saw quite enough, and gathered quite enough from its contents to drive her nearly to the verge of desperation.

During her long and anxious ride, she painfully revolved in her mind what she should do, and in so revolving it, she banished all other considerations save those of actual and mere personal safety, and was quite willing to adventure anything, however desperate it might be, for such a purpose.

Then, when she came to consider that it was evident from all she now knew that Sir Anthony Wyvill had been alarmingly ill, the thought of how fortunate a thing for her it would have been had he actnally died, gave the first impulse to a dark and horrible idea that such a consummation might yet be effected.

The more she reflected upon this idea, the more tangible was the shape it assumed, until at last she began to think it an admirable and a desirable thing—a thing which ought to be looked forward to as of the first consequence to accomplish, and which would easily and quietly rid her of all uneasiness.

"Shall I hesitate now," she said, "I who have already gone so far? Shall I now pause in an undertaking which so materially concerns my welfare, and which is of such vast importance to me, just because a human life stands in my way, a thing which I have always held in such deep contempt ; and which, although I have never yet actually adventured the taking of, I have not hesitated to tell myself over and over again, if it was at all necessary to my purposes. Shall I now, from any weakness, pause in my great resolution, because such a thing as a human existence stands in my way?

"And what to me is the accidental fact that Sir Anthony Wyvill is my brother? What to me is it that mere chance gives him the same name as myself? I am far above caring for such circumstances unless they bring with them collateral advantages. What is it to me, if a life is to be taken, whether it be the life of one person or of another? If a murder!—I do not shrink from the word, although many who would perpetrate the deed do so. What is it to me, if a murder is to be committed, who it is to be committed upon? If the deed, as pretended, be a deep and a damnable one, it is equally so be it committed upon whom it may, and I will not shrink from it."

The more she thus reasoned, the more she seemed to convince herself that the death of Sir Anthony Wyvill was a thing so much for her own sake to be desired, that she actually began to plunge quite into details concerning it, and to consider in what manner it could, with the least danger to herself, be accomplished.

"If he were dead," she said, "there would be nothing in the world to prevent me from producing a will which should place everything at my disposal, and leave Emily and her child to my liberality. Then I should be for ever at once free from all fear, for the dead cannot be troublesome, and under the circumstances, no one would be fool-hardy enough to dispute with me the fact that Sir Anthony had made such a disposition of his property."

"Moreover, if Emily still lives, although this letter seems to hint a doubt of her continued existence, if she still lives, I can and will be so liberal towards her that she shall not have it in her power to make any complaints, without seeming most ungratefully to regard what shall be made to wear all the aspect of great munificence."

Before, however, she could take any steps to accomplish these dark and unholy purposes, which were rapidly finding a home in her breast, it became necessary that she should have more information than she already possessed, and how this was to be obtained she could not imagine.

What had become of the lad whom she had appointed to attend upon Sir Anthony Wyvill, likewise to act the part of a spy for her, baffled all conjecture; for she could hardly suppose it possible that Emily could, upon the occasion of his taking the letter to her, have had any suspicion sufficiently strong to induce her to tamper with this lad in the least, so as to get from him the letter of introduction, and to personate him; and yet that seemed to be the only means by which she could have placed herself in the position mentioned and alluded to in her letter.

When she got about ten miles out of London, and while she was engaged in these ruminations to the greatest possible extent, so much so indeed as to be oblivious of every circumstance but those which occupied her own guilty thoughts, the wearied horse, by suddenly stumbling, gave an unequivocal testimony to the correct judgment of the groom, who had prognosticated such a result, if she continued on her present course, without giving the jaded animal rest or refreshment.

She was nearly thrown from her seat, and however she might despise danger, there can be but little doubt that she would have been seriously injured but for great projects of mind at the moment, and she considered, correctly enough, that a trivial accident happening to her now would have all the effect of destroying her schemes and prospects, and placing her completely at the mercy of circumstances over which she could have no control.

This consideration was the only one which induced her now to exercise what appeared to be ordinary discretion, and to the great joy of the groom, she turned at once, and said to him,—

"I will halt at the next place I come to."

"There seems to be an inn, madam," he said, "about half a mile further on, and I would reccommend that you pause there, and walk the horse gently till you reach it, for it's not worth while, madam, meeting with a serious accident to save, perhaps, five minutes of time."

This Margaret agreed to, although she said nothing, and she allowed the horse to walk the remainder of the distance which had to be traversed before they reached the inn which the groom had spoken of, and the swinging sign of which stood far out in the road-way.

A very short time sufficed for them to reach it, and Margaret then resigning her horse to the care of the groom, who was not a little gratified to find her in a more tractable mood, demanded a private apartment, into which she was immediately shown, for her haughty imperious manner, if it did not inspire any affection or good-will on the part of those that encountered her, at least begot some amount of fear, and that suited Margaret's purpose quite as well, for so long as she governed, and her authority was given way to, she cared not whether she owed that circumstance to affection or to dread.

She had made up her mind, during the short progress from London, that the situation in which Sir Anthony Wyvill was placed, was one which precluded the possibility of his taking any immediate and active measures against her, and the fact of the position of affairs at the hotel, and the place in which she had found the letter, tended much to convince her that he had but just received it.

These considerations induced her to feel that although delay was dangerous yet, that there was no great hurry in her proceedings, and that too much haste might be equally if not more so.

"I will give two hours," she said, "to a calmer consideration of what has happened, and during that time I make no doubt but I shall be able to make up my mind to some course of conduct which shall be clear and distinct, and which I shall be able to pursue without more trouble and difficulty than may naturally belong to the circumstances."

She told the groom that she would be two hours, and then having ordered some refreshments, for she began to feel the necessity for them after the great fatigue she had undergone, she shut herself up alone, to think.

What must have been the nature of the thoughts of such a person—how could she hope that reflection would bring any solace to her mind full of evil thoughts, as it was, and possessed with strange fancies? How could such a person as Margaret Wyvill ever hope to know peace when her mind was filled with a consciousness of the actual commission of many crimes of great amount, and she was actually then considering how she might commit others equally serious?

Wast his the sort of woman to derive any solace from reflection? Was this the sort of woman to rise up from the company of her own evil thoughts with anything like satisfaction? It was indeed wonderful that she, with all her great tact and experience, and with all her real talent, did not, or could not, perceive or perhaps would not, that she was placing herself in a worse position by every step she took and that she was really only more and more involving herself by the plunging efforts she made to rescue herself from circumstances she could not control.

The first thing that struck her particularly during the progress of her reflection was, that she had not sufficient evidence to go upon, and that she would run great chances of defeat from defective information; but how she was to obtain any more accurate knowledge than she at present possessed appeared to be a proposition most difficult of solution, and in fact almost impossible to arrive at a correct conclusion upon.

Had her juvenile spy upon whose services she had in the first instances so much counted, but been faithful to her, she would have been released from this great difficulty, and now her only chance consisted in finding some one upon whom she could rely, to play the part of a spy upon the actions of Sir Anthony Wyvill.

"I need not hesitate," she said, "so much as I hesitated before, in having an accomplice, or in trusting any one to gather information for me, because already Sir Anthony knows the very worst that he can know, and nothing further can occur in the way of information to him, that can make me hold a worse place in his opinion. All I want is to know what he is going to do—to receive early information as to where he betakes himself, and to ascertain fully and clearly what are his intentions."

After a time she thought to herself, that surely the groom whom she had with her, might accomplish this much, and reasoning upon the not very improbable assumption that money will accomplish a great deal, she made up her mind to tempt him to play the part she required, at all events of some one, she cared not who.

"He can but betray me," she said, "and if he does, I am no worse off, for without a doubt Sir Anthony Wyvill, after the reception of that letter which no doubt he has read, although I am possessed of it, surmises all that it does not tell him, and looks upon me in the worst possible light he can.

CHAPTER XXXV.

THE INSTRUCTIONS TO THE GROOM.—HIS ADVENTURES ON THE ROAD TO LONDON.

MARGARET rung for an attendant, and desired that her groom might be sent to her.

When he appeared—and he certainly was rather surprised at the summons—she spoke to him with less asperity than she usually threw into the tones of her voice, and said,—

" If you are inclined to do me good service, and likewise to earn for yourself an ample reward, attend to me now."

The man was astonished at what she said, and wondered what was going to happen next, but he made no remark upon the subject, and merely waited for her to continue to say what she pleased to him regarding the service she required, of him.

No. 29.

"1 have been to London," she said, " for the purpose of endeavouring to excite my brother's passion for the Lady Emily, his wife, but I have failed in doing so, although I hoped to have succeeded. Although he is on a bed of sickness at present, I much fear that he meditates some harsh treatment towards her, and therefore am extremely anxious to know what he is about, that I may put the Lady Emily upon her guard, and save her, perhaps, from disastrous consequences."

The groom signified that he should be very happy to assist in any such matter, although certainly as yet, he did not see his way to do so.

"I do not expect," she said, "that you should dictate any course of conduct; what I want you to do is to obey what I shall propound to you, and all I require of you is to be faithful and discreet—I do not ask impossibilities of you, and you may find insurmountable obstacles in the way of what I wish you to undertake, and in the way of what I have no doubt you will endeavour to do, therefore do not shrink from the task because it may possibly be unsuccessful."

" I will not, madam, you may be assured, and I am quite certain that nobody can be more sorry than I am, although all the servants at the Hall are sorry that any disagreement should have taken place between master and the Lady Emily, and although they all think that it wasn't at all likely, and, indeed that she has not done anything wrong, none of them can think so, more than I, or be more willing to do her any service."

" That is well, and what I expected of you; and what I want you to do, then, is to go to London, and as quickly, and as secretly, as possible discover all the particulars you can regarding Sir Anthony Wyvill. Do not hesitate to write to me because you may think I must be acquainted already with what you hear, but write everything, whether it be trivial or important, and you may count upon a reward from me which shall not be measured by the amount of intelligence you give me, but by the zeal which you display in endeavouring to do the duty to which I appoint you."

" I am willing to do my best, madam, but I am afraid it will be difficult for me to find out anything."

" Not at all; you must make acquaintance with the servants at the hotel to which I shall direct you, and as I pay you for finding out information for me, you shall have the means of paying them for what news you require."

" I dare say I can manage that, madam; and I shall do it with all the better grace when I think, as I of course do, that it is for the advantage of Lady Emily."

" Yes, yes, it is so."

" I am sure we all wish her back again to the Hall. The old place has not looked like itself without her."

" Certainly not, certainly not," said Margaret, impatiently.

" And as for the poor people who lived about, and to whom she was so good, I am sure they would make a general holiday if she were to come back again."

" No doubt, no doubt. I think now you fully understand me, and have now your precise instructions. There is money for you : be prudent in its expenditure, but never stint it in the purpose for which it is intended ; and recollect, I shall expect to receive a letter from you, addressed to Wyvill Hall, by every morning's post—and remember, I expect this whether you have anything to communicate or not, and I shall be satisfied if it merely contains a statement that you are vigilant upon your post, and that no change has taken place since last you wrote to me."

" I shall obey you, madam, cheerfully."

" Begone, then, at once ; take your own horse with you, and place the creature somewhere in London, where it will be in safe keeping. In a few hours' time I shall again proceed towards the Hall. Be vigilant, punctual, and faithful, and then you may name your own reward for the service you render me."

She waved her hand, in her usual imperious manner, for Margaret had much of the manners about her of an autocrat, and scrupled not to treat her dependants after a very sovereign-like fashion, which many persons would not have admired, but which, whether they did or not, they would have been compelled to submit with at her hands, if they expected to remain in any way connected with her—for she was one of those individuals who will not endure any divided rule, and who will govern entirely, or not at all.

Having thus, as she considered, satisfactorily taken the only step she could under the circumstances, for the purpose of securing her interest, and of discovering what course Sir Anthony Wyvill was likely to pursue, she inquired anxiously of the people of the inn when they thought the horse would be ready to resume his journey, for she had no wish now to meet with an accident before reaching Wyvill Hall.

To her mortification, she was told that the animal was completely knocked up, and unfit to proceed further on that day; but this information was accompanied by another, that tempered it considerably, which was, that they could provide her with a horse that was perfectly fresh, and which would be able to perform the journey she meditated, for she had mentioned the distance she was going with great care.

"Let me have it instantly," she said, "for I am most anxious to get on."

The steed was speedily at the door, and, although she more than suspected that the declared incapacity of her own horse was in consequence of the wish of the people at the inn for her to make use of one of theirs, she made no cavil at the proceedings, but allowed them to please themselves in the matter.

The day was now considerably advanced, and let her make what haste she could, it would be almost impossible for her to reach Wyvill Hall by sunset; but, nevertheless, she started, and being heedless as she was, and totally free from those ordinary fears which would have beset most women if travelling alone, she started from the inn at a good pace.

There are two classes of females who can always travel with perfect safety alone, viz., the ignorant and the highly educated. In either of these cases no mischief is likely to accrue; but in the intermediate class numerous difficulties are likely to present themselves, for there is sufficient attraction to induce a sort of persecution, under the name of gallantry, while, at the same time, there is not sufficient dignity and tact in the individual to repress it.

Margaret, certainly, belonged to the highly educated class, for there was scarcely a branch of human knowledge that she had not made some progress in. Her restless intellect must always be at something, and when she saw no opportunity of carrying out plans for her own aggrandisement she would turn to some branch of knowledge—to the study of a science or of a language, which ordinary persons would never have thought of encountering.

As she proceeded onwards, she asked herself seriously the question of whether the circumstances that had occurred were really such as to strike at the root of her prosperity and power, or whether there was a possibility of her successfully combating with them.

"Shall I endure," she said, "such a defeat as this, and not make some gigantic effort to retrieve it? It is life or death with me; for if I saw that all was lost—if I saw that there was no possibility, or remote chance even, of escape from the circumstances that beset me I would rather take my own life than continue to exite in the scorn of those whom I have commanded, and from means wrung from the charitable consideration of those whom I have attempted to destroy; and as for condescending to the drudgery that is nicknamed industry in the world, and doing anything for society in exchange for a subsistence, I would not dream of such a circumstance, nor for one instant calculate upon such a vile resource."

She rode on, heedless of the many natural and exquisite beauties of scenery by which she was surrounded, and although she was passing through about one of the loveliest tracts of country that England could present, it had no charms for her.

She was buried deep within her own thoughts, and they were not such as at all assimilated with the beauties of nature—they were not such as would enable her to look upon the green fields, the majestic trees, and all the beauties of hill and vale, wood and river, with eyes of contentment and satisfaction. No ; harmony, and the quiet, gentle scenes of nature, were distasteful to her. They presented too great a contrast to the war of evil passions which found a place in her own bosom

She rode on, taking the proper road mechanically, without thought, and still intent upon manufacturing all sorts of combinations, and in arranging circumstances of a probable as well as of an improbable nature, which were likely to occur in the progress of time, as regarded her own affairs.

As yet, she had scarcely wished to avail herself of all the advantages which her possession of the Wyvill estates and their great revenues presented to her; for although she knew that the income was extremely large, yet she was not quite so secure of it as to justify herself in bursting out with that grandeur of display which was congenial to her spirit.

And at first glance it would appear strange that in such a person as Margaret Wyvill there should be such a love of the glittering gauds of existence ; but if we look below the surface upon such a subject, and cast our eyes round for examples, we shall find that the spirit of magnificence and the love of the costly and the beautiful belong entirely to the highest intellects, and those which have received and are susceptible of the greatest amount of cultivation.

It is among those small spirits destitute of genius, and who are content to grovel because they want the capacity to aspire, that we shall hear a defence of what is mean and contemptible, and as bitter tirades as their small imaginations give them the capacity to utter against beauty of display and all that glitter of existence, in which higher and more choice spirits love to indulge.

We do not intend for one moment to bestow any commendation upon Margaret, although, from her being a highly intellectual woman, she certainly had a taste for the magnificent, which, be it remembered, is as widely different from a vulgar love of finery as any high attribute of the mind can be from any low one.

And this it is people of small minds run their heads against, and mistake for that glorious and beautiful taste which lends a stimulant to all the graceful arts of which the world is capable.

It is truly a sad thing to think that high intellect and great mental resources are not always associated with correct notions of right and wrong. If they were, Margaret would not have been the character she is ; but that they are not, is a truth as apparent as the sun at noon-day to any one who has taken the least trouble to inquire into so deeply interesting a subject.

Education will do much, but it cannot do everything. A vicious intellect may be made less vicious by the force of precept and by example, but nothing will materially alter the natural bias of the mind ; and such a person as Margaret, educated or uneducated, was quite certain to become such a character, and must meet with universal reprobation, and be capable of producing the greatest possible amount of evil, to those by whom she may be surrounded.

CHAPTER XXXVI.

EMILY AT THE PHYSICIAN'S, AND THE GOOD ADVICE.

ALTHOUGH Emily Wyvill had done what she had to conceal the fact of her existence from her husband, she could not be unmindful of his condition, but with an anxiety which vividly proclaimed its existence in her countenance, she earnestly besought those kind friends with whom she was now remaining, to make for her every possible inquiry into his condition.

This, as a matter of course, we may expect that they would do, and Dr. Hammerton made it his especial business to call upon the surgeon—who was in attendance upon

Sir Anthony Wyvill; and, without going any round-about way to the matter, he said at once—

" I have a private reason for feeling interested in knowing how Sir Anthony Wyvill is going on, and shall feel obliged if you will tell me his precise condition."

This, the surgeon to a professional man, did at once, and he said—

" If you are at all anxious for his recovery, I have the pleasure to inform you that it will be complete, and that he is going on as pleasantly and well as it is possible he can; and he owes, by-the-by, almost all to the excellent nursing he has had from, I believe, his sister."

" Is she handsome ?"

" Oh, most decidedly, and she is a widow, but as handsome a woman as I think I ever saw, and as perfectly a lady in all she says or does, that it is quite delightful to speak to her. I can assure you, if you saw her, you would be quite taken with her. You could not avoid it, for certainly she is the most fascinating creature I ever saw."

" You are quite in raptures ?"

" In truth, I am."

" Then you are not aware that she is Colonel Wyvill's mistress ?"

" The devil, she is."

" Yes, I happen to know; and, from what you say of her, I certainly must compliment him upon the good taste he has shown in his selection."

" Well, you surprise me for she is the most modest, quiet, creature that ever I came near, without exception. Oh, you must be mistaken."

" Well, as you please. I was only told so, you know, so I cannot of course avow it of my own knowledge. But you have no fear of any relapse ?"

" Oh dear no. Not unless something very extraordinary indeed was to take place; but really, medically speaking, he is convalescent."

The doctor brought this news to Emily, and added—

" Now, in order that you may recover the tenour of your own mind, and be able to take such steps as may soon be necessary and agreeable to you to take under the circumstances in which you are placed—you should now take as much mental repose as possible—I do not mean mental inaction, but I mean that you should occupy your mind in some other way than that which has distressed you."

" Mrs. Hammerton has been so kind," said Emily, " as to place your library at my disposal. I am now so satisfied, by the accounts I hear of the apparently complete recovery of Sir Anthony, that I shall without anxiety be able to avail myself of such an indulgence."

When Dr. Hammerton had left her, a sensation of almost happiness crept over her as she drew a book towards her, and banishing for a time her fears and anxieties, she read a tale, as follows :—

During the period that England and Scotland were separate countries, and long before either country thought there was either policy or right to keep peace on the borders, between the two nations, many terrible calamities were perpetrated by the hostile natives of either soil.

Sudden irruptions have been made from one side the border to the other, for the purpose of foray or revenge, as the case might be. The English Beeves were great temptations to their poorer neighbours the Scots, who had less to lose, though they were occasionally the victims of similar inroads.

There was one homestead situate not many miles from the border, and which enjoyed more peace than those lying more immediately close to the borders—but it was not entirely exempt from the attacks of the moss troopers, and hostile attempts of the Scots: the truth of this might be seen, in the way in which the homestead was built.

It was of circular form, with towers on either side of a gate-way, besides the main building; altogether it was as strong a place of defence as any farm-house could well be converted into, and was a strong enough to resist any assault that could be made upon it by the ordinary incursions of the Scots; unless they sat down to reduce it with something more than the usual numbers which formed a foray, and where the loss of men as compared with the importance of the object was not a matter of consideration.

The walls were thick, and there was little chance of setting fire to it, and the only way in assailing, would be by artillery or by assault, which if attempted would ensure upon the assailants a heavy loss, if the defenders were at all resolute and courageous.

The place belonged to one Mason—the eldest of a numerous family. The father had died about ten years. Mrs. Mason, the widow, still lived, as well as several others of the family, who remained and aided the son in the farm.

There were many men always in the house quite sufficient to defend the place against sudden attack with advantage.

But there came no sounds of war, or the clank of the jack boot, the clash of sword or clang of trumpet, but these sounds were all changed for the pipe and tabor, and the merriment of a wedding-party.

There was much feasting and revelry that day ; the young men and maidens were decked out in their holiday attire, and the dance was begun ; no sounds but those of mirth and revelry could be heard.

The joyous, happy laugh rang through the halls, and not a face was there present but bore the happiest auguries for the future.

Mason had been that morning wedded to the daughter of a thriving family at Appleby. The bride's friends accompanied them home and promised to stop till a late hour, and then, when the hour of parting came, the bridegroom and his friends insisted upon seeing them some part of the way home, and not being people of a warlike disposition, they were glad enough to accept of the offer, though they made an attempt to dissuade them from leaving the farm.

" We will not keep you away from your bride," they said. " It is not to be expected ; and we will not accept of such services at such a sacrifice.

" I will see you fairly on your way," was the rejoinder, " and for that matter I am sure they would aid us by her company ; she can ride as well as any of us, I am sure of that."

" I'll come and enjoy the ride," said the bride, with pleasure sparkling in her eyes; " a moonlight ride is of all things what I most enjoy."

" Then for once," said Mason " you shall be indulged in a ride ; we'll just go over the hills and then we'll return ; it will not be half an hour's ride there and back again, you know."

" To be sure not ; I should like it above all things. I must now begin to be used to the country at night, and then I shall make a farmer's wife."

" So you will, Mary, and a better no farmer need seek for, and if he should he will not find one."

" Well. well," said her father, " you shall come as far as the hill, for I must say this is a wild country, but I dare say that it wears off when you become used to it. Is it not so ?"

" Yes," said the farmer. " I am at home here, and can find my way about on the darkest night that ever hung over the moors of Cumberland."

" I should be something worse than dead," said the mother of the bride. " Be sure you wrap yourself up well, Mary," she added to the bride ; " you are not used to this keen air. While at Appleby, you never went out after dark, you know, and now, dear me, how chill is the air !"

" Ah ! town manners and country habits differ much, and if you reside about here, you would not meet with the some misadventure or other."

" That may be, but——"

The horses were now ready, and all further speach was cut short, and the whole parted mounted and rode out in the rude Cumberland fashion of the day.

There was much chatting and laughter among the members of the party, and all appeared in high spirits, and many excellent jests was uttered by the party.

They now came to very near the hill-side, where they came upon a small wood, and having passed through the end of it, Mason said, as he was emerging from it to the hill-side :—

" Now, our ride ends, and we must bid each other good-bye; we part here."

He had scarcely uttered the words, when some words were spoken in a strange language—they were short and hasty—stern and harsh. Mason too well knew their import, and turned to speak to his party, but before he could fly, he was struck off his saddle by a spear, and in less than five minutes every one of the party were made prisoners.

The fact was, a party of border robbers were out, and having accidentally come upon the party, made them all prisoners for the sake of ransom.

There was, besides, something more. Mason had killed one of the clan some years before, but as that was in battle, his fate did not appear any great hardship to any one, save that the Scots bore bitter hatred to the band that slew him, and all shared in the blood of the foeman.

It was a planned thing with them to make an incursion into Cumberland, and if possible, carry off Mason's cattle, horses, and house, and, as they knew, the strength of his place; they determined that it must be a surprise.

This they knew could not be better done than on some occasion, when there was some festivity and revels carried on, and news being brought that Mason was to wed a rich tradesman's daughter of Appleby, they determined they would make an attack that night and carry off the bride, and thus strike a deeper blow upon Mason's happiness than could have been stricken by any other means.

The plan had nearly miscarried, for they could not march with sufficient celerity through the hills of Cumberland, to reach the house of Mason before it was made secure for the night, and in that case, they reckoned it would be difficult to get in—certainly not without some loss, for the inmates would have time to rise, and arm themselves in defence.

They could not set out earlier from their own hills, else the alarm would have been spread, and they chased back again to their own country, if they escaped being made prisoners or killed.

As they were making the best of their way towards Mason's house, they fell upon him and his party, who, being unarmed, were totally unable to withstand the Scots, and were at there mercy.

There was now a party despatched to the house, and while the other, and much smaller party remained in charge of the prisoners; and these, after a short time, began to move towards their own country, leaving the others to follow them at a more rapid rate than they could move at, encumbered as they were with the prisoners they had so unexpectedly made.

There was a thrill of terror that ran through the whole party, which had been thus suddenly made prisoners. The moment the bride saw her husband struck to the earth, she screamed and fainted.

In this state she was lifted on the horse of one of the troopers, and when such of the men who had been taken were secured and bound to the horses, they were easily withdrawn from the scene of the attack.

The sudden change from joy and peace to wars and alarm was so great that everything that had passed appeared as though it had been some terrible vision, upon which they had not yet awakened.

They rode on slowly, but surely, avoiding all parts were they were likely to be met by any of the inhabitants, and pursued.

* * * * *

There poor Mason remained upon the earth—for some time bereft of all motion—and was looked upon as dead by the foemen who retired, leaving him where he fell, and they rode away.

For nearly ten minutes he remained thus, after they had gone; then he turned and opened his eyes. Slowly rising, he sat up in a sitting posture, and he endeavoured to recollect what had happened.

No sooner, however, did he become fully sensible of his loss, than he started up, and hastened, with all the speed he could muster, towards his own house; but a very short distance served to convince him that in this matter he was too late, for the flames that enveloped his own dwelling were now but too perceptible; and he instantly turned aside to raise what force he could at the houses of some friends.

He made the best of his way to the nearest house, and by the time he got there he found the inmates all armed and sitting up, anxiously waiting for intelligence.

To them he related how he had been used, and knocked senseless down upon the earth, and begged they would assist him to recover his wife and her friends, his cattle and his gear,—for all were now gone.

" Can you tell me how many there were ?" inquired his host.

" About a score."

" Oh, that is about four times the number of men I can raise; it would be no use : and besides, who can tell how many parties are to be found out—the whole border may be alive."

" Well," said Mason, " if I am not to have your aid upon this pinch, lend me a horse, that I may find friends elsewhere."

" Stop a minute—not so fast," said the other: " do you think there are any more parties out ?"

" I do not."

" Well, we will go with you, and can gather strength as we go ;—I can reckon upon ten or twelve at the next house we call at — so mount and be off."

In a few minutes more there was a clattering of horses' feet in the yard, and the sounds of armour, the gingling of spurs, and the clang of the sword.

It took but a few moments to set the whole party in motion, and, including Mason, there were but six. He was furnished with a horse and arms, and forthwith they rode ; but Mason, when he had ridden about half-a-mile, said to his friends,—

" Which way do you go ?"

" To the right, to raise the Fullertons — I can reckon upon eight or ten men there."

" And I will go to the left and raise the Grahams—I can reckon upon as many more ; by that time we can meet on the main road."

" Good," said the other ; " in an hour I will be there—in company or by myself."

They parted ; and Mason rode to the Grahams, whom he reached in less than half-an-hour. They were all asleep, save a watch they set ; and Mason soon threw them into alarm when he showed them the red sky, and related the tale of his woes ; and in a moment the generous sympathy of the whole party that heard him were aroused, and with hearty execrations they swore to be avenged and not rest until they had restored Mason his bride, and till they had taken goods and cattle from the enemy to the same amount as that of which he had been despoiled, and moreover taken revenge upon them for the mischief they had committed, which was what they could not repair.

In less than an hour the whole party met at a cross road, on the main road into Scotland. The Grahams had mustered fifteen men well armed and mounted, while the other party consisted of about thirty good men—all ready and willing to inflict vengeance upon the Scots.

In all there were about five or six and forty men well mounted, and preceded by an old moss-trooper, whose services had been retained, and they all trotted forward in pursuit at a good round pace.

Before three hours had elapsed they suddenly came upon the party that were riving the cattle they had taken from Mason's land.

This party were immediately attacked ; they consisted of but five and twenty, they were all killed or left for dead on the field of battle. A party of five then were entrusted with the cattle, and to drive them back, while Mason rode on with the remainder of the body, and seek those who held his bride in captivity.

They were a-head they had no doubt, so accordingly they put their horses to their mettle, and galloped onwards for some miles. After awhile they were close in upon the enemy's country, the very hold of the clan who had made the descent upon the English.

Here they proceeded more cautiously until they came upon a small body of men who halted at once, but who no sooner heard the approach of the party and saw them, than they immediately endeavoured to mount and ride off.

But in a few moments they were surrounded, and the whole party endeavoured to defend themselves, but unsuccessfully, for they were hewn down without mercy, and the whole of their horses and arms became the prey of the victors, and then began a search for Mary.

The house at which they stopped, would give no information as to wha had become of her, but after forcing the doors, and bursting in a panel or two' they found her bound and gagged.

"Mary!" said Mason, as he rushed up to where she sat, not observing how
No. 30.

she was secured; he uttered an execration, and with his bloody sword he cut her bonds asunder, and then she fainted in his arms.

There is no describing such a scene; they remained locked in each other's arms for some time until Armstrong came up to him, saying,—

"Well, well, Mason, there is a time for everything, we are in an enemy's country and day fast coming down upon us, and there is yet much to do."

"Enough," said Mason, "the moment is passed—thank God, she is safe—I thought—I feared worse."

"And worse there would have been," said one of the party, "for, had they got clear off, you would never have seen her back again."

"No, they would have feared that they would have been recognised and sworn to by her," said another.

"Well then, Mary," said Mason, "you must ride with me; but before we leave this place, we will leave one house in Scotland to tell the tale of our presence, and if they forget coming so far across the border, it will be no easy matter."

They all remounted and applied a torch to it in several places, and when it was fairly on fire, they proceeded homewards by another route, but in going this road they came upon the valley in which were placed the houses of those who had so lately made a foray upon them, and here they halted.

A short consultation was held among them, when it was agreed they should set fire to the whole of them.

This they only partially effected, after a skirmish, in which were killed many men; houses were fired, and cattle driven off, and then the whole party returned.

The sun rose high before each party reached their homes, and many kindly greetings took place—many a hearty farewell and good wish uttered.

But when Mason reached his home, it was merely blackened walls, having been completely gutted; he was compelled to reside at some neighbour's until his ow house was rendered habitable and secure, which took a month to do.

Mrs. Hammerton had come so quietly and gently into the room, that Emily had not observed her; and now, when she looked up, she met her eyes, in which beamed a cheerful light, for she was well pleased to see that Emily could thus divert herself.

The mere fact that she was able so to do was a convincing proof that her mind was greatly at ease, and that the change in her situation that had taken place, since she had been found by Dr. Hammerton in such disastrous and afflicting circumstances, and so deeply depressed at the lodging she occupied, had been one of great advantage and comfort to her.

"You are happy now?" remarked the Doctor's wife.

"Much happier," said Emily. "The fact of the complete recovery of Sir Anthony has removed from my mind a great source of anxiety and absolute fear. I can indeed look forward with something like a feeling of hopefulness to happier times. I may be wrong, but something seems to tell me that such a man as I know him to be must awaken at last to better feelings than have possessed him, and think and feel that true happiness is to be found in honour and comfort in his own home only."

"He may do so."

"Yes, he will; I am almost certain that he will. I would not destroy that thought for worlds. And the manner in which I shall be better able to judge of what he thinks, and what course he will be likely to pursue, will be from his behaviour to his child."

"You will. A note has been sent to him, as you wished, informing him of your death; and, if that do not move him, he is indeed invulnerable, and past all chance of better feelings. Every inquiry shall be made, and that frequently, too; so I think you may now really be at peace."

"I will; I feel that I ought, and that I can be so now. Oh! if happier times should ever dawn upon me, what an intense pleasure it will be to me to turn to such a dear friend as yourself, with a consciousness that you saved me from that despair which might have ended in my destruction."

" I do hope that the day will come when we shall yet see you happy at Wyvill Hall, and forgetting all your cares in the society of those who are dear to you. This may be but a temporary state of things—a mere trial, although a most melancholy and most grievous one."

" I will strive to think so."

CHAPTER XXXVII.

THE STEPS TAKEN BY SIR ANTHONY UPON THE RECOVERY FROM HIS SWOON.

WE left Sir Anthony Wyvill and his kind and attentive nurse, each in a state of mind transcending all description, on account of that letter which had been received from Emily, and which had removed from before their eyes such a fume of mystery and misconception as, perhaps, never before had passed any human beings.

The clear, explicit statement which that most agonizing epistle had made, carried with it at once all the impress of truthfulness. To read it was to believe it, for there was not a word of it which did not breathe that spirit of innocence which we may truly call divine, and which formed so essential a part of the character of the devoted and the persecuted Emily Wyvill—she who, with all her beauty, all her accomplishments, and all her simple-minded truthfulness, had not een able to escape calumny or reproach.

It was a strange thing—a very strange thing, that Margaret Wyvill should have had the opportunity of entering the sick chamber so entirely unobserved, but in an hotel such an opportunity was likely to occur with more certainty than under any other circumstances, and the way she had made her approach so quickly and unannounced, was this :—

She walked into the hall of the hotel, and, being completely ignorant of the fact of Sir Anthony Wyvill's indisposition, she merely asked which was the way to the apartments he occupied, and the waiter to whom she propounded this question never for a moment dreaming that any one could come to see Sir Anthony Wyvill without knowing what had happened to him, gave her the necessary directions without making any futher remark upon the subject.

It was not until she actually reached the apartment and opened the door, that she became aware something disastrous must have happened.

She had glided in and glided out with so little noise, that she who was attending upon Sir Anthony Wyvill with such care and assuidity, although she did faintly hear the sound of some one's footsteps, thought that they proceeded, naturally enough, from some of the attendants of the hotel, who were in the habit of thus stealing in and out of the sick chamber, whenever they had occasion so to do, with extreme caution and gentleness, so as not to disturb the wounded man.

It was merely what might be called a swoon that the captain's widow had fallen into, but yet she was not perfectly insensible, as Sir Anthony Wyvill now was, nor would he, under any ordinary circumstances, have fallen into that sad state ; but when we come to consider how much all his physical energies were sure to have been depressed by the serious wound he had received, we cannot wonder at the circumstances attendant upon such a shock as that letter from Emily gave him.

How long he would have lain in such a trance, or what really permanently injurious effect it might have had upon him, it is hard to say, for his disinterested and kindly nurse the moment she recovered[herself sufficiently to do so, turned all her attention towards restoring him.

She would not procure any assistance while she had a chance of success alone, because she felt that the grief to the consciousness of which he would soon recover, was of too sacred a nature to become a subject of idle comment ; and, for aught she knew to the contrary, his first words, upon recovering, might convey some strong impression to by-standers of the cause of his emotion.

Her efforts were crowned with success ; and after a short time, she had the satisfaction of seeing that he was on the point of recovering. With a deep sigh he opened his eyes and looked her imploringly in the face, and, contrary to what might ordinarily have been expected, he seemed at once to awaken to a consciousness of all that had passed, as the deep dejection that was upon his countenance sufficiently testified.

"You are better," said the widow, "tell me that you are better."

"Emily, Emily," was all he replied, "and the tone of voice in which he pronounced the name, had in it such an amount of exquisite anguish, that it was painful in the extreme to hear it, and suggestive of such utter desolation of heart, that the tears gushed to the eyes of his nurse, and despite all the necessity she felt for upholding him as much as possible in his present weakly state, she fairly gave way to her own emotions, and, sitting down by the bedside, she wept bitterly.

Sir Anthony Wyvill was silent for a time, and then he spoke to her, saying,—

"Do not weep ; I can understand the sorrow of sympathy that fills your bosom, but I pray you to subdue it."

"It is more," she said, "than the sorrow of sympathy—I cannot but feel—for I feel that I have been the cause, the most unworthy cause truly, but still the cause, of all this vast amount of suffering to those who are so entirely innocent, and who should have suffered nothing. I cannot but feel that the generous sympathy which has made you such a friend to me, has made me—Heaven knows how unwillingly —such a foe to you."

"Speak not thus," said Sir Anthony Wyvill, "I pray you speak not thus, for by so doing you inflict upon yourself the most serious injustice. Heaven knows how free you are from even the shadow of reproach in these matters. Oh! these cruel wounds, that keep me thus imprisoned when I should be searching for her who has already suffered so much, and so wrongfully! Emily—Emily, where shall I look for you—where shall I hope to find you? Heaven help you, and Heaven grant that justice may sooner or later overtake those who have done you so much evil!"

"Justice will and must overtake them. Oh! could any one have believed it possible that there was so much wickedness in any human breast."

"Give me her letter again," said Sir Anthony, "give it me again, and let me look upon the writing. I know her hand well, and it will be something to feel that she has gazed upon the same paper which will meet my eyes. It will be something to trace in each written word a remembrance of herself. Give me the letter, —I pray you give me the letter."

"I am searching for it," was the reply, "but I cannot see it."

"It must be here."

"Most assuredly : blinded by grief, and overcome by the sadness of my feelings, I dropped it from my hands, and there it should have lain ; but—and that most most mysteriously—it has disappeared, I know not where. I cannot see it."

She searched the chamber through, and then, feeling convinced that it could not be there, she approached Sir Anthony Wyvill, and spoke gently to him, saying,—

"It is gone, I cannot find it. Heaven only knows what can have become of it !"

He was silent for several minutes, during which a strange expression crept across his countenance, and when he spoke, he said in a low whisper,—

"Was it nothing but a delusion? The real and the unreal have been so mingled together of late in my imagination, that I almost doubt the evidence of sense. Was it a delusion after all?"

"No, no, it was real, do not fancy it was otherwise, but believe, as you may well do, that the Lady Emily has become the victim of the cruellest and most criminal persecutions which all that is beautiful and good ever endured."

"She must be saved—she must be saved, let the effort cost me what it might. I ought to be up and stirring—I must search for her. Who but myself ought to undertake that duty? Oh! is it not sad and strange to think upon, that I, who loved her so well, should not have known her, but should have suffered her to tend upon me with all her love and gentleness, and yet not for one moment to suspect to whom it was I was indebted fo so much devotion!"

"Alas, alas! what must have been her feelings when I came and supplanted her, taking her place by your bed-side, while she, who had all the right to be there, was, so to speak, driven from it; alas! how little I felt or suspected the pang I was inflicting by such conduct."

"But you have no self-reproach; it is I who ought to have known her under any disguise. Oh, Margaret, Margaret, may Heaven forgive you your deep iniquity, for I cannot! But I must rise, sick and wounded as I am, I must rise and seek her. My child too, that little innocent, who has scarcely yet known a father's blessing—I must seek my child."

"Oh, be calm and patient. Remember, that upon your life may yet hang the happiness of her who is so dear to you."

"Let me think—let me think. God of Heaven, I remember now the letter spoke of coming death. She wrote it to me with the consciousness that her end was near, or else I had not heard from one who conceived she was so deeply injured. Have mercy upon me, great Giver of life and health, and preserve her. Grant me, o, strength, that I may yet seek her out, and cast myself at her feet to implore to forgiveness for injuring her even in thought, and then I am content to die."

"Nay, rather hope to live yet many years of happiness, when the remembrance of this sad episode in your existence shall have passed away, or, if it still linger in your memory, it shall serve but to make the joy of the succeeding time more exquisite by contrast."

"I dare not have such hope. Emily, why have I sat down so supinely when I ought to have been searching the wide world over until I found you? Why did I for one moment allow the natural indignation which first seized upon me when I heard the accusation breathed against you, subside only into a doubt of its truth, and afterwards to take the form of a belief, that one bad or ignoble thought could inhabit such a breast as yours."

"But what could you do?"

"I should have rejected all evidence whatsoever but what came from her own lips. Oh, I am justly punished for my treason against all that is great, and good, and virtuous; for it was treason—treason only second to a doubt of Heaven itself. Yes, yes, I have been the cause of all this. When, oh when, will self-accusat'on leave me? If I had had a moment's thought I might and must have known what sort of tale could be carried to a wife's ears, in consequence of my innocent association with you."

"I cannot hear you blame yourself when you are entirely innocent. Yes, innocent in intention and in deed; but if you were generous and noble enough to place yourself for my benefit, in a position from which false inferences might be drawn, it was my duty to have prevented it, and to have set you right again. There it is that I have failed, and there it is that I feel all the accusations of self-reproach. Can I ever hope that Lady Wyvill will forgive me?"

"If she lives to forgive me, she can surely forgive you, who are so much less guilty, or rather, I should say, so entirely innocent. Will you order me a coach? I must rise and leave here in search of her."

"Oh no, no, that would be your death; you have quite enough, more than enough, to contend against, in the deep anxiety that now besets you; fatigue added to it might prove your destruction. Besides, where would you seek her?"

"I know not, care not; but, be she hidden where she may, the perseverance of deep affection will surely discover her."

"Nay, nay, leave that to me. Do you fancy that my endeavours would not be dictated by such an earnest desire to know where she was that I should fail to find her from want of perseverance? Ah, no; leave the search for her to me, and with the feeling, that in undertaking it I am endeavouring to atone, in some measure, for the evil that I have done. I will leave no spot of earth untrodden which may afford me a chance of her recovery."

"I do not doubt you, I cannot doubt. Emily, Emily, instead of writing this cruel and yet too kind epistle, why, oh why, did you not come to me yourself and say to me are you faithless, or may I dare to hope that I may yet call my own, the heart which plighted to me, its vows. Then, then, indeed, all would have been well."

"It is even so," replied his companion, sadly, "it is even so. True affection shrinks aghast from anything that looks like treason, to its purity; and so she who might have resolved all doubts, if she had doubts, by a single question, hesitates to put it, and resigns herself to despair. But here are other letters: will it not please you to read them, or let me read them to you, for Heaven knows but some one may contain news of a more cheering character. Here is one, shall I read it to you?"

"'Tis sealed with black."

"I did not notice that, but it is so. I will not open it. We want no bad news at such a time as this."

"No, no, let me hear it. I shall be tortured by a thousand doubts and fears if I hear it not; let me hear it at once, I implore you."

Thus urged, she opened an epistle which had upon it a massive black seal, and which she trembled as she tore asunder, lest it might contain the very worst and saddest intelligence that could at such a time be brought. And Sir Anthony Wyvill, too, looked on with such an interest, that his life seemed to hang upon the fact of that letter containing pleasant or disastrous intelligence. He drew his breath short and thick, and as he did so he fixed his eyes so earnestly upon the countenance of the captain's widow, in order that, from its expresion, he might learn, before she uttered any words, whether the intelligence were sad or otherwise, that, upon taking a casual glance at her, and observing that expression, he trembled for the result.

But the letter must be opened, and it must be read likewise: there was no escaping the going through that frightful ordeal, and the moment her eyes fell upon the words, which were brief but terrific, that the epistle contained, Sir Anthony Wyvill uttered a cry of despair.

Inured as she was to conceal her emotions, or to school her features to an expression that did not belong to them, the moment she discovered the tidings the letter contained, that those tidings were of a most disastrous character might be legibly seen upon her countenance.

"Read, read," cried Sir Anthony, "for the love of Heaven read, or this suspense will kill me."

"I cannot—I cannot—I dare not."

Having risen from the couch on which he lay, he took the letter from her trembling grasp. For a few moments his bewildered eyes felt dazzled, and he was utterly unable to decipher a word which the epistle contained, but gradually this sort of mist that was before him cleared away, and he was able to see distinctly—dreadfully distinctly, the few lines of writing that were upon that piece paper.

They were nearly to the following effect—brief but frightfully significant:—

"Sir Anthony Wyvill is informed that Robert, who attended upon him, and whose real character he probably by this time is well aware of, is no more. Buried by friendly hands, the victim of faithfulness, he has at last found rest in the tomb."

*   *   *   *   *

And this was all which the epistle contained, two brief sentences, containin g in themselves sufficient to drive Sir Anthony Wyvill to the confines of delirium.

He sank back with a deep groan, and while the captain's widow let her face rest upon her hands and wept convulsively, he was as silent as the very grave.

Such a letter as this would have been, after all, but a just punishment upon Sir Anthony Wyvill if he had been guilty, but being really innocent as Emily herself, it was sad indeed to think that he should have been subjected to it. The motive in adopting such a course, and the motive of Dr. Hammerton and his lady in aiding and abetting such a plan, were of the best character; and it was thought possible enough, that by such means Sir Anthony might be awakened from the dream-like delusion in which they supposed him to be, to a better state of things.

It was thought by the parties who had concocted this epistle that it would give such a shock to Sir Anthony that he would abandon the evil connexion he was so erroneously supposed to have formed, and that his bitterness of regret would be so great, that, after a long period of repentance, it might be hinted to him that Emily was no longer dead to the world, although she was dead to him, and then, she could use her own discretion as to whether she ever again resided under the same ro f with him.

It was a long time before he spoke, and when at length he did so, she alone who listened to him felt that she had never heard such tones of frightful, heart-breaking despondency from any human being.

They were really most terrific to listen to — tones that were likely to linger upon the memory, and to intrude themselves even upon the slumbers of the individual who had had the sadness—and a sadness it was indeed—to listen to them.

"And that is all," he said, "that is the end of my human career. God of Heaven! what have I done that I should be thus marked out for special and terrible vengeance?"

He was silent; and then after a time she spoke to him, and her voice was scarcely audible from the tears that choked her utterance.

"Sir Anthony Wyvill," she said, "I dare not now remain with you a moment longer. The sight of me must be hideous, and would continually suggest the most sad and gloomy memories. Farewell for ever, and may Heaven help us both!"

He looked upon her but he did not speak, for the power of utterance seemed to be dead within him. He made a faint gesture with his arm as if he deprecated her leaving him, but that was all, and she did not see that, but passed out of the chamber, carrying with her such a world of grief, that she would have been thankful at that moment to any friendly hand that would have taken her life.

And so, like a moving statue rather than a living person, she slowly descended the staircase and passed across the hall of the hotel into the street, leaving Sir Anthony Wyvill and his sorrows to their own sad companionship.

Perhaps it was a mistaken notion of her to do so, but, for all that, every one who looks at the circumstances, of the case, will be inclined to think that it was an extremely natural one, for, believing as she did, that Emily was now no more, she felt that she could not remain any longer with Sir Anthony without incurring the suspicion that she had an intention of making a closer connexion with him now that she was at liberty to do so.

Moreover, she had spoken the truth when she said, that the sight of her must awaken in his mind the most uncomfortable sensations, and while she was about him, he never could forget, even for a moment, his domestic disasters.

CHAPTER XXXVIII.

SIR ANTHONY'S NEW INDISPOSITION, AND THE REAPPEARANCE OF THE CAPTAIN'S
WIDOW.

IT was a considerable time before any one went near Sir Anthony Wyvill, because the people at the hotel were so accustomed to her who officiated as his nurse,
making known any of his wants and wishes, that when a long interval elapsed
during which they heard nothing of him, they generally assumed that he was
asleep.

In the present instance this was the supposition, and consequently he was lef
for two hours perfectly alone before any one came into the apartment, and then
if the surgeon who was attending him had not called, no one would have though
of intruding themselves.

Heaven only knows what must have been the thoughts of Sir Anthony Wyvill
during that weary two hours of time—what dreadful ideas and sensations chased
each other through his brain! Probably he himself would have a difficulty to describe; for when the mind is in that fearful state of confusion, so many distorted
images arise, and the thoughts and feelings intermingle with each other in such
inextricable confusion, that it is impossible, or next to impossible, afterwards to
separate them.

And poor Sir Anthony lay there like a man dreaming, yet awake, and endeavouring to think, while he was yet incapable of adopting anything like a rational course,'
or arranging any regular routine of thought.

When the surgeon entered the apartment, of course he expected to see the same
indefatigable nurse whom he had praised so highly to Dr. Hammerton and concerning whom he had received a piece of information which so much astonished
him. But when he found she was gone, he walked up to the bedside, and addressing Sir Anthony Wyvill, he said,—

"For the first time, Sir Anthony, I find you alone."

"Yes," said Sir Anthony, "alone, quite alone. Heaven help me, I am now
indeed alone."

The surgeon saw at once that something had happened of a character to make
a strong impression upon the mind of his patient, and drawing a chair, he sat down
by the bedside, saying,—

"Sir Anthony Wyvill, I sincerely hope and trust that no one has been allowed
to see you with agitating news. I grieve to say that you seem to me certainly
altered for the worse. Your pulse indicates a frightful extent of fever."

"I am alone, quite alone now."

"But, but Sir Anthony Wyvill, allow me to say that you certainly ought not to
permit the absenceof the lady whom I have recently seen with you to affect you so
strongly."

"I think I see her now," he said, "as I first knew her, in all the pride of her
young beauty, e'er her heart had known a pang! Alas! alas! where is she
now?"

"What mean you?"

"Look look, how she glares upon me, and calls me her destroyer. Emily!
Emily! do not fix those eyes upon me! Have mercy, and remember that even I,
too became the slave of circumstance. Fix that stony glance upon Margaret!
look upon her heart as you now look upon mine, for she is the fiend who has
been our utter destruction."

"He raves," said the surgeon.

"Away, do not hover so closely around me: I cannot breath?" The air is thick and heavy, with the sighs of those who, like myself, are bereaved of all they love ! Have mercy—Heaven, have mercy !"

The surgeon now rung the bell, and when the people of the hotel answered him, and he asked them what had become of Sir Anthony Wyvill's attendant, they knew not, but replied they supposed she had been there, for that they had no notice of

her leaving, and were as much surprised as he could possibly be to find S:r Anthony alone.

" This state," said the surgeon, " is extremely critical now, for he has seriously relapsed. Something has happened to produce a great effect upon him. Heaven knows whether it be the departure of that lady or not, but a nurse must be immediately procured to attend upon him, and I now have serious doubts if he will recover."

No. 31.

This intelligence took everybody by complete surprise, and the greatest confusion prevailed in the hotel, and as the delirum of Sir Anthony Wyvill each moment increased, an experienced nurse from one of the metropolitan hospitals was immediately sent for, under whose care he was placed, and who was directed to use the utmost vigilance in looking after her patient, for in the state that he was in, which was evidently one of great mental despondency, there was no saying what he might do, or how he might dispose of himself.

It showed that the surgeon was alarmed concerning the state of his patient, when he waited himself until the nurse came, in order to give special and most particular directions ; and then he left, promising to call again in six hours at the latest, when he said he would bring a physician with him, for the case had assumed now far more of a medical than a surgical aspect, and required the utmost vigilance and care to counteract any evils that might arise from it.

Poor Sir Anthony, was quite unaware of all the commotion he had excited, and remained, perhaps happily for him, so far lost to all around him, that he neither knew his own danger, nor retained any recollection of those sad events which had led to them.   He continually fancied that Emily was near him, and sometimes he called her by her assumed name, Robert, and implored her to speak to him, and not to look upon him with that silent deadly look of reproach.

" It's an odd thing to me," said the nurse, after she had been an hour or two in her vocation, " it's an odd thing to me, for I never saw anybody so mad in all my life.   He don't know girls from boys, that is as clear as possible, for he keeps on calling Robert a she, that he does."

" The deuce, he does," said the waiter, to whom this remark was made ; " we certainly had a young fellow of the name of Robert, he who was attending upon Sir Anthony ; he bolted off all of a sudden without saying a word about it : the deuce is in all the people, if I can make out what they mean."

" That's all very well," said the nurse, " and very proper, for it's my opinion as people who is not regular nurses oughtn't to attempt to nurse nobody, but what astonishes me is calling Robert a she—I can't make that out at all ; not that I cares ; it's all one to me.   I has so much a week, and he just says what he likes ; I can tell you, young man, that it aint a trifle as any patient can say, as puts me out of the way."

" So I should think."

" You are very right, young man, for once in the way, and now you can tell your master, 'cos I think it's right he ought to know at once, seeing as this is a hotel, which, to my mind, is a genteel public-house, that I never drink anything."

" Well, you are a nonsuch, for I never heard of a nurse before that didn't drink till all was blue."

" Then, you know it now, young man, and I can tell you that never a drop of anything passed my lips except hot water."

" Hot water ; why, that's enough to make anybody ill."

" Do you think I don't know that, stupid—I that's been a nurse a matter of twenty-two years?   What do you suppose I put brandy and sugar in it for, but to prevent it making me ill ?"

" Damn it that's remarkably like brandy-and-water, is it not ?"

" Stiff, always stiff.   I wouldn't give a pin for slops, and as this happens to be just the time of day I always feels a sinking, you had better bring me some at once, but mind not slops—half and half, you know, with three nobs of sugar and a little piece of lemon peel.   As I don't drink anything, what I do have ought to be wholesome."

" I tell you what it is, old lady," said the waiter, " it strikes me that if you say anything about your hot water peculiarity here, you will run a good chance of getting discharged, for they won't stand it, I know, so you had better not try it on."

" What ! is a person to be starved while they are attending upon the sick ? Young man, young man, you don't know what sick people are ; you have no idea of what iron chains and roaring lions they are, and it takes a lot of something, sometimes, to drink, before a nurse can be expected to put up with them."

"Well, there is something in that," said the waiter, "and I'll tell you what, old girl, we will manage it somehow ; you shan't be without a trifle to drink if I manage by hook or by crook to bring it you myself, which I will contrive to do somehow, so make yourself easy."

CHAPTER XXXIX.

WHAT BEFEL MARGARET ON HER ROUTE TO WYVIL HALL.

SHE still rode on, but the beauties of the landscape, hill, or dale, meadow land, or the winding rivulet, the bending corn, or the towering plantation, were all alike to Margaret Wyvill. She heeded not the changes in the scene ; she urged her horse onward, and passed all her own thoughts, being of that character which disregards all other things, and smarts under disappointments, and raises the ire against all living things.

The finest spot on the earth would have been to her a place devoid of interest, and to look at it would have been but a vexatious diversion of thought from subjects that were of more interest, but yet not so pleasant and placid in character.

Margaret's mind was a choas of those feelings under which all the gentle affections give way. Sternness and acerbity of disposition were all that was left her. She was lost in reflection, and of no pleasant mood of mind as she came to a hill top, and saw the sun setting in the west.

The evening was balmy; there was not a cloud in the heavens—all was calm and still ; the sun was sinking in a dusky horizon, the heat was great, and there was no mitigation of this ; the sun had beat down with his rays all day, and now they were aslant, and losing their intensity. The radiated heat from the earth was more than sufficient to repay the loss, and keep up a suffocating warmth.

Little heeded Margaret Wyvill heat or anything else, and more than once did the horse she rode evince signs of distress, and, having stumbled twice, drew down upon himself a sharp rebuke, in the shape of words and blows, and he trotted forward anew at a pace that better suited the temperament of his mistress, than the brute, from the fatigue it had undergone.

The spots of sweat burst out on the animal before, but now his panting sides became dappled with streams of foam, from one spot to another, until even its rider noticed the condition of her steed, and then she reined up her steed, muttering,—

"Oh, well, I suppose I must see about putting up for the night ; you cannot go on without rest no more than I, but I would have gone another twenty miles or so ahead before I did stop. It is the worst of brutes, they want as much attention as human beings, aye, more. I could ride this creature longer than he could carry me."

She appeared to consider it was a defect in the nature of the animal she rode that it could require rest and food, and not go on as long as she wished, or as long as was convenient.

Then pausing, she cast her eyes westward towards the setting sun, and seeing in the distance an inn, she determined in her own mind to push forward until she came to it, muttering to herself,—

"Ay, ay, we'll stay there when we get there, so don't flag now, good horse, but do thy work well, and plenty will reward your exertions."

She struck the horse with her riding rod, and in less than half an hour she drew up before the door of the hostel.

It was one of these clean white-faced inns, of which there are many on the main roads, where the coaches used to change horses, or rest on their journey, for the fifteen or twenty minutes that used to be allowed travellers for refreshment.

In a moment an ostler came up, and, touching his hat, or rather cap, laid his hand on the bridle, while a waiter came out, and assisted her to dismount, and the wearied animal was led away to the stable, and its mistress entered a private room, which was immediately placed at her disposal, when, ridding herself of her riding dress, she at once threw herself into a chair, and looked through the dwarf blinds at the scene below.

In a few minutes after her arrival, the sound of a horn attracted her attention, and in the next, several horses were led out of the stables, and placed before the door, all harnessed, with cloths thrown over their backs, and men waiting in attendance.

Soon after the coach came up, and the mail pulled up exactly where the horses stood : the four were instantly unharnessed, and the other four put in their place. Scarce three minutes were occupied than away rattled the mail, and the bustle that had been caused for a minute or two subsided, and the whole face of things appeared as though such an occurrence had never taken place.

The horses and ostlers disappeared, and the whole scene was changed as suddenly as a pantomime trick, leaving no trace behind.

There was no mark of what had been ; a stone thrown in the water makes a few eddying circles, and then disappears, and is seen no more.

"Jack," said one of the ostlers, as he came out of the stable, and spoke to another, who was filling a pail at the pump,—"Jack."

"Well, what ?"

"Why, did you see the new whip?"

"Yes, he's a big 'un."

"He is. He's an extra three hundredweight for that coach to carry."

"You're right ; he's a nob, he is. Did you twig his coat, and the rosebush in his button-hole?"

"Yes, it would have filled a tub ; his coat must have cost him something."

"Yes, it must ; why, it's seamed all over."

"I dare say he gets tipped pretty handsomely on the road, I dare say—he drives hard."

"Does he ?"

"Yes, the cattle show it, and there's the way he'll get into trouble if he does that, for when the proprietors find the horses falling off, they won't like it."

"I should think not."

The two men parted, and they went about their respective employments, and all was again reduced to silence and still life.

There came no more disturbances for some time. Margaret Wyvill sat musing upon the scene before her, and there she sat for some time without moving, and without even lifting her eyes from gazing upon one spot, from which at length she did withdraw them, and then rang the bell.

A waiter appeared.

"Bring me some refreshments," she said.

"What will you have, madam ?"

"Tea."

This word was pronounced as if she did not desire to be troubled with any more words, and the waiter at once closed the door, and disappeared ; and when next he reappeared he brought in with him what she had ordered, as well as a cold joint of meat to which Margaret objected, but she sat down to the table, and to what was brought her.

"Anything else, madam," inquired the waiter."

"Nothing."

The waiter bowed, and withdrew, wondering, in his own mind, what sort of a woman he had got there, and whether she was always as she was then. If so her conversation would be but useful—not interesting.

Margaret's mind was filled with vexation and anger ; she knew not how to vent it. She was unwilling to commence with any one, and then there was no one with whom she could at that moment.

When she had finished her meal, she rang the bell, and inquired "if they had anything with which she could amuse herself for an hour or two—any books?"

"Books! ma'am?"

"Yes, books; they will do very well."

"We haven't one except the Directory, and the Ready Reckoner; would you like to have either of them, ma'am, I'll fetch them."

"No, no, dolt, that will not do; but never mind, you never do have books in these parts. I suppose they do not know how to read."

"Oh yes, madam, we do, only we haven't much time to spend in reading."

"That will do."

Margaret was vexed; she had been annoyed enough by her own thoughts which often recurred to the disappointments she had suffered.

Soon, however, her thoughts were directed to another channel, which served the purpose she sought to be effected, which was this:—A chaise rattled up to the door, and out slipped a young man fashionably enough attired, and with him was lifted out another young man; but he was suffering from illness and starvation—his attire bespoke want and distress.

There was so great a contrast between them, that they were the immediate cause of much conversation among the people present, who could not understand the cause of a beggar riding in a carriage with a gentleman; they thought it was something extraordinary, and so it certainly was.

"A private room," said the young man, as he entered the inn.

"Yes, sir."

"And just help this invalid into the room; you had better bring a chair, and carry him in."

This was done immediately, and the men carried him into the room which was next to that in which Margaret was seated.

It was one which had been partitioned off from the one in which she sat. The two rooms made one, and that one had been cut off to make a greater number of private rooms, so that they could accommodate a greater number with private rooms than they would otherwise have been able to do.

It was therefore easy for one party to overhear what was said to the other, if they spoke at all distinctly.

Margaret was somewhat interested in the occurrence, and wondered in her own mind what could be the cause of so singular a companionship, and her curiosity was not long without its reward.

In a few moments she heard them both enter the room, and sit down. The voice of the young man she heard giving orders to the waiters to bring them some wine, and then some refreshment."

When the waiter had left the room, he said, as he poured some wine out,—

"Come, Bennett, come, drink some of this wine; it will do you good; it will not hurt you: your illness arises from want."

"Alas! it does."

"Therefore, drink; it will prepare your stomach for something stronger—we shall have a joint up; in the meantime, tell me what brought you to this wretched plight."

"I will, I will; but first may you never split upon the rock on which I have."

"And what rock is that?"

"A woman!"

"Oh!" said the other, with a shrug, "I am not such a fool as to do so, though I must not take too much credit to myself for that, because I had very near done so. I have had a narrow escape."

"Indeed!"

"Yes, a very narrow escape."

"And how was that?"

"I married," said the other, quietly.

"Good God, you are never so unfortunate, are you? but I beg your pardon, you may not have been so unfortunate as I have been, but you are no doubt happy?"

"Yes I am, very."

"Then you are what I believe few married men can say; you are satisfied with the fetters that have been put upon you."

"By no means, I am happy, I say, as to the escape I have had."

"I don't understand you."

"I am free again; I am a bachelor, that is, as much of a bachelor as a widower can make."

"Oh, your wife is dead, then?"

"Yes, thank God."

"What, had you an unhappy choice?" inquired his friend.

"No, no, I had not; she was as good a woman as you will meet with, but the fact was, I began to find out, that amiable as she was, she was likely to become too exacting, and wished for an explanation of everything that happened, and if I did not always tell the exact truth, it was remembered and brought up in judgment against me."

"The old story."

"Exactly, you cannot be master when you are married; you must give up so much personal liberty; but it will never suit a man of any mind or spirit, and so my wife and I, though we never positively quarrelled, were like to do so at a future day."

"I understand you."

"Well, she died with her first child."

"You grieved?"

"I did; and felt sincerely sorry for her and the child, for I would have done my duty by them, notwithstanding they would have been a millstone round my neck."

"And any other man."

"Well, I say, I regret the event, though I say, I thanked God for it."

"That is paradoxical."

"It appears so, but I was sorry for the event, as an event, but then I thanked God for it, as one that shifted a heavy burden and enormous future misery off my shoulders, and I have never thought of marriage afterwards without a shudder. A girl is one thing, and when she is a wife, she is another; she is not able to help it, I believe, but so it is; and the fact stares any married man in the face most plainly."

"So it does. Well, I am happy you are no longer in trouble about this matter."

"I am clear."

"Then take the advice of one who knows what marriage is, and what women are; and rather than be tied to a woman during my life, whose temper is the bane of my life, I would and do suffer this."

"Good God, you don't mean to say that a woman has reduced you to such a condition?"

"It is so, but you shall hear all from the first to the last."

"You had a good property."

"All gone."

"May Heaven defend me from the fair sex."

"Amen."

The waiter now entered the room, and produced some refreshments, and the noise of plates and knives were sufficient to interrupt the conversation which was of a general character while the waiters were in the room, and then, when all was cleared off, the waiters gone, and they were once again alone, the two friends again began the same subject as before.

"Well, you promised you would relate your misfortunes to me."

"And so I will—may they be a lesson to you. You will be amazed."

"I dare say."

"You remember when last we met."

" I do, you were driving about in your own cab, and just returned from a tour on the continent, where you had spent some pleasant hours."

"Ay, that was it; but I have had a tour that was not on the continent—a tour in search of bread ; but how I came to take such a step, you shall hear :—"

Soon after you saw me, I was introduced to the society of Mr. and Mrs. Templeton ; they were a friendly couple with a good fortune, and a family of seven children, the greater part of whom were girls."

I visited them, I saw them at all times, and took a great fancy to one of the daughters, who were all grown women ; the youngest, Ann Templeton, was the object of my choice.

She was the youngest, as I have said, and I thought he appeared to be rather ill-treated by the others—I do not mean what is usually meant by ill-treatment—but neglect, and spoken ill of.

This I laid to the score of jealousy, and have lived to repent my error, and make better amends for the evil I thought of others.

Well, I courted the lady, and all the sisters appeared sorry, and were, I dare say, somewhat vexed at seeing themselves passed over for the youngest in the family. Had I made a different selection, I fancy at times my fate would not appear so hard. But upon second thoughts I think women are but women, and if one has not this fault, she has some other defect which is quite as bad as the one we most complain of, because we feel the most, being the most prominent part of a character, and against which we are often compelled to rub. But enough of that—well, we were married. She had no fortune—something I believe, but she had it all herself, I cared nothing about it.

Well, she was tolerably well satisfied with her lot, though if any matter displeased her, she was ready to sulk—a very sulky creature she was.

This was a dreadful annoyance to me; I could not bear to be at enmity with any one.

" No, no, you used to be a warm-hearted man, always ready to forgive."

Well, this went on for a twelvemonth, Sunday and other days, it mattered not, she was always an eye-sore to me to see her wander about sulky, but it was of no use, I was compelled to endure it.

After a time, use becomes a second nature. I could endure her fits of sulkiness very well, I began to imitate her, instead of arguing the matter with her, I left it to her own imagination, and held my peace, interchanging as few words as possible.

After a time this would not do, and instead of being sulky, she became abusive, and dinned in my ears, whenever she could find me, something or other about which she thought she had been ill-used.

Well, sir, that was at length so intolerable, that I took to leave home, and sought pleasure where I could best find it, and on one occasion and another I found this so much more agreeable than in sitting at home, and listening to the noisy and dissonant alarum rang by a woman's tongue, which never tires.

" You are right."

Well, home was no longer home, and I became heartily sick of it, and never went home more than I could possibly help, and then it grew still more unpleasant.

Of course my absence from home was ascribed to my gaiety, my want of taste for the enjoyments of home—everything was my fault.

I was told I had a good home and a very obedient wife, who was a slave to my wishes, and who did all she could to make me happy and comfortable.

" Of course, every wife does that if you ask her."

Exactly—well, she had sacrificed herself to me, and now I was ungrateful for it. Everything was my fault, my own vicious courses arose from the viciousness natural to me.

Of course, nobody ever thought of the provocation, and who could explain—who paint the reality—why men will not even believe it, for there are many who are not fit for any office in life, beyond that of an overlooker in a nursery.

Well, from one excess I was driven to another, and, finally, I took to gambling.

" That was bad."

It was bad, but it was a very natural transition for all that—it was bad.

"Yes, yes; one thing leads to another, and who can tell where to stop?"

That is exactly my case. I could not stop because home was more uncomfortable than ever; we never agreed, and she never saw me without some very malicious remark or other, so that I could not venture to see her, and then I found myself embarrassed.

Yes, I became dreadfully embarrassed; of course I was extravagant and all that—I lost money at the gaming table—who does not, when they have once gone there?—and to retrieve my losses, I still went there.

My turn will come by-and-by; go on—go on, and you must win—you must have a change of luck, for it is changeable, and never can always be on one man's side. So I did go on.

These are every man's maxims, when he begins to lose; no man likes to turn away, when he finds himself suddenly deprived of half his fortune.

I thought it would be death to go home, and say, " I have lost half my wealth— we must retrench."

No, no; I was resolved I would not do that, for well I knew the kind of conversation that my wife would treat me to.

I had not the courage to face a woman's tongue, though I have faced my enemy in the open field.

" You have."

Well, I went on, and a little luck that I had there was enough to induce me to believe my luck had turned, and I went on until I lost every farthing—every acre I had!

" This was a climax."

" It was, indeed, a terrible one, too."

Well, I shall never forget the feelings that came over me; I was still sorry for my wife, and yet I knew not why I should have been sorry; she would have had no sorrow for me, none at all.

How to break it to her, I knew not. I had not sufficient nerve to make her acquainted with what had happened; I could not.

Everything I had, save some jewellery, I had lost, and I was determined to pay everything off, if I destroyed myself afterwards, and this I did.

The affair was broken to her, but in a manner I had not anticipated.

I went home one evening, with the intention of arranging some papers which I had there, before I gave up possession of the house. It was some days after I had been required to do so.

When I entered the house, I heard an altercation in the parlour, in which my wife's voice was sounding in a very high key, and then I heard a man's voice. I could not tell what was the matter, and at once opened the door, and walked in.

I was petrified. There was my wife, red in the face, and her eyes flashing fire, and several severe-looking men, who seemed to have been laughing.

" Will you teach these men how to conduct themselves, and that this is not a tavern. They have nothing to do here, at all."

" Oh, but we have," said one of the men.

" What is your business?" said I.

" We have brought this—we have come to take possession of the house and furniture." At the same time he handed me a legal document.

" Well," said I, "your employer is rather peremptory. I did not expect he would have sent so soon."

" We don't know anything more," replied the man. " We are sent to take possession, and can do no more nor less, since we have possession."

" You don't mean to say that they are going to take our house about our ears, and that we must leave it in their hands?"

" Yes, I do."

My wife uttered a loud shriek, and fell in a fit to the floor, at the same time.

I was too desperate to heed what had happened to her. I rang the bell, and desired some of the women to carry her away.

"You must do your duty," I said to the men.

"In course we must," they replied.

"Exactly; but you may as well do it with as little obtrusiveness as possible. You will meet with no hindrance or obstruction, and I shall not remain on the premises much longer."

"Very well, sir; we don't want to be disagreeable; and a gentleman as is a gentleman, why, we will do anything for; so you have only to say where we shall locate ourselves, and we will remain as much out of sight as we can. We know what it is to be unfortunate ourselves, and we aint proud."

"You can quarter yourselves where you like, my friends, and in doing so, you

No. 32.

will not disoblige me; interfere as little as may be with the women, and you will oblige me indeed."

"We will do that, sir, never fear."

"There is some ale in the casks below—you can help yourselves; but, for your own sakes, be moderate, for it is strong."

"We'll take care of that, too, sir; we don't want to be hocussed, and lose our places, so we'll take care."

To make a long matter short, the men were right enough, and did their duty very well. I had no cause of complaint, but I did not expect it to be done so soon.

As to my wife, she raved, and made a thousand words, of course. I was all that was vile and bad; my vices had brought her thus to poverty and ruin—I was a disgrace to mankind.

Of course, I admitted all this. I had long since seen the folly of quarrelling with a woman who had just understanding enough to see her present inconvenience, and who had abundance of ill-nature, so that she could ascribe all to me, and nothing to herself.

I listened; and when she had entirely raved herself out of breath, there was uttered the usual desire that she wished I would come to some understanding.

This I was glad to hear.

"Yes, we can come to some understanding," I said; "we can do that now. I have nothing to give you, and nothing to take; therefore, do you do your best. I am penniless, and have no home—what will you do?"

"I have friends, and shall leave you."

"Thank God for that, then," said I. "If I be poor, I have my freedom, and am no more galled by the chain by which I was united to a woman."

"You ungrateful wretch! have I not sacrificed all to you, and this is how you treat me?

"Sacrificed, indeed!" exclaimed I; "you have made me a sacrifice, and I now am penniless."

"I must go to my friends," she said.

"You may go anywhere, so I have no more torment," I replied. "I am a beggar."

"Then you may beg for your own support," she replied; "for I will have nothing to do with such a man as you are—a beggar!"

More altercation took place, and we parted. She returned to her friends, and I took what things I had found to live upon, and upon them I lived very nearly eighteen months.

Then I met with an accident. I was knocked down in crossing a road, and had a couple of ribs fractured. I was carried to an hospital, where I remained many weeks, and when I recovered from the injuries I received from the accident, I fell ill with a fever.

How long I remained I can hardly say, but a good many weeks, I believe. I was weak, ill, and scarcely able to crawl; my clothes were unfit to be seen, and my family all shut their doors against me.

Under such circumstances I knew not what to do. I could go nowhere, and had not one penny piece to pay for a meal's victuals.

I then determined to see my wife, to know if she would spare me a pound or two to help me to obtain some means of support, but that was an absurd notion of mine.

I saw her, and she appeared astonished at my assurance, and wondered what I could want—she dared say it was money.

I told her it was money, and then related to her how I was placed, and begged her to lend me a few pounds, which I would repay her.

This was peremptorily refused, and I was told her friends did not allow her any money, conceiving I could not be so abandoned as not to support her. It was in vain I laid before her the state of the case : she was deaf, and affected to believe that she could give no credence to what I said to her.

"I left her with a hearty execration, and since that time I have never set eyes upon her but once."

"And when was that once?"

"One day when I was begging—for it came to that at last ; and she drove up in a carriage, opposite to a large draper's. She gave me a penny piece very unconcernedly, and walked in.

"I turned away stunned, but I ought not to have been surprised at a woman's weakness. I ought to have known such would have been the case. I was not there but by accident.

"Since that time I have been wandering about the streets, a common beggar, obtaining the meanest and poorest pittance that man can exist upon, and when you saw me I had not eaten food for two days."

"Good God !"

I had not indeed. I was wandering about, and going to lie down and die under the first hedge I could find, when I could walk no longer.

"Thank God, I met you!" exclaimed his friend.

"I do thank Him—but where this is to end now I know not, unless I can obtain some means of supporting myself, and I see not how I am to do that."

"We'll provide for you for some time at least, and then I will see if I cannot do something that will render you independent of any one."

"You will do me one of the greatest services you ever rendered any one ; but if you could put me in some situation abroad I should be glad."

"I will endeavour to do so. Money will procure everything, therefore do you not be cast down. I tell you what, we'll endeavour to exchange your present attire for a better—perhaps the waiter will help us, he may have a suit to sell ; if not, we can make it worth his while to do so."

Thus the two friends conversed for more than an hour afterwards. It was evident that the one had seen the other, and took him up, and thus attempted to restore him to society.

* * * * *

Margaret Wyvill sat and mused ; but how the shades of evening had deepened into those of night, and the waiter entered the room with candles. She ordered a slight repast and some wine and water, and then, when she took that, she desired to be shown to her apartment, which was done by the chambermaid.

She entered her room, and felt fatigued, and she felt it would not be long before she was fast in the arms of slumber. She threw herself upon the bed, and lay meditating upon what she had heard—she fell into a sound slumber.

* * * * *

The next morning at an early hour Margaret Wyvill descended to her room, and summoned the waiter, and demanded if her horse had been fed.

"He has been fed a short time," said the waiter.

"Tell the ostler I shall want the horse in an hour at the door."

"Yes, ma'am," replied the waiter, and he withdrew.

The breakfast was placed on the table, and Margaret partook of it in silence ; she said not a word beyond what was necessary to express her wants, and occupied with her own thoughts she was almost unconscious of what was passing around her.

The hour had scarcely expired when the waiter appeared with the bill in his hand, saying,—

"Your horse is at the door, ma'am."

"Very well," she replied, "I am ready."

"The bill, if you please, ma'am," said the waiter, placing it on the table.

Margaret saw the bill—read the sum total, and then threw the money down with a gratuity for the waiter, which was acknowledged by a low bow ; she then left the inn, and once more was on the road to return by the west to Wyvill Hall.

This **day she rode h**ard, and passed over many miles of ground, stopping to rest her horse when necessary, and now she urged him on with all the strength he could muster. Margaret, however, knowing very well there was a limit to human as well as animal power, determined to put up once more ; but she thought she could push on another ten mile stage before she was obliged to draw rein for the night.

She was passing through a wild tract of country, through which, indeed, she would hardly have cared to pass, but then she could not avoid it. It was wild and desolate, partially moor, and partially woody—stunted and badly grown timber, which showed the earth was of an inferior quality and not cultivated.

She was pushing the horse through rapidly when she came to a turn in the road, and her view was intercepted by the trees, which began now to grow closer and taller, and a great ditch ran on either side. When she had reached the corner, and was looking up, a couple of men started out of the ditch and seized her horse.

" Your money or your life !" were the only words.

Margaret for a moment hesitated, but being in not one of her best humours, she struck her horse sharply and then one of the men, exclaiming,

" Leave go, sirrah ! what do you mean by such insolence ? leave go my horse's head."

" Ay, ay, I will," replied one of the men, " when you are off," and at the same moment he came behind her, and with one effort lifted her from the saddle, and then putting his arm round her waist, he added as he held her tightly—

" You are my prisoner, at all events, and if you talk big I shan't stop here."

Margaret Wyvill saw what men she had fallen in with, and said no more ; murder seemed not to be strange to them.

" Come, come, your money ?" inquired the man, " give it to me, else I shall have the trouble of hunting after it, and I won't leave a whole piece of cloth about you, if you can't give it to me."

" Yes, ma'am," said the other man, " you had better be pretty sharp and do it at once ; we aint very particular when we commence."

" Here is all I have," she said, giving her purse to them, " give me something to carry me on the road with, as I am travelling."

" What is that to us ? "

" But, as you are men, do not act so barbarously ; I shall not get food if you do not leave me something ; besides, the horse will starve ; have some pity, if for nothing else, have some on that."

" We will, we will ; you have looked a little into our faces, ma'am, we can't part with you directly, but we'll take care of you for a short time."

" What do you mean, have you not got my money, what more can you have ?"

" We'll tell you, by-and-by ; come, no resistance, come with us, and don't utter a word."

Thus urged and admonished, she followed the man who led the way, and another followed her closely, with the horse at her heels.

" What made you bring that brute here with you ?" inquired the first man, when he first noticed animal.

" I thought if he were seen at present he would cause some one to commence a search before one was at all necessary or requisite."

" Oh, well, only it's an incumbrance, and leaves a trail that might be followed, and bring us eventually into trouble—it's no use in being over-cautious."

" I am not, and as for a trail, I should like to see one on the earth we are now walking over, it is as hard as a brickbat, feel it."

" Don't want, and haven't got time."

They all proceeded onwards through a very winding path indeed,—it was a wild track, which led through many grounds, among trees and shrubs and rocks ; the ground was uneven, and large pieces of rock were every here and there visible, and not a single mark by which she could remember the way.

The character of the scenery was completely changed, and it now became rugged and uneven in places, rocky and hilly.

The route was tiresome and difficult, and at length they paused at a large stone.

Margaret could not divine what was their object, and looked from one to the other as if she feared they had brought her there to destroy her more at leisure, and with less chance of being discovered afterwards, and a tremor ran through her frame.

The men paused, and one took his dagger out and tapped gently and in a peculiar manner, and then with their united strength they removed one of the stones, and an entrance was plain to her sight, and a man came out and said, as he looked at Margaret,—

" Well, what made you bring this hag of paint here, haven't we enough bother as it is in the cave ? "

" Always on the grumble."

" No, but who's to be eternally watching a woman ? I'm quite sick of it, quite."

" Very well, be quiet, it will be all right by and bye, she must be put somewhere where she can be taken care of securely for a short time."

" Well, well, come in, ma'am, come in."

" But what do you want with me, you behave very wrong ; surely my life cannot benefit you. Spare me and I will take an oath,—do anything that you propose—never to divulge your abode, which I could not find again if I were to try."

" Come, come, no talk, but walk in."

" Spare me !"

" Go in and don't bother."

But Margaret endeavoured to elude the grasp of the man and began to scream out dreadfully ; but she was instantly thrust towards the cave with no gentle hand, and pushed under the entrance to compel her to enter the cavern.

" I'll split your head open if you don't hold your noise !—this is always the way when any of your cloth is brought here—damn me if it aint, they ought to have stopped your chatter before they came here."

So saying the man pushed her forward until they came into the interior of the cavern, which appeared a long, natural excavation.

There were one or two smaller places, some natural and some artificial, which served to give the place the convenience of more than one apartment.

" There !" said the man, pushing Margaret into a room and rolling a large stone against the entrance that effectually put a bar to ingress or egress—a bar much beyond Margaret's strength to remove, had she attempted to do so.

Then she seated herself upon a projecting piece of rock when she recovered herself so far as to be able to think of what she was about.

The place was dark, quite dark, and when she first entered it she fell down, and now she sat on the stone against which she had been thrown by the violence of the man who thrust her in.

This was a state of affairs she knew not how to deal with ; what was the end of the adventure she could not tell—perhaps a great misfortune might be hanging over her—her life, or her liberty, might both be taken from her.

She sat in silence and in dread,—she listened to the sounds of the men as they were gathering together, and much whispering was going on among them.

" Well, what have you done ?" inquired a strong voice, apparently the leader, by the deference that was paid him,—" what have you done this evening ?"

" Captured a woman!"

" Ho! ho! ho!" laughed a deep bass voice—"ho! ho! ho!—What made you do that ?"

" Because we thought she was too cunning and too clever, and would recollect us."

"Ay! ay !"

" Yes, she began to talk too, and looked hard at us, and moreover we thought there would be something gained by the clothes of the traveller, as no doubt she has some money about her."

" She'll make noise enough to stun the whole cavern, and awaken the echoes in the bowels of the earth until it splits in two."

" That would be an enormous—"

" Yes, but true!"

" You forget, it's only a woman."

" I know that, but she can scream all the same, and a little worse than any other animal you can name.   What's to be done with her ?"

" Ay, that's the question,—What's to be done with her ? I'm for putting her out of her misery at once, and then there's no further fear of bother attributed to it, a hole can be made and the carcase thrown in, and who's to know anything about it ?"

" That's very well argued certainly," said another man, "but I know a case in which people used to be made prisoners of, and then kept till they turned out handsomely to get away, and paid a good ransom."

" But you are never sure."

" O yes, you must not bring them home—keep them in different places."

" They may escape."

" Take care of them : only consider what a sum that brought in; why our fortunes will be made in a few years, I'll be sworn to that."

" Ay, and so would I ; we should have a short rope to cling to as our only hope, and an ugly one it would be—a dance upon the clear air, without any impediment to kicking one's heels, till one's tired, which would not be long I anticipate—not time to say a short prayer."

" Shouldn't want one."

" Well, but what shall we do with her ?"

" Tell her at once, that the best that can be done will be to kill her."

" How ?"

" Oh, anyhow ; there are more ways than one of killing a dog, you know, besides hanging him ; you can have her strangled, knocked on the head, smothered, or shot by a pistol."

" Oh, I think smothering as good a plan as any."

" Very well, but who is to do it ? whose turn is it now ? but you had better do it by ballot, and he who draws the prize shall do the deed ; he shall go in and smother her."

" Why not let the youngster try his hand, it will be his first trial, it will do him good, and will be quite an unexpected treat for him."

"Ho ! ho ! ho !" laughed the deep-toned voice—"what a treat ! Ho, ho, ho ! but let the boy do it ; if he cannot smother her, he had better kill her by means of a dagger."

" A pistol."

" Ah well, that will do as well as either, and will suit him well ; the youngster is as good a shot as I know off ; he is a regular good hand."

" So he is : well, let him come forward—here, youngster, we want to get your hand in for good work— you are to kill to-night."

" Very well," said the boy ; " a man ?"

" No, not a man yet ; besides, we have not a man to kill yet, it's only a woman ; but that is something for you to begin with."

" Very well," said the boy, " better luck next time ; I shall kill a man soon, I dare say, and would now, if anybody was to offend me."

" Ho ! ho ! ho !" laughed the man with a bass voice—"ho, ho, ho ! you are a forward cock, to crow so early, but you'll do—ho, ho, ho ! good boy ! good boy ! fine chick, you'll make rare broth some of these days."

" Not so soon as you will, old Growler, your turn for spitting will be before mine."

" Don't talk too fast, young weather-cock, you may find more men than you can manage ; but do your duty, and that's all you have to mind."

" Where is the pistol ?"

" Here, go in and do the business at once, make haste over it ; but don't be in too great a hurry lest you miss your shot, and that will be worse than all the rest; take a cool aim, a cool hand is worth two unsteady ones."

Great was the consternation of Margaret Wyvill when she heard the foregoing conversation. The voices came to her in subdued tones, and many of the words were to her indistinct and inarticulate, and it was only from the general tenor of what was said that she could gather the fearful intention they were about to put into practice of taking her life.

"Give me a light," said the boy, "I will have some talk with the old woman."

"Do what you like, but make no blunder over the affair,—there, go in while we get ready to go; but we shall be ready soon."

"Very well, you shall hear the report, and that will tell you the news."

"So it will."

So saying the men rose and went to the other end of the cave where the ammunition was kept, while the youth was taking the light; and pushing the stone half round he entered the cell.

"Well, now, mother——"

"Hah!" exclaimed Margaret, as she heard the youth's voice, with surprise.

"Well," said the youth, holding up the candle so as to throw the light upon the features of Margaret Wyvill, whom he no sooner saw than he started,—"what, Margaret Wyvill!"

"Ay, boy; but how came you here?"

"Nay, what business have you here?" retorted the boy; "I am at home."

"At home! you ungrateful dog, what do you mean? Is this the return I am to expect at your hands?"

"What is the matter?"

"What! have I not done for you—clothed, fed, educated and schooled you, and set you up in an honest course of life—did I not send you to London to make your entrance into life in a manner that was at least likely, and sure, with due care on your part, to be profitable—honest, and would place you above temptation?"

"Well, but that is a mistake, I am not above temptation; and you see I am now embarked in a more profitable enterprise.'

"Yes, it will be so profitable that it will lead you to the gallows."

"I shall have had my swing out first, though."

"It would indeed be hard to deny you that poor consolation—you would have your swing out; such as the life that you lead is sure to be terminated. But leave this place."

"Leave this place! why I am too much at home, and besides that I have come to shoot you and I have no time to spare."

"Ungrateful boy! Is this the return I am to meet with at your hands? is my life then forfeited, because I have done you good? You return evil for good—Let some other hand be stained by my blood, not yours; and yet I know not why, if it must be, but one crime more will, and such a crime, convince you of the errors of your way."

"But I have not said I would do it."

"You came here to do it, and you were but too glad to obtain the chance of committing such a crime."

"Not exactly, I knew not you were here; but others will not save you."

"Can you?"

"I think there is a chance, but it is only a chance."

"And in what does it consist?" inquired Margaret, whose new hopes of life changed the current of her thoughts, and her sterner thoughts gave way to hope, and that hope was a new life.

"It is this—I will fire the pistol off, and you must lay down as dead, and if they do not disturb you, you will be safe."

"Very well; do you think they will not discover me? will they not come in to examine how you have done your first deed of blood?"

"No, no, I think not."

"Cannot you let me out of the corridor, and then I can make my way?"

"No, no, you cannot—I do not believe you would be gone five minutes before they would have you again, on every side you would be surrounded."

"What can be done?"

"Wait till they have gone out at night, and then I will risk all and tell you all."

"Do so."

"I will lay down as if shot.

As the boy spoke Margaret Wyvill sank upon the earth, and he fired the pistol at the same moment, and then after a pause he came out.

"Well, boy," said the deep-toned voice of the captain—"Well, boy, hast done it?"

"Ay; she fell without a groan."

"Capital! Where is she?"

"Yonder; she's hardly dead yet, at least there's a kind of motion in her limbs."

"So there will be, boy; you'll generally find something of the sort, but it's nothing. Put the body out of the way, if you can, before we come back."

"Am I to stop here?"

"Yes, for a time; you shall have your turn very soon. Time enough for all things, especially for that; you'll go out with us very soon; don't be too fast at first, else there may be a sudden movement that may put a stop to your career."

"I must take my chance of that," replied the boy; "but I'll do duty out or at home, as the turn comes, so there's no grumbling."

"That's right, boy. Now, then, comrades, are you all ready?"

"Yes, all!"

There was a movement among them, and they all quitted the cavern, and went into the wood without; and when they had gone, when the boy had seen the last of them turn his back upon the cavern, when the last dark, dusky figure had vanished from his eye, when the last rustle of the distant leaves had subsided, and when all was quiet and still, he re-entered the cavern, and proceeded to the cell of Margaret Wyvill.

"Well," he said, "it has succeeded."

"I am free!"

"Not yet: you must remain a little longer—an hour or nearly so; and then you shall quit this place securely. I shall put you on the right road. Do you spur your beast until you reach the nearest market-town, where you had better put up."

"Well," said Margaret, "this advice I give you—remember it may be well if you follow it, and evil if you persist. Leave this den of crime and infamy—seek some other mode of life. You may yet be saved from an infamous end."

"Ah! well," said the boy, "there aint so much to be said about that as you may think; but I tell you, you must reserve your advice for some other occasion; and I'll tell you what—keep quiet until you get away. I came here, and how long I may remain may depend upon two circumstances—the first is my life and my own will ——"

"Let that determine you to leave at once."

"It would be barely safe to do so; but now, are you ready? The time is now come when you may with safety travel, and you cannot do better than be quick and silent."

Margaret Wyvill arose at these words; they were so impressively uttered by the boy, that she followed him implicitly. He led her through the passage that she had come down, and then by great exertion he contrived to move the stone so much, that they were enabled to crawl out, and once more they stood in the open air.

"Wait a moment," he said, "and you shall have your horse. I heard you were mounted, and I know where it must be placed."

He left her side for a moment, and in ten minutes he returned to her; but the ten minutes appeared an age to Margaret Wyvill, for each minute was an hour; however, when he did return, he brought the steed with him, and then he aided her to mount.

"Now be silent and quick," he said; "I will lead your horse until the path is plain, and you cannot miss your way."

In silence, broken only by the sound of their feet, they trod the wild woody place, where there were so many impediments to travelling, that Margaret wondered how they got along at all. At length she emerged into a broad, open path down which the boy told her to ride, and not once look behind; but continue on until the main road was reached; and before she could speak to him, he was gone; and she rode onwards quickly and safely.

CHAPTER XL.

MRS. ANGERSTEIN'S VISIT TO THE CHILD.—THE DEEP DEJECTION OF SIR ANTHONY WYVILL.

The shock which the proceedings it has been our painful duty to relate had given to Sir Anthony Wyvill, was in every way calculated to exercise the most powerful influence upon his health, and to retard considerably that recovery which, under ordinary circumstances, would have proceeded without any fear of a relapse.

No. 33.

But when we come to consider what a frightful state of mind he must have been reduced to, now that the awful plot, by which he had been made to believe that Emily, who was the very soul of innocence and purity, was guilty, we may well imagine that again that life, which had been declared safe, was in great danger.

This was a new cause of exquisite pain to Mrs. Angerstein, who, in addition to the other most wretched feeling of considering herself the innocent cause of all the dreadful evils that had taken place, had now the pain of thinking that, after all the death of Sir Anthony might be the climax of those miseries.

She knew that when he found what an amount of mischief she had produced unwittingly, her first impulse was to fly from the possibility of being any longer made by designing persons an instrument for working out their desperate resolves. But when she saw the sad state to which Sir Anthony was reduced—when she heard the medical man declare that now he knew not what to say to the case—she felt again that she had a higher duty to perform, and she resumed her station by his couch.

It is night again, and all is still in the chamber. Sir Anthony, for the first time since that dreadful hour which had awakened him to a full sense of all his miseries had dropped into slumber—exhausted Nature would no longer be defrauded of repose.

And she who had tended him in what she had certainly considered most distressing circumstances, but which were quite happy and delightful, compared to the present, sat absorbed in deep grief, and unable to think collectedly upon any subject.

It seemed to her as if she were some doomed being who, by Providence—for people give poor Providence the credit of everything—was condemned to bring misfortune, death, and disaster upon all who had become in any way connected with her ; and although such an idea partakes really something of the character of an hallucination of intellect, we can scarcely wonder that, under the circumstances it took possession of her.

And as she reviewed her past life, it assumed a greater and still greater garb of probability, until she could almost have persuaded herself it was her duty to leave a world in which she was condemned, if she lived in it, to do so much mischief.

"Alas, alas !" she murmured, "I remember that the misfortunes of my father commenced so soon as I became his only companion, and my husband fell on the field of strife, while thousands escaped ; and now I have brought misery upon this generous-hearted man, whose evil destiny prompted him to step forward to my relief."

Tears gushed to her eyes, as well they might, at such a thought as this taking possession of her, and it was some time before her better reason came to her aid and told her how wrong, and, indeed, how impious it was to charge Heaven with even the conception of a purpose so every way unjust.

When she came to consider this, and to take a much more rational view of the question, her mind became calmer, and she was better able to feel and comprehend her real position.

"To be sure," she said, "but for the wickedness of one individual, all would have been well, and Sir Anthony Wyvill would have had no cause to regret extending the hand of kindness to one in my desolate condition. But for his sister, might even have succeeded in increasing the happiness of him and his family, instead of being productive of all this serious evil."

Sir Anthony Wyvill slept on for a considerable time, but when he awoke his dejection of spirits seemed even to be greater than before ; and Mrs. Angerstein spoke to him imploringly, saying,—

"Oh ! remember, Sir Anthony Wyvill, remember, that notwithstanding all the misfortunes that have befallen you, that although the hand of Providence has fallen heavily upon you, you have yet a sacred duty remaining which ought, and which I am sure will yet bind you to existence."

"No, all is lost ! all is lost !"

"Nay, it is not so ! Do you forget that you have a child—a living image perhaps, of its poor mother? Do you forget that you may recompense, by your care and attention, that infant for the grievous loss it has sustained—a loss, certainly, to all appearance irreparable, but still one which a father's love may do much to overcome."

"Dare I look in that infant's face again, feeling that I am its mother's murderer?"

"It is not so! you judge too harshly of yourself; and that, instead of remembering you, as well as she, have been a victim to the cruel machinations that have been brought to bear against you, you talk of yourself with feelings of self-accusation which you know you do not and cannot deserve."

"I deserve all; I should have doubted Heaven first, before I doubted the faith of Emily. I never can look upon my child's face now without such pangs of mental reproach as will surely kill me."

"Do not speak to me, I pray you, of that little innocent; it is better that it should never in this world look upon its unhappy father."

He turned aside, and from the expression of his countenance as he did so, she saw that nothing but some powerful excitement would rescue him from the condition in which he was.

She rose without a word, and walked from the room.

In an adjoining apartment she had a bonnet and shawl, which she hastily put on, and then requested one of the waiters of the hotel to get a coach for her, which was done very quickly, for her gentle and unobtrusive manners had won for her the affection of the whole establishment.

It was most fortunate that in the letter which Emily Wyvill had addressed to Sir Anthony, she had inserted a separate slip of paper, on which was the woman's address who had the child to nurse; and as the letter had fallen on the floor, that slip of paper had become disengaged from it, so that it did not fall into the hands of Margaret along with the letter.

Mrs. Angerstein had picked up this slip, and although it contained nothing but a name and an address, she guessed at once to what it alluded, and her present determination was, what the reader has no doubt already guessed—viz., to fetch Sir Anthony's child, in order that it might exercise its gentle control over his disordered spirits.

The distance was considerable, and her great anxiety to be back quickly made it appear doubly long; but at length she reached the humble but comfortable home in which Emily had succeeded in placing her child; and with some misgivings as to whether the woman would feel herself justified in parting with her charge, she entered the house.

She thought it the best plan to be explicit, and candidly to state the whole affair, which would explain why she wanted the child so hurriedly taken away; and the narrative had such an air of truth about it that the kind-hearted woman who had the child to nurse, did not hesitate a moment, but considered that, certainly, if anything was calculated to restore Sir Anthony to serenity, it would be the presence of his child.

She was astonished, however, to hear that the seeming lad, who had represented himself as the brother of the child, was in reality its mother; for although, she said, she had suspected there was some mystery in the whole transaction, she had not thought it was one of that character.

This good woman was rather garrulous, and would have talked a great deal more, had not Mrs. Angerstein feelingly represented to her how anxious she was to get back, in order to try the experiment upon the feelings of Sir Anthony Wyvill, which she hoped and expected would win him back again to the world, which, at present, he seemed anxious only to forget.

Accordingly she started, promising to let the woman know the result of the affair, and by an extra reward to the coachman, she got back with much greater speed than she went, and was well pleased when she drew up again at the door of the hotel.

The first inquiry was how it fared with Sir Anthony, and she was told that he had not stirred since her daparture, and that, although they had several times been to see him, they could not extract a word from him, and it was their opinion that he was fast lapsing into a state of melancholy madness.

"I hope to Heaven," said Mrs. Angerstein, "that I am, in time. If anything in the world will restore him, it will be this child, and if that fail, I shall have no hope whatever."

The child was silent through astonishment at the sudden changes of place and person, so that there needed no injunctions to the little creature to be still, as Mrs. Angerstein carried it up to the chamber of its father.

Sir Anthony was lying in precisely the same position as she had left him; and placing the child upon a chair out of his sight, in case even he should turn his head, she approached him, saying,—

"Perhaps you have thought it unkind that I have been so long gone from you?"

"No, no," he said, mournfully, "but I think I am going mad, for strange visions have been flitting across my brain. Alas, alas! is that to be the end of my career? Is the gloom of insanity to take the place of every other feeling which from time to time has made itself a home within my heart? What will become of me, what will become of me? Why will not death come to relieve me from such a world of suffering as this?"

"You half promised me that you would conquer this despairing mood."

"Alas! I cannot, for it has become native to my heart, and while I live now I shall know nothing but despair. I shall have no hope but that life will soon depart from me, and then, in another world, I may have an opportunity of imploring the forgiveness of her whom I have so deeply injured."

"Nay, nay, think again—think again. Is there any living creature who would have acted otherwise than as you acted? Think of the circumstances in which you were placed, and the many, the very many, apparent proofs which you had of the faithlessness of her who has now turned out to be all faith."

"Yes, yes! all faith and all purity, and she has died to prove it. Oh! what a martyrdom hers has been."

"Will you not live for justice? Will you permit that person who has injured you so deeply, and who has been the real cause of all these afflicting circumstances, to triumph in your ancient home, and to rule at Wyvill Hall? Have you nothing to do as regards retribution in that quarter?"

"That feeling stirs me a little, but I can depute others to see that retribution exacted. I feel that I dare not trust myself to look upon Margaret Wyvill; and had I a sword, it would leap from its scabbard, woman as she is, for vengeance, were I face to face with her."

"Do you not think it is a duty you owe to your tenantry and to your servants, and to the many persons who are dependent in some way or another upon the proper management of your large estates, that you should rescue them from such a rule as Margaret's, which surely cannot be for good?"

"That can all be done while I am dying. Justice shall be done; but I have so little concern now with the world, and all its uses and usages, that I cannot of myself undertake these things, but must depute them to others more competent to do them. Do not ask to move me into earthly toils again—I am very, very content indeed to die."

"To die while your child lives?"

"How can I presume upon the fact of its continued existence? I dare not think so, now that she whom I loved has gone from me. Was she not young and beautiful, and has death spared her? Oh, no! oh, no! Talk not to me of earthly ties."

"And yet you have one of the strongest."

"In years to come, it may be that I shall be able to look upon that form which may ever remind me of her who is now no more—but now I think it would break my heart. But do I talk of time to come? Alas! there will be no time to come for me."

"You wrong your own feelings and your own judgment."

He turned aside, and with a deep sigh paused in the conversation, as if it were too great an effort to him by far to carry it on ; and Mrs. Angerstein turned to the child, and taking the little thing in her arms, laid it gently on the bed by its father's side.

"The goodness of Heaven," she said, gently, while her eyes glistened with tears, " and the claims of nature, will avail my plan ; and I shall live to see the father smile yet upon his dear little one."

She retired to the farther end of the apartment, and sat down, trembling with excitement, and scarcely able to see, from the tears that would start to her eyes, as she waited for the moment when Sir Anthony should discover the presence of his child.

About three minutes elapsed, and Sir Anthony had not turned himself, nor had the child, who was rather terrified than otherwise at the whole affair, uttered any sound whatever indicative of its presence. But this was a state of things that was not to last long.

The child itself put an end to it, and, as if intuitively feeling that some act of its own would be required for the purpose of rescuing its father from the state of mental thraldom in which he was, the little innocent placed her small soft hand upon the rough face of Sir Anthony, and spoke gently, saying,—

" Will you love me ?"

Sir Anthony Wyvill started, and uttered an exclamation of surprise, as he half rose in the bed, and cast his eyes upon the little intruder, whose sweet cherub countenance [betrayed some alarm, but not so much as might, under the circumstances, have fairly been expected, considering its strange situation, and that Sir Anthony, although so nearly allied to it, was in reality but a stranger in form, voice, and features.

" God of heaven !" he cried, " what is the meaning of this ? Who is this ? Is it true that my heart tells me ?—I is my own little one !"

It would seem as if indeed his heart had told him so, for he immediately clasped the child to him, and covered it with kisses, as he said,—

" Yes, yes ! Earth has me back again !"

*   *   *   *   *   *

We will not attempt, by any laboured powers of description, to profane the sanctity of a father's feelings, but willingly draw a veil over the proceedings of the next five minutes in the chamber of Sir Anthony Wyvill.

And more willingly do we do so, because we know that those who accord to these pages their attention will be well able of themselves to picture all that such a man as Sir Anthony was sure to feel at such a moment.

Suffice it for us to say, that in the course of a short time, Mrs. Angerstein was sitting by the bed-side again, and endeavouring to allay her tears, while the child reposed upon the breast of its father.

" Oh, how can I thank you, kindest and best of friends," he said, " for thus rescuing me, by the only means that could have been successful, from myself ?"

" I am," she said, " indeed I am most amply rewarded by the success of a stratagem which you must pardon for the motive which prompted it."

" Pardon ! pardon ! Can you use such a word in reference to that which you have done for me, when it is I who should ask you to pardon me for so much perverseness, as to make it necessary you should take so much trouble for me ?"

" And you now feel differently ? You now do feel that you have something to live for ?"

" I do—I do indeed ! and this child who, I said, I dreaded to see, lest it should remind me of her who is now lost to me for ever, shall never part from me ; and by such affection as I can show to it, I will endeavour to make it not miss a mother's fondness, however it may regret a mother's loss."

" Oh, how deeply then am I rewarded for all that I have suffered ! what a world of satisfaction now beamed over my soul, to think that you will not be wholly stricken down by this blow which you have received, but that you will both live to promote the happiness, and to deserve the best love, of this little one."

" I will endeavour to deserve it," he said, as a tear gushed to his eye ; " and when a few years more have rolled by, I will tell this child the story of its poor mother's w. ngs.

" Yes, and < . your wrongs—have you not been wronged most abundantly ?"

" I have, I have, and where I most trusted. Oh, who could have supposed it possible that one in whose veins flowed kindred blood with myself, could have played towards me so terrific and so base a part."

" Pride and avarice will achieve wonders !"

" They will, and from the earliest girlhood, I have always known Margaret to possess a proud and arrogant spirit ; and although such qualities in a woman do not by any means tend to make her more loveable, I became in a measure reconciled to them, from the thought that they would at least diffuse sufficient self-respect into her as to make her free from vice and iniquity."

" A fatal confidence !"

" Most fatal ! Oh, most fatal ! But the day of retribution has nearly come ; and although no act of mine may recal from the cold grave her whom but to look upon for one brief moment is life, I would barter freely the half of my remaining existence, and in the sacred name of justice, avenge her wrongs. Tremble, Margaret, tremble ! for you have, by the spells of your own evil passions, raised a spirit you may seek in vain to quell."

" It would be a mockery to ask you to think of these matters calmly,—a perfect mockery of what must be your feelings concerning them. But still let me, if I have any influence upon you, pray of you to take no positive revenge upon Margaret."

" What mean you ?"

" Leave her punishment to Heaven, and let it be sufficient that you take that negative vengeance to which all good men are fully entitled, namely, that you place it completely out of the power of the person who had once behaved unworthily towards you, to do so again."

" I understand you; you would have me temper my just resentment with so much mercy as to make it stop short of any positive act of vengeance, but content itself with an utter and complete repudiation of her who has worked me all this woe."

" I would have you do that,—I would have you, with this little one in your arms, go down to your own halls, and when you reach them, say nothing to Margaret, for she is unworthy even to hold converse with, but point silently to the threshold of your house, and she will understand you, and cross it, feeling and knowing that her reign of deceit, of dissimulation, and of triumph is over."

Sir Anthony Wyvill was silent for a few moments, and then he said, in a voice of more emotion and sadness,—

" You are right ! you are right ! that will be the way, and the only way in which I can or ought to express my indignation, which in after years will fully bear reflection. You are quite right, and it is a great mercy to me that at such a time as this, I have not been abandoned to the suggestions merely of my own maddened imagination, which might have prompted me to acts which the repentance of a life would not have atoned for."

" You will then adopt that course ?"

" I promise you that I will ; and a promise made to you is not one that I think so lightly of, as easily to break. You shall yourself see that I adopt your advice."

" No, no," said Mrs. Angerstein, " if there was before a necessity for any such conduct on my part as should remove the least impressions from my mind that I held a position in your esteem which I ought not, that necessity has become now strong and overwhelming, and I implore of you to let me leave you."

" You implore ! do not use that word where you may command. I feel that to you I owe my very existence,—to you, I owe all of happiness that I shall ever be able to call my own, and I will not inflict upon you the pang of even asking

you to remain with me as my most honoured guest, when your own high and nobl
principles and feelings prompt you to act otherwise."

"I cannot say," she replied, falteringly, "I cannot say how much I feel beholdei
to you for this most generous consideration. I shall, perhaps, when some few year
have passed away, be glad to come to look upon the face of this little one, for whon
I cannot but feel the deepest sympathy, but till those years have passed away
which will be sufficient to stifle the tongue of rumour, and to stop the smalles
vestige of a benevolent remark, I will remain here in London."

The good sense of this proposition on the part of Mrs. Angerstein was too eviden
to allow it to be slighted, and if possible, Sir Anthony's opinion of her was mor
favourable than ever from the manner in which, in such an emergency, she acted
and the candour too, so rare a quality, with which she enunciated her motives fo
so acting, instead of adopting some lame excuse to give a colour to a proceedin
which could only be excused by the feeling which did so p operly possess her upoi
the subject; and in which all our readers, both ladies and gentlemen we are sure
will have much pleasure in coinciding, for they as well as we know well, that in thi
every-day, artificial world, it is really not sufficient to be virtuous, but everythin
must be done to seem so likewise, or all the consequences of the worst derelictioi
will be visited upon the most innocent person that ever breathed."

To be sure, we cannot but feel with Sir Anthony Wyvill, that, if with pro
priety Mrs. Angerstein could have gone home now, and taken up her abode at Wyvil
Hall, his child would never have felt the loss of a mother ; but a moment's thought
of course, was sufficient to convince him that he ought not to dream of one such a
she was so completely sacrificing herself to him, and to his interests and feelings

And yet he knew not the great mental struggle that she endured when sh
came to the conclusion to leave him—he knew not how the feeling of gratitude whicl
had possessed her had deepened into one of the highest affection ; and that. althoug
she dreaded to confess the same to herself, she did love Sir Anthony Wyvill.

Situated now as they both believed themselves to be, there could not be tha
amount of impropriety in an attachment, had it been reciprocal, which, before th
supposed death of Emily, would have characterised it ; but, as regarde
Sir Anthony, the wound his heart had received, by the news of the death of Emily
was too green and fresh to allow it to be covered over with the thought of a nev
affection ; and although he entertained all such affection for Mrs. Angerstein
that the most devoted of brothers could feel for a sister whom he doated on, n
other feeling as regarded her had as yet found a home in his heart.

Nor indeed did he suspect that she entertained any other feeling than one of th
most exalted friendship for him, or perchance some sensations might have beei
awakened in his own heart which would have induced him to make an attempt t
alter the aspect of affairs.

As it was, however, they, after some more conversation, agreed between then
that she should remain in London in an establishment which he would keep up
while he went to Wyvill Hall, to execute the mild justice that Mrs. Angerstei
had persuaded him ought to suffice, against Margaret, and then endeavour, by ai
austere performance of the duties of his station, to forget to some extent th
painful past.

But he could not yet think of leaving London, until some vigorous exertions ha
been made for the purpose of endeavouring to discover the particulars of Emily'
supposed death, and where her mortal remains had been deposited—facts which he
Sir Anthony, considered it was cruel to keep from him, and which, unquestionably
he ought to know. But where and how to make the necessary inquiries wer
difficulties that appeared to be almost insurmountable, from the absence of all clu
to her place of retreat after she had left the hotel.

CHAPTER XLI.

THE INQUIRIES INSTITUTED BY SIR ANTHONY WYVILL FOR EMILY'S GRAVE.

HAD it not been that Sir Anthony Wyvill had been suffering from his wound, and the information he had received relative to the death of Emily, he would have at once proceeded to his estate in Wales, and have taken possession of it without any delay; but now his feelings and intentions were altered, and he longed to know where the last resting-place of his unfortunate wife was situated.

It was, however, a search to be made in the dark; and where to begin at he knew not—that was the main difficulty. The anonymous intimation he had received of her death did, he thought, appear to give him room to suppose she had been buried in some of the metropolitan churches; or, at least, in some of the suburban ones, but where, or even at what end of the town, it was wholly impossible to say.

Often did Sir Anthony Wyvill sigh as he thought of the adverse circumstances that had attended this unhappy affair, and he longed more than ever to ascertain the last resting-place of Emily.

It would be found, he thought, in some obscure spot where there would hardly be a name to indicate who lay buried beneath the heap of superincumbent earth; but it should be his care to erect such a memorial to her name that would at once testify his sorrow and love.

He determined to consult with Mrs. Angerstein upon the best plan of proceeding in this matter of the discovery of the burial-place of Emily.

"Women," he said, "if they have not the strong masculine hand of man, have, nevertheless, much acuteness, and may strike out some new light which might give him some more hope than the plan which he proposed to adopt on the present occasion."

Accordingly, when he felt himself equal to the task, he sought her, to consult with her upon the propriety of doing what he had imposed upon himself. He then stated to her his intentions with regard to his proposed search.

"It will be almost an endless search," she replied, "and one that will take much time and attention; for it will not do to miss one single burial-ground, for if you do, you are very likely to miss the one you most want to visit."

"Yes," replied Wyvill, "I am afraid it will be a long, tedious job, but it will be one of love. I would above all find out the grave of poor Emily."

"It would be desirable," returned Mrs. Angerstein; "those who gave you so much information ought to have given you what they must not only have been possessed of, but what they must, also, have known you would have been most anxious to learn—the resting-place of the unfortunate lady."

"I should have been most glad; but perhaps it might have supplied some link by which the writer might have been discovered, and that might have been a motive for his withholding the information I so much desired."

"It might so, certainly; but you will, I suppose, commence your search very soon."

"Almost immediately."

"When will you make the first attempt at discovery, and how will you begin, or set about it?"

"Thus I will begin—Heaven direct me, for I know not where I will begin—here, and so go on through the whole county, until I find where she is. It will be a long search, and yet if conducted well, may be successful; and I would undergo every kind of fatigue rather than I would forego the discovery. I will traverse every foot of graveyard to be found, and read every inscription, so that I shall have less chance of passing by the spot."

"But that would be unnecessary labour," said Mrs. Angerstein; "besides, you know, she must have been buried within a certain time, and it would not be necessary to examine older tombs—nay, I think that, by a careful inquiry of the sexton, or examination of the parish registrar, much labour and loss of time might be saved."

"True, true, it might," said Wyvill, thoughtfully, "it might; it will be well to do so, for I shall have none to spare when I come to consider the extent of my task; but your hint will certainly be the best to act upon."

"What I may be able to effect towards the attainment of your purpose, Sir Anthony, I shall be most happy to do; if you can only point out how I can be of service, I am sure it will be done with pleasure."

"No, no," said Sir Anthony, "I know not in what way you could possibly aid me here; far from it, save now and then, when you feel disposed, and the occasion suits, you may prosecute the search with me."

"And that I will do right willingly," said Mrs. Angerstein, "and the sooner the better; for delay will but put off the day of your success; at the same time the longer it is put off, the more difficulty in the search."

"I will begin to-morrow," said Sir Anthony; "that is settled upon, and in the meantime I will make arrangements for my adventure to-morrow, for I anticipate I shall meet with troubles and some strange occurrences."

"You will come in contact with some singular people in the course of your travels."

"Yes, but more of that another time."

*   *   *   *   *

The next day Sir Anthony Wyvill left his hotel, and proceeded upon this strange inquiry through the metropolis, where he determined he would not be baffled by any circumstance whatever—that no rebuff should induce him to turn aside.

When he got out, he walked on till he came to a small church, the graveyard of which was about the size of a town garden, behind a second or third-rate house, and one that might have been paved over without costing the parish but very little —indeed the tombstones themselves might have been used for the purpose, and they would have been enough.

It was some time before the sexton could be found; he was doing something to the churchyard, that is to say, his tools were there, his boards, pick, and mattock.

"Where is the sexton?" inquired Sir Anthony Wyvill of an aged woman, who was peering about the churchyard.

"Ah, where indeed!" she replied. "And where could be expected such a drunken fool as he, but at the alehouse. Yes, I'll warrant, if you find the sexton, you'll find him there—I'll warrant he's always here or there."

"Well," said Sir Anthony, looking round, "I imagine that he must oftener be there than here, seeing the extent of the ground is not very great."

"Ay, sir; but he does an uncommon deal of business for all that, I am sure."

"Indeed, it is very surprising," said Sir Anthony, looking about, "very surprising, indeed. I cannot think how he does it."

"Oh! burials, burials!"

"That is yet more astonishing than ever, for I cannot see the room which he can find for business."

"Ah!" said the old woman, "this place holds many bodies—some on 'em are eight and nine deep; and then they dig up all the old ones and burn them."

"Burn what?" exclaimed Sir Anthony.

"Burn—why, burn the coffin and bones, to be sure. I know they'll deny it; but what of that? It doesn't take a schoolmaster to tell how many dead bodies will fill this place over and over again; and what becomes of them, I wonder?"

"They decompose, I suppose," said Sir Anthony.

"Ay, ay! decomposed indeed, and so would you be decomposed in a very short time, and the coffin-lids do so too; but at the same time, you'd lay there many a long year before you would do so natterrally."

"But the sexton?"

"Is over the way, I dare say, as I told you before; he has had to do too much work lately, and has more money than he knows what to do with."

"Have there been many burials lately?"

"Yes."

"Has there been one of a lady—a young, a beautiful woman, unknown here?"

"Not that I know of; beautiful indeed, beautiful, well, they are all pretty well of one complexion in the grave, and the most beautiful will make but an indifferent corpse."

Sir Anthony was tired of this, and turned away, leaving the old woman to mumble and mutter her indignation upon everybody, and to prove her assertion that one be as good as another in the grave, and that none were beautiful, but only ghastly and hideous corpses that were horrible to look upon.

After he quitted the churchyard, he went over the way to the Pumpkin and Poker public-house, where he could hear some signs of jollity, but of rather a curious character; the sounds of pots and voices were quelled in the deep voice of a man who was singing something about the churchyard yew and the jolly old crow who cried, ' crow ' on the same tree, whenever a body was being lowered into th grave—so ran the song, though Sir Anthony could not hear the whole of the words of this delectable production.

"Well done, old Mattock," said a voice, "well done."

"Ay, ay, it's easy to say well done," answered another voice, "but whoever heard old Mattock in mirth save at a burial. The passing bell is to him the sweetest music, far sweeter and more merry than the Christmas chimes."

"And so I ought to think," said old Mattock, "seeing they bring me my bread; I know then there is business to be done, and I begin to get the jobs out of hand."

"Well, well, you ought to be and are grateful to Providence, I suppose, to think it kills people that you may bury them."

"Providence never finds me unthankful for his favours; were it my own wife, I hope I should continue to ' praise him from whom all blessings flow.' "

"Ha, ha, what a sly jolly dog you are, Mattock; where did you learn to be such a character?"

"In the churchyard beneath the yew-tree; it was as good as a hawthorn to me."

    *   *   *   *   *

Sir Anthony Wyvill waited not to hear the conclusion of the conversation, but seeing one of the people of the house, inquired if the sexton was there.

"Yes," was the answer; "do you want to see him?"

"I do, I will wait here for him," said Sir Anthony; "I wish to speak with him, and shall not detain him long."

"Here, I say, Mattock," said the man who went in, "I say, old crow, you are wanted outside: your comfort is broken in upon for this afternoon, I see."

The old crow made no reply, but hastily shuffled to the door, and then Sir Anthony saw the singular being who had not been denominated unhappily, "the old crow."

He was short, broad, and bony; with thin, straggling, jet-black locks hanging about his head; while his deep black eyes, looking upward towards the stranger (for he had a stoop), gave him a very singular appearance, for he was a very aged though an able man.

"Did you want me?" he inquired.

"Yes, I did."

"Parish business, eh?"

"I wish to make some inquiries respecting a burial that has taken place recently."

"Yes, there have been a good many lately. Who was it you wanted to hear about?"

"This," said Sir Anthony, handing the man a description of the unfortunate Emily, for he dared not trust himself to pronounce her description, for it would have been her eulogium, which would have caused him to have betrayed too much emotion. This will tell you exactly what I want."

"Well," said the old man, reading it carefully, "I haven't buried anybody of that name."

"You may not have had the right name given, but some anonymous one or mere initials."

"No," said the old man, "I haven't buried anybody but what I know very well these six months; we seldom indeed have anybody but parishioners here, nobody but what we know, or else of a different description."

"Then I must seek elsewhere. I have plenty of room."

"And a long search, if you don't know either time or place."

"Nothing more than what is there. This is the first place—I must proceed: I am sorry I have disturbed you."

    *   *   *   *   *   *

Sir Anthony Wyvill toiled from graveyard to graveyard, and saw more sextons that day than he could have believed to have existed before; but yet after many hours thus spent, he returned to his abode with an air of dejection and disappointment.

The day had been one of some toil to him, for his exertions were great, and the fatigue was no less, and yet it was not as yet rewarded, but would have to be persevered in until he had made a round of the whole metropolis.

It was singular what a quantity of churches there were in London, and that shows what a rich city it must be where such costly luxuries are to be found and paid for by the citizens, for the Church has but little to do with giving.

Receiving is as much as she can spare time and attention for; it could not be possible that any one of the cloth should give anything towards supporting the calling, save the attention and exertions of the various members when they are paid for it, but not otherwise; for I am sure no Churchman ever yet looked upon it in any other light than as a means of living, whose income was more than enough to live humbly upon.

It is the layman who gets imposed upon. Much mystery and many hard words terrify him to endow, or help to build and endow, a church, while his fellow-man stands by, crying and sickening with disease and hunger!

While such things exist the system must be vicious,—bad from the core.

No one could credit the quantity of metropolitan churches, unless they went upon some such interminable errand as Sir Anthony Wyvill's; and then, when you are going from church to church, and anxious to get to the end of them, you suddenly find out what a stock you have before you.

This was Sir Anthony's case, and a singular method it was to make an inquiry; but he deemed only his own personal exertions at all adequate to the exigencies of the case, or at all likely to be satisfactory to himself.

He would have been for ever doubting the accuracy of his information, and would, moreover, have believed that some error or other had been committed; and he would have had the extra trouble to go over again, and if he did not succeed, it would be a double aggravation and cause of disappointment, besides additional toil.

*   *   *   *   *   *   *   *

Several days passed, and no success. This was an uncomfortable state of things, —far from agreeable; for there was not one single event that enabled the mind to look back upon, and say, this much has been made.

When he spoke to Mrs. Angerstein about it, he could not extract any hope from her beyond what his own mind told him; and that was, he might stumble upon his wife's grave accidentally; or, indeed, upon what was as highly probable as anything, and that was, he might miss the object of his search through some means that might be used to prevent recognition by any one.

But still hope buoyed him up, and he continued his search day after day, until he had made a circuit, and so had completed his inquiries; and then he determined to do the like in respect of the suburban towns or places.

Here, too, was a wide field; everything was to be done, but it would give him some trouble.

She might, he argued, when she found herself growing ill,—she might have requested to be conveyed to some near country-like spot, and there have remained until she died, and, of course, at such a place she would be buried.

Thinking there was more probability in this last opinion than the first, possibly because it was exploded, and not because the last was more likely, he set about it.

He then took several days' tour at once into the country, to examine thoroughly each suburban district, so that no part might be omitted; for he felt that everything depended upon the strictness of his search.

At length he came to a pretty, retired spot, where there was a quiet rural population, closely connected with the metropolis, where its church was an ornament, and the graveyard a pleasant saunter for the rustics who lived in those parts, and for the more adventurous from London who would walk as far.

Here Sir Anthony stopped one afternoon, and gazed upon the spire of the old-fashioned church; indeed, he was stricken with its beauty, and the secluded nook in which it stood surrounded, at least in part bounded, by high elm trees, in which the rooks had built their nests for ages, and yet had never been disturbed by the villagers.

Sir Anthony entered the churchyard; he saw nobody about, and he pushed open the gate with the view of examining the tombstones, and thus ascertaining in part whether she whom he sought was there or not]; but he had scarcely turned an angle of the building when he came upon the sexton, who was busy in his avocation.

He was shoulder-deep in his grave, throwing out shovelfuls of earth and stones not unmixed with human remains, but which now were not to be identified to be other than human bones : the traces as to whose grave he had trenched upon were all lost long ago, and the grave of some one who once occupied and whose remains were now nearly returned to their original elements, and entered into the chemical combination with the surrounding soil, and what yet remained of the less destructible parts were thus thrown up with other rubbish.

The sexton paused to wipe his forehead, which streamed with perspiration—the effect of his work, for the soil was heavy and difficult to work, besides which the position he worked in was constrained.

Sir Anthony gazed upon him for a few moments in silence, and when the sexton turned his eyes upon him, he said,—

" You are busy in your vocation."

" Yes, sir," was the reply.

" It is a large grave," said Sir Anthony, noticing the extraordinary length of the grave.

" Why, yes, sir, it is for a long man ; he stood six feet eight without his shoes, and his coffin will be seven feet, so, you see, the grave must be a little beyond that, or it would not be long enough to let it down."

" An inhabitant of this place ?"

" Yes, he was known as long Jemmy the Idiot : he was very thin, and stooped ; quite harmless though ; fine man too, of his inches ; very tall ; the ladies used to say he would have been a pattern, only he was so silly."

" What ! stooping and narrow-shouldered ?"

" Yes, sir ; why, you see, height is the great thing, though in my young days, a well-proportioned man of any size was considered handsome, or at least passably so."

" Have you been busy lately ?"

" Why, yes, reasonably so—I musn't complain, being pretty brisk—had an epidemic, which carried off a few—a dozen or two —sad thing ; but what's one man's meat is another's poison, and it's an ill wind that blows nobody any good, you know, sir—put a little into my pocket, and I am thankful to Providence for its goodness to me.

" Have you buried any one lately—a lady—who has been buried somewhat privately ?"

" Yes, I have."

" Where ?—Was she sinking from illness and grief ?"

" Yes, that was it, poor thing ! she did seem to take on about something sorely ; her friends brought her down to the White House, hoping, I suppose, she would recover, but she was too far gone. There's the grave, yonder."

Sir Anthony strode towards the grave, and there, upon a small head-stone, were the initials E. W., and the date of the death, but nothing more. He reeled and staggered, for he felt here was Emily's grave.

He fell upon his knees, and offered up a prayer for her and for himself; he was much agitated ; he scarce knew what he was about ; however, he remembered the direction of the gravedigger, and went there to stay for a while, and in the meantime he made inquiries respecting the grave about which he felt such emotions.

" Yes, sir," said the landlord, in answer to his inquiries, "the lady was very beautiful, very beautiful I should say, only she was very melancholy, and very sad ; she was brought here by her friends, and nobody knew whence,—she was buried so very quietly.

" And did you learn nothing respecting them or the servants ?"

" Oh dear no ! sir, they were all as close as could be, for we were at one time very curious about them."

" Ah ! it must be her I am in search of. Oh, Emily, Emily, you shall not sleep in so obscure a corner, beneath such a simple monument, if not to extol your virtues, at least to show my estimation of them, and to vent my grief: it will be some slight consolation to know you sleep not unknown and unhonoured.

    *   *   *   *   *   *

The monument designed by Sir Anthony Wyvill was erected to the memory of Emily ; he saw it, and was satisfied : such a splendid mausoleum was never before seen in the churchyard. The inscription expressed the virtues of her who had gone, and the sorrow and lamentations of those who were left behind to bewail her.

This employed Sir Anthony some time, though he urged the work on with all possible dispatch, and when it was done and completed, he prepared to leave the place.

That morning, however, was filled with events to which he was a stranger. A stranger drove up to the house, alighted, and then went to the churchyard, and there remained for some hours until, coming back, he inquired who it was that had erected the monument, and, when he learned who it was, he desired to see him. Sir Anthony admitted him; and, when he saw him, he ran up to him, and embraced him, saying,—

" Generous man, you have a heart that sympathises with me; you can compassionate the undeserved misfortune and the suffering of innocent beauty."

" What do you mean," inquired Sir Anthony, annoyed and amazed at this strange kind of address.

" You have raised, generously raised, a monument to the memory of my Emilia White."

" Eh? What? Your Emelia?"

" Yes, yes, I was detained—cruelly detained, and kept in ignorance of all, but I have now received proof of her unfortunate decease ; her letter to me in a few hours before she died told me all—here, sir, read it, and tell me what you think of it."

Sir Anthony caught sight of the letter—it was enough—he had been mistaken, and at once quitted the spot, followed by the thanks of the stranger, who kept on extolling his goodness and generosity.

CHAPTER XLII.

MARGARET'S AGREEMENT WITH FOSTER FOR THE MURDER OF SIR ANTHONY WYVILL.

WE left Margaret Wyvill under the guidance of the youth whom she had so unexpectedly recognised in the cavern of the robbers. It was night, or rather it had long since turned the midnight hour, and the youth led her for some distance through the forest, until they came to an opening, a kind of road, where he paused.

" Are you not going on further, boy?" inquired Margaret.

" No," replied the boy. " If I do, there will be no time for me to return before they are back, and you will be in greater danger than you are now."

" Ay, indeed, I might ; but as they believe me dead, I think they would scarce look for me, though they might for you. There would be ample time to escape."

" No, no," said the boy. " If they found your body gone, they would naturally conclude we should be off together, and therefore a stricter search would be made ; besides, they will not, if I go back, think of looking for you; they will deem it all right."

" You do not intend to remain there all your life, do you? Your fate will be one that will reflect but little credit upon you—one that will end in a painful death."

" That death will not be painful, because it is a speedy one," said the youth, "but I am sure that will not be mine. I have liberty and strength."

"But you may soon be deprived of both," said Margaret, "and fetters can bind the strongest hands. Take advice, and go to London, and seek some honest way of living : I will not forget you."

"Ah!" said the boy, "I have tasted of the freedom of the forest, and the constraints of society sit ill upon my shoulders—so, farewell; and ride forward down this road, until it merges into another, but still keep on without slackening your speed; ride till day dawns, and till your horse can go no further, then take shelter in the first inn."

"Farewell, boy."

"Farewell, and take my advice ; ride on while you have the reins, and when called upon to stop, ride through at full gallop ; you will do better thus than by any other means."

She waved her hand to him, and he let go the bridle, and in a few minutes more the clattering of the horses' hoofs alone were heard, and then the boy turned away, to retrace his steps towards the den of infamy he had left.

Margaret rode away from the spot with much haste; she cantered her horse, and trotted him forward at a round pace, until she had got at least several miles from the place ; and then day broke upon her suddenly, for she had been riding in some low valleys, when she suddenly emerged from deep wooded roads into the open country, upon rather an elevated situation, and then the beauties of the day disclosed themselves.

Here Margaret Wyvill drew breath, and looked behind her, and in the dark masses below she could not see anything that gave her the slightest uneasiness. She was alone, and no soul near her at that moment. She was free.

Before lay a long road—the skies were glowing with all the colours that could be imagined ; and she thought that she could from the elevated spot where she now stood, see the mountain—if not the particular pass that she would have to enter to go to the Wyvill estate—she was near home.

"A few hours more, and I shall be there; but Nature requires something to recruit her exhausted energies—and rest to one's weary limbs ; besides my horse must now be dreadfully winded. Yonder is a pretty inn, if the inmates are yet about —push on, good steed, soon you shall have your reward."

As she spoke she struck lightly the horse; and, as if he understood her words, he started off afresh, willingly though languidly; and in not a very long time she arrived at a small road-side inn, where she stopped and looked about her, fearful lest she should not see any means of getting in.

However, to her great relief, she observed a man in the stable, which was close at hand. The door being but a few yards from the main entrance, she immediately rode up, and called to him, upon which he came out.

"My friend, can you accommodate my horse with stable room, and myself with shelter in the house ?"

"Your horse can come in, but as for yourself, ma'am, I don't know what to say—our people aint up."

"You can wake them, can't you ?"

"Yes, I can wake them, you see ; but the consequence of that might be, that I should be very soon sorry for having done so ; missus is, you see, such a precious vixen."

"Tell her I have been stopped and robbed, and I am very ill; surely she cannot complain of opening the house under such circumstances as these," said Margaret; "try, and I will reward you!"

"Very well, ma'am," said the man; "why, if she do, then I can't help it—so here goes; but first I'll rack up the horse, and then I'll run up and call 'em, and let 'em grumble how they will!"

Having done this, he posted off to the house, which he entered by a back way, and began hammering and calling for his mistress, who appeared excited with anger at being thus unseasonably disturbed by the ostler.

"You noisy varlet !" said the hostess, "when I get up, I'll lay the cart-whip about your ears, I will, for disturbing me in the midst of a pleasant dream. I was dreaming about a white horse, and all the world knows that to dream of a white horse is lucky, and now, you varlet! you have spoilt a piece of good fortune for me!"

"Please, missus," remonstrated the man, "please, missus, it aint a white horse but a chesnut mare."

"Oh, you villain, do you think I don't know more about my own dreams than you; go along and let me try to sleep again; it's pleasant to have lucky dreams."

"But the lady——"

"The lady! what lady?"

"Why, the lady that's come on the chesnut horse; she's waiting; she's been robbed, waylaid, murdered, and maltreated; she's wanting to come in; won't you let the traveller in? She'll go down below at the Old Ale Tun if you don't."

"Yes, yes, I will come, I will come; but at the same time take the horse, and put it in the stable."

"I have, marm."

"Then she can't go yet awhile, but call up the wench, and I'll be down; call the gal; kick at the door; God bless me, how one must be about in this world to do anything at all. Servants do nothing unless one is ever upon their heels, and then it is just as hard a work as in doing it all by one self, oh dear!"

She gave a great yawn, and began her toilet with some haste, while the ostler found the wench's apartment with marvellous and suspicious haste, and alarmed her.

These things done, the inn doors were opened in a little while, and Margaret Wyvill entered the best room they had to offer her, and a fire was about to be laid, when the landlady said—

"I am very sorry we aint better prepared, madam, for a lady like you, but we do not often have such early travellers, nor do we often have ladies."

"I dare say not, but accident alone makes me a traveller; however, you need not put yourself out of the way to light a fire: a couple of hours' repose will better suit me than anything else at this moment."

"Ma'am, eh, what will you take?"

"A bed."

"Oh yes, a bed," said the astonished landlady, who had some notion that the visitor would require an infinity of eatables and drinkables, the moment she got up.

"I have not slept since yesterday morning, and I am very weary: I will have breakfast when I get up."

"Certainly, ma'am, certainly."

Margaret was speedily shown into a bed-room; upon the couch she soon threw herself, tired and exhausted, and in a short while she fell into a sound sleep.

When she awoke, she knew not how long she had been there; but there was much bustle and noise below: she jumped up, and went to the window, but she saw nothing to excite any alarm in her mind,—only the country people were bustling about on their own business.

She thought it must be mid-day, and as she desired to ride home by the day-light, she determined that she would at once see about getting on the road again; therefore, she left her room, and going down stairs she encountered the landlady, who was employed in scolding the girl in a very high strain, from which she desisted when she saw Margaret.

"Ah, your humble servant, ma'am—hope you slept well—hope we haven't disturbed you!"

"No," said Margaret, "can I have breakfast now?"

"Yes, certainly, ma'am. What would you like for breakfast?" inquired the landlady, obsequiously.

"I am not particular, but let me have it immediately, as I wish to leave here as soon as I can."

Thus urged, the landlady soon produced the meal she requested, and with it some substantial viands, but which she would like to have had some especial orders, as they always contrived to charge double, because they are asked for.

However, having given traveller all she thought necessary, she placed herself at the table before the fire, and began to talk to her guest while employed in the process of eating.

"And so, ma'am, they say you were robbed this morning, and that you had been ill-used?"

"Yes, I had been detained by the roughness of their treatment. I have a few bruises about me now."

"Nothing more!" exclaimed the hostess, who had an appetite for the horrible, which was by no means appeased by a few bruises—a smash or two would have been more agreeable food to feed her mind upon.

No. 35.

" Nothing more," replied Margaret ; " and would you really have had me suffer more than I have ? You couldn't feel pleasure in hearing that I had been hurt."

" Oh, no, but I thought you had been nearly killed, by what my ostler said."

" Indeed ! do they usually hurt people much about these parts ; or are they subject to brutality as a common occurrence ?"

" Why, I can't say it is exactly ; but this I must say, sometimes people are killed."

" I never heard of it," said the lady, " though I must say there are bad people enough to do anything in that way."

" That is very true," said the landlady ; " but the fact is, there are the Welsh only a few miles off, and who knows who comes here ? and then they go back again, after having committed often very desperate acts indeed."

" Is that the Welsh you are speaking of ?"

" Yes."

" Are you sure that you are right?" inquired Margaret ; " I have found as many bad characters in England as Wales."

" It is all very well for you to say so, ma'am, but you haven't had the experience I have ; you haven't suffered what I have, and therefore you think otherwise."

" What have you seen to prove this ?"

" Oh, quite enough to make me have the most determined hatred against them. They are a vile set altogether, without any exception at all. I never thought to have got over that day."

" What day ?"

" The day upon which my poor husband was barbarously murdured," said the landlady.

" Murdered, did you say ?"

" Yes, poor man! he was cruelly and barbarously murdered ; that was as plain as ever any man was murdered."

" By whom?"

" The thieving Welsh, our neighbours over the hills," said the landlady, who felt perfectly infuriated when the Welsh were mentioned to her by any one.

" How has all this come about ?" inquired Margaret, who thought she would exhaust her ill-temper in telling the story of the murder of her late husband.

" It's now about six years ago since he was killed, poor man, and that took place in the middle of the day, by a party of Welshmen who came to seek harvest work, or, I think they had harvest work, and were returning home ; yes, that was it, because they were going home.

" They all came here—there were five or six of them ; and having entered the room below, they called for beer and some bread and meat, also some cheese. Well, they were all served with enough, and began to eat and drink.

" All the while, however, they began to talk about the meat, and cheese and beer, which they said was bad.

" ' Bad,' said my husband, ' it is good, very good beer—none better to be found anywhere within twenty miles of this ; I am sure there is none better.'

" They declared it was bad, nay, too bad to drink, and they wanted him to get them some stronger ; but this he refused to do, but told them to leave the house.

" ' Leave the house,' said one ; ' yes, we will do that when we take you with us and drag you through your own pond ; you shan't do this for nothing—we are not to be talked to in this way at all—bring some strong ale.'

" ' I will not,' said my husband.

" ' You won't ?'

" ' No, I won't ; and what is more, I want the money for what you have had. Come, come, pay me for what you have had, I want the money.'

" ' And you are likely to want.'

" Now this was more than my husband could well bear, and he said he would have his money, or would take means to punish them for their want of honesty.

" ' Punish us !' they exclaimed ; ' we will punish you, if you don't do what we tell you ; fetch us some more ale—some strong ale—and, d'ye hear, be quick.'

"My husband was glad to get out of the room, for he thought they meant mischief; so he sought out the ostler, to whom he told all that had happened.

"'If you don't mind, master,' said the ostler, 'they'll get the better of all here, and turn the house inside out. You had better let me go down to the town, and get what force I can.'

"'That is just what I was about to tell you what to do,' said my husband.

"'Then the sooner the better,' said the ostler.

"'Go at once,' said my husband, 'and go as quickly as you can, for I fear they are impatient, and will proceed to the worst before you can come back with aid.'

"Thus admonished, the ostler set off as quickly as he could, and he ran very fast, for he was partial to his master, and he thought these Welsh would do some evil to him.

"The ostler had no sooner gone, than one of the Welshmen came out and saw the man running. This was enough; he guessed what was the matter, and immediately called out to his companions something in Welsh.

"I did not understand what it was about, but they all came out upon the signal; these words seemed to inflame them greatly, and they all looked after the ostler, when one of the men said,—

"'So, you have sent for men to turn us out, have you? you want to do us mischief, do you?'

"'No,' said my husband, 'I do not, though you have tried to do me evil. Why, have you not thrown my things about, eaten and drunk of my best, and now you refuse to pay me?'

"'We will pay you,' said one.

"'That is all that I want,' said my husband, 'all that I want, and only fair; live and let live, you know.'

"'Our payment will not be of the sort,' said another Welshman; 'you must take in out in kind; but first, you must give us some money.'

"My husband refused. 'He had no money to give them,' he said, 'and how could they expect it?' He began to get away, and suddenly made a bolt into the stable, for he thought by their eyes that they meant him mischief.

"He had no sooner gone there than he locked and secured the door, and proceeded to arm himself with a pitchfork, and began to cry out for aid.

"This is a lonely spot," said the hostess, "and nobody was near, and the Welshmen immediately made a rush at the door; but it did not give way easily, and some of them attempted to get in at the window; but the prongs of the fork gave sore wounds, and they were compelled to desist, until one climbed up and got into the loft on the top, and then he came down the ladder, and as my husband couldn't keep them out of more than one place at a time, they got in and opened the door.

"Here my unfortunate husband was driven into a corner, where he defended himself very well, until one rushed upon him, and he was run through, and fell dead; but the others had passed the fork and laid their hands upon him, and a blow he received on the head brought him on his knees.

"'Mercy, mercy,' he said.

"'None, none.'

"'You shall have all you ask for—everything in my house, but spare my life.'

"'No, you shall die—you shall die.'

"They beat and knocked him about dreadfully; the place was literally wet with blood.

"He broke away from them, and rushed, all bleeding as he was, towards the house, but received a heavy blow on the head, which brought him to his knees on the threshold of his own door, and he was unable to rise.

"'Mercy,' he said, in a hoarse voice, 'mercy; spare my life, I will do you no harm.'

"'Kill him,' was the only answer they made.

"'Yes, yes, spare him,' I cried, as I rushed to the door; 'I am his wife, do not murder him before his eyes, do not let me see him die; spare him, for God's sake.'

" I was struck on the head, and fell senseless, and my husband was killed out-right.

" When I came to my recollection I found some people about me, they had come soon after; but as I was the only person in the house living, they had no knowledge which way the murderers had gone, as no one could give any knowledge Nor could I, for I was insensible before the murder was completed."

" Were they never punished for this deed ? "

" Never, for they were never taken; they must have gone back to Wales, from which place I hope they'll never come, unless it is to be hanged."

*   *   *   *   *

There was a pause of some moments' duration, after which Margaret Wyvill said she wished her horse to be brought to the door for her, as she wished to leave for her journey was lonely, and she wanted to get over it before the evening came on

Her wishes were complied with, and discharging her obligations to the hostess's satisfaction, she left the roadside inn.

It was then scarcely mid-day, and setting her horse to its work, she pursued her journey at a good round pace, that, in as short a time as could be, she was ascending towards the rocky pass that led to the valley in which the Wyvill estate was situated

This she gained, and looked down from the elevation along the narrow road, and then she encountered the Dyke House in which the Fosters lived, where the traveller had been murdered, as here she intended to call before she reached the estate as she had something to say to the inhabitant.

It was not long, though at a slower pace, before she reached the Dyke House, at the door of which she tapped with her riding rod, and Foster himself came out.

" I want to speak with you, Foster."

" Yes, Mrs. Margaret ; will you please to alight and come in ?"

" Yes, I will; my horse you must secure for me, as I cannot remain long."

" As long as you please, Mrs. Margaret."

The man immediately secured the bridle in the ring and hook that was close by the door, apparently for that very purpose, which done, he aided Margaret to alight, and they both entered the Dyke House, in which at that moment only Foster and Margaret were to be seen in the kitchen or principal room.

" Are you alone, Foster?" inquired Margaret, with a familiar emphasis.

" Yes, quite, nobody within car shot."

" That will do : now I want to tell you Sir Anthony Wyvill is coming back to take possession of his estate, which will make a sad difference to more people than to us."

" It will," said Foster, thoughtfully.

" And of course it is their interest to prevent it. Now, Foster, what do you say to putting it out of his power to reach Wyvill Hall? then all will be safe."

" Yes, yes; if I could see all safe and clear, and it was worth while—why—"

" You shall have a handsome reward, a very handsome reward, if you will do it fully and fairly."

" If you make it worth while, Mrs. Margaret," said Foster, with a slight grin, " I can do my best, and you shall have no cause to complain of any part of the bargain."

" I will be true, and you shall have a royal sum."

" Good ! but I must have a watch; I must have scouts, &c. out so as to watch him coming up the other side, and then before he can get up I will send to you, so you shall come and see I did it well and thoroughly."

" Yes, yes; that will do, that will do very well. I will come when you send to me, but be sure you do not miss him, that would ruin all."

" No, no, I will take care of that; but I want money in hand, Mrs. Margaret, to keep the game afloat ; in the mean time, when they are upon the look-out, they are not at work, you know that, Mrs. Margaret ?"

" I do," said Margaret, as she handed Foster a sum of money, and then she added as she rose,—

" Now, do we understand each other ?"

" Yes," said Foster; but some more conversation passed, and then they parted. Margaret Wyvill remounted her horse and quitted the Dyke House, while Foster accompanied her for a short distance on foot. He returned, and she pursued her way to Wyvill Hall by herself, where she arrived, after a journey of some danger and interest.

CHAPTER XLIII.

THE MURDER.

WE have now arrived at that dreadful epoch in our story which compels us to request our readers to be ready to keep in their memories, or to refer back to the first part of our tale, in which we described the passage of Sir Anthony Wyvill through the dyke, with his child in his arms, towards his ancestral home.

It will be recollected that one of those storms which in mountainous districts are so common had ensued, and that, contrary to his intention, Sir Anthony had been compelled to seek the treacherous shelter of the Dyke House for himself and that sole relic of his dear and well-remembered Emily, as he thought.

After the unsuccessful search in London and its vicinity for the tomb of her whom he believed to have gone broken-hearted to the grave, he had with melancholy earnestness turned his steps at last homeward, at all events determined to displace from her arrogated authority the one being who had been the malignant cause of all the terrific mischief that had taken place.

Before starting from London, he had had a long and deeply interesting conversation with Mrs. Angerstein, the object of which on his part was to persuade her, after some time had passed away, to banish from her mind those scruples she at present had, and consent to take up her abode at Wyvill Hall, as one of the most honoured guests that had ever crossed its threshold, and bestow upon the little Emily the benefit of her society.

It may be well guessed by the reader, with his knowledge of the feelings of Mrs. Angerstein, what a crowd of emotions such a request, evidently urged with such great sincerity, were calculated to awaken in her breast.

" My affections," said Sir Anthony, " are, as you know well, in the tomb with my lost Emily, wherever that tomb may be, but still I cannot but picture to myself the vast advantages which my little one, who is deprived of a mother's tender care and solicitude, would have from your society, if I could but prevail upon you to disregard the ideas and remarks of a malevolent world, and take up your permanent abode at Wyvill Hall."

" I will not," said Mrs. Angerstein, " I cannot say absolutely no to the proposal, because I am well aware of the pure and good motives that prompt it, but time must elapse first, and then, if I could bring myself to think that the sight of me really would not always, as it appears to me now it must, awaken disagreeable reminiscences, I should not feel that I ought to deny you."

" I will be satisfied then," said Sir Anthony, " with the conditional promise, and the duration of the time you mention I must leave to yourself, only hoping and entreating that it may be curtailed as much as possible."

This Mrs. Angerstein promised it should be, and it was with such an understanding that Sir Anthony set out upon his return to his home accompanied by the child, with whom he may be said to be only just commencing to form anything like a great intimacy, although he soon succeeded in acquiring the little [creature's best affections, for children soon accord their love to those who speak gently to them and use them kindly.

And so was it, as our readers may well imagine from a knowledge of his character, that Sir Anthony Wyvill soon won all the dearest affections of that little creature, who was as yet too young to know or to be told the dreadful story of its poor mother's wrongs. The separation, too, which had taken place between the child and Emily, had tended, to some extent, to weaken the tie that bound them together, on the part of the former, so that when Sir Anthony came, with abundance of caresses and kind words, the child looked up to him as its kindest, and indeed its only friend in the world, and seemed to lavish all its love upon him.

And no wonder was it that he cherished that little living image of her whom he had loved with all the devotion that a noble nature was capable of, and lavished upon it that concentrated fondness which we ordinarily do not see exhibited, but which, in the outpouring affections of Sir Anthony's nature, he now permitted to flow completely in one channel, and that, too, without the least restraint.

We have said nothing of the groom who was employed by Margaret to watch the proceedings of Sir Anthony; but it will suffice for us now to state that he did make one experiment upon the baronet, without succeeding in inducing him to accept of his services; for, whether it was a hesitation on his part, or really something in his appearance that Sir Anthony did not like, certain it is that, although he did want an attendant, he refused him at once, although at considerable inconvenience to himself.

The only thing that annoyed the man in this was, that he might fail in getting more money from Margaret; and he set his wits to work to try and mend such a state of things. The best way to do that, he thought, would be to conceal the disappointment, and to write to Margaret, saying that Sir Anthony was still staying in town, but that he required more money for the purpose of following him about from place to place; and that he had got a promise from him of being taken into his employment in the course of a short time—or, at least, as soon as circumstances would allow.

This letter, so far as securing money was concerned, produced the desired effect, for she at once sent him a sum beyond his expectations. But what was money to her, if she could succeed in what she wished now most ardently, namely, the destruction of Sir Anthony Wyvill? for as she, not unfrequently, now muttered to herself, as she wandered, restless and disturbed, about the various rooms of the Hall,—"His death will be my life."

It was the great wish of Sir Anthony to get down to Wyvill Hall without Margaret having the least idea of his coming; for although, partly at the intercession of Mrs. Angerstein, and partly from his own natural impulses to mercy, he had determined upon doing nothing beyond discarding her from his home and his affections for ever, he certainly did wish to see her, to tell her, in a few words, what he thought of her conduct.

Those words would not be words of violence, for such were altogether contrary to the habit of the baronet to use; but like Hamlet, when he proposed turning his mother's thoughts inwards upon her guilty soul, Sir Anthony Wyvill would speak daggers, although he used none, and he felt that his sister deserved little consideration at his hands.

On the way he regretted that he had not made greater efforts to combat with the feelings of Mrs. Angerstein, which had induced her to decline, probably for a considerable length of time, becoming an inmate of his house, and he said, as he revolved in his mind the many excellences of her character,—

"Would that I could truly love her sufficiently in time to ask her to become my wife; but the very thought of a successor in my affections to poor Emily sounds like sacrilege, and I cannot entertain it for a moment. No—as dear friends—as loving intimates—more affectionate than ever was brother and sister we will remain, and nothing more."

Notwithstanding the thoughts that were passing so rapidly through his mind, he never once wavered entirely as regarded proceeding, and it required all his strongest resolutions to enable him to do so.

This feeling kept on increasing until he came to within twenty-five miles of the valley in which Wyvill Hall was so delightfully situated, and as he reached this valley towards sunset he made up his mind that he would remain there that night, and make a strong endeavour to shake off the nervousness that oppressed him.

He found an old-fashioned country inn that had at one time been a farm house, and which was one of the most picturesque buildings he thought he had ever seen, and there he paused; nor was he, upon entering the place, disposed to repent doing so, for he found the people homely and agreeable, and resigning, therefore, for a time his new-found treasure—his darling child—into the care of the landlady, he after taking some refreshment went for a stroll among the green lanes and meadows by the sweet soft light of a young moon.

Cooped up as he had been the whole day by sitting in a carriage, it was a great luxury to walk in this way for an hour or so, and he unconsciously extended his stroll to a greater distance than he had at first intended.

But then the night was so tempting—there was such a soft, delicious, balmy air stirring the flowers in many a garden that he passed, and forcing them to part with their most delicious perfumes, and the moonlight spread such a mild and beautiful lustre among the trees, and tinted as if with liquid silver every wild flower in his path, that he could not refrain from wandering on, although now and then melancholy thoughts would sweep across his mind.

"It will now," he said, sadly, "be more so. All that is beautiful and good will remind me of my Emily, for was she not the best and most beautiful of all?"

He still walked on, until suddenly he found his view of the moon completely obstructed, and upon suddenly arousing himself from his reverie he found that he was close to an old, ruinous looking building, which he had never before observed, although he thought he knew tolerably well every object of interest or curiosity that was within fifty miles of Wyvill Hall.

Upon looking at this old place intently he found that it had been some ecclesiastical structure, that had sadly fallen to decay, and that adjoining to it there had, at one time, been built a house of more modern design, which appeared to be indebted for the greater part of its materials to the ruined building by its side.

That newer structure had, however, likewise given way to the progress of time, and had fallen into decay with the exception of some portion of it, which, to judge from a bright light that came from one of the windows, was still in a state of habitation.

This light, however, as he watched it, rather surprised him; it was so strange and flickering, and inconstant—at one moment it would seem to be almost expiring, and then again it would shoot up into fresh brilliancy, and be almost too intense and dazzling to look upon.

Suddenly, then, just as Sir Anthony was about to turn away, and take no more notice of the strange light that came from the window of the inn, he heard a loud explosion, accompanied by a cry of alarm; and fearful that some accident had occurred, he, with the impulse of his generous spirit, rushed forward at once, and dashed through an open doorway among the ruins. All was darkness of the most intense character; and after going on for some short distance, he thought it would be undoubtedly better to make himself heard, which he attempted to do by shouting in a loud voice,—

"Hilloa! hilloa! Is any one hurt? House! house!"

His cries were reverberated; and, by feeling before him, he found that he had come upon a staircase, which, as he trod upon it, creaked ominously, and seemed at each moment quite ready to give way and to let the adventurous individual down; but as, unquestionably, some one had ascended before him (for it was from above that the explosion and the cry of distress had come) he persevered, and clutching by the crazy balustrades, he reached a landing-place, after ascending about thirty of the really fearfully crazy steps.

When he got to that point, he saw a glimmering long streak of dim light at some distance off, which seemed to have come from the narrow crevice of a door, and as he was debating in his own mind whether to advance at once towards it or endeavour to make his presence known by again using his voice, the door, from the small crevice of which the light issued, entirely opened, and he saw a most strange unearthly-looking figure, with a most cadaverous-looking countenance, standing on the threshold with some sort of glass-lamp in his hand which he held above his head as he said,—

"I thought I heard a voice. Is it the spirit of the old prior, or a mortal, who comes at this moment of intense bitterness and disappointment?"

"I am a traveller merely," said Sir Anthony; "and, as I was looking at the ruins, I heard a loud explosion, and, as I thought, a cry for help, which tempted me to make my way into them. Has any accident occurred?"

"The worst—the very worst. Come this way, and your curiosity shall be satisfied. You may step with confidence, for there is nothing in your way. Come, and I will tell you what I and the world have lost."

Sir Anthony Wyvill, in his own mind, had no difficulty in setting this man down as a madman; and, for all he knew, he might be a dangerous one, although he certainly looked nothing more than some harmless enthusiast. Curiosity, however, overcame any prudential considerations, and Sir Anthony walked onwards, guided by the lamp, from which there came a most peculiar charnel-house kind of odour, and soon entered an apartment, which at once proclaimed to him the pursuit of the occupant of it, for it was filled with chemical apparatus of all kinds and descriptions, and a furnace now threw out some dull red rays on to the floor.

He found, too, that it was from the lamp that the horrible unearthly tint of colour came that made the singular inhabitant of that place look more like a corpse than a living man, for it threw the same pale, dirty looking, green tint upon every object in its immediate vicinity.

"You have come," said the alchymist, "to hear of the destruction of all my hopes. Ha, is it so?"

This latter exclamation arose from the sudden fall of something in the wall, which produced a clear silvery sort of sound, and then the alchymist took up the lamp again, and approaching Sir Anthony he narrowly scanned his countenance, saying,—

"I shall know you again when I may chance to meet you, when your great danger is over,—yes, I shall know you again; and as your motive in coming here was a good one, I hope I may yet live to aid you in your fearful extremity."

"What danger, and what fearful extremity do you allude to?"

"That I cannot tell you; but, as sure as you are a living man, you will come to some great evil before many hours have passed over your head. When that object which was on the wall falls and makes the sound you heard, it indicates great danger, but not death. When there is no sound, death is certain."

"But may it not mean you?"

"No. My doom is already fixed. I am not as common men are, but bear a life that is at once charmed and accursed; I am doomed to live for ever, until I can, by research, find out the principle of life."

Sir Anthony Wyvill had it upon the tip of his tongue to say, that if the stranger lived till then he might be quite sure of reaching a great age; but he forebore to utter the words, for a second thought convinced him that he was speaking to one of those enthusiasts in the cause of science who engage in the pursuit of an impossibility, and then convert some of their failures into such food for the imagination that they may be considered as positively insane. He contented himself, therefore, by merely saying,—

"Indeed! And can you tell me the particular danger which will beset me, in order that I may take some steps, at all events, to avoid it?"

"No, no, I cannot. There human knowledge fails; we can see the shadow, but the substance, in its proper forms, hues, and colours, is far beyond our ken."

"The knowledge then is not very desirable, since it seems to be such an insuperable condition of it that it shall not be useful."

"It is not desirable. Knowledge is unhappiness. Oh, would that I, instead of knowing what I do know, had fed sheep upon some verdant wood, and dozed the hours away, knowing nothing—hoping nothing—and fearing nothing!"

There was a strange and wild philosophy in this which pleased **Sir Anthony** Wyvill much, and spoken too, as it was, with a deep and melancholy voice, it certainly sounded like one of those great practical truths, which a man, after years of research and patient study arrives at, and which, at the very first, it appears wonderful, did not show itself to him long before, with wasted energies and an exhausted frame, he with a sigh was taught by bitter experience to acknowledge its truth.

" And what," said Sir Anthony, " was the experiment you were trying ?"

" It was to discover the principle of life, but the crucible exploded, and the labour of the last three years has gone in a puff of smoke ; but I have this consolation, that among men generally the labour of a whole life ends in the same manner."

" It does so indeed. That, at all events, is a piece of philosophy in which you are correct ; but as I find that you are unhurt, I must now leave you, for I have come further from where I thought to pass the night than I intended."

" Can you not pass it here ?"

" No. I have a child dependent wholly upon my care and attention, whom I have left at an inn, whilst I merely came to take a walk beneath the bright moonlight ; so I will now bid you farewell."

" Farewell, farewell ! But something occurs to tell me that we shall meet again, yet, and that shortly too."

" It may fairly be so, and I will at once promise you a visit within the next month, for I reside not much more than twenty miles from here, and can easily ride across the country and see you."

" I thank you, I thank you. I like sometimes to see a human face without the vain smile of ridicule upon it, and to hear a human voice that does not scout the labours of my life."

The philosopher lit Sir Anthony down the rickety staircase, and, as he did so, the latter could not but perceive how extremely weak and wretched-looking he was, and that he trembled in every limb. Whether he was distressed or not Sir Anthony could not discover, and, for fear of a mistake, he did not like to make any offer of assistance to him ; but he made up his mind to come over some time in daylight from Wyvill Hall, and visit the old enthusiast, and then he thought he should be able to judge more accurately of his condition, for an intimate acquaintance with the sublimest secrets of Nature, is not to be compared to an intimate acquaintance with the butcher and baker.

CHAPTER XLIV.

SIR ANTHONY CONTINUES HIS JOURNEY, AND SEES THE PREMONITORY SYMPTOMS OF THE STORM IN THE DYKE.

SIR ANTHONY WYVILL was very far from being so superstitious as to place any belief in the prognostications of danger which the alchymist had made to him, but as he certainly had been away from the inn much longer than he intended to have been, he hurried back again as quickly as he could.

As far as regarded the child he need not have hurried, for the little creature was in as good hands as it could possibly be, since it had been confided to the care of the landlady of the old-fashioned inn, and was quite happy, and asleep, when Sir Anthony arrived.

He made some inquiries then concerning the ruins which he had visited, and he found that it was the remains of an old priory, and that, about fifty years since, an attempt had been made to build a house close to it out of the fallen materials of the original structure, but that the house so built had quickly fallen to decay, as some people said, because it was built of consecrated materials ; but, as others insisted, because of bad mortar, and Sir Anthony Wyvill, although by no means what might be called a sceptic, certainly inclined himself to the latter opinion.

As for the strange man who now resided there, very little was known of him, except that he had come from a distance, and taken possession of the place, in which no one had shown any inclination to disturb him ; that he was out of his senses, and supposed to have been a doctor, the landlady likewise added, so that the desire to revisit the singular being was rather increased than diminished in the breast of Sir Anthony Wyvill.

He slept that night calmly and comfortably at the inn, and indeed the fatigue of his journey enabled him to taste of a better night's repose than had been his lot now for many weary weeks, during which physical suffering, added to his deep mental distress, had played sad havoc with his slumbers.

The morning was one of the brightest and most beautiful he had ever beheld ; in fact, if anything, there was quite an unnatural clearness and transparency in the air which those who pretended to be weather-wise shook their heads at, although they did not know exactly why.

Now Sir Anthony banished from his mind, as much as he could, the uneasy sensations that had existed as he neared his home, and after partaking of a hasty breakfast, and rejoicing in the healthful looks of his child, he proceeded onwards in the travelling chariot at an easy pace, for he did not wish to reach the Hall till the latter part of the day, and indeed he would have preferred it to have been in the dim twilight of the evening, so that no intimation of his coming could have reached Margaret, in order to enable her to make her escape before his actual arrival, or to concoct some new piece of artifice, which, while it could not have had now any effect in her favour upon him, would certainly have increased his disgust.

By the time, however, that they had gone about twelve miles, and just as they were looking about for some place at which to bait the horses, there burst overhead one of those sudden drenching rain-storms common to the region, and accompanied by such a furious gale of wind that it was really with great difficulty only that the horses could keep their feet, and succeed in dragging the carriage and its occupants to an inn.

Thus Sir Anthony remained for more than two hours, which, if it had no other effect, at least afforded to the horses an excellent rest ; and, although the fury of the storm seemed to have passed away, the whole aspect of the heavens looked strange and threatening, while huge masses of cloud would now and then sweep over the entire sky ; but still at intervals the sunshine would and did peep out with great beauty, to be in another moment completely obscured from sight.

This was not a pleasant state of things, but still he knew the evanescent nature of storms in that vicinity, and that the one which had then suddenly broke over head might not at all, although it seemed, be the herald of any others, notwithstanding the ominous appearance of the sky, which in some quarters, and more particularly from whence the wind blew, presented a strange aspect, but virtually the storm was truly over ; and under such circumstances he thought that it would be better to proceed at once, because if he did but get once through the mountain pass, the route to the Hall was clear and easy, and could present nothing in the shape of danger or difficulty, even should the storm break over them, which it might or might not do for hours to come.

The idea of waiting for the chance of the angry and threatening clouds that appeared on the horizon, when it was a matter of doubt as to how long that period of waiting would have to be, was extremely uncomfortable to him, so that, considering all things, he ordered the carriage to proceed.

And it did proceed for another two miles until they reached the valley, which was on the other side of the mountain pass from that on which Wyvill Hall was situated, and then Sir Anthony's attention was aroused by hearing the horses plunging violently, and feeling the carriage running down on one side. The postilion succeeded in quieting the affrighted animals, but a wheel had come off the vehicle and rolled a long distance away, thus effectually stopping the further progress of the travellers.

After this it seemed as if, perforce, there must be an effectual stop put to the wish of Sir Anthony to proceed to the Hall that night, although he really was but a very short distance from it—a distance which, had he been alone, he would have had not the smallest hesitation in walking.

But he did hesitate, encumbered as he was with the child, to do so, and when he found that no carriage was to be had, and that the wheel of his own was so broken that to repair it was almost a matter of impossibility, he did begin to think that he should have to stay where he was.

But yet, after a time, when he thought that he saw by the appearance of the weather that everything in the shape of storm had vanished, and considered how small a burden he had to carry, even if he should have to do so all the way, as regarded little Emily, the wish to get on came strongly across his mind again.

That wish grew at last, towards nightfall, into a determination, from which nothing could stir him. " What danger can there be," he said, " in a walk of a mile or two from here to my own home? Surely none ; and it is downright timidity not to undertake it."

And so, with the child grasped in his arms, and partially folded up in the ample travelling cloak which Sir Anthony had brought in the carriage for its use, in case of a cold wind blowing in the mountainous region, Sir Anthony Wyvill entered, contrary to advice and to prudence, the dyke which separated the valley in which his mansion lay, from the one where he left his carriage and servant.

Alas ! could he but in the dimest manner have foreseen a tithe of the horrors that awaited him, with what precipitation he would have shrunk back from that pass. But he was doomed, and who shall avoid their destiny? His was a terrific one. The reader already knows something of it.

CHAPTER XLV.

THE GRAND ENTERTAINMENT PROJECTED BY MARGARET.—THE HORRORS OF CONSCIENCE.

MARGARET WYVILL was successful !   Yes, she was a living exemplification of that divine truth, " that for a time the wicked shall seem to prosper ;" but was she happy ? Fearful question to one who has bartered her soul's salvation for the fleeting and hollow enjoyments of a world which may not endure for her beyond an hour.

What had she gained by her intense wickedness, and what had she lost? Fearful questions still to Margaret Wyvill, the bold and the ambitious.

She has gained, and so she would say if she were upon her oath, and intent upon keeping the sacred pledge to speak the truth—she has gained the possession of Wyvill Hall and its rich dependencies ; but she has paid such a price as never was paid before by any human being for such a possession. The price of peace here, and happiness hereafter.

Oh ! who, from the very lowest depths of misery, would exchange with Margaret Wyvill, when she sat in those lordly halls, and told herself that the dead alone could oust her from her dominion ; and the dead she strove to tell herself she feared not—but oh ! how bitterly she really feared them !

Can there be a more idle boast than that of any one who fancies that conscience is to be defied? Margaret found that it was a very idle boast indeed. The day-time she might contrive to get over by bustle and by activity, but the night-time, never ! Oh ! no ; then it was that fearful visions disturbed her, and she became maddened with the horrors that fancy conjured up to terrify her, and drive her to despair.

Day after day she looked worse and worse, and at last the thought struck her, that she might possibly lose the consciousness of her deep and desperate wickedness in a whirl of enjoyment. The resources of Wyvill Hall were ample, as regarded the seeing company, and Margaret had two reasons for filling the saloons with the gay and the thoughtless.''

One of those reasons was, to lose a recollection of her own crimes, in the bustle of such pleasures, if such a thing could be. And another was, to find herself a husband, for she had made up her mind to have the society of some one. She determined upon wedding a poor gentleman, if she could find one willing to wear the golden chains ; and she thought that then, even if he whom she chose should suspect that she had not obtained her power very legitimately, self-interest would keep him silent. Margaret judged of everybody by herself—self-interest was to stifle all scruples.

But most unquestionably now her greatest source of disquietude consisted in the difficulty of satisfying the Fosters. Old Foster was continually coming to the Hall, and there was about him a look of positive madness, which inexpressibly alarmed Margaret. He kept from her the frightful fact, that in lieu of Sir Anthony Wyvill, it was his own son whom he had killed at the fatal chamber, at the Dyke House. He knew that if he told her so much, she would hold him at defiance, whatever disquietude she herself might suffer from the reflection, that, for all that, the knowledge of such a dreadful event nearly drove him mad. He had never slept since, and he was the shadow of his former self.

There appeared to be some idea ; upon his part, of leaving the country. He hinted at such a step several times, and, when Margaret eagerly caught at the idea, he avowed it ; but he had the audacity, as she considered it, to demand five thousand pounds as the price of his expatriation and his silence.

This was a demand which the avarice of Margaret would not permit her to comply with, and she accordingly put him off from day to day, constantly giving him money, and constantly hoping that he would die. Perhaps she had some vague idea of assisting in the last desirable confirmation. She was quite capable of taking such a measure, and we cannot but consider that the villain, Foster held his life upon a very frail tenure indeed.

From further information Margaret fancied she could rely upon, from London, she was led to believe entirely in the death of Emily, so that she now satisfied herself that never again in this world would the eyes of those whom she so much dreaded be cast upon her.

It was then that suddenly getting possession of about a couple of thousand pounds of the rent-roll of the Wyvill estates, she determined to commence the career of glitter and extravagance to which she looked for the means of rescue from the horrible thoughts that continually oppressed her.

No doubt she would have gone to London or elsewhere for the purpose of commencing this new existence, but she dreaded the Fosters too much to leave the neighbourhood in which they were, until something more decided had been done regarding them. So for a time she made up her mind to remain at Wyvill Hall, and brave the terrors of recollection.

She gave out that her brothers had retired to the continent, but had told her to keep up by every possible means the ancient hospitality of the mansion, and that it was in compliance with his wish that she did so. She then issued invitations to a splendid entertainment, which was to be upon a scale of surpassing magnificence, and to comprehend in its arrangements a masked ball, and a supper. It was a wish of Margaret's that the ball should be a masked one, simply because she wished her own countenance to be covered, from a sort of dread that otherwise her guilt would be read in her changing colour.

Every family of note and consideration, and many of no note nor consideration, in the neighbourhood was invited, and on the evening before the day on which all this gallantry and magnificence was to take place, Margaret sat alone with the back of her chair against a wall, as was now her invariable custom, as if she feared that otherwise some horrible shape would come behind her.

She had continued during the day, by dint of continued bustle, to keep herself tolerably free from horrible thoughts, but now the evening was stealing on rapidly, and she knew that her imagination would soon commence its wonted activity, and nearly drive her to distraction before she could venture to take the opiate, without which she now never sought her couch.

Suddenly there came a tap at the door, and in another moment a servant appeared, and said,—

"If you please, madame, Mr. Foster desires to see you."

"Admit him," was the brief reply.

Now these visits of Foster were the most intolerable burden to Margaret, but she dared not forbid them; and although the servants were far indeed from suspecting the nature of the secret which existed between her and Foster, yet they knew that there was some secret, which induced their haughty misstress to be always accessible to that man.

It was with a half-familiar, half-crouching air that Foster came into the apartment, and advanced towards the place where his principal in crime was sitting. He felt that he could command her to see him; and yet he could not wholly get over the feeling of how much she was above him in rank as well as in education and wealth.

"Well," she said, in a low tone, "I saw you yesterday, and gave you some money; what want you here again to-day?"

"You are about giving a masked ball," he said; "I know why you give it. You want to drive away thought. Well, hang me, if I haven't got my uneasy thoughts as well as you have, so I want to come and see if the music, the gay company, and the sparkling wines will not have some effect even upon me."

"You come?"

"Yes, and why not, Margaret Wyvill? We are equals now."

Margaret felt with a shudder the dreadful truth of that remark. They were equals. A community of spirit in crime had brought her, proud and haughty as she was, to an equality with the base-born, ignorant, brutal Foster! No wonder that a frightful groan came from her lips, and that she looked like one more dead than alive, as she, after a brief pause, replied to him,—

"Foster, you must be mad to think of such a thing. I will give you money wherewith to enjoy yourself; but by attempting to mingle with my guests, you only expose both yourself and me to suspicion."

"I am nearly mad."

"Hush! not so loud, not so loud. I cannot understand the change that has come over you. I am quite sure you had dipped your hands in human blood before that deed, which you now pretend so much affects you."

Foster groaned, for he knew well that what she said was true, and he did not want to tell her that, although it was true he had never, until then, taken the life of a son of his own.

"Peace, peace," he said; "why do you rake up the past? Give me a ticket for your entertainment; you have nothing to fear. I will be dressed, and, moreover, it being a masked ball, there is no possibility of my being discovered."

"You persevere in this wild intention?" said Margaret, knowing well that if he did so persevere she had no resource but to yield.

"I do—I do."

She was silent for a few moments, and then with trembling hands she took from the table a ticket for the ball, saying,—

"There is a card which will admit you, but let me implore of you, for your sake as well as for mine, to be careful, and to keep yourself well disguised; but oh, above all, Foster, be sober: do not drink anything but what I give to you, and they shall be light French wines. You will promise me so much, and, in order that I may know you, tell me what costume you will come in."

"Oh, that's easily told; I don't dance, so I only come in a cloak, mask, and hat with one black feather in it, and the colour of the cloak will be brown, as I happen to have one by me."

Margaret dreaded to ask him how he happened to have it, and whose it had once been. Her conscience told her that it was the cloak of her poor murdered brother, Sir Anthony; and she only shivered as if a sudden chill had come over all her system, and had deprived her blood of all its warmth.

"All's right," said Foster; "I shall be there."

"And you promise me what I require?"

"Oh yes, yes; I have as much to dread as you from any indiscretion, so I promise to take nothing to drink but what you invite me to yourself. Will that satisfy you?"

"It will, it will. I shall be at ease in my mind then, and to-morrow, Foster, if you behave youself as I wish, you shall find that on the succeeding day I will be most liberal towards you. I have been thinking of your proposal to leave the country, and I may possibly entertain it, and give you the large amount you require."

With this they parted upon very tolerable terms indeed, and, after he was gone, Margaret rested her head upon her hands for a while, and was evidently in deep thought; suddenly then she rose, and approached an Indian cabinet of rare inlaid wood that was in the room and opened it, muttering as she did so,—

"It is a stern necessity which is always sure to arise, that we must get rid eventually of the tools with which we work our way to the goal of our ambition; and, Foster, you must die."

There was a secret drawer in the cabinet which Margaret now opened, and she took from it an exceedingly minute phial, which she held up to the light, and saw that it contained a small portion of semi-transparent fluid.

"This must suffice," she said. "I procured this for myself in case of failure of all my schemes—one drop of it in a wine-glass, I am assured, holds such enmity with life, that, in a few minutes, whosoever partakes of it will surely die. It will rid me of Foster, who daily is growing more troublesome and importunate. Yes, to-morrow night there will be a sudden death at the masked ball, and that is all—a week's wonder from the guests, and then I shall surely breathe more freely."

Margaret seemed to feel happier and gayer now that she had made up her mind to the death of Foster; and certainly she did not feel anything in the shape of compunction at this new crime, but, on the contrary, began to wonder to herself that she had never before thought of so easy a mode of getting rid of her greatest living torment.

In a short time she retired to rest herself; but she did not forget to partake of the opiate from which she hoped to derive the oblivion of repose. She was that night, however, most frightfully disappointed, for her sleep was tormented by the most horrible images; and she rose at break of day so pale, so haggard, and so wan, that her appearance would have excited the pity of her direst foe.

Truly it was not all sunshine with Margaret Wyvill.

CHAPTER XLV.

THE MYSTERIOUS ARRIVAL AT THE LODGE OF WYVILL HALL.—THE TRAVELLING CARRIAGE.—THE BALL.

THE guests to Margaret Wyvill's grand entertainment were expected to arrive exactly at seven.

Not less than one hundred persons were invited, and the principal ball room

of Wyvill Hall—a most magnificent apartment, which had not now been opened
for a considerable time—was placed in order, for the reception of the largest party
that had ever assembled within the walls of the mansion within the memory of
any of the servants.

The bustle and excitement of the day kept Margeret's spirits up; and she carefully carried about with her a wine glass, into which she had poured, early in the
morning, two drops of the poison, and there let it dry on to the side of the glass,
so that if wine was poured into that vessel it would take up sufficient of the mortal
drug to produce death.

She was satisfied that she must succeed, nor did there indeed seem to be in the
ordinary course of events any likelihood of a failure.

But Margaret could not be everywhere at once; and something was going on at
the lodge of Wyvill Hall, which, if she had known it, would have filled her with
conjecture and alarm.

Just about an hour before mid-day, there came a young man on horseback to
the lodge, and he gave a letter to the old couple who were there, and who, it will
be recollected, were such warm friends of Sir Anthony Wyvill and the Lady
Emily. What that letter contained will be well enough guessed at as we proceed.
Suffice it to say, that the old woman fainted when her husband read it to her; but
he called for no assistance, and she was, by the aid of a little water, recovered.

During the remainder of the day it was wonderful to see what efferts the old
lodge-keeper and his wife made to render this little humble abode cheerful-looking
and pleasant, and towards evening he went up to the Hall.

When he got there, he made his way into the kitchen, where all the discourse
was, as a matter of course, turning upon the approaching ball.

"Ah," said the old lodge-keeper, "they tell me that even the cards of invitation
are handsome things."

"They are indeed," said a footman; "there's one, and you may stick it upon
your chimney-piece in the lodge as an ornament, for you see it's quite a picture."

The old lodge-keeper looked highly gratified, and promised to do so; after which
he made a few common-place remarks, and then went back to the lodge with an
air of great satisfaction upon his face. When he reached his little house, he filled
up this card of invitation with the first names that came uppermost to his mind,
and carefullly laid it aside. For what purpose this was done we shall know speedily.

At the appointed time for the arrival of the guests, the carriages began to arrive
quickly, and various parties went up to the Hall; but one party, consisting of three
persons, two ladies and a gentleman, went into the lodge, from whence they,
however, shortly emerged, and went likewise to the mansion.

As the hour had approached for the arrival of the guests, Margaret found her
spirits rise. The brilliant lighting of the rooms, and an occasional burst of music
from the orchestra of the great ball-room, gave a sort of fulness to her spirits,
and she almost began to think she should really succeed in [stifling the pangs of
conscience, in enjoying the wealth she had waded through such frightful iniquity
to obtain.

Vain hope! When was the fearful inward monitor—conscience, lulled to sleep
by the glitter of the results of the iniquity that called the unslumbering voice into
existence?

For a time Margaret might succeed in not being so wholly miserable as usual,
but that was all; Retribution would most surely and justly come again.

The glass which contained the small but, as she well knew, most effectual dose
of poison, she kept in her pocket, trusting to her own dexterity to use it when
Foster, as most assuredly he would, should come to her for wine. And now it is
nearly an hour after sunset, and some of her guests have already arrived, so that
it is necessary she should make her appearance in the reception-room.

Margaret was most magnificently attired, and but for the frightful jaded aspectly
of her countenance, she might have merited some of the compliments which her
guests thought themselves bound to pay to her upon the auspicious occasion of the
giving of such a gorgeous and satisfactory entertainment.

To all, she replied with ready courtesy and an appearance of great self-possession, although Heaven only knows what efforts it cost her to appear quite at her ease.

The ball-room was not opened at once ; but, with a judicious eye to effect, Margaret had arranged that not until the greater portion of her guests had assembled in the principal reception-room, and it should begin to become inconveniently crowded, should the doors of the splendid saloon be flung back. This arrangement certainly did produce all the effect she expected.

And now strains of ravishing and delightful music began to echo through the place, and after some of the guests had taken refreshments, the dancing commenced with great spirit ; but no one could induce Margaret to join in the dance Truly she was thinking of other things than such a frivolous amusement as threading the mazes of a quadrille. She wandered among the guests looking for her victim, Foster, whom she wished as early as possible to accommodate with the dose.

For a long time she looked in vain, but at length she thought she saw some one bearing a close resemblance to his figure, and habited as he said he would be.

It was the work of three or four minutes before Margaret, without exhibiting a haste that might have drawn attention to her movements, found her way to Foster, and then she whispered in his ear,—

"I know you !"

"Yes," he replied, "it is I."

"Will—will you drink ?"

No. 37.

"Not just yet, madame," said the mask, as he walked away.   And then Margaret, as she glanced at the figure, thought she had committed a fatal error.

In vain she strove to restore herself to confidence. "All must be well," she
said to herself.   "They are all dead—dead, and as for Foster, his impeachmen
and denunciations of me would be his death-warrant, for he it was who did the
deed.   Oh, yes! I am quite safe from Foster's treachery, and who is there else
who can tell anything? I will be calm and serene.   But where is he?   Oh! how
I pant to give him the potion that will silence him for ever.

After this adventure, Margaret was much more careful how she addressed any
one; but at length, standing close to one of the side tables, she saw a figure which
she supposed must be the one she sought, wearing a large brown cloak and a hat,
in which was one large feather.

"It must be he," she said, "yes it surely must be he;" and when she got near
enough, she whispered to the mask, "Do I know you, Foster?"

"Really I don't know," was the reply; and as before some one whom she mistook for Foster, walked away; and as the person did so, she became convinced
of her mistake.

All this was very strange, and Margaret began to be horribly nervous and apprehensive that everything was not exactly as she could wish it, but yet she could
not reconcile to herself the idea that there could be any real danger; and she often
upon reflection blamed herself for the mistakes she had made, telling herself how
very likely it was, that persons who did not come to dance, should adopt some
such cosume as she expected to find the villain Foster in.

Margaret certainly by her notion of giving a masked instead of a plain ball, had
succeeded in concealing her own features from minute observation, during the
principal part of the evening; but it had likewise the effect of preserving her from
making those recognitions she wished to make.

She felt too late that it was quite an error of judgment; but yet she hoped t
retrieve it at the supper table, when it would of course be necessary for the guest
to unmask; and then she thought she would make sure of Foster, for she still ha
the glass with her that contained the deadly poison.

"He shall die!" she muttered; "I am resolved upon it, he shall die!"

The dancing now went on with great spirit indeed, and the masked ball in th
ancient halls of that mansion might be said to be at its height.

Nearly two thirds of the company were dancing, and still with anxious eyes di
Margaret go from group to group of maskers in search of him whom she so much
wished to see; but she found him not. Indeed, after the two disappointments sh
had had, she began to dread addressing any of the maskers, and she began to thin
that she had really better give up the affair until twelve o'clock, at which hour th
supper was to be announced.

Just as Margaret might be said to have made this resolution, she in common wit
every one there present was startled by a loud clap of thunder, and there immediately followed such a rush of wind, that it seemed as if, substantial as the ol
stone-built hall was, it could hardly stand the fury of such a gale.

"A storm!" she muttered. "Well, well, be it so; there cannot be a greate
storm without among the elements, than there is in my heart."

Margaret did not wish the bustle and the festivity of the guests to diminish
because of the war of the elements, and she did all she could to keep matter
going, and to raise the spirits of any who seemed to be flagging; and still sh
looked earnestly for Foster, but she could not find him.

The storm raged with unabated fury, so much so indeed that the affrighte
guests stood huddled together in groups; and the dancing which had been goin
on so merrily, was suddenly suspended.

At this moment, a gentleman and lady took off their masks suddenly, and th
former said, in a voice which betokened some anger as well as surprise,—

"Are we all prisoners here, I should like to know? I and this lady have jus
made an attempt to leave the saloon, and were told by a man at the door that w
could not be permitted to do so: I should like very much to know, as I am
stranger to the family, if that is what they consider hospitality and courtesy."

CHAPTER XLVI.

THE CONCLUSION.

THESE words were just calculated to produce a wonderful commotion in a ball-room, and probably in no ball-room could they have produced so much effect as in that at Wyvill Hall.

For a few moments no one moved, and no one spoke; surprise kept every one fixed and silent, but then, when this kind of paralysis of surprise had passed away, there arose a perfect din of voices, which, however, were all hushed again, when one voice, loud, and clear as a trumpet, cried,—

"Peace! Hear me speak, for I suspect I have the right!"

A stately form sprung into the centre of the ball-room, and while the guests shrunk back, so as to leave him the centre of a circle, he tore off his mask, and cast his cloak to the ground.

It was Sir Anthony Wyvill.

A person, attired in a domino of blue cloth, sprang forward, and clung to his arm. A mask dropped from before the face, and revealed Emily.

Margaret was so far outside the circle, that she could not see what was going on, and she only imperfectly caught the sound of the voice that had stilled all other sounds. But she cried frantically,—

"Make way! make way! For the love of God, make way!"

"Let her approach," said Sir Anthony, and in another moment they were face to face. With a loud shriek Margaret fell upon the floor.

"Remove her," said Sir Anthony; "and I desire all my friends here to unmask."

The request was obeyed by all, except one man in a brown cloak. Sir Anthony sprung upon him, and tore the mask from his face. It was Foster.

"Officers!" cried Sir Anthony, and six strong men advanced—"officers, there is your prisoner. My friends, you see me like a man recovered from the tomb. I live, as does my long-lost, best, and greatest treasure, my wife. We—we had a little one——"

"And here it is," said a voice, as the idiot, who, it will be remembered, was at the Dyke House, on the night of the projected murder of Sir Anthony, darted forward, and placed the child in his arms. "I took care of it in a cave among the mountains. I aint quite such a fool as people take me for. How do you feel, Foster, eh?"

What pen shall paint the rapture of Sir Anthony and his wife at recovering their child! It is easily explained how he and his much-injured wife came together again. By the exertions of the kind friends that Emily had found, all had been happily arranged some short time after Sir Anthony's escape from the Dyke House, and they had planned with Mr. Beauclerc, who now stepped to their side, giving Margaret this not very agreeable surprise in the midst of their visitors. They it was who arrived at the lodge so mysteriously.

The card of invitation, promised by the old lodge-keeper, had been filled up, to admit a Mr. Smith and party, which included Sir Anthony, the two ladies, and six active police officers.

How completely the storm was forgotten in the midst of all these exciting circumstances! The wind still howled without, and the thunder rattled, but the guests that were assembled at Wyvill Hall, heard them not, so completely engrossed were they in what was going on within the ball-room.

The scene within truly was more stormy than that without, for what can compare with the wild exuberance of human passions when powerfully excited.

When the villain, Foster, saw, as he did now, that all was over, he cried aloud,—

"I denounce Margaret Wyvill—I denounce her as the instigator of my crimes. Take her into custody as well as me, and I will tell a tale that will make you wonder if she be a woman or a devil."

Margaret had sufficiently recovered to hear those words, and she spoke faintly, saying,—

"I have an all-sufficient answer to whatever can be alleged against me—an amply sufficient answer. But I am weak and can scarcely speak, and I feel faint too."

They raised her, and placed her on a chair.

"Before you take me away upon that bold man's accusation," she added faintly, "I have an accusation to give which will at once dispose of his accusation. But I—I am faint."

"Let her have some wine," said Sir Anthony; "God send she may have some sufficient answer, I would give Wyvill Hall and everything it contains for a proof of her innocence."

One of the police-officers who had accompanied Sir Anthony went to a table that was in a recess, and brought from it a decanter of wine and a glass. He approached Margaret, but she held up her hand, saying,—

"I have a glass and was going to take some wine. I have a glass in my hand.'

"Oh, very well," said the officer, and he poured the small glass she held towards him full of wine, which in another moment she drank off. Then turning her eyes upon Sir Anthony Wyvill, she said, in a strangely altered tone,—

"All this may be a dream, but, if so, it is wonderfully like reality. I told you I had an answer ready—a most complete answer—it is Death!"

Even as she spoke, she fell from the chair on to the floor, and when they picked her up, she was a corpse. The subtle poison had done its work most effectually. The guilty spirit of Margaret Wyvill had winged its flight to another world, where let us hope that, bad as she was, she has found justice tempered with mercy.

But little now remains to tell. The guilty Foster expiated in some measure his crimes upon the scaffold, for he was executed upon the most unquestionable evidence of having committed numerous murders.

The poor idiot who had reared the child was most munificently provided for by Sir Anthony Wyvill. Mrs. Beauclerc resided permanently at the Hall, nor was there one human being who had done a kind action or said a kind word to Emily Wyvill during her pilgrimage from her home forgotten. Even Adolphus Dacre often shared the hospitalities of the Hall, and was permitted, without any bad consequences, to tell to the Lady Emily the anecdote of the charming woman and the charming ladies.

* * * * * *

The lives of Sir Anthony Wyvill and his beautiful wife passed onward like a summer streamlet, full of beauty, and with no storms to disturb the even and musical tenour of its way. They were blessed, and in their case it was a blessing with many children, and the old Hall for many and many a year resounded with the clear, musical laughter of happy and innocent childhood. May they too be happy, without knowing the perils that had surrounded the earlier years of their now delighted parents.

THE END.

LONDON : Printed and Published by E. Lloyd, 12, Salisbury Square, Fleet Street.